THE CURSE OF MOOSE LAKE

ALSO BY BETHANY HELWIG

International Monster Slayers:
The Curse of Moose Lake
The Bite of Winter
The Ghosts of Yesteryear
The Dark Whisper
The Brood of Nightmare
The Lone Hunter

~

Darkest Light

INTERNATIONAL MONSTER SLAYERS
BOOK ONE

THE CURSE OF MOOSE LAKE

BETHANY HELWIG

BRIGHTWAY BOOKS

Second Edition: April 2019
ISBN-10: 1-946639-20-6
ISBN-13: 978-1-946639-20-2

For my father and those
troublesome twins that inspired
another pair of troublemakers

1

My eyes travel up the daunting height of Werevine Pharmaceutical. The skyscraper boasts so many windows it's like one giant mirror reflecting the noonday sun over Minneapolis. I squint against the burning light and move for the double glass doors, taking care to walk at a normal pace. Cars honk and rev their engines on the road behind me, their shapes ghosting across the reflective windows of the front entrance to the building. I try not to shove people out of my way on the sidewalk ahead of me. My brother says I'm too impatient and today I have to agree with him. I take a deep breath and reach for the handle of the door.

There I pause as I catch my reflection. Sharp green eyes squint back at me beneath my tidy blood-red hair pulled back into a ponytail that seems to soak up the sun's rays and glow. My skin is pale but that's no surprise. On my best days I look like curdled milk with a dash of freckles for texture across my nose and cheeks. I have a heavy amount of makeup on today to make my eyes seem brighter and my face fuller. I'm trying to look the part of a twenty-something FDA agent and wore my only skirt for the occasion, but I'm afraid my seventeen-year-old gangly limbs are going to give me away.

I exhale through my mouth to release the tension in my shoulders and shove my way through the glass doors.

The foyer is bedazzled with mirrors, glass, and shiny decorative objects. The sunlight jumps in after me playing a game of tag through its various reflections. I squint as I walk to the front counter where a girl sits stiff-backed in her chair, hands glued to a phone and keyboard simultaneously. She doesn't smile or look up when I approach.

I smooth out the front of my silk blouse and wait impatiently for the girl to end her call. I'm fidgety and feel out of place. If my brother was here, like he's supposed to be, he would have waltzed in like he owned the place and schmoozed right up to the receptionist, probably even gotten her to smile. I'll be lucky if I can make it through a conversation without saying something stupid.

The girl finally looks up and ends her phone call. A smile plops into place on her face but it looks rehearsed.

"Can I help you?" she says sweetly with just the slightest bite to her words. She must be having a bad day.

"Yes. Right, just a second," I say and start rummaging through my purse. I don't usually carry a purse and it's something I borrowed so it takes me longer than your average girl to find what I'm looking for. The receptionist starts strumming her fingernails on the desk and her smile stiffens. I finally manage to pull out my mostly authentic FDA badge and hold it up for her to see. Now *that* catches her full attention.

"Agent Jane Roe with the FDA," I roll off, rather impressed with myself for saying it like it's true despite the generic name sitting foreign in my mouth. For a split second I almost said my real name. "This is just a random check on the company. My partner should be coming along shortly. Is it okay if I wait here in the lobby until he arrives?"

"Of course." She gestures to a row of plastic chairs along the wall. "Just let me know if you need anything. I'll pull up some passes for access to the building while you wait."

I can't believe how simple that was. "Thank you."

"If you don't mind my saying," the receptionist continues, her eyes narrowing ever so slightly. "You seem awfully young for an agent."

"Yes, well . . ." I fumble for something appropriate to say in response and end up spitting out a half-truth. "This is my first assignment." And it is. Just not for the FDA. Not that I'm going to tell her that.

Before I say something else that makes her distrust me, I sidle over to the plastic chairs and take a seat, clutching the purse to my stomach while I wait for my slow, *late* partner to catch up. To keep my hands busy, I dig into my purse and run my fingers over the cool metallic surface of the bio-mech gun to reassure myself it's still there. Right now it rests dormant and shaped like a heavy makeup case. I'm not technically supposed to have it—let's just say it's on lease—but I feel better having it with me. It's my first mission out in the real world, a routine check on this company, but I'm anxious and expecting something terrible to happen. It's basically the plot of every spy movie I've ever seen.

I tap my foot while I wait and glance at my watch every now and then. Ten minutes pass before my partner arrives, and by partner I mean my twin brother, Hawk. He's dressed up for the occasion as well in a suit trying to look like he's from the FBI but looks more like a high schooler going to prom. His shock of red hair and bright green eyes match mine except his hair is cropped short and today is combed neatly for once. He's slim to a freakish degree but once he smiles and draws back his shoulders, he actually manages to look like he belongs in his navy blue suit.

He runs a hand down his front lapels and walks directly to me. I stand to meet him and he plants his hands on his waist before leaning in to whisper.

"Cobb isn't coming."

"What?" I hiss. Cobb, our useless mentor, is supposed to be guiding us through our mission. We've never done this before. "Why not? We can't do this without him."

"He figured this is so low key and routine that we don't need his assistance. That, and he said he needed a smoke break." Hawk adjusts his tie and rolls his eyes. "He said we just need to run through the checklist with the CEO and then grab the latest printouts on production of the serum."

I'm fighting back anger and no small amount of panic. Heat radiates from my face. My brother seems to find this amusing because he smiles and laughs under his breath.

"Calm down. It'll be fine, Phoenix."

"It's *Jane Roe*," I say and glare at him.

"Yeah, whatever, you walking panic attack. Come on."

He leads the way across the lobby, all confidence and self-assurance, and leans on the countertop to smile at the receptionist. She gives him a real smile instead of the forced one she gave to me.

"Hi, there!" he says. "I'm Agent Jim Roe. Sorry to keep you waiting. That is a lovely blouse by the way."

"Oh, thank you." She blushes and I turn away slightly to hide the roll of my eyes.

"As I'm sure my partner told you, we're here for a random compliance check on the company. Normal FDA procedure. We promise we won't take up more of your time than necessary. I was hoping you could point us in the direction of your CEO and lead bookkeeper."

"Of course." She points us to another set of double glass doors bordered by metal detectors and a security guard. She hands us passes and after a little more small talk between her and Hawk, we move on. The security guard kindly takes my purse and I step through the detectors unhindered. It's the moment my purse is scanned that I have to force myself to keep steady. My set of ordinary keys, left there for the purpose of seeming normal, sets off the alarm. They're placed in a plastic bin and my purse passes the check. The highly advanced bio-mech gun goes through undetected, impervious to the sensors. The guard hands me my items with a smile, directs me to the correct elevator, and offers a kind farewell. Hawk passes through as well and we enter the elevator. As soon as the doors close, we turn to each other and I hold out my fist in my palm for rock, paper, scissors.

"If I win, I get the printouts." I don't want to run through a checklist with the CEO. I don't think I can be convincing enough but Hawk will probably make me do it just to get me to try.

He shrugs back his sleeves and copies my posture. We hit our fists in our palms three times and Hawk beats my scissors with his rock. I punch him in the shoulder but he just laughs and presses the button for the twenty-fifth floor. We ride the fast moving elevator up until Hawk reaches his floor and leaves in search of the bookkeeper. A young paperboy steps on at the same floor and shoots me inappropriate looks as we continue up. I fight a losing battle with the flush trying to take over my face and grit my teeth.

The elevator dings when we reach the forty-ninth floor and I step out onto a long open floor covered in various shades of gray from top to bottom. Workers cower in their cubicles and don't make eye contact. The clicking of keyboards, the loud thrum of a copier, and the shuffling of paper are the only sounds. The atmosphere is too quiet and contained with fevered work, like final exams in high school. *Pixies*, I hated high school.

The paperboy jogs off and pushes his cart to the right. I stand awkwardly by myself for a moment before I start walking slowly along the wall on my left to look for the CEO's office. I try to make as little sound as possible in my heels as I thud across the hard carpet searching for the correct door. A few cubicle workers glare at me over the top of their computer monitors as I pass.

Just past the cubicles I find another receptionist's desk. The women sitting behind it has red-rimmed eyes and the largest mug of coffee I've ever seen in my life in front of her. She startles when I come up to the other side of the desk. I smile to ease her anxiety but her eyes remain wide and she glances around like someone looking for an escape. Definitely not a good sign.

"Hi, I'm Agent Roe." I flash my badge. "I'm looking for the CEO. Is he around?"

"Mr. Bole is—he's . . . well, he's busy." The receptionist's eyes keep flickering around like she's waiting to be attacked. I lean forward and she twitches.

"Are you okay?" I ask in an undertone.

The force of her nodding throws her bouncy blonde curls around. "Of course, but Mr. Bole is not currently here."

"Where is he then?"

"He's on the top floor but he's not to be disturbed." Her eyes water a little when she says this and I imagine the CEO must have yelled himself hoarse at the poor receptionist for disturbing him before. "If this is an emergency, I could call up to him."

"Don't bother." I wave a hand to let her know it's all right. The woman looks stressed to the point she might start pulling out her own hair. I don't want to add to that. "I'll run up there myself. It's no trouble."

The receptionist tries to tell me I can't, that I shouldn't, Mr. Bole will be really angry, but I ignore her and move back to the elevator. I hit the button for the fifty-first floor and rise.

The doors open to some kind of paper disaster. There are additional cubicles here, wider and more lavish than before with leather swivel chairs and multiple coffee machines, but each is covered by piles upon piles of paperwork in every nook and cranny. There are heaps on the floor, some knocked over and fallen like snow drifts while others tower over me. It looks like someone's pulled together every single piece of paper the company has ever printed and stuffed it up here. I exit the elevator and have to pick my way carefully through so as not to step on scattered invoices and data charts.

It's eerily quiet and there's not a soul in sight. I wonder if the receptionist was wrong about Mr. Bole being up here but then I hear a faint sneeze from the far end of the open room. I work my way down the long row of cubicles until I reach the back office with a semi-opaque glass screen as its wall. The door is ajar. I take a deep breath and step forward to stand in the doorway.

Two of the walls are made completely of bookshelves filled with thick volumes bound to cover all things pharmaceutical, but directly opposite me the wall is a single yawning window overlooking the city and parking garage below. The dark blue carpet is plush in here and I hardly make a sound as I walk forward to announce my presence.

A massive hardwood desk fills up most of the office all by itself and behind it sits a plump man with round glasses. It's clear he's attempted, and failed, to use what hair he has to comb-over the large bald spot on the top of his head. He sits far down in his chair like he puddled there, his body squashed down into a thick middle and pudgy fingers. The golden buttons of his expensive striped suit strain against the taut fabric. He looks up when I enter and his frown pushes his lips out in a hideous pout.

"Who are you?" he snaps. "What are you doing here?"

I'm ready this time with my badge and step closer so he can see it before I tuck it back into my purse. "Agent Roe with the FDA. I'm performing a random routine check on the company."

"A check? Why?"

I take the empty seat in front of his desk and set the purse in my lap. "A number of flags were raised in our system because of some recent activity. We're just checking in to make sure everything is . . . kosher."

His eyes rake me and I stare evenly back. I can see the same distrust in his eyes as the first receptionist. I don't look the part of an FDA agent. I'm too young. I try to ignore his suspicion as I pull out the checklist Cobb gave me. Mr. Bole grumbles under his breath and reaches for a cup of coffee on his desk. His fingers close around empty air a few inches short of the cup so he tries again and manages to grab the handle. His hand trembles as he brings the cup to his lips and takes a slow sip.

I stare. His clumsy attempt to pick up his coffee just set off warning bells in my head and I wait for him to do something else so I can gauge his movements again but he remains still except for the slight shake in his hands.

"So?" he snaps. "What do you want?"

I clear my throat and try to act normal but now I'm on edge and wary. Thinking fast, I dig around in my purse and pretend to be exasperated.

"I can't find my pen," I sigh. "Could you pass me one, please?"

He moves very slowly as he picks a blue pen off his desk and offers it to me. His reach is a bit short, which he seems to notice, so he leans forward so I can grab it. My fingers brush his hand and his skin feels somewhat waxy.

"Thanks," I say and then smile even though my heart is racing. That simple act of passing the pen tells me everything I need to know.

I see the man for what he truly is. All the signs are there—

the lack of spatial awareness, the slow methodical movements, the trembling in the hands, not to mention the odd texture of his skin. He wasn't able to grab his cup on the first go because he isn't used to his short arms. He moves slowly because he knows he isn't acquainted enough with his new body. That waxy skin of his isn't normal for a human.

I set the checklist on top of my purse to hide the fact I'm moving my hand inch by inch to wrap my fingers around the bio-mech gun, because this man sitting in front of me is not Mr. Bole.

This man, setting his coffee cup down with careful precision, is a shapeshifter.

I hadn't been lying before about the red flags triggered by the company and it seems I've found the source. A shapeshifter has infiltrated the company, this place of all places, and now I don't know what I'm supposed to do. Dang it, I wish Cobb had come along. He's a lousy mentor but he would know what to do. Should I go through the checklist like normal and leave so I can find Cobb? Should I take the shapeshifter out right now? Should I make a run for it?

"Ask your questions or whatever it is you need," Mr. Fake-Bole grumbles and makes a shooing motion at me with his hands. "Get on with it. I have work to do."

Okay. I guess I'll play it normal for now, maybe even figure out what this shapeshifter is doing here.

I clear my throat. "Like I said, there were a number of red flags triggered by our security measures. There's been a large amount of client data pulled recently—"

"We're always pulling data," he says gruffly.

"Client data on a very particular group of people, specifically those taking the serum designated Y-S." I say it in a flat tone and watch his reaction. His eyes narrow. "And from the look of this floor, all that data is being printed out and combed through by you. Why don't you explain that to me? What are you doing with all that data? What are you looking for?"

We have a staring contest and eventually he asks, "Who are you really?"

That's it. It's over. No cat and mouse for us. We'll have to do this the old fashioned way. Since I'm on my own, I have to make my own call.

"The better question is, who are you?" I say. "I mean, it must be killing you to have to sit around in that squat man's body all day. I bet you're just itching to change back into your home form."

He doesn't show any sign that I've touched a nerve, that I've caught onto his secret. In fact he doesn't move at all. He freezes up and even the trembling in his hands stops as he clenches them together.

"That's right," I say, fingers curling around the bio-mech gun to activate it. The smooth, flat surface begins to transform. "I know what you are, and by now I suspect you know who I am."

The muscles around his tiny mouth tighten. "You're too young to be with them."

"Let's just say I'm a special case. As for you, you're in violation of about a dozen Federal Title 51 chapters—impersonating a human with malicious intent, interference with commercial trade, probably serum tampering. Shall I go on? Or are you going to answer some of my questions?"

He tenses as though to spring forward. I raise the bio-mech gun, which now actually resembles a silver gun fitted to the curve of my hand, and level it with his chest. He freezes again.

"Where is the real Mr. Bole?" I ask, the gun in my hand steady. "What have you done with him?"

The fake Mr. Bole smiles but says nothing. I'm getting irritated. Before I can keep at him, he moves faster than I anticipate. He snatches the coffee cup off his desk and flings it at my face. I dodge to the side but too slow. The cup clips me on the shoulder and scalding hot coffee splashes all over the side of my neck and shoulder. I let out a yelp of pain and automatically clutch my arms in towards my chest. The shapeshifter launches himself from behind the desk and throws us both to the ground. We roll apart for a mere second but it's enough. I bring the bio-mech gun up and fire. A pulse, visible as a streamlined shockwave through the air, strikes the fake Mr. Bole in the chest and he stumbles backwards onto the floor.

Panting hard through the pain and surprise, I keep my gun trained on him but he doesn't get up. Careful of the reddening burn on my shoulder, I push myself up and brace myself against the opaque wall behind me. I need to call Hawk. We need to get this shapeshifter out of here somehow before security figures out there's been an incident. I grab my purse, yank out my cellphone, and hit the speed dial for my brother.

It rings three times before he picks up. "*Agent Roe, what a surprise. What do you—*"

"I need help carrying a body."

Silence ticks by until he says, "Uh, what? Sorry, I must not have heard you right."

"The CEO is a shapeshifter. Top floor. You better hurry."

This time he doesn't hesitate. "On my way. Hang tight."

The line cuts out and I throw the phone back into my purse. I cautiously approach the unconscious shapeshifter, keeping my gun trained on him the whole time. Parts of Mr. Bole's features have begun to melt away like wax on a candle. I've seen this kind of transformation before but it's still unnerving every time to see two people morphed into a single body when the magic of the change is no longer held together by the shapeshifter. My shoulder aches as I step around him and look out the window. The parking garage almost touches the building it's so close. If we could get there with the shapeshifter in tow . . .

A black cable catches my eye. I press my face against the window and spot a window washer's scaffold hanging a floor down. It's not exactly subtle but it might be our only option if we can't find another exit.

I walk back out to the cubicles as I contemplate how to even get to the scaffold when the hairs on the back of my neck rise. I spin about and find a lady with a narrow, unpleasant sort of face staring at me from another office further along the glass wall. Her hair is wrapped in a bun as tight as her smile. I thought Mr. Fake-Bole had been the only person up here. I gulp and glance at the gun in my hand.

"Sorry, miss, I'm with the—"

"IMS, I can tell." She laughs, the sound high and sharp. Okay, so clearly not just some office worker. "Aren't you a little young to be with the International Monster Slayers? I want to see your badge. Your real one, not that FDA garbage."

I swallow my pride. "I don't have mine yet. I'm a junior agent."

Her smile twists into a cruel shape. "Oh, I see. Well, why don't you put down that toy of yours, little girl, before you get hurt?"

"How about you tell me who *you* are first?" I snap.

An angry red flush crosses the woman's face—then the red keeps spreading until all of the woman's skin is the fierce color of blood. Her entire body expands like a freakish balloon and her fingers lengthen into hideous spike-like claws. She's a shapeshifter but not a normal one. A crazy powerful, super angry version—a berserker.

I draw up my gun and fire. She ducks but the blast hits her in the shoulder. She slams against the opaque glass of her office, creating spider-web cracks through it. I begin to advance to make sure she's down when she kicks out and sends a water cooler flying towards me. I try to leap out of the way but it catches my right leg and sends me spinning. A deluge of water falls around me as I fall flat on my face four feet away and taste coffee-stained carpet.

Without even looking behind me I push myself up and begin running back through the building. A loud, hideous shriek follows me so I start to zig-zag through the cubicles. I fire blindly over my shoulder and accidentally hit a computer. I keep running as its box frame explodes and sets fire to the stacks of paper surrounding it. The berserker pauses at the flames, giving me a chance to slide under a desk and get out of sight.

A few heartbeats later a storm of paper flies up into the air a couple of cubicles away from where I'm hiding. Shredded scraps rain down all around bearing client data in cramped typeface. Invoices and spreadsheets continue to fly until it's hard to see anything clearly. Smoke rises and flames crawl across the loose papers.

I pant and clutch onto the bio-mech gun desperately. Peering out from beneath the desk, I can barely make out the cracked glass of the office down the length of the open room. I listen for movement but can't hear anything over the rustling and crackling of paper still falling and catching fire.

"There you are!"

I gasp and roll onto my back. The berserker is standing almost directly over me, one enormous clawed hand raised, ready to rip me to shreds. It pulls back its lips with a hiss to expose sharp, shark-like teeth, its blonde hair now the shade of blaze orange.

A shockwave ripples the air above me and the berserker is jerked back by the pulse of a bio-mech gun. I scramble away out of reach and get to my feet as Hawk strides forward with his own gun in hand. His expression is furious and he marches unfazed through the clouds of paper. When he reaches me, we stand shoulder to shoulder and face the berserker with guns raised. It's grasping onto the sides of a cubicle, sinking down and effectively crushing a computer monitor. Wheezing escapes its repulsive form.

"You'll never stop us!" it shrieks.

"You're under arrest," Hawk and I say in unison. Our fingers are on the triggers at the same time and we unload. Blast after blast jolts through the berserker until it's spread out on the floor, the redness fading from its skin and its body slowly shrinking to the size of a normal human. Once we're sure it's really down, I let my gun hand drop and we survey the room. The paper has settled on the floor and everywhere else like some kind of peculiar snow. Flames spread out to each cubicle, eating up the abundant source of fuel.

"Well," Hawk says and tucks his gun into an inner pocket of his suit jacket. "That could have gone better."

The next second the overhead sprinklers turn on and we start getting dowsed. An alarm rings through the building.

"Oops," my brother says nonchalantly. "Time to go. I hope you have some sort of a plan or we're screwed."

Police and firefighters are sure to be on their way soon. There's no way we can go back down the way we came and escape before they arrive. It's not even an option with two bodies to carry. I stride past him to the office at the back, raise my gun, and fire into the glass wall. It cracks, spiderwebs, then blows outward from the force of the bio-mech pulses. Hawk stares at me when I turn around to start hauling up the berserker's limp body.

"There's a window washing scaffold," I say.

He gestures widely to the window I blasted out. "You could have *opened* it."

I shrug. "Too late to argue now."

Together we drag the unconscious berserker and shapeshifter to the blown out window. Hawk holds my hand to anchor me as I lean out far enough to grab the cable to the scaffold. I'm breathing fast as I cling to it, water dripping from my hair, and slide down into the scaffold. I'm dizzy and lightheaded at this height. I avoid looking down, focus on the pulleys, and hoist the scaffold up to the window. Hawk shoves the bodies over and I make sure they don't fall off before he climbs in. The first thing he does is look over the side and his entire body shudders.

"I'm starting to think I really don't like heights," he says in a high-pitched voice. "Do you have any idea how high up we are? You wouldn't be able to tell the difference between me and chili if I fell from up—"

"Hawk," I say sharply. "Focus. You're not going to fall. Tie yourself in." I toss him a line of rope lying in the bed of the rickety scaffold. He wraps it around his waist and ties himself to the railing. I do the same.

Hawk mans the lever for the pulleys and we leave the destruction of Werevine Pharmaceutical's executive floor behind. Bright flashing lights of police cars and fire trucks pass below on the main street as we begin the long descent to the ramp of the parking garage directly below us. Hawk is right—we are *very* high up.

"Crap, they're moving fast," Hawk says. Men in blue uniforms and firefighter gear surge towards the building. We both hunker in the scaffold hoping not to be seen. "Hold onto your guts, Phoenix."

"What? Why?"

He yanks on the lever and we begin to skyrocket down. My stomach slips into my throat. Half of me feels like throwing up, the other half wants to scream like I'm on a roller coaster ride. The floors of the building flip past like slides of old film—each one an image of startled workers staring out from cubicles, spilling cups of coffee, or jumping out of their chairs in surprise.

Once we pass thirty some floors Hawk hauls on the lever and a billow of smoke rises from the cables with a shriek worse than that of the berserker. The scaffold shudders and comes to a very jerky, unpleasant stop. It takes me five seconds to remember how to breathe properly again and uncoil my numb hands from around a bucket I didn't realize I had been clutching. Holding back my breakfast, I look over the edge of the railing and see we've stopped nearly level with the ramp of the parking garage.

Hysterical laughter finds its way out of my throat and Hawk joins in as he throws an improvised hook on a rope to catch the cement side of the ramp. Together we pull ourselves over so the scaffold leans at an awkward angle and the two unconscious bodies thump together against the thin railing. I hear shouts as the police spot us.

"Go, go, go," I urge my brother. He hops the cement wall and holds the scaffold steady as I heave up the bodies and dump them onto the ramp. Hawk lets go of the scaffold once I'm out as well and it swings back to bang against the windows of the glass building. He dashes into the structure to find our car while I sling one body over my shoulder and drag the other. It's times like these when I really appreciate my strength. I might not be as special as the shapeshifters but I have gifts of my own. Well, really just the one gift. I am strong.

I stumble along in the dark of the parking garage and hear Hawk begin arguing with another familiar voice. I finally reach our black SUV and bang on the hatch door.

"Hey, open up! These guys are starting to get heavy!"

Hawk shouts some more and the door clicks open. I lift the bodies into the open hatch and hear him arguing with our supervising agent.

"Cobb, we had no choice," Hawk says. I shove the fake Mr. Bole—who looks like a completely different man—into the back. He's become a lot taller and I have trouble fitting his legs inside.

"It was supposed be a routine check!" Cobb shouts. I catch sight of him in the driver's seat when I flip the berserker on top of the shapeshifter. Her face catches on the edge of the SUV and I have to really shove her in.

Hawk laughs nervously, the sound of the police sirens nearly drowning him out. "Oh, it *was* routine up until some crazy shapeshifters decided to kill Phoenix."

"Are you two insane? You managed to attract the attention of half the police in the city!" Cobb is nearly hysterical at this point. I can see his floppy mop of brown curls shaking above the driver's seat. I tuck the berserker's foot into the hatch, slam the door shut, then rush around the side of the SUV and hop into the second row of seats.

"Why are we still sitting here?" I ask loudly. "It's too late to argue about what we should have done. Get us out of here, Cobb."

He turns around in his seat to give me the crazy eyes, but Hawk fastens himself into the passenger seat and we both look at Cobb expectantly. The sound of sirens is hardly muted inside the car. Cobb's crazy eyes grow wider but he finally puts the car into gear and we fly out of the garage to the sound of squealing tires.

2

I never appreciated how well Cobb could drive until he manages to evade every police car trying to find us. I also never realized how many profanities Cobb knows. He lets them out in a spew until he regains himself enough to phone in to the director of the Minneapolis Division of the IMS. Cobb explains the situation and requests agents to secure the Werevine Pharmaceutical building and scrub the surveillance footage before the police can identify Hawk and me.

I stare out the window and listen to the director yell through the cell phone. Hawk and I share a look of apprehension. It's not like we had a lot of options at the time when the shapeshifters were trying to kill me, but this is bad. Drawing attention to our work is one of the worst things we can do, but that's exactly what happened. I gaze out at the Mississippi River on my left. The sun is still high and the water reflects painful shards of light into my eyes. The trees bordering the river are nearly bare as fall creeps over Minnesota, each October day growing colder. The leafless birches and poplars wave boney fingers at me as the SUV curves along the road.

"Yes, sir," Cobb says into his phone, holding it slightly away from his ear as the director continues to shout at him. "I'm on Main Street right now. We'll be at the top of the laboratory in a few minutes." Cobb glances back at me in the rear-view mirror. "Yes, sir. I will."

As soon as he hangs up, Cobb chucks the phone into the cup holder in the center console. "Why do I have to be the one to babysit a couple of delinquents? Are you two insane?" he snaps at us.

We both remain silent. We quickly discovered from the beginning to keep silent during Cobb's frequent tirades. Interrupting him only makes him angrier.

He swings off Main Street and into the Supra Energy Power Park. After a quick chat with the guard and a flash of Cobb's badge, we're let through. He pulls into the parking lot just past the power park and before the Flumen Laboratory. He backs up to a small cement bunker on the rear side of the lot shaded by trees, rams the shifter into park, stalks out of the SUV, and slams the door behind him.

"How bad do you think?" Hawk asks quietly.

"I don't know," I answer. "Optimistically, they'll just suspend us. I think. Worst case, we get kicked out of Underground."

I see the muscles in his face tighten and I know he's thinking the same thing I am. If we get kicked out there's nowhere for us to go. We've been orphans since we were four and Underground is the only home we know. The IMS and its world are our family.

Cobb opens the rear hatch and just gestures to us, apparently unable to look us in the eye. His mop of hair continues to shake with his suppressed fury. Hawk and I ease out of our seats and meet him at the back. He points to the bodies, points to us, then starts to walk to the cement bunker. Taking the hint, we lift the bodies ourselves, sling them over our shoulders fireman style, and follow Cobb into the building. Inside are two guards bearing the IMS logo on their uniforms—a dragon crouched over a shield bearing the division's name. Cobb complains to them, uses a few more swear words, and the guards let us pass through a thick metal door.

I'm familiar with the room and the procedure. This is just one of the many entrances for humans like us to enter Underground. Its walls are all gray cement and there's nothing in it except for two black platforms that can hold a good twenty people each. We gather on one and Cobb hits a button on the top of the platform's control pedestal. The platform shudders and starts gliding down an angled tunnel. I have to readjust the berserker across my shoulders to keep my balance as the platform picks up speed.

Cold, wet air blows into my face from intervals along the long tunnel down, down, down. I can almost hear the roar of the Mississippi River as we pass beneath it to the very bottom of the riverbed and a little deeper still until the platform slows to a stop in a nearly identical cement room as the one up top. Bernie, the guard at the bottom of the chute, is snoozing in a chair. His graying hair nearly hides the little horns sticking out of the top of his head but is unable to conceal his deer-like ears. A pair of cloven hooves sticks out of the bottom of his maroon slacks.

When Cobb shoves open the metal exit door and it gives a whiny creak, Bernie jerks awake with a snort and nods to us.

"Hey, kids," Bernie the faun says with a smile. I always liked Bernie. Every time I see him he's got a smile and friendly greeting waiting for me. He's the poster child for faun hospitality. "How did your first mission go?"

"Not well. Idiots," Cobb growls and hustles through the door.

I grimace and promise to tell him later before Hawk and I chase after Cobb to keep up, our captives nearly slipping off our shoulders.

As soon as we step through the doors it's like entering a whole different world. Colors, sounds, and smells blend together into something fantastic and instantly familiar. The cement walls stretch up fifty feet high and are covered in bright banners bearing different crests and depictions of all the legendary races that reside within this hidden city beneath the Mississippi River.

I take a deep breath of the aroma coming from the center of Market Square twenty feet in front of us. Buildings designed after different ancient structures—from the red-titled temples of Japan to the arched basilica of Rome to the mud-brick shops of Mesopotamia—stand brilliant and draped in even more color. Down the first row I spot the source of the mouthwatering smell—Old Man Two, a crabby but gifted centaur, is mixing a massive cauldron of stew. Farther down I see a group of young fauns fighting over muffins sold at Giant's Reach, a pair of water sprites and nymphs bartering over soil at Madame Rush's Emporium, and a doddery unicorn giving a ride to a young elf. Up high on the roofs are the gargoyles, hulking stone creatures animated by magic to act as Underground's vigilant protectors. Home sweet home.

I still have vague memories of when I first came here with Hawk. Only four years old, we were terrified by the strange otherworldly things until a kindly faun became our guardian and eased us into the world of legendary and mythical creatures. Now, having spent most my life here, I can't imagine living anywhere else. It's the outside world that seems strange. An unpleasant twinge twists my gut. I hope our recklessness earlier today doesn't cost us this place we've learned to call home.

As I stand there considering what it would be like to live somewhere mundane like Chicago, a group of IMS agents pulling two hospital gurneys part the crowds through the middle of Merchant Square. They don't speak a word to me or Hawk but whisper in undertones with Cobb, so we plop the shapeshifters onto the gurneys. I roll my shoulders trying to work out the kink I got from hauling a berserker around and eventually Cobb motions for us to follow the agents pushing the gurneys through Merchant Square.

I try not to make eye contact with any of the shopkeepers or customers. I know all of the creatures that live in Underground. My brother and I have been here for fourteen years. Most of the creatures buying fried snails or trading ancient coins I recognize or know by name.

We pass shop after shop until we reach the colonnade. Long rows of cherry trees covered with pink blossoms lead directly to the heart of Underground. Shallow fountains stand at regular intervals down the lane and flecks of water touch my skin when a couple of water sprites decide now's a good time to invite me to play with them. Their child-like shapes formed of water sit giggling in the pool of a nearby fountain and beckon me towards them. I wave them off and keep moving. Warm light filters through the branches overhead by the magic of a fire sprite to keep the trees alive all year long and dries some of the dampness out of my clothes. This is one of my favorite places in Underground. I wonder vaguely if this will be my last time seeing it.

The trees end and we stand before the very heart of Underground. Another agent comes out to greet us and talks with Cobb. I stare up at the glossy black wall of IMS Headquarters that stretches almost all the way up to the ceiling. The artificial sunlight behind me gleams off its surface and illuminates golden letters etched in bold above the entrance. *Protectors of legends. Secrecy is our shield. Knowledge is our weapon.*

The shapeshifters are carted away to the right towards the penitent cells but Cobb takes us straight to the head offices. We enter the black door and it's as if someone flicks a switch and everything magical in Underground never happened. The inside is like any generic human building—off-white walls, tan carpet, ordinary sized chairs, two sofas, and a front desk. The only things exceptional are the pictures of various dragons hanging on the walls. The receptionist greets us with a smile but her expression quickly melts into shock when Cobb whispers to her. She nods after a few words and dials someone, speaking quietly into the receiver before hanging up.

Cobb turns back to us. "You two stay here and don't do anything stupid. Think you can handle that?"

"Uhh . . ." Hawk says in a dull drone, clearly done being his usual charming self. "Like right here? Freeze where we're standing? Or can we sit down?"

Cobb doesn't even respond but sweeps away down the only hallway and disappears from sight. Once he's gone we collapse onto separate sofas. Now that my adrenaline has worn off, the coffee burn on my shoulder is really starting to ache. I gently rub it and stare down the long hallway. The only sound is the receptionist clicking away at her keyboard.

An old memory surfaces of the first time I was brought here. After all the strange things in Merchant Square, the normal rooms of headquarters had been a welcome relief. Nowadays they feel grossly out of place. We had come here during a storm. I remember dripping a puddle of water onto the floor in the exact same place I'm sitting now. I quickly push the thought out of my mind, of being that scared little girl. Such thoughts will only lead to painful memories.

We sit in the reception area longer than I can control my patience. Hawk and I stand at the same time and begin to pace. Every time we cross paths we reach out and give each other a low five. It has always been our way of saying we're there for each other.

The phone rings at the receptionist's desk. She picks up and doesn't speak a word before hanging up again.

"Director Knox will see you now," she says.

I take a deep breath and walk step in step with Hawk down the hallway. We turn left, go up a flight of stairs, and then go right. A glass wall opens up on our left along the next hallway. While the interior of the building may seem generic, what stands through the glass is anything but. I look out on a stone courtyard nestled in the center of IMS headquarters with nothing in it except a peculiar archway. It's of the same glossy black finish as the exterior of headquarters and bears golden letters but they are in a language I don't understand. The script is jagged and sharp, then fluid in other places—the language of dragons. I don't know why but it's always sent my heart thundering whenever I see it. If I stare at it long enough, the air around the arch seems to waver and spark with hidden power. I quickly look away and turn down another hallway on our right.

A single door stands at the end with a nameplate boasting DIRECTOR DAVID KNOX across its lacquer finish. We both pause in front of it. I've only been in this office three times before—twice for "unruly incidents" and once to be granted junior agent status. Hawk stands frozen so I reach up, wrinkle my nose, and knock.

"Come in," a deep voice says muffled through the door. I obey and enter followed by my brother. "Close the door."

I swallow involuntarily and do as I'm told. I turn back around, stand straight, and clasp my hands together behind my back to mimic my brother's stance.

This room is like the rest of headquarters except there are black and white photos of dead presidents hanging on the walls alongside medals and military commendations in neat frames. A single tinted window overlooks the colonnade. Before it stands a heavy desk bare of anything except a single open file and a cup of coffee. The smell of it makes me realize I'm still wearing my silk blouse with a huge coffee stain along the top.

Cobb stands with his back to us and his hands twitch like he wants to strangle something. Standing across from him behind the desk is Director David Knox. He's a good foot taller than any of us—I used to think he had giant blood in him—and his skin is a shade darker than his mahogany desk. The fluorescents reflect off his bald dome but are unable to touch his dark eyes. He's in a crisp suit that puts the rest of our attires to shame and makes him seem even taller. His even stare makes my palms start to sweat. He's always been intimidating.

"Cobb just finished explaining what happened," he says, his deep baritone loud in the office. "Do you have any idea what you two have done?"

I'm not sure if I'm supposed to respond or if it's a rhetorical question. I wait it out but when Director Knox continues to stare, I sputter, "We were just—"

"Doing everything the IMS is *not* supposed to do," he booms. I have a feeling he was waiting for an answer just so he could cut me off. This isn't looking good. "Tell me what our motto is."

Hawk and I say in unison, "Protectors of legends. Secrecy is our shield. Knowledge is our weapon."

"Exactly!" He begins to pace and gestures out the tinted window to the colonnade beyond. "The whole point of Underground is secrecy, to keep this world hidden from those who would fear it. You've nearly exposed us all! I had to send in a team to clean up your mess and try to make excuses to the local authorities."

"With all due respect," Hawk says, "we stopped two dangerous shapeshifters."

"By nearly destroying an entire floor of a building!" The director slams a fist on his desk and we all jump. "Do you even know what Werevine Pharmaceutical does? You two of all people should know what they produce."

I glance uneasily at my brother. We're broaching a very touchy topic. "They produce the werewolf serum," I say quietly.

"Yes!" Director Knox rolls back his shoulders and takes a deep breath, making a clear show of reining in his temper. "They're one of the largest manufacturers of the medicine that keeps *your* kind in their human minds." He points at Hawk for emphasis. "Now who knows how long before the company will be back up and running?"

"That was the whole point, sir," I interject, suddenly angry for him badgering my brother for something that isn't even his fault. It's not like Hawk chose to be bitten and become a werewolf. "What were the shapeshifters doing at the company and why were they going through the records of werewolves? We were just trying to—"

"I don't care what you were trying to do. If you figured out there were shapeshifters, you should have gotten out of there and notified your superior so we could send proper agents in to do the job." The director massages his bald head and stares out the window. "I should have seen this coming. You've always been troublemakers. I still remember when you convinced a water sprite to haunt a high school water fountain. You've never fit easily into the human world."

I clench my jaw and fight back raw emotion in my throat. I'm furious but the director's also right. Once Underground became our home, the rest of the world became odd. We don't belong there anymore, not since my brother became a werewolf and I became something of an oddity myself.

"I knew your stint of field training as junior agents was going to end in disaster," the director continues, pacing again behind his desk. "If you two didn't have a certain dragon pushing to get you into the action, I never would have agreed to send you out."

My head snaps up. A dragon has been campaigning for us to become agents? I thought we got into the IMS because they finally got sick of saying no to our staggering number of requests to join.

"Which dragon?" I ask.

Director Knox gives me his signature hard stare and plants both hands on his desk to level with me. "You know which one."

"Sir," Cobb interrupts. "What are we going to do with them?"

"All three of you will be suspended."

Cobb leans forward, his mop of hair shaking yet again and his face turning red. "Excuse me, all *three* of us?"

"That's right. You were supposed to be in Werevine with them. Instead, you let them run free and destroy part of a company while you were on a smoke break. Get out of my office, Cobb. Go turn in your badge and weapon at the armory."

I flinch as Cobb hurtles past me and slams the door on his way out. A hollow feeling fills my chest. We're being suspended. What are we supposed to do now? I suddenly imagine myself chopping up pig feet in the back of Old Man Two's shop for the rest of my life. I can't let that happen.

"Your suspension will be more permanent than Cobb's," the director says once it's just us. "You've done enough damage. I'd like to kick both of you out of here for good but you'd probably cause even more destruction on your own." He drags a hand down his face and gives a heavy sigh. My heart beats a jagged, painful rhythm in my chest. "However, you're still both special cases and have clearance to stay in Underground. For now, I want you both to report to Junior Agent Wallowitz to return whatever weapons you *borrowed* from the armory without authorization."

He points to the door and it's clear our time is over. Hawk opens the door for me and we both exit, our feet dragging on the tan carpet. As we trudge along the hallway and go down the stairwell, Hawk whispers, "What do we do now?"

3

I always find something new whenever I visit the armory. The room itself looks like an enormous cave with blue LED lights embedded throughout the ceiling that give a diffused glow similar to moonlight. A few brighter spotlights shine down on three computers in the very center that catalog the various weapons strapped to the walls. There are several metal racks holding bio-mech guns. Next to those are rows of swords, staves, axes, hammers, crossbows, and longbows that hang along the walls, held up by near invisible holders so the weapons appear to float in the air.

At the back are glass cases where famous weapons are on display. There are golden swords etched with dragon script, a flamethrower branded with a skull, and even a chainsaw with a plaque that reads *"Used by Rae Lightfeather to decapitate the infamous Siren of Mississippi River at the water entrance to Underground."*

I peer into the newest glass case while Hawk swings a monk staff at invisible monsters on my left. He's changed into a plain t-shirt and jeans—I did the same after that terrible meeting, ready to get out of that coffee-stained blouse as soon as possible. We didn't put on our junior agent uniforms just in case Director Knox decides to take those away too. I sigh and try to focus on what's inside the glass case illuminated by blue light. It's something that looks like a bio-mech gun but longer with silver gills down the length of the barrel.

"What's a phase-repeater?" I ask offhand, reading the plaque inscription.

A wheelchair rolls up beside me carrying one of my oldest friends, Aaron Wallowitz. We just call him Witty. He came to Underground around the same time as us and under similar circumstances. A blanket covers his scarred legs that are defunct after he suffered a hydra attack when he was five. His parents—a pair of IMS agents—were killed in the attack. His godfather, who still works for the IMS, brought him here for healing. They couldn't do anything for Witty's legs but they let him stay in the protection of the magical city.

Witty peers into the glass case beside me and brushes his dark hair out of his bright blue eyes. "It's new dragon tech," he says. "The latest model of the bio-mech gun—fully automatic and with extra kick. They're for use against level five monsters."

"Ah, I see." I straighten and dodge Hawk's attempt to smack me in the back with the monk staff. Witty returns to the computer he had been working on so I follow him. "What are you up to?"

"Just entering data on the two bio-mech guns you guys said you were using for *target practice*." He quirks an eyebrow at me then strums on the lighted keyboard, plugging notes into some database. Witty's lucky he has top-notch computer skills—he's so good that he was asked to work the IMS systems before officially becoming a junior agent. At least he has a job.

Hawk comes around the computers popping into various kung fu stances with the staff and flashes a wide smile at us. He's playful despite everything that's happened but there's something lingering in his eyes. I'd say it's fear because I feel it too—fear of not knowing what's going to happen to us now. "We did use them for target practice . . . just on moving targets. Right, Nix?"

"Right" I say. "One pudgy, the other bright red, big, and freakin' scary." I hold my arms out at my sides like a gorilla and make a high-pitched shriek, attempting to be as playful as my brother so I don't have to think about anything else. Hawk fake attacks me with the staff complete with sound effects.

Witty holds up a hand and shakes his head. "No way. You two fought a *berserker?*"

"Yeah," Hawk says and throws a fake blow at my head. I grab the staff and start to shake him. He's trying not to laugh as he says, "We kind of weren't supposed to, though."

"Hence, the permanent 'suspension'," Witty says with a sigh. "Well done."

I push Hawk away to glare at Witty. "Hey, we've already gotten enough crap from the director. We don't need it from you too."

"I'm just saying, you won't have much of an excuse to come visit me now that you aren't on active duty. I'm always stuck in this cave, remember?"

I roll my eyes. "Oh, how will you survive without us?"

Hawk jumps behind Witty to grab the back of his wheel-chair. "We'll still come around for races!" He starts to push Witty forward at a fast clip out of the armory, Witty yelling the whole way.

We run a few laps around headquarters, Witty holding onto his wheelchair for dear life, but eventually an agent comes out and barks at us to knock it off after we nearly crash into the doddery unicorn near the colonnade. Witty wheels himself back to the armory after Hawk and I are banished from headquarters. Without the company of our friend and without any training or missions to look forward to tomorrow, our shoulders slump.

I suggest getting cheesy noodles at Old Man Two's. Hawk shrugs noncommittally but follows me to the centaur's restaurant anyway. The noise and mixed aroma of the market surrounds us from the various eateries, apothecaries, and emporiums. I glance at each of the shops morosely.

"I suppose we'll have to get a job somewhere," I mutter.

Hawk clenches his jaw and keeps his eyes straight ahead. "Yeah."

I don't mention jobs again. There's always been prejudice against werewolves in general throughout the magical community and Hawk is no exception. Werewolves *are* diseased, infected with an evil magic. They aren't legally considered monsters anymore since the invention of the serum that lets werewolves keep their minds, but still, it's not easy being a werewolf. It certainly won't help Hawk's job prospects.

We reach the restaurant and an airy voice calls my name. "Phoenix! Over here!"

Celina, a faun with long golden locks and a permanent

smile, waves me over to the seating area outside the restaurant. She's wrapped in a red silk, brocade dress and her crossed hooves stick out from under the table she shares with Doocan the giant. He's got a bowl the size of a gallon bucket in front of him. He waves his dinner-plate-sized hand and gives us a gap-toothed smile before attacking his soup. I take the chair opposite Celina and Hawk plops down beside me.

"Oh, darling," Celina coos and reaches across the table to grasp my hands in hers, the soft fur on the edges of her palms like velvet against my skin. Her deer-like ears flick back and forth in agitation. "You two look terrible. What happened? You must tell me everything and not squander a detail to the void." She waves over Old Man Two. "A couple of bowls of raisin soup for my friends, please!"

The centaur grumbles something and clomps off into the restaurant. I worked for him a couple of summers ago but you'd think I'm some impolite customer by the indifference he shows me. I heave a sigh and spill the story to Celina. She's one of the only people I can talk unabashed to apart from Hawk. Celina was the one that took care of us both when we first came to Underground. She's the closest thing I have to a mother. She listens with rapt attention despite Doocan loudly slurping his soup beside her. My story is eventually interrupted as Old Man Two returns to shrug two bowls of soup onto the table in front of me and Hawk.

"Thanks," I say but the centaur ignores me and stalks away.

"Oh my dears," Celina sighs. "I'm so sorry. I truly wish there was something I could do for the pair of you."

Doocan finally speaks and stares wide-eyed at me. "You discovered the shapeshifter by yourself?"

"Yeah."

"You are smart."

"Thanks, Doocan."

He stares off into space and doesn't rejoin the conversation, ignoring us again. None of us take any offense. Tuning out is just something he does.

"We'll figure something out," Celina assures us. "I promise. Hawk, dear, how are you doing? You haven't spoken a word."

Hawk shrugs, then pushes out his chair and walks towards the eastern end of Underground, most likely going to the stadium near the water entrance. I let him go. I know what becoming any agent means to him, what it means to me. With everything that's happened, I wouldn't be surprised if he runs a few laps on the track to let it all out.

I lean back in my chair, blow out an exasperated breath, and stare up at the cement ceiling a long ways up. Celina starts suggesting a slew of other jobs we might try for but they're mostly custodian work or cooking. My mind wanders as I watch a couple of air sprites that look like child-shaped clouds run across the ceiling and stop at slated vents to circulate the air. Then they're off chasing each other again.

When Celina puts a hand on my arm I almost jump. She pulls me up out of my chair and pats Doocan on his forearm to get his attention.

"Come on," she prompts. "We haven't watched a movie together for some time. I heard they're playing one of those spy movies you love. It'll be fun."

I don't fight the pull on my arm and allow myself to be led away from the market to the north side of Underground. We grab ourselves a couple bags of smoked paprika popcorn from the nymph vendor outside the entertainment arcade and make for the movie theater. We slip past a group of rowdy elves having a dance off and I almost get stepped on by a centaur trotting down the row carrying rolls of video game tickets. We hurry into the safety of the dark theater and worm between the wide spaced seats to the back right corner. We're late for the movie tonight. It's already in the opening credit sequence with ladies dancing in some bizarre flashing color intro.

I stuff a fistful of popcorn in my mouth and try to focus on the screen. Right now I just want to forget everything that happened today. I wish Hawk were here though.

I zone out as the hero sneaks into a secret facility in the mountains. I sink into a stupor and the tension in my shoulders begins to ease away. I've been coming to watch movies here since Celina first told me everything was going to be all right. She was the one who brought me and Hawk to the theater and showed us the video game room—the fun, semi-normal side of Underground. She shared her love of smoked paprika popcorn and introduced us to Doocan, the friendliest giant you'll ever meet.

The movie picks up in pace and the hero uses some crazy gadget to blow open a grate.

"That's not possible. That's not possible . . ." Doocan mutters beside me in a hypnotic-like trance.

Celina reaches over me to pat his knee. "It's okay, Doocan. He's allowed to do these things in his own movie. He's special."

Special—it's a word people have used to describe me on more than one occasion. I automatically reach for the silver mark under the sleeve of my shirt on my right shoulder. It's an odd discoloration of the skin in the shape of three vertical lines trailing off. A mark left by a powerful dragon—the same dragon I suspect rallied for me and Hawk to join the IMS. I'm what they call Blessed—people touched by dragons. The few other Blessed I know can levitate things with their mind, melt metal, or control electricity. All I've been able to do is lift heavy things. So much for being special. At least it gives me a free, lifelong pass to Underground.

I don't pay much attention to the movie after that. I just nibble at my popcorn. Every time a song plays, even a sad one, Celina gets out of her seat to dance. Fauns are like that. She pulls me up one time and makes me dance with her. Once she sees that my heart isn't into it she doesn't do it again. As soon as the movie ends, I leave my friends behind and shuffle back through the arcade, across Merchant Square, and to the apartments on the other side.

I pass the cement housing for the giants, the fields and forests for the fauns, centaurs, and nymphs, until I reach a row of Roman inspired houses complete with marble columns and balconies. I reach the one in the middle with a red door and step inside. Almost everything inside is made of marble, from the staircase, to the parlor benches, to the columns supporting the apartment complex. Hawk and I share it with other agents on three separate floors but most of them are hardly ever at Underground anymore. I tramp up the winding flight to the top floor and enter our apartment.

The main living space only has a sofa and one tiny table in the center. I glance out the open balcony to the lights over Merchant Square before turning into the connected kitchen. As usual, there's a mess of bloody meat wrappers left on the counter. Grumbling, I shove them into the trash and push open the door to Hawk's room. The inside looks like a couple of air sprites played a game of toss—clothes are scattered all over the floor, there are crumbs spilled from open packets of crackers, and stains of drool mark the rumpled bed sheets. Hawk is already sound asleep on his bed spread out on his stomach, mouth open, a pool of drool forming to create yet another stain. I quietly close the door and slip away to my own room.

Despite the fact Hawk and I are twins, our rooms are like night and day. Everything in my small square of life is tucked away in its proper place, the bed is made, and not a layer of dust dirties any surface. My coffee-stained blouse and skirt are the only things sitting out at the foot of my dresser, ready to be washed the next day.

I sit on the edge of my bed and carefully strip off my shirt. The red burn on my shoulder sticks out painfully, just like my wounded pride. I take a deep breath and slip into my pajamas.

So what if I can't be an agent? At least I get to stay here in this world that I love. I'll just never get a badge and be able to protect legends like all the other Blessed do. I reach for the ripped picture on my nightstand. A happy couple beams up at me clutching onto their two squirrelly, red-haired kids, IMS badges visible on their jackets.

I set the picture back with a sigh. "I'm sorry, Mom and Dad."

4

I'm not sure what to expect after being summoned by Director Knox early the next morning. Hawk and I stand shoulder to shoulder in his office wearing our junior agent uniforms, which are basically just black tactical boots, black pants, a black shirt, and a black fitted jacket with the IMS logo above the heart. They haven't asked for the clothes back at least. Director Knox is sitting in his chair reading and rereading a memo in his hand. He doesn't look particularly happy but at least he hasn't started yelling yet. The clock on his wall ticks loudly like a bomb counting down to detonation.

"I received a call from the DODA this morning," he begins, sets the memo down, and temples his fingers together.

I stand a little straighter. The Department of Dragon Affairs is the secret federal branch in charge of the IMS in the United States. Did we screw up so bad that the head honchos are calling? Do they want to send us to lockup? Or worse, kick us out of Underground?

Director Knox sighs. "It seems you two have a rather influential friend. They've remanded my order from yesterday and are reinstating you as junior agents." He shakes his head in disappointment. I can't hear the clock anymore over the thundering of my heart. "However, we've all agreed that you need a better mentor than Cobb. You need to experience the real world if you're going to function properly in it."

Oh, no. The last time they wanted me and Hawk to experience "the real world" we were sent to high school along with Witty. Worst three years of my life. Things improved after we got kicked out, though.

"You will be escorted to the Moose Lake Field Office where you will train under Agent Barnes. I've already arranged transportation. You'll leave in an hour."

"Uh, sir?" Hawk raises his hand like he's in class. "Where exactly is the Moose Lake Field Office?"

The director studies the watch on his wrist. "It's roughly two hours north of the Twin Cities. Pack your bags and meet Agent Snow at the top of the chutes. You're dismissed."

We walk as calmly as we can out of headquarters but as soon as we hit the colonnade outside we're jumping in the air and giving each other high fives before we're racing to our apartment. Giddy in my relief, I wave to the different shopkeepers in Merchant Square for my hasty goodbye as we rush past them. We're still going to be agents. We're being given a second chance.

By the time we reach our apartment it begins to sink in that we are also leaving our home. This will be the first time since we were four that we will be living somewhere new. At that thought, I take a few deep breaths to calm myself while I stuff my clothes into a duffle bag. Before any true panic sets in, Hawk turns on a rock song in the living room. The music settles my nerves and I finish packing my things at a blazing pace.

I take a turn around the apartment looking for anything I might have missed but realize I'm already set to go. Hawk is still trying to cram the disaster that is his room into a travel bag so I go stand on the open balcony. The music coming from our apartment is so loud that a group of fauns passing by on the street below stop and dance to the beat. I watch them giggling from the balcony and break out a few moves myself.

Hawk comes flying out of his room and joins me in a manic, bizarre jive. We've always been a little crazy, especially when it's just us, and dancing is our expression of happiness. Just as the song stops, a thought pops into my head and I gasp.

"We have to tell our friends goodbye!" I shout.

Still laughing, we leap over the couch, turn off the music, and race down the marble steps with our bags slung across our backs. We run to the armory first where Witty is working at a computer as usual. It's hard to feel bad about how unhappy he looks when I feel like there's a balloon of pure helium expanding in my chest. I'm ready to fly away right then. We promise to call and I give Witty a hug before we're racing off again.

We find Celina and Doocan eating around a table at Giant's Reach. Doocan pulls on a grumpy frown at our news but Celina instantly bursts into tears and starts blubbering about not having anyone to watch movies with. By the time we manage to extricate ourselves from her deathly tight hug, we're running late. Boots thudding against the cement floor, we burst through the door to the chutes, pass an out-of-breath goodbye to Bernie the guard, and then rise on a platform up to the world above.

A kindly, balding agent is waiting for us beside a dark SUV. Once our bags are loaded in the back and we each have a bag of smoked paprika popcorn for the road, we pull out of the power park and move onto I-35 on our way north out of the Twin Cities.

The only city I've ever known flashes past me. Cars veer around us, fishing in and out of lanes like a swarm of bees following familiar paths to freedom. The skyscrapers and towers gleam in the morning light but fade away in the distance. Agent Snow navigates the traffic with experienced ease and soon we are flying out of the city. The highway shrinks down one lane at a time until trees close in on either side before giving way to fields, some with cows and horses, others barren and brown.

I prop my chin up in my hand, brace my elbow against the door of the vehicle, and stare out. We pass a few of the outlying cities until the land rolls on almost uninterrupted except for billboards punctuating the scenery with bright splashes of color. I haven't been away from the constant babble of Underground or the restlessness of Minneapolis since I was four. The silence surrounding the hum of our SUV is unnerving. Where on earth are we heading?

Time feels stagnant in the vehicle like we haven't passed any time at all. Hawk and I start up a game of Monster Snatch, imagining which kind of monster lives at the places we see flickering by and have to say how we'd kill or capture it before the place disappears out of sight. The longer we play the louder we get, shouting things in a big rush trying to capture monsters before old silos and barns disappear behind the trees. Apparently we get too rowdy and Agent Snow yells at us to shut up. Boredom sets in again and we pester him to turn on the radio. I almost want to cover my ears when he cranks it up to some rap song.

We sit still, clutching our now empty bags of popcorn while being shouted at by an angry rapper about taking someone's sneakers. When Agent Snow lets out a very loud, relieved sigh, I realize we must have reached our destination but as far as I can tell, there's nothing actually here. He pulls off the highway and makes a left. A white water tower stands in the distance, the only real marker that we've found a town. There's a hotel and restaurant right off the highway but then we go a ways without seeing anything else. Houses start to pop up, a church, a vacant general store, a police station, until we find the first stoplights.

I get a sinking feeling in the pit of my stomach when we enter the main drag, which is more like a pit stop than a city. A lake opens up on our right with a single dock and a bubbling stream feeding into it.

"Is that Moose Lake?" I shout over the rap music, pointing to the lake now obscured by trees and buildings.

Agent Snow shakes his head. "No, that's Moosehead Lake. The real Moose Lake is outside the city of Moose Lake."

"Because that makes perfect sense," Hawk grumbles beside me.

It takes thirty seconds to reach the halfway point of the city. We pause at the second pair of stoplights and I spot a worn down movie theater near the corner. Instead of it making me feel better, my chest aches. We turn off onto a county road and are quickly out of the city again and into the country. Houses are sporadic and tucked back from the road. Everything just feels so . . . empty.

Five minutes later and we're turning onto an even smaller road without a shoulder, back deeper and deeper into swamp and trees. We slow as we reach a gravel driveway on Soldier Road guarded by towering pines that form a wall in either direction fifty feet long. I spot some kind of camera attached to a tree that overlooks the front of the driveway as we pull in. More pines guard the long, bumpy drive, the tires crunching on gravel, until we hit a brown field.

The driveway circles back around on itself outside a log cabin where we at last come to a stop alongside a truck that's shedding so much rust it's sitting in a halo of orange flakes. The cabin certainly doesn't look like much. There's a stump out front with an axe imbedded in it, a pile of wood beside it, and what appears to be an ancient barn looming behind. There are uneven colors on both roofs, as if someone tried to patch holes with different materials. A wooden fence starts along the back of the cabin and extends into the pines. Some of the posts are rotting and held together by something that looks suspiciously like tape. If we were playing Monster Snatch, I would have guessed a near dead troll lived here and all you would have to do to kill it is tap the side of the cabin and the whole thing would collapse on top of it.

"Welcome to the Moose Lake Field Office," Agent Snow announces, gesturing wide with one hand before getting out of the vehicle.

"You've got to be kidding," I say, my stomach dropping into the soles of my feet.

"Considering how much Director Knox doesn't like us," Hawk says, throwing open his door, "this probably *is* his kind of a joke."

We grab our bags and stand outside the cabin as Agent Snow begins digging through a backpack in the hatch of the SUV. He pulls out two cell phones and passes them to us.

"These are for you. The numbers for IMS headquarters and the landline for this field office are already programmed in. Either you or your supervisor needs to call and report in to headquarters every two days per the director's orders."

I glare at the offered cell phone and shove it into my pocket. Agent Snow doesn't offer us anything else. "That's it? No bio-mech guns?"

He actually laughs. "After what happened at Werevine? I don't think so. Besides, you aren't even supposed to carry a handgun until you're twenty-one out in the real world."

"Underground *is* real," Hawk argues, flipping his cell phone over and over until he almost drops it.

Agent Snow snatches the cell phone out of Hawk's hand and sticks it in the top of his duffle bag. "Not out here it isn't, and you'd better remember that."

The door to the cabin creaks open and we all stop to stare. A man steps out in a flannel plaid shirt carrying a dead rabbit by its ears. His gray hair falls a good two inches past his ears and waves lifeless in the breeze. Scruff covers his jaw, building up into a goatee around his thin mouth. His dark eyes are nearly hidden beneath his low brow and, with his wrinkles, it looks like he's been stuck squinting his entire life. He stares at us for a whole silent minute before suddenly turning and whipping the dead rabbit through the air. It sails above us and crashes into the pines, hitting a trunk with a loud thump and catching branch after branch until it hits the ground. Despite feeling a little disturbed, I have the urge to laugh but bite my lip to hold it back.

"I thought they were sending me agents," the man growls, his voice deep and scratchy. "Not some snot-nosed kids."

"We're not kids," I snap.

His eyes widen just enough so I can actually see his entire pupils. "Oh? How old are you exactly?"

"We're seventeen."

"Well, unless the definition of adult has changed recently, I'm pretty sure you're still kids." He turns to Agent Snow, ignoring us. "Really? Since when does the IMS let kids work topside for them?"

Agent Snow just pulls out a file from the backpack he's holding and passes it over. My face burns when I catch a glimpse of my photograph on the outside of the folder. I wonder how much of my history is in that flimsy manila folder. How much of my life have they kept track of?

"Phoenix Mason," the old man drones, pronouncing each syllable with a kind of mean humor. "Hawk Mason. These are your real names?"

"Our parents had a bird fetish," Hawk says calmly and crosses his arms over his chest. "You still haven't told us your name."

At that Agent Snow smiles and starts to backtrack. "I'll let you three have fun. Everything you need is in the file, Agent Jefferson Abraham Barnes."

He chuckles and jumps into the SUV, quickly throwing it into drive, and rolling down the driveway, leaving us quite alone and forsaken.

"So," I say, dropping my bag and crossing my arms as well. "Jefferson Abraham Barnes." I say his name in the same distasteful way he did mine.

"A president fetish is better than stupid birds," he mumbles. He slaps the file closed and retreats into the cabin without another word. We pick up our bags and follow him inside.

Considering what the outside is like, I shouldn't be surprised by the inside but I still am. It's tight, cramped, and messy. Of course, maybe it wouldn't feel so small if there weren't so many random boxes overflowing with paper everywhere. They sit haphazardly on a table, across the narrow kitchen counter allowing just enough room for a pile of dirty dishes, and are stacked precariously as a couple of towers against the far wall. Three doorways split off from the main entrance and there are visible trails through the paper to get to each.

"So, was this paper fort on purpose or the cause of a troll hoarder sneaking in here every night?" Hawk says, gazing up and all around.

Jefferson ignores him and stands in the center of one of the aisles paging through our file. I puff out my cheeks, anxiety levels rising already, and pick up a random sheet of paper from a stack. It's a list of prescriptions and patients out of a local family clinic. From what I can tell, all the prescriptions are for the werewolf serum from different pharmaceutical companies. Werevine Pharmaceutical is prominent on the list. I swallow and put the paper back on its loose stack.

"Does it say what our mission is?" I ask in the hope of prompting a response while thumbing through some other miscellaneous papers.

"Mission?" Jefferson looks at me over the top of the file. "There are no missions out here, little girl. We don't chase after harpies, put down hydra, or even find trolls in the garbage.

No, the Moose Lake Field Office handles one problem and one problem only. Werewolves."

I can sense Hawk tense without even looking at him.

"Werewolves aren't classified as true monsters," I say. "Under Title 51, subtitle 6, chapter 606—"

"*Beings infected with magical decay but are not, by their own nature, of malice or perceived to be hostile.* I know the law." Jefferson closes the file again and tosses it onto a nearby stack. "Our job isn't to kill them, it's to regulate them. Do you know how easy it is to spread the werewolf disease? Now throw in a bunch of teenagers that don't care and a pack of toddlers who don't know the difference. It's a population explosion." He throws his hands up and accidentally disturbs a pile of papers, turning them into an avalanche at his feet. He steps nonchalant out of the mess and continues on.

"What do you think all this paperwork is about? I've been trying to handle it on my own, making sure each one gets the serum so they don't go wolf crazy out in the woods. It's for their safety and the safety of the whole city."

I gaze around at the thousands of sheets littered everywhere. "How on earth do you keep track of any of this?"

"Can't you just put it all into a computer?" Hawk says.

Jefferson brushes away some leaflets to uncover a tan box. "The stupid thing hasn't been working and I don't trust computers. Hard copies are always better."

He turns it slightly so I can see the box is actually a monitor. It's sitting on an equally as large box that is the computer itself. I push my palm against my forehead. I sense a headache coming on.

"Well, you better stow your things so you can get to work," Jefferson says.

"Work on what?" Hawk asks.

His laughter is absolutely no comfort. "Organizing!" Jefferson points to the first door before vanishing through the second and slamming it behind him.

Hawk looks to me and shrugs. "It could be worse?"

"Yeah," I say and head for the first door. "We could be dead."

I push it open with my foot and flick on the light. There's more paper stuffed in here too, so much in fact that it takes me a moment to realize this is a bedroom. A set of bunk beds is pushed against the wall and there's a single wooden dresser hardly visible beneath more boxes. With a sigh I wade through and open the shade on the only window. It creaks and a waterfall of dust rolls off it. The window itself is cracked and kept together by a mix of duct tape and hard white paste. I peer through its frosty surface to the barn behind the cabin and a system of pulleys set up in a flat backyard. I can't be sure but it looks like a homemade firing range.

"Charming place," Hawk says behind me. He throws his bag onto the bottom bunk and a cloud of dust rises making us both cough. He waves the cloud away with his hand and sputters, "It's like a soft blanket of flaky, dead people on everything. Nice and homey."

"*Piping Pan!*" I cough and let my bag slide to the floor. "It's like a person disintegrated on the bed. We should have packed our bed sets."

"Oh, we'll be fine," Hawk says and tries to brush off the thick layer of dust but just creates a bigger cloud. We escape the room to the breathable air of the main area and stare around at the paper.

"Think we'll find a body under all this?" I ask.

"Probably two," Hawk says.

The door behind us swings open with the unpleasant smell of a used bathroom and Jefferson rejoins us. "Not human bodies any way. I think I heard a mouse trap go off about three weeks ago."

Hawk sniffs and wrinkles his nose. "Yeah, that smells about right. And whatever just died in the bathroom."

"Everybody poops, kid." Jefferson fans a newspaper in front of his face then heads for the outside door. "You two better get started on that. Best to sort them alphabetically, I think."

"Where are you going?" I ask loudly before he abandons us.

"I'll be back at dusk," he says over his shoulder and disappears outside.

Silence follows. I brace myself against the back of a chair sticking out from the mountains of paper. I feel dizzy and angry. Just this morning we had a dragon backing us up and remanding the director on our behalf. Now we're stuck handling the Rockies of paperwork in a dusty, smelly, old cabin bound to collapse on top of us at any moment. My throat starts to constrict and I'm desperately homesick.

I look to my brother for some kind of support. He looks just as upset, arms tight across his chest and his mouth a thin line.

"I'm hungry," he says. "Think there's anything edible in the fridge?"

Leave it to my brother to break my shell. I start to laugh and clamp a hand over my mouth. He throws me a big smile and steps carefully over to the fridge that looks like a gigantic bar of soap.

"Probably not," I say, still laughing. "What do you want to bet there's paper folded up to look like food?"

He shuffles aside paper blocking the door with his foot and yanks it open, bending down to peer inside. "Well, I think he's got enough alcohol in here to make a giant pass out. And Mr. Presidents-Man seems to like leftovers as much as paper. It's like a temple in here."

He pulls out a white Styrofoam container, opens it, and then holds it out so I can have a look.

"Great," I mutter. "Unidentifiable meat. It could be one of the many mice victims he's trapped in here."

My brother lifts it to his nose and takes a deep whiff. He shakes his head and stuffs it back in the fridge. "Just venison."

Sometimes I forget how good his sense of smell is. Eventually, after hunting through the cupboards, we find a bag of only slightly stale chips. We split the bag and inspect the rest of the cabin. It's obvious Hawk and I will have to share the one room with the bunk beds. The only other rooms are the bathroom, complete with a stained washer and dryer squeezed in next to the toilet, and Jefferson's room. His is the only room that doesn't have paper in it. In fact, the room is mostly bare except for a locked gun cabinet and a picture of a little girl riding a pink bike with her two braids flying behind her.

"His daughter?" Hawk suggests. "Niece? Dead girl buried under the paper?"

"Only one way to find out," I sigh.

We tackle our designated bedroom first. The piles of paper

and boxes are pushed out and, after Hawk's suggestion, placed inside Jefferson's room. As he says, Jefferson is clearly lacking a healthy amount of paper. We rip the bedding off the bunks and beat the dust out of them outside. Once we have a decent place to sleep, we both bunch up around the computer and press buttons but can't get it to turn on. It's older than any computer either of us is used to and after ten minutes we give up.

The door creaks open and Jefferson stomps in, his boots covered in mud and leaves. He pulls them off and sets them at the door, walks in, stops at the fridge, turns around, and freezes when he sees us as if he had forgotten we're here. He blinks, then steps around us muttering into his bedroom. I lean back—Hawk mimics me—to peek into the other room. Jefferson fumbles with the lock on his gun safe but eventually cracks it open and pulls out a camera. He fishes a card out of his pocket, shoves it into a slot on the back, and starts scrolling through pictures. Hawk shrugs at me.

"Uh, Agent Barnes?" I say loudly, in case he tries to ignore me again. "What are you doing?"

He holds up the camera and shakes it. "What does it look like I'm doing? I'm looking at pictures."

"Of what?"

"My game cams I have set on the back forty acres," Jefferson says and keeps clicking through the pictures on his camera. "Considering the amount of wolf tracks back there, I had a feeling I'd be able to snap a photo of the culprits killing livestock in the area."

Hawk shakes his head and moves to lean against the open doorframe. "It has to be regular wolves. Werewolves that take the serum keep their human minds when they transform. They wouldn't be killing cows or whatever."

Jefferson jerks his pointer finger in Hawk's direction without looking at him. "Firstly, step back out of my room." He twitches his finger shooing Hawk. With a scowl my brother takes a few steps backwards. "Second, who's to say there aren't werewolves out there running around unaccounted for without the serum because their friends don't want to rat them out?"

"Why would anyone *want* to run around like an animal?" I argue. "That doesn't make any sense."

He rapidly hits a button on the camera then marches forward and shoves the lit screen under my nose. "Because some people get a high off the hunt."

I glare at him for a moment before taking the offered camera to get a better look at what he's trying to show me. Hawk stands over my shoulder as well to see a pack of four wolves running through the trees. They're frozen mid-stride in the picture. One is looking directly at the camera. There's something odd about the eyes. The color and shape are all wrong. They're human.

"Werewolves," I murmur.

Jefferson snatches the camera back and nods. Sharing time over, he glances around at the piles of paper and snatches up our file that he left sitting out. I bite my lip—I should have looked at it when I had the chance. Stupid me.

"I see you two have hardly done anything," he grumbles.

"If you haven't noticed," Hawk says, "there's enough paper here to build another cabin."

"Then I suggest you get started." He slams the door to his room, probably to keep us out, and shrugs past to the fridge.

I throw my hands up and slam them back down on a stack of paper. "You're supposed to be training us, not turning us into your servants because you haven't learned how to alphabetize your own crap!"

He pulls out a Styrofoam box, balances his camera on top, and takes a bottle of beer before shutting the fridge with his foot. He points the bottle at me. "Half of being an agent is paperwork. Better get used to it now. If you want to do something else, then finish that first."

His squinty eyes flash over the pair of us before he stomps out of the house. I peer through the small window in the kitchen and watch him carry his dinner into the barn.

"This is so bogus," I growl.

"We're being punished, remember?" Hawk sighs. "We might as well get started. I have a feeling we won't be going anywhere for a while."

The truth of that sinks in and I shuffle over to him morosely. The first thing we do is clear enough room around the computer and chair so it's usable. I'm determined to hound Jefferson into getting it to work or getting a new one. I wish Witty was here—he can reanimate any dead computer.

After we clear that small space, we start picking up random sheets of paper trying to figure out what we're sorting. There are medical records, prescription lists, newspaper articles of wolf sightings, a few handwritten grocery lists, old credit card offers, and every kind of map imaginable for Moose Lake.

"Does this guy throw anything out?" Hawk scoffs, tossing aside a letter promising $50,000 in cash if Mr. Barnes transfers money into some shady account for fees.

By the time night has fallen we've barely made a dent. I

glance out the window and the lights in the barn are still on. Jefferson hasn't shown his face again since he went out there. We heat up one of his venison steaks after nearly blowing up the stove and find a can of orange pop in the back of the fridge that we share. We work another two hours under the dim light of an old incandescent bulb and manage to uncover a garbage bag beneath the mess that we dump all of Jefferson's useless items into it.

Moonlight creeps in through the window and we finally quit, both bearing paper-cuts on our hands. We turn out the lights in the cabin and I can still see light from the barn. A shadow moves now and again, which I assume is Jefferson working on something secret he doesn't want us to know about.

I'm nearly asleep in the top bunk when I hear howling in the distance. The bunk below me creaks and I know Hawk is awake. The howling continues louder and is joined by others. Hawk exhales sharply and the floorboards squeak under his weight. I slide out of my bunk and hit the ground with a thud before he reaches the door.

"Hawk?" I whisper. "Where are you going?"

He pauses with his hand on the knob and looks back at me. His expression is one of pain. I close the distance between us and rest a hand on his shoulder. The howling only gets louder and I can feel his muscles coil under my palm. I mean to comfort him but it feels like I'm holding him back.

He grits his teeth. "I haven't had an urge like this in a long time," he forces out and gives another big exhale.

I tug his shoulder back and forth. He stands stiff and rocks with the movement. He's like corded steel. "Who's your family, Hawk?" I ask.

He sighs. "You are."

"And who will always have your back? Me or a pack of psychopathic teenage werewolves?"

My words hang between us and I can feel him start to relax. Sometimes I have to give him these reminders, ground him in the fact that he's human and doesn't answer to animal instincts. It's been this way since he was first infected. I keep him focused. I've helped him through the hard times, held his hand when he needed it, stayed quiet during his darker days, or pushed him back into life when he deserved a kick in the butt.

"You always have my back," he says quietly. His hand falls from the door handle.

I give his shoulders a squeeze and lean back with a smile. "Of course I do."

A loud crack makes us both jump. I swing around to the window and see Jefferson standing outside the barn, the door thrown back against the wall.

"I know that's you, Ben, and your flea-bitten friends!" he shouts towards the dark woods, cupping his hands around his mouth. "Go home or I'll tell your mother!"

The howling instantly stops and the silence is tangible. Jefferson stands in the glow coming from the barn for a moment longer before stomping back inside and slamming the door shut with another loud crack.

5

By the time I wake up, a good hour before sunrise, Jefferson is already in the kitchen cooking scrambled eggs. Slipping past him to the bathroom, I put on my spare junior agent uniform and wrap my hair up into a ponytail. Once done, I stand in the open and wait but Jefferson ignores me.

"Good morning," I say.

He finally glances at me with a grunt by way of a greeting and starts to scoop eggs onto a chipped plate. I turn my back on him to survey my and Hawk's progress from last night. The stacks of boxes we had put in Jefferson's room have mysteriously reappeared behind the computer and the garbage bag full of credit card offers and junk is gone. I can't help but smile darkly and shake my head.

I take the seat in front of the computer and rap my fingers on the keyboard. "So . . . you knew who was howling last night? How could you tell who it was?"

Jefferson speaks around a mouthful of scrambled eggs. "It wasn't hard to guess. He and his delinquent buddies have been trespassing on my property for a couple of weeks trying to harass me, but I finally found his weakness."

"His mother is his weakness?" I quirk an eyebrow.

He lets out a low, rumbling laugh and jabs his fork at me. "That woman is scarier than a berserker on steroids."

I quickly look away, my face warming as I'm reminded of the berserker I fought at Werevine. Jefferson crams the rest of the eggs on his plate into his mouth. To my surprise he comes over by me. He presses the power button on the computer then gives it two hard whacks on the side and a loud slap on top. The computer beeps and the monitor flickers to life.

"Uh, thanks," I say.

He grumbles something and tramps to the front door, grabbing his coat off a hook on the wall.

"Where are you going?" I ask, rising from my seat to follow.

"I'm going to pay Ben's mother a visit. I'm sick of those kids howling at night."

"Can I come?" I ask hopefully, even though I already know what he'll say.

His smile is dubious. "It looks like you're already busy. Help yourself to some eggs." And he's out the door.

Left alone to paper once again, I decide to wait for the computer to boot. Ten minutes pass but it's still trying to make it to the home screen so I decide to eat what's left of the scrambled eggs. I stand with a plate staring at the monitor when Hawk sluggishly walks out of the bedroom, his hair sticking straight out in every direction. He's in the middle of rubbing the sleep from his eyes when he notices I have food.

"Eggs?" he asks past a yawn.

"I'll make you some."

He twitches his leg and pulls at the jeans he's wearing. "These pants feel weird."

"Maybe that's because those are mine," I say and finish my plate.

"Oh." He turns about and stumbles zombie-like back into the bedroom.

While he's back changing and I start up another batch of eggs, the cell phone in my pocket starts to buzz. I pull it out and the ID reads "IMS Headquarters." *Pixies*, they're calling early. Do they think we couldn't manage a single night here without an incident? I groan like a deranged bear and answer.

"This is Junior Agent Phoenix Mason."

"ID number?" a polite woman's voice asks on the other end.

"0919-32."

"Please wait while I transfer you."

I glower at the eggs frying in the pan and prod at them with malice. I sure hope it's not going to be Director Knox coming on next or that's really going to ruin my morning. He'll probably want to gloat over successfully getting Hawk and me as far away as possible from Underground.

"Phoenix?"

I release the breath I didn't realize I was holding. "Witty? Giant's feet! It's good to hear a friendly voice. I had no idea you'd be calling."

"Didn't they tell you?" He sounds confused and speaks a little too loudly—probably trying to drown out what sounds like a walrus bellowing in the background.

"Tell me what?" I ask and put him on speakerphone so I can whip up the eggs with both hands.

"I'll be the agent you report in to every other day."

"Really? That's surprising," I say. "I thought for sure I'd have to describe every detail of my day to someone like Knox." I purse my lips as I try to think of a logical explanation for the director allowing one of our friends to handle something like this. There's a particularly loud bellow from the phone and I flinch, flinging a spoonful of eggs over my shoulder.

"Ouch!" Hawk shouts from behind. I spin around as he peels steaming bits of egg off his face. There are already red marks.

"Hawk! I'm sorry!" I shriek. "Don't sneak up behind me like that!"

He scowls at me and moves to the sink, turning the faucet on high. "I didn't realize you chuck eggs over your shoulder at random intervals when you're cooking." He cups cold water in his hands and splashes his face. "If I would have known I would have ducked—or held my mouth open."

"Phoenix?" Witty says in small voice from the phone on the counter. "Is everything okay?"

"Yeah," I say and pass Hawk a dishtowel. "Hawk just got breakfast face first. But what on earth is going on there?"

"Oh, that?" There's another bellow that makes my phone vibrate. "Just an irate berserker, that's all."

Hawk shuffles around me to the phone, dabbing at his face. "A berserker? You mean the one we caught?"

The bellows slowly fade like Witty is moving away. I can hear his breathing pick up, probably from pushing his wheelchair along. "I'm sorry, guys," Witty finally says, "but I can't talk about that. Director Knox told me not to tell you anything."

"Why?" Hawk and I say in unison.

"He says it's none of your business," he says matter-of-factly. "That's not why I called though. I'm supposed to get a report from you two. Make sure you're toeing the line, you know."

I roll my eyes and finish cooking the scrambled eggs. Almost as soon as I take them off the stove, Hawk starts to attack them. I pick up the phone and shuffle through paper to the center of the room with it still on speaker.

"Oh, it's been great," I growl and go on a tirade. "We're just stuck in a moldy old cabin, swimming in paper, working for the undertaker himself. He has us trying to organize his crap that I think he's been stockpiling for twenty years. I'm still waiting for the computer to finish booting but I swear this thing is older than the dragons. Everything here is a huge waste of time."

Witty's silent for a moment before he says, "Oh, I'm sure it'll get better. Just . . . just hang in there, Phoenix. Everything will work out. You'll see."

"And if it doesn't?"

"Hey, at least you've still got friends. I'll always be here if you need me."

I rub the back of my hand across my forehead. That would be more comforting if I was back in Underground where all my friends are. "Yeah. Thanks."

"I'll check back in with you guys in two days, okay?"

"Sure thing, Witty."

The line clicks dead and I stow my phone in my pocket. Hawk is strangely silent and stares at me with a superior smile like he knows something I don't.

"What?" I snap.

He holds his hands under his chin and gives me droopy eyes. "I'll always be here if you need me, Fifi."

I grab a piece of junk mail and chuck it at his head but he ducks and it misses. Talking to Witty equally brightened and darkened my mood—I got to talk to a friend but it only made me more homesick. I take the chair in front of the computer and start paging through paper while it whines and brings the screen up at last but I don't think it's even worth trying to use it. It's obviously busted like Jefferson said.

The rest of the day we spend going through paper, paper, and more paper. We've started to sort it into general piles—names starting A through E there, F through L there, and so on. We comb through medical records, newspaper articles, profiles, and toss junk into another garbage bag we uncover. We're starving by noon and Jefferson still hasn't returned. The fridge is raided for more venison, which seems to be in every container, and we're back at it.

The afternoon drags on and I can't get rid of the frown on my face. I know Jefferson said he regulates the werewolves but I'm astounded by the amount of private medical data he has. I get an itch in the back of my mind. Is this all legal? What right does he have to hoard so much on everyone?

Jefferson finally returns after the sun has gone down. He gazes around and whistles. There's still plenty of paper but it's certainly more orderly than it was before. There's more room to walk at least. He doesn't speak to us but grabs his camera, food from the fridge, and is about to leave again.

"Keep at that," he says. "At the rate you're going, it might be done next year."

"Hey!" I shout at him before he can escape. I toss the papers in my hands to the side and they billow in a cloud. I haven't felt this kind of pure anger towards someone since a centaur falsely accused me of stealing. "We've *been* doing what you asked. You don't have to rub our noses in it. We already know we're being punished, all right? *We get it.*"

His squinty eyes widen and his eyebrows shoot up. "Excuse me?"

"We're doing the best we can!" I shout, my frustration getting the better of me. Hawk doesn't back me up but stands next to the sink, his eyes frozen on the piece of paper in his hands. "You don't have to treat us like slugs that snuck into your house. All we ever wanted was to become IMS agents. And yeah, we screwed up. I understand that. I'm not proud of it, but you could at least treat us like human beings. You gave us almost no direction, no help, no supplies—you didn't even let us know if there was food we could eat!"

Jefferson angles more towards me, his eyes turning squinty again. "You've been helping yourselves to my food."

"Maybe that's because we don't have transportation to go buy our own!" My throat burns I'm yelling so hard. I can't seem to stop. "We've got nothing! And now we're stuck here out in the middle of nowhere with no support, no friends, no guidance, and no family!"

I'm panting and my whole body is shaking. I can't even remember the last time I've let loose like this. A muscle in Jefferson's jaw bulges as it tightens then relaxes again.

"Is there anything else?" he asks calmly.

I feel almost manic and shrug half-heartedly, wishing I could curl up into a ball somewhere. "We could use some more boxes," I say weakly. "There's a lot of paper."

He doesn't nod, he doesn't shout, he doesn't say anything— he takes his dinner and retreats outside to the barn. Continuing to shake and feel weak in the knees, I slide down against the wall and sit on the floor holding my hands against the sides of my head. Hawk comes to stand next to me but keeps quiet and doesn't offer a hug or anything. I'm glad he doesn't. I'm so angry and frustrated right now that doing either would probably only make me more upset.

Part of me wants to cry. I don't cry often but when I do it usually comes like a flood and there's no stopping it. Instead I bite down on my tongue and close my eyes for a couple of minutes. Hawk puts a hand on my shoulder then and I let the tension ease out of me. There's nothing I can do about anything right now except the paper mess. So, I rise to my feet and pick up where I left off on the paper stacks which signals Hawk to do the same.

The one thing about my outburst is that it's given me a do or die drive. Hawk heats up supper but I hardly eat. I'm too focused. It gets darker and my eyelids become heavy. I slap my arms and face a few times to stay awake and keep working. Hawk ends up sitting on the floor against the kitchen cupboards to look through paper and yawns constantly. I'm not sure when he falls asleep but I don't wake him. Thankfully it remains quiet and there's no howling to disturb him tonight. Jefferson's talk with Ben's mother must have gone over well.

The light bulb starts to flicker. I sit in the chair in front of the computer, which has died again, and the dimming light puts me in a kind of hypnotic state. I keep paging through a stack without really looking at it anymore. I struggle on and keep glancing at the progress we've already made to boost my drive. We've uncovered the rest of the table the computer is sitting on along with three other chairs. Boxes are stacked high against the walls and a trap with the skeleton of a mouse sits on the floor.

I don't know when I fall asleep. I dream about Witty interrogating the berserker, asking it where it put the Styrofoam containers. The berserker starts to puff up and turn bright red, reaching across the table and grabbing Witty by the throat—

I jerk awake with a gasp and find myself still in the chair in front of the computer. Something crunches under my elbow when I shift. I look and find a roll of crinkly green wax paper. I unwrap it to find a turkey sub sandwich. It smells delicious, but for whatever reason, I can't understand what it's doing there. There's a loud snort and I see Hawk spread out on the floor against the kitchen cabinets still asleep. Pushing back in the chair, I see there's also a new stack of empty boxes sitting just inside the door. Faint sunlight filters in from the lone window.

The door behind me creaks open and I just about launch out of my chair. Jefferson laughs under his breath and passes me carrying a bag of something that clinks when he moves. He stops by Hawk and prods him with the toe of his boot. It's only then I realize there's an identical wrapped sub next to him as well.

"Wake up," Jefferson says in his croaky voice. "No time for sleeping."

Hawk jerks and glares at Jefferson in a daze until he pushes himself upright. I rub the sleep out of my eyes and hold up the sub next to me like it's the most beautiful thing I've ever seen in my life.

"You got us breakfast?" I ask.

"Nah," Jefferson says. "I'd never do that." He looks at me over the rim of the coffee cup he sips from. I can't be sure but his eyes seem to be testing me.

I unwrap the sub completely and take a bite. After eating reheated venison for nearly every meal since we got here, it tastes like heaven.

"That's too bad," I say. "If you had, I would have said thank you."

I rip into the sub like I've never eaten before and Hawk does the same. My brother gives Jefferson a thumbs up and devours his sub with little deference. Once the food has disappeared, Jefferson sits on the edge of the table we cleared and sets down the bag which makes a loud thud. Whatever's in it must be heavy.

"So, you two want to train?" Jefferson asks, continuing to take steady sips from his coffee. Hawk and I nod. "Okay, then. I'll make you a deal. I'll ask you a series of questions to see what you know about our work. For each one you get wrong, you have to organize twenty-five more pieces of paper." When we start to groan he holds up a hand for silence. "For each one you get right—" He digs into the bag and pulls out a small, shiny, copper capped bullet. "—you get one of these for target practice out back. Deal?"

There's no hesitation—we both nod vehemently. He flips a coin in the air then slaps it back down onto his hand.

"Phoenix, heads or tails?" he asks.

"Heads?"

He looks at the coin before tucking it into his pocket. "Okay. You start. First question—who founded the IMS?"

This is going to be easy. "The dragons." I allow myself a smile. "Why?"

"Because there's so few of them. They needed agents all over the world that could help keep the monsters in check." I don't know why he's asking something so simple. It's in every history book related to the IMS.

Jefferson tosses a bullet in the air and I catch it. The weight is heavier than I expect. I've actually only seen human guns and bullets in movies. Hawk and I trained solely with bio-mech guns—dragon-designed weaponry—at the Underground armory. Most average, human weapons aren't very effective on the things the IMS hunts and bio-mech guns are more humane anyway.

"Hawk," he continues, angling himself towards my brother, "Who does the IMS answer to in the United States?"

"The Department of Dragon Affairs," he says looking eager. "The dragons made a treaty with our government when it was first formed."

He tosses another bullet and my brother catches it.

"Phoenix, how are monsters classified?"

I sit a little straighter. This is my kind of game. "They are classified by their power, abilities, and potential for destruction. There are five levels."

Another bullet. We spend the next twenty minutes going over elementary IMS history and procedure. Our stockpile of bullets grows and I start to mound them in the green wrap my sub came in.

"All right, smarty pants," Jefferson growls, checking inside his bag for more bullets. "Phoenix, how far can you run flat out before you have to stop?"

I blink. "What? What does that have to do with anything?"

"Just answer the question."

"I don't know. Maybe—"

"Wrong answer!" he says loudly over me. "Twenty-five pages to sort for you. Hawk, what about you? How far can you run flat out?"

Hawk holds his chin in a generic thinking pose and narrows his eyes. "I've held my longest sprint for ten minutes over four miles. After that I have to slow down."

The surprise is clear on Jefferson's face. "Seriously?" he says and tosses my brother another bullet. "That far?"

"Yeah. I run the track at Underground all the time. I keep in shape."

I roll my eyes and jingle my stash of bullets. "Yeah, and running that time as a wolf has nothing to do with it," I mumble under my breath.

The questions turn back to me. "How many pounds can you lift?"

"I can bench press six hundred ninety pounds and squat eight hundred eighty pounds," I answer immediately with a wide smile. When Jefferson doesn't toss me a bullet, I hold my hand out. "Really? You believe Hawk but not me? Honestly, I've been keeping track. That's the one thing I can do really well."

He squints at me, clear distrust in his eyes, but eventually hands a bullet over anyway. After that he quizzes us on social nuances and mathematics. Hawk and I both start to stumble through answers and we're assigned more paper. When Jefferson asks a slew of questions about physics, chemistry, and ordinary household objects, I get flustered and shout "Idaho!" for responses because I don't have a clue.

"Okay," Jefferson says and stows his remaining bullets into his jacket pocket. "It's obvious you know the legendary world but don't know a pickle from a slug when it comes to our world. Come on. Might as well use those bullets before you forget what they're for. Meet me out back."

He disappears into his room and I can hear the lock on the gun safe click. I cup my green wrap full of bullets to my chest and follow Hawk out into the cold air outside. There's a breeze that ruffles the lifeless brown and yellow leaves tumbling across the dry grass. It's nearing the end of October and I can feel it. The fresh air rejuvenates me and Hawk sniffs towards the sky like a dog on a scent.

"Anything good?" I ask him off hand and walk back towards the barn.

"I don't know," Hawk says, his voice distant and detached. "There's just something that smells . . . familiar about this place."

"Hmm." Standing beside the barn I get a better look at the range I saw when we first got here. There's a system of wires and pulleys up and down the length of the open field behind the cabin. I pull on the closest one and a piece of cardboard holding a red target starts to squeak towards me from the opposite end. None of the parts look like they belong together. Some are shiny and clearly newer while other pulleys and metal rods are rusted or patched with duct tape.

Jefferson comes around the side of the cabin holding two rifles with a handgun strapped to his waist. Hanging off his left arm are three bulky things that look like headphones from fifty years ago.

I point to the elaborate pulley system. "Did you make all this yourself?"

He nods and begins unloading what's in his arms onto a rusty metal platform that I suspect may have once been a barbeque grill in its former life. Jefferson gestures us over to the makeshift stand and rests a hand lovingly on one of the rifles.

"Have either of you ever shot one of these before?" he asks.

I bite my lip and lean back. I'd like to say I have but the closest I've ever gotten to human-designed guns is looking at them on a projection screen.

Hawk pats the end of the rifle and nods slowly. "Ah, yes. The old rifle. Shoots straight and true long distance. Would this one be, ah, considered a . . . long barrel? Since it's so long?"

The look Jefferson gives him could have frozen a giant mid-charge. "You've never held a real gun before, have you?"

"Not even once!" Hawk says cheerfully.

I grimace on my brother's behalf. "We've only handled dragon tech. Don't you have any bio-mech guns here?"

"If you haven't noticed, the Moose Lake Field Office isn't exactly swimming in funds and sophisticated technology," he growls. "You have to make do with what you're given and use it for as long as possible until it just can't be fixed anymore."

"Hence the duct tape everywhere," I say, glancing at the pulley system.

"Duct tape is God's Band-Aid. Now pay attention."

Jefferson spends the next ten minutes explaining the different parts of the guns he's brought out, where the safety is on each, how to load a clip, and sighting in a target. The point and shoot part certainly comes the easiest. That was basically it for handling a bio-mech gun. He gives us the dorky looking headphones and has us put them on. Once they're snug on our ears, effectively blocking out most sound, Jefferson pins up a new target on the line and reels it out using his pulleys. Once it's thirty feet away, he draws his sidearm, loads it faster than I can see what he's doing, and begins unloading the clip.

I clamp my hands on the headphones and press them down because they certainly can't drown out the explosive sound of each shot. It rattles through me and adrenaline makes me shaky in a matter of seconds. The movies don't do live fire justice in its volume and intensity. The bio-mech guns make a faint pulse sound when they discharge—the difference between it and a human gun is like a kitten purring and a dragon roaring. My ears have a faint ring in them once Jefferson finally stops and starts reeling the target back in.

I claw my headphones off. "How on earth does anyone stand that?"

Jefferson actually laughs. "Don't worry, princess. The .22s I'm going to let you shoot are a lot quieter."

He looks past my shoulder and pauses. I turn around and see Hawk shell-shocked, staring at the target. I look too and see the holes shredded through the very center, ripping the target apart.

"I thought you said you just regulate the werewolves," Hawk says in a deadly quiet tone.

The October air seems to drop a few degrees and I shiver. Now I can't stop staring at the precise, gaping holes in the target that Jefferson took apart so easily. The movies don't do justice to this kind of feeling either, of something being so real and dangerous.

"These aren't for werewolves," Jefferson says. He digs into his thick, brown jacket and pulls out what looks like a small needle attached to a glass tube. "*These* are for werewolves—the ones that try attacking, anyway. Don't worry. They aren't poison. They're tranquilizers."

"Do you ever use them?" Hawk's tone doesn't soften at all.

"Only on the ones that try to rip my face off. Are you done?" Jefferson raises his eyebrows and starts loading one of the rifles.

Hawk exhales sharply and stalks away to lean against the side of the barn. I remain where I am, clutching at the headphones sitting around my neck. There are times I know I should comfort my brother but there are no words that come to mind. I can understand why this would upset him so much, that some people treat werewolves like animals rather than humans suffering a disease, that they should be put down like dogs instead of helped. It makes me angry too.

"Hey." Jefferson nudges me with the end of the rifle. "Is he going to come back over here?" I shake my head. He sighs. "All right, fine. He can wear his fussy-britches all he wants. Here, take this."

I do as I'm told and Jefferson instructs me on how to hold the rifle properly. He readjusts my grip and makes sure the stock is tucked snug into my shoulder. He stands directly beside me and shows me how to look through the sights and aim. I nod that I understand, but he asks me again to make sure before he has me put my muffs back on. He reels out another target and backs away to give me room.

"Whenever you're ready!" he shouts since we both have our shooter muffs on.

My hands are still shaking from earlier. I take a deep breath and try to relax, my cheek against the stock, my eyes focused through the scope at the center of the target. I pop the safety and squeeze down on the trigger. Jefferson is right—it's a lot quieter than his handgun but the sound and kickback into my shoulder is enough to make me jump. Even though I saw how much Jefferson's hands jerked when he fired his gun, I'm still not expecting it.

"Pixies!" I shriek. "It kicked! Is it supposed to do that? Is that normal?"

I can see Jefferson fighting back laughter, his mouth twisting and pursing, his eyes flashing. Heat crawls up my face and neck.

"Yes, it's supposed to do that," he shouts over the muffs. "Keep going!"

Shaking some more, I focus back on the target. After nine more shots I start to get a feel for the rifle and discover something unexpected—this is *fun*. Jefferson has me make sure the chamber is clear then load another clip, snap it in place, pull back the bolt, and slip a bullet into the chamber. I fire ten more times until my clip is empty. When I hold out my hand for more bullets, Jefferson shakes his head.

"You used up your quota. Why don't you get your pansy brother over here? And grab another target while you're at it. They're leaning against the other side of the barn."

"He's not a pansy," I growl but do as he says.

I jog to Hawk carrying the rifle, appreciating the weight in my hands now. He doesn't look so angry but he's still touchy. After I describe the feel and power of the gun, explosions kicking back into your shoulder and all, Hawk finally agrees to give it a try. I know how much he likes explosions. He shuffles up to Jefferson, head bowed, and takes up the other rifle. I fight back a smile and run around the side of the barn looking for more targets.

I find a cardboard box covered by a weatherworn tarp. The targets are there, a whole stack of them. I grab a handful when the hairs on the back of my neck rise. I deliberately put the targets on the ground, stand straight, and then wheel about with the rifle still in my hands.

Standing on the edge of the trees not thirty feet away is an enormous black wolf. Its yellow eyes cut through me. Normally when I see werewolves I don't feel afraid. I've been living with one long enough that the sight of a wolf doesn't make me jump, but this one makes me want to crawl right out of my skin. There's something darker about it than its black fur. It stands perfectly still apart from those deeply intelligent, horrible eyes looking me up and down, studying me.

I draw up the rifle, forgetting that it's empty, and aim. The werewolf doesn't even flinch. My breath catches in my throat and for the first time in a long time I feel truly afraid. I want to call out but I'm afraid what it will do if I shout for my brother. So, instead we have a stare down. Eventually it lowers its head and its lips pull back exposing red-stained fangs.

Well, it clearly isn't friendly. If I run for the others, I'll leave my back exposed and this werewolf will easily reach me before I reach help. There's nothing else for it.

"Hawk!" I scream and start backpedaling as fast as I can. The wolf takes a step forward. I'm moving backwards blind so I end up clipping the side of the barn and stumble to the side, falling to my knees. The rifle slips from my hands. Heavy footsteps thunder towards me. My hands slide on the grass as

I try to crawl and my face meets the cold, hard ground, the rifle under me. I grab the gun, flip onto my back, bring up the barrel—a pointless gesture—and aim.

The werewolf is gone.

Hawk skids to a stop on the ground beside me. Jefferson moves around the side of the barn with his handgun raised, eyes darting to the woods then me. I'm panting hard and can taste dirt in my mouth. My brother grasps me under the arm and hauls me to my feet, taking the rifle out of my hands that I've refused to let go of.

"What happened?" he asks, roughly scrubbing dirt off my forehead with the edge of his sleeve. "Are you okay?"

"There was a—a—" I gesture wildly to the trees. "A *huge* black werewolf."

"Are you sure it was a werewolf?" Jefferson asks, his handgun still trained on the woods.

I nod and brush the rest of the dirt off my face and clothes. "Yeah, I'm positive. And there was something . . . off about it. Something dangerous. I don't know."

"Did it do anything?" he asks, an edge to his voice.

"It just stood there eyeing me." I run my hands over the top of my head and smooth my hair back into place.

Hawk grips my shoulder far too tight. "You never freak out like this. You faced that berserker down without blinking an eye."

"I know that," I snap at him and brush his hand off. My rush of anger isn't really directed at him, but he points out what's bugging me, too—I'm overreacting. Maybe it's the adrenaline left over from shooting. Some primal instinct is forcing fear down my throat and that makes me irritated.

The breeze rustles our jackets and Hawk sniffs the air, slowly walking forward until he's at the tree line. He bends down and brushes his hand over the dirt. "Wolf prints. Big ones."

Jefferson inspects them too but I stay where I am. After a moment of keenly staring at the ground, Jefferson straightens and makes shooing motions at Hawk and me. "Okay, fun's over. You two go back to the cabin and keep working on that paper."

"You aren't going out there, are you?" I ask, the pitch of my voice higher than usual.

He shakes his head. "I'm going to put the guns away. Go on you two."

The wind picks up and we turn our backs against it on our way to the cabin. Once inside I feel like I have a fever. I'm itchy and need to do something.

"That was weird," Hawk says and stares out the kitchen window.

"You're telling me."

"No, I mean I couldn't pick up a scent at all on that werewolf. I can usually smell *something* but there was nothing."

Well, that's not comforting in the least. I hastily return to the mounds of paper and start going through them like they have all of life's answers.

"Are you sure you're okay?" Hawk asks and helps me shuffle through the stacks.

"It's got to be in here somewhere," I mutter and scoop stacks towards me. Flipping over a piece of junk mail and snatching up a loose pen, I start drawing a table so I can categorize what we have.

"What are we talking about?"

"That werewolf," I say and jab the end of the pen at the window. "There's so much here that there has to be *something* about who that was."

Hawk places a hand on my arm. "Well, you're starting to freak me out, so . . ."

"We have to organize this anyway. Just help me."

He falls silent and his motions sync with mine. I read a page, scribble down notes in my table about what it is, and pass it on to Hawk who files it into one of the empty boxes Jefferson gave us. I'm not even sure what I'm looking for, or how I'll know it when I see it, but I go at it like a three-headed dog on a steak. By the time lunch rolls around, Jefferson still hasn't returned from "putting the guns away." I start to worry he went into the woods looking for the black werewolf and was attacked. A shudder ripples through me and I try to focus on the medical records in my hand.

My obsession keeps my focus but eventually Hawk starts poking around at other things in the cabin. He finds an old radio somewhere and tunes it to a self-proclaimed oldies station. It's white noise to me in the background as I tick through record after record. The floorboards creak as Hawk dances behind me but I'm determined not to be distracted.

It grows dark, supper passes, and I'm still in a funk. Hawk goes to bed but I stay awake. I'm trying to reason with myself now. So what if it was a werewolf? Jefferson said himself that there's been a population explosion. It could have been a teenager standing there. For whatever reason I feel like there's something I'm missing and it's in the back of my mind but I can't find it.

I pull out my cell phone now and then to check the time. It's nearly midnight. My energy starts to wind down but my mind is still wide awake. At least I've made significant headway. I've filled the empty boxes with orderly medical records and have moved on to miscellaneous items. I'm scanning through old police reports when the front door creaks open. I'm instantly hit with a flood of adrenaline and am halfway out of my seat when I realize it's only Jefferson.

He looks tired—I don't know why that surprises me considering the time. He's got shadows painted on his face and his eyes are bloodshot. When he spots me at the table, he manages to look even older and the shadows on his face darken like he's haunted by some deep sadness. He stops at the fridge and pulls out a bottle of beer, pauses, then grabs another. With both bottles in hand he skulks into his room and locks the door behind him.

I'm not sure what I'm supposed to make of that but his unexpected appearance managed to wake me up once more. I become twitchy and glance to the window more than once like I might find someone watching me. It's unnerving and significantly slows my progress. The feeling might just be from the police report I have in my hands. It's dated nearly fourteen years ago. Police and first responders were dispatched to a residence in the middle of the night. The unidentified father said a rabid wolf had burst into their house. By the time the police got there the wolf was gone, a little girl was bitten, and the mother was dead. The father—

The rest of the page is blotched over with a coffee stain that smears the ink into an illegible mess. I flip it over but the back is blank. I dig around some more but can't find the rest of the report. Deciding I should probably call it a night before I go completely mad and paranoid, I leave the report where it is on the desk and head for bed. Hawk is sound asleep on his bunk. I lay a hand on his forehead for a second, reminding myself that I'm not alone and there's nothing to be afraid of, before climbing into my own bed.

Sleep doesn't come easy. I dream I'm in a police squad riding with first responders to the call of a wolf attack. When we get there I'm standing outside a white house with green shutters. There's an oak tree in the front yard and a swing hangs from one of its thick branches creaking in the breeze. Police officers swarm into the house and I chase after them. Inside there are claw marks on the walls and drops of blood. I look for the little bitten girl but instead find two children huddled together under the kitchen table, a boy and girl. The boy is crying and clutching at his side. The girl holds him in her arms, silent as a graveyard, and stares up at me with big, round eyes.

I flick on the flashlight in my hand and hold it over them. Their red hair stands out like fire in the beam's light.

The whole bunk bed shakes as I fly awake with a gasp. I clamp a hand to my forehead and come away with cold sweat. Below me I hear Hawk muttering in his sleep—something about giants throwing boulders. I stare straight ahead and listen to him rattle away in his sleep. It's still dark out and a quick check of my phone tells me it's 3:00 a.m. *Pixies*. Freakin' nightmares.

A faint glow outside the window catches my attention. I lean forward and realize it's coming from the barn. It's either Jefferson out there or . . . someone else.

I slide out of bed and hit the floor on the balls of my feet to absorb the impact quietly. I sneak out of the bedroom, my eyes quickly adjusting to the dark. Jefferson's door is open. A quick check inside tells me he must be the one in the barn. Why on earth he would be out there at three o'clock in the morning is anyone's guess. Curious, I pull on my shoes and one of my old hooded sweatshirts with *Go Fire Sprites!* in faded red across the front. I push open the front door and freeze in the frame. It's near pitch black outside and the only light is what shines from the windows and underneath the door of the barn. If that black werewolf is out there right now, I'd never see it coming.

My hand clenches on the door handle, the metal screeching under my death grip. I've never been afraid of the dark before. There is no reason to be scared now . . . except for giant were-wolves lingering in the woods. I take a deep breath, throw the door shut, and sprint as fast as I can for the barn. I nearly ram my shoulder against the door in my haste to get inside quickly. The wood groans, one of the hinges cracks, and I fling myself inside the barn before slamming the door shut behind me again. So much for a sneaky entrance.

My unreasonable panic subsides and my mind focuses enough on my surroundings to realize there's a gun pointed at my head. Jefferson lets out a choice swear word and lowers the handgun, tucking it back into its holster.

"Are you crazy?" he shouts at me. "What are you doing barging in here in the middle of the night!?"

Reasonable thoughts evade me and I blurt out, "It's morning."

There's a strong smell of something foul coming off Jefferson and it only gets stronger as he continues to shout at me, "Get out! You don't have any right to be in here!"

"I'm sorry! I just—I saw the light and I—I . . ."

"Thought you'd snoop where you don't belong? Huh?" He waves his hands at me, one clutching a dark bottle. "Go back to bed before I kick your butt out of here!" he thunders. It's clear he's deranged, and furious, and I believe in earnest he really will physically punt me out of his barn.

I glimpse just a few things in the room—a tarp draped over something huge, file boxes, stairs leading to a second level, and a map with pins on the wall—before I'm clawing at the door and barreling back out into the night. As before, I sprint across the open ground and fumble with the door handle to the cabin before I slip inside and shut it firmly behind me.

My heart is hammering against my ribs and it's only then I really consider that Jefferson pointed a gun at my head moments ago. It's obvious he's expecting trouble—that or he's paranoid. I'm just glad he stopped to make sure what he was aiming at before pulling the trigger. Then I start to think. What is Jefferson hiding in that barn that's so secretive he doesn't want me to see it? The fact he wanted me out so badly only makes me that more intent on finding out what he's hiding.

I slink back into bed and lay on my side to stare out the window. I'm exhausted and eventually fall asleep. The next time I wake, Hawk is roughly shaking my shoulder. His eyes are bright and his smile wide.

"Wake up, sleepy head," he says and starts tugging on my pillow until my head thumps onto the mattress. I reach out and push against his face. He only laughs and shakes my shoulder harder.

"*Okay,*" I snap. "I'm up, I'm up."

He rushes out the door and shuts it behind him. I get dressed and brush my hair up into a ponytail, all the while glaring out the window at the barn. If Jefferson follows his usual routine today, he'll disappear for an extended period of time. It's a window of opportunity if you ask me, and I plan to take advantage of it.

My brilliant plan comes crashing down once I step into the main room. Hawk and Jefferson are both sitting at the table enjoying cinnamon buns out of a white box and scrambled eggs fresh from the stovetop.

"Look!" Hawk says triumphantly, holding aloft a glorious, delicious-smelling bun.

Jefferson looks at me over the top of his ceramic mug. I can see the hint of a grin behind it. "I figured you two have been working so hard you ought to have a reward for your efforts. And I thought it was past time I helped you through all this. Plus, once it's done, we can really focus on your other training." He leans back and sips at his cup of coffee—evil, stupid coffee. "I've been neglecting you two. I'm going to stick around like glue and give you my full attention."

Clever. Very clever. I take the seat Hawk offers with my eyes locked onto Jefferson to make it very clear that I know exactly what he's up to. He wants to keep me out of that barn? Fine. He has no idea who he's dealing with.

The cinnamon buns do look good though. I dig into the one my brother passes over and aimlessly scan the papers in front of me as I try to think of a way to ditch Jefferson. An obvious piece of paper is missing and I stare at the blank spot where I had left it the night before—the stained police report involving the little girl. When I meet Jefferson's eyes again, they are frosty cold.

"You know," I say casually. "Maybe if you told us what you were looking for, we'd be able to find it faster."

"I don't know what you're talking about," he says as calm as can be. "I just need this organized so I can keep track of the werewolves better."

"Uh-huh." I blatantly turn away from him, giving him the cold shoulder.

Since he seems content to stay here, I decide to pursue his papers anyway and see if I can't figure out what he's looking for before he realizes what I'm doing. A calloused hand pushes a cup of coffee across the table to me. I glare at the hand and snatch the coffee, draining half of its scalding contents in one gulp. My mouth is on fire but I ignore the pain and the stares I'm getting from the other two. It's time to work.

The effort we've put into organizing is finally paying off. Despite the sheer volume of information, I'm beginning to see patterns. We've managed to string together profiles for each werewolf Jefferson has identified. There's several of his own handwritten notes and photos of livestock attacks or peculiar break-ins. His notes identify the behavior of a new werewolf and tracks them in his field reports until he finally confronts whoever it is. The werewolf serum is ordered and kept track of through the family clinic. There are newly updated prescription reports for each person. Jefferson has been keeping a close eye on each identified werewolf, making sure they have been taking their medication. How he managed to do that considering the mess this place had been, I have no idea.

"Isn't some of this stuff confidential?" I ask out loud, paging through a twenty-page physician's report by one Dr. Rosewell. The doctor is clearly in the know—her findings specify the werewolf symptoms and stages of a bite healing in a report not printed from a hospital server.

"Werewolves are classified as special cases," Jefferson answers without looking up from an old newspaper in his hands. "We're allowed specific information to make sure the disease isn't spreading to others and that the ones who do have it are in control."

Hawk scoffs. "How do you judge that?"

"It's just like addicts and their sponsors. We make sure they aren't giving in to the animal nature of the disease. That's all." Jefferson folds up his newspaper and tosses it onto a random pile. I snatch it up and put it along with the other newspapers. "Speaking of which, I'm scheduled to do a welfare check on Ben and his family this afternoon. You two can tag along if you promise not to do anything stupid."

"Ben?" I ask, the name triggering a cache of information in the back of my mind. "Ben, the howler in your woods that one night? What's Ben's last name?"

"Ferguson. Why?"

I hold up a finger for him to wait and start paging through

the stack closest to me which lists all the werewolves with a last name starting with 'F.' I find the Ferguson family and wiggle out their pile of papers held together with a rubber band.

"I noticed something earlier but didn't think much of it." Thumbing through, I stop on the family's most recent prescription order. "Ben isn't the only werewolf in the family, right?"

"His mother, too—the scary one."

"Okay, then why are they getting enough serum to treat at least five more werewolves?" I toss the paper across the table and Jefferson catches it. His eyebrows rise into his hair.

"I guess we better ask them," he says and gestures to the pair of us. "Come on. Grab your jackets."

We dash into our shared bedroom and throw on our junior agent uniforms. Hawk blocks the door before we go anywhere and leans in until his mouth is nearly at my ear.

"What's going on with you and Jefferson?" he whispers.

I roll my shoulders and adjust my jacket. "He's hiding something. He basically screamed me out of the barn when I tried going in there last night."

"Okay. We're going to try and get in there, right?"

I nod. "Right."

"We'll play it cool?"

"We play it cool."

We give each other a low five and hurry outside where Jefferson is waiting. The old, piece of junk, green truck is thrumming with life, shaking more rust flakes off its body. I'm surprised it actually works.

"Are we riding in . . . that?" Hawk says and points to the beastly thing.

"What did you expect?" Jefferson glares at us both. "What are you two wearing? You're going to spook the Fergusons dressed like that."

"Dressed like what?" I look down at my black uniform. I honestly have no idea what he's talking about. Isn't it normal for agents to dress in their uniforms when on business?

"You look like you're about to draw a gun on someone or whip out kung fu moves. You don't want to look dangerous. They don't trust us enough as it is."

I don't mention that I *do* know kung fu. It was part of our training and I loved it.

Hawk leans in towards the old man. "Why don't they trust us? We're supposed to be their protectors, aren't we? That's the whole point of our job."

"Maybe if our organization didn't have *slayers* in the title, they would be more at ease," Jefferson grumbles. "Doesn't matter. Go change into some normal clothes."

I sigh and slouch back inside with Hawk on my heels. I grab clothes at random and hustle into the bathroom to change. My brother and I meet back outside in our "normal clothes"—plain t-shirts, cargo pants, and worn tennis shoes. He pulls on a hooded sweatshirt against the chilly air as I button up my faded green, military-style jacket and walk to where Jefferson waits.

The truck rumbles and growls as we approach. There's only one extended cab seat so Hawk and I squeeze in next to Jefferson who sits with both hands resting on the overly big wheel. I press myself against the door and try to give my brother as much room as possible but he seems to take pleasure in causing discomfort to Jefferson by getting in his personal space. The older man draws in his shoulders to keep from touching my brother and cranks on the shifter that makes a horrible grinding sound before the truck lurches forward.

Once we're on the road, I roll down the window a crack to get a breath of fresh air. The cold wind brushes stray red hairs out of my face and I strum a finger over my lips in my boredom. Hawk tries to fiddle with the radio but all that comes in is the oldies station we found at the cabin. Jefferson eventually slaps his hand away and we listen to a deep voice sing about blue shoes as we pull into the heart of Moose Lake.

We take the main road straight out of town and keep heading north past raised railroad tracks and a cemetery. A paved trail follows the curve of the road on which a handful of runners and bikers are out enjoying the October weather. The truck turns and we cross the path to another road, going several miles until we are well back in the trees, and stop in front of a weatherworn farmhouse. The house itself is squat with big bay windows, and a story-book red barn sits behind it enclosed by fences this way and that. The truck lurches to a stop at the end of its rutted driveway.

Before I can get out, Jefferson reaches across and holds the door shut. "I don't want you two to touch anything, say anything, or do anything. Just let me do the talking. You can *watch*."

He releases the door and I push out as hard as I can. The door groans and I slam it closed again after Hawk gets out. Being treated like I'm a five-year-old gets old fast. Together we trek up the porch steps and Jefferson knocks on the frame of the screen door. Footsteps echo across hardwood floors and the door opens to a thin, severe looking woman with curlers in her hair. Jefferson flips out a badge from his jacket and holds it up against the screen door.

"It's just me, Mrs. Ferguson."

Her glare is fierce and she wraps her pink bathrobe tighter around her shoulders. "And who are they?" She jerks her head in Hawk's and my direction.

"Interns. They're shadowing me. May we come in?"

Mrs. Ferguson purses her lips and shoves the screen door open. We slip inside to a dark foyer leading to a flight of stairs with rooms opening up on either side. Jefferson has clearly been here before because he turns right into a living room and sits on a flower-patterned sofa. Mrs. Ferguson takes the recliner across from him but remains perched on the edge, stiff and hands clasped in her lap. Her scowl never fades.

Unsure where we're even allowed to sit, I stand in the doorway to the living room with arms crossed. Hawk leans against the entrance beside me. Everything in this house makes it look like a perfectly normal family lives here. Photos of Mrs. Ferguson smiling and holding hands with a little boy line the mantel over the fireplace. I notice the lack of a father in any of the family portraits but there is a single photo in the center, a sign of its importance, of a young man in hiking gear grinning in front of a snowy mountain.

"Mrs. Ferguson, this is simply a check-up," Jefferson begins, leaning forward slightly, hands braced on his knees.

"There's nothing to report." Her tone is snippy and she hoists her chin like she could use it as a weapon. Considering how sharp her jaw and cheekbones are, I wouldn't be surprised if she could.

"How's Ben doing?" Jefferson continues unfazed.

She rolls her thumbs around each other. "He's a teenage boy. He likes to be active."

"I see." Jefferson pulls out a piece of paper from his jacket pocket. "How about we just go over the usual, okay?" She sniffles indignantly and nods. "All right, let's start with transformations. Have you noticed any unusual patterns? Anything out of the ordinary?"

"No."

"Any lingering sensations or urges?"

"No."

As he continues down the list, I hear a creak in the floor-boards above us. I know Hawk hears it too because he cocks his head ever so slightly. It could very well be Ben, the teen that had been howling on Jefferson's property. It's possible he knows who that black werewolf was that scared the crap out of me earlier. They certainly could have crossed paths if they've both been sneaking around Jefferson's property. I can't help it—I'm curious. I clear my throat and take a step forward.

"Mrs. Ferguson?" I interrupt. "May I use your restroom?"

Her head snaps about and she glares at me. "It's the first door at the top of the steps."

"Thanks." I shuffle out of the room at a casual pace. When I pass Hawk he holds out his hand and I give him a soft low five.

I move quietly up the stairs but instead of taking the first door, I follow the sound of the creaking floorboards and pad down a short hallway. The last door has a length of what looks to be yellow police tape angled across it that repeats "Keep Out" over and over again in black letters. The door is slightly ajar. Even from out in the hallway I can smell the distinct odor of wet dog. There's more shuffling and a stereo cranks up playing rock music.

Light flickers under the edge of the door as someone moves back and forth. I stand there thinking how to properly an-nounce myself when the door suddenly flings open. I flinch back and try to hastily compose myself. A boy freezes in the doorway, his hand still clutching the knob, and stares at me. He looks to be my age but taller with dark shaggy hair that's damp. His cheeks are flushed and he's breathing hard like he's been running. There's a sheen of sweat on his skin that makes his white t-shirt cling to his chest and shoulders and his feet are bare beneath the hem of his jeans. A thick leather cuff encircles his wrist. All and all an ordinary boy.

But I can detect the differences, even in my current state of shock at being caught outside his door. His red face and the sweat combined with the smell of wet dog are a good indicator that he recently transformed out of his wolf state. His entire body would be tingling right about now like it's been pinched, hence the flushed skin. As for breathing hard, I notice an open window with scratch marks around the frame behind him leading out to a section of the roof. He probably climbed up and transformed within the last few minutes. And—the most peculiar thing—is the faint ring of yellow around his irises in his otherwise gray eyes. It's the most telling factor and one that shouldn't be there at all if he has been taking the werewolf serum regularly.

"Oh," I say breathlessly, hoping to sound flustered and confused instead of guilty being caught where I'm not supposed to be. "I was just—" I point down the hallway and back to him. "Looking for the bathroom."

"Who are you?" he growls. When he speaks I can smell the metallic tang of blood on his breath. In fact, I can see blood on his tongue and the corners of his mouth. That's when my other senses kick in—the ones honed into me during my combat training. My hand instantly goes to my hip before I forget that I'm not allowed to carry a bio-mech gun, or any gun for that matter, like I did while training. I brush the movement off as tucking my hand into my back pocket. I'm not afraid but wary.

"I'm Junior Agent Mason with the IMS. Can I talk to you?"

Before he can respond, I put my hand on his chest and push him back into his room, closing the door with my foot so we're alone. He slaps my hand away and looks like he's about to start shouting at me so I clamp my hand on his mouth and press a finger to my lips.

"There's another agent talking to your mother right now," I say quietly. "They don't know I'm up here. It's just you and me. I want to ask you a few questions, that's all. What you say doesn't have to go outside this room. Okay?"

His eyebrows draw together but he nods. Once I pull my hand away from his mouth he takes quick steps backwards to put distance between us. He even glances at the open window like he might make a dash for it. I plant my hands on my waist and stare him down.

"It won't do to run," I warn him. "You won't get far. I promise."

He smirks and shakes his head. "You couldn't catch me."

"Maybe not, but my brother waiting downstairs could. If you transform for speed, he'll just do the same. And he's fast."

That wipes the smirk off his face. "Your brother's a werewolf?" I nod. "Prove it."

"He's got a silver bite mark just under his ribs on his left side." I pat the area on me for emphasis. "A werewolf bit down and tried to throw him across a room. I stopped it."

His expression is incredulous. "Yeah, right. How?"

"I punched it in the nose." I shrug. "And I'm guessing you have the same kind of mark on your wrist. That's why you wear that wristband, yeah?" I point to it and he clutches it to his chest like he might still be able to hide it. "It looks handmade. Odd thing to wear nowadays unless you're trying to hide something."

At last I can see he's starting to believe me. "What do you want?"

I gesture to his bed covered in a patchwork quilt. "Why don't you take a seat?"

Sunshine reflects in his eyes as he glances outside, at me, then slowly sits down on the edge of the bed. I go to lean against the frame of the open window to make sure he doesn't bolt that way. Plus, the breeze is a nice relief. With the door shut the smell of wet dog is nearly overwhelming. You'd think I'd be used to it by now having a brother as a werewolf but it still makes me want to wrinkle my nose.

"It's Ben, right?" I ask. He nods. "Okay, Ben. Have you been taking your serum doses lately?"

His eyes dart to the side. "Yeah. Of course."

"I know you're lying, Ben."

"I'm not lying!" he says sharply and a bit too loudly. I worry Jefferson might hear and will quickly realize I'm not actually in the bathroom.

I make a circle motion around my own eyes. "Then why the coloration? That yellow in your eyes? That tells me your werewolf instincts are trumping your human ones. That doesn't happen when you take the serum."

"I *am* taking it," he argues and starts to rise from the bed. I tense again but try not to show it. Like my instructors always told me, let your opponent think they have the upper hand but never let your guard down.

"Sit down, Ben," I say evenly and keep my eyes trained on him.

He doesn't listen and stands, running his hands through his damp hair. "It hasn't been working lately, I swear. I've even been taking extra doses but I've been losing track. I've had these . . . urges I can't control anymore." As he talks he takes one step forward, then another, and another until he's a lot closer than I want him to be. He stops there, takes a deep whiff, and closes his eyes. My hands curl into fists.

"Why do you . . ." He sniffs again and opens his eyes. The yellow rim around his irises is prominent. "Why do you smell so different than everyone else?"

I angle my feet into a better stance in case I need to defend myself. "It's probably the jacket."

That brings him up short. "What?"

"I wouldn't be surprised if someone died in this jacket. It smells a bit like dead person." I take a sense of satisfaction in his confused expression before I say, "It's from a thrift store."

"Oh," he breathes but the furrow between his eyebrows remains.

Before this conversation takes another turn in a direction I don't want it to go, I press on and ask, "Where did you just come from, Ben?"

His blank expression certainly seems genuine. I release a small breath as he steps back, running his hands through his hair again and returning to his spot on the bed. "I don't remember."

"There's blood in your mouth."

As if in a trance, he reaches up, swabs his finger inside his cheek and pulls it out. The tip is slathered in pink saliva. He stares at it.

"What did you do?" I continue. "I need you to remember. You could have bitten someone. If you did, we need to help that person as soon as possible or they'll have to deal with these urges the same as you. Do you want that?"

He shakes his head and wipes his finger on his white shirt,

leaving a faint pink stain on the hem. He bends over and puts his head in his hands. "I don't think I bit anyone. I think—maybe I . . ."

I lean forward eager for an answer when the door is thrown wide. We both jump and find Mrs. Ferguson standing in the frame, Jefferson and Hawk hovering over her shoulder.

"What do you think you're doing in here?" she shrieks. "You are not allowed to question my son without my permission! Get out! Get out NOW!"

Ben holds a hand out towards his mother. "Mom, she just—"

"NO! I SAID GET OUT!"

She stands aside so I can hurry out. Before I exit I look back and lock eyes with Ben. He looks terrified. Mrs. Ferguson hustles us out of her house and slams the front door, hitting my heel on the way out. I'm scowling and limping and if that weren't enough, as soon as we get back in the truck Jefferson starts yelling at me too.

"What did I say?" he thunders. "Don't speak, don't touch, don't do. And what do you do? You do all three! You need to obey orders, not let them slip in one ear and out the other—"

"The serum isn't working," I say and he falls silent. "The extra doses were for Ben. He's been having urges and blackouts despite the serum."

"That's not possible," Jefferson says almost to himself.

I don't say anything. Arguing with Jefferson won't change his mind. Maybe he hasn't read my whole file, or maybe it wasn't even in my file, but I know about the shapeshifters. I know they were trying to control a pharmaceutical company, and that company just happens to be one of the biggest werewolf serum suppliers on the planet. Now Ben's serum isn't working? I'm not buying that as a coincidence. Not for one second.

We return to the cabin and Jefferson herds us inside. I'm sat down at the table and yelled at some more.

"But we need to do something about this!" I eventually counter. "We need to track the werewolves or something."

Jefferson lets out a hard laugh. "*You* are going to stay here. *Both* of you. *I* am going to try to make amends with Mrs. Ferguson before she sets fire to my house and then *I* am going to figure out the werewolf problem."

He shakes his head and goes back outside with a cell phone glued to his ear—I can hear him trying to apologize to Mrs. Ferguson. It doesn't sound like it's going too well and I watch Jefferson disappear into the barn.

"Keep an eye on him?" I ask Hawk and dig into the files.

He leans against the kitchen counter and stares out the window. "Looking to see if the Fergusons' meds are from Werevine?"

"You read my mind."

The family's file is right where I left it. I page through the medical records, find the exact type of werewolf serum, and look up its manufacturer on a separate page. Just as I suspected, the Fergusons get their medication from Werevine Pharmaceutical. I whip out my phone, nod to Hawk, and dial headquarters. I wait on hold for Witty for nearly ten minutes before he comes on the line.

"Phoenix . . ." He sounds nervous.

"Is something wrong?"

There's a rush of wind and I picture him wheeling fast down a dark hallway. "I had to sneak away from Director Knox."

I bite my lip. "You're not in trouble are you?"

"No. Not yet anyways," he says. "He just wanted an update on you two." I can hear the clicking of a keyboard.

"Okay . . . well, we may have bigger problems than worrying about us getting into trouble. Have they interrogated the shapeshifters yet? Have they learned anything?"

"Uh . . ."

"Come on, Witty. I think we may be on to something. Were they manipulating the serum?"

"What?" The genuine surprise in his voice makes it clear they have no idea about the shapeshifters messing with the serum. "No, they were accessing patient files. They were cataloging and . . . well, I think they might have been looking for someone in particular."

"Who?"

"I don't know."

I start gesturing with my free hand even though he can't see me. "Witty, you have to convince Director Knox to take a closer look at the serum. It isn't working. I don't know what the shapeshifters want but they must have changed the werewolf serum. Even extra doses aren't helping now."

Witty's breath almost comes through the phone as he says, "Do you have any idea what Director Knox would do to you if you're wrong?"

"I'm not. We've got a solid lead."

"You're not on a mission! You're supposed to be training!"

The phone clicks and for a second I think he's hung up on me. I'm ready to start dialing his number over and over again if I have to when I hear him sigh.

"I'll see what I can do but no promises," he says and then the phone clicks into a dial tone.

I wriggle the phone at my brother. "You get all that?"

He nods. "Well, we can't just sit by. If the serum isn't working and headquarters isn't going to do anything about it, and Jefferson won't let us help, then we have to take matters into our own hands."

Being twins has its advantages—I can already tell what he's thinking. I sit on top of the table and roll my phone around in my hands. "Track the werewolves ourselves?"

"I can sniff them out and follow in wolf form. They'll just think I'm another kid in town that's been infected recently. You can keep an eye on them from a distance and we can see what they're doing while not under the serum's influence, see if we can figure out what Ben was doing and if anyone else needs help."

It could work, but it's not much of a plan. "Well, I'm not going to walk around all night," I say. "I'll need a car."

"I'm sure we can borrow Jefferson's truck." Hawk winks at me and smiles. He must already know how to get the keys.

"Okay. One problem solved, but we need more information."

We look to the boxes of files at the same time. What am I thinking? We have all the information we need right here. I dig out a map of Moose Lake and tack it up on the wall. File by file, we find each known werewolf's location, mark the map where they live, and put a red dot on those taking serum from Werevine Pharmaceutical. If Ben is feeling a little too in touch with his wild side, then maybe the others are as well. We spend most of the day marking up the map, reexamining what we know, and going over our plan.

A part of me wonders what on earth we're even doing. I reason that we're making sure Ben and his friends don't bite anyone else but there's no telling if they'll even change tonight. New werewolves tend to change spontaneously or sporadically depending on what calls of the wild they encounter. Ben could sleep through the night in his bed, normal and non-dangerous. Yet right now I feel like I have a purpose, a reason for being stuck out here in the middle of nowhere. That, and it's something to do. It even sounds *fun*.

Jefferson comes in late that evening. We hardly talk over our dinner of eggs and reheated venison. I swear it's the only thing Jefferson knows how to cook. Hawk and I sit around the table pretending to read files and eventually Jefferson moves back out to the barn and the lights flick off.

"Is he sleeping out there?" I ask, staring at the dark outline of the barn.

Hawk shrugs. "Who cares? Come on. Now's our chance."

I throw on my agent getup—black is best for night work—and make sure I have my cell phone in my pocket. Hawk finds the truck keys tucked under Jefferson's pillow—I don't ask how he knows where they are—and then we creep out to the truck. It's quiet tonight except for the distant hoot of an owl. I hop into the truck, put the key in the ignition and turn one click to release the column lock, then put the shifter into neutral and hop back out. There's no sound from the barn but we wait a good five minutes before we grab onto opposite sides of the truck and push it down the driveway, our feet pressing hard against the cold ground.

Once we're past the wall of pines and out of sight of the cabin, Hawk passes me his cell and slips around the back of the truck. Using a roll of duct tape I stole from the kitchen, I fashion a gray rope and tape each end to the sides of Hawk's phone to create a makeshift collar.

From behind the bed of the truck I can hear Hawk groaning and there's a shuffling sound. A few bits of gravel roll towards me. An ache goes through my chest. No matter how many times I've heard it before, it hurts me to hear Hawk in pain when he transforms. We're not meant to bend from one shape to another. We're supposed to be human our entire lives. Changing into something other than what we're meant to be is agonizing. I know there are a few werewolves that actually enjoy the pain of the transformation. I can't see how.

A minute passes before a great furry shape stalks around the edge of the truck. Real werewolves aren't like a lot of the imaginings I've seen in the movies. They aren't half man and half wolf, looking like neither and standing up on two legs. My brother looks like a regular timber wolf with a strong dash of red through his fur. I can faintly make out the lines of the shirt he had been wearing. Scientists and scholars have tried to explain why werewolves morph with their clothes but like my good friend Witty always says, the werewolf disease is a magical one and magic is weird.

The top of his head comes up to the bottom of my ribs. His ears perk forward and he stares up at me. The greatest tell of a werewolf is the eyes. If I focus just on his sharp green eyes, I can see my brother again.

"Are you ready?" I ask.

He flips his tail once. That's a yes. After fourteen years of living with a werewolf, we've worked out our own system of nonverbal communication. I kneel down to his level and slip the duct tape collar around his neck. His hot, wolf breath blows in my face as I press a few buttons.

"Geez, Hawk. Brush your teeth sometime."

He headbutts me and, unable to keep my balance, I fall back and land on my rear. For a second I'm stunned but then almost start laughing out loud. I clamp a hand over my mouth and swat him on the nose before trying to set his cell phone up again. After initiating a call and leaving the line open, I test to make sure he can hear me. Then I flip on a GPS app we installed earlier and see a red dot flash on my screen letting me know exactly where Hawk is.

"Okay, I think we're good." I toss my bag into the cab of the truck after making sure I have the map we marked up. "Let's go, wolf-man."

I drop the tailgate for him and he clambers into the bed of the truck. Night is well and settled so no one should notice I'm carrying around a timber wolf in the back of the truck. I slide into the driver's seat and quickly familiarize myself with the controls, thanking my lucky stars for all those hours learning how to drive every vehicle under the sun at an IMS training facility when I got my license. The truck lets out a loud whine—that hopefully Jefferson doesn't hear—when I shift it into gear, and I ease it down the rest of the driveway. Guided by my memory, and a long study of the Moose Lake map, I take us on a back road skirting around the town itself to get to the Fergusons' farmhouse. The half moon shines down on the trees, shrubs, and old wooden fences giving everything a little depth. The headlights of the beater truck blaze a path and the world becomes a ghostly field.

It's quiet apart from the growl coming out of the truck's engine. I glance in the rearview mirror now and then to spot Hawk's ears sticking up, the only part of him that's visible. We're almost to the farmhouse when he scratches against the rear window. I bring the truck to a rumbling stop and slide open the window panel behind my head.

"Got a scent?"

One thump of his tail and he vaults out of the bed. He vanishes into a row of towering pines, leaving me alone in the darkness. I shut the panel against the cold outside and watch the little red dot on my phone slowly inch away from the road. He heads at an angle from the farm so I continue to pull ahead and park at the end of the Fergusons' driveway. Through the cell phone I can hear his wolf pants and the rustle of foliage. While I wait for something to happen I pull out the marked map and spread it across the seat beside me. Using a flashlight I find in the glove compartment, I keep track of where Hawk is in comparison to the spots on our map.

"You're heading towards the Moose Horn River," I warn him. "If you *have* to cross, try not to soak your phone or I might lose you."

A gruff grumble lets me know he heard. I listen carefully to the sound of leaves crunching and branches snapping until the sound of his running stops and the churning of a river fills up the speaker. The red flashing dot stops on my cell phone and I wait for him to make a move. His panting suddenly picks up followed by a loud splash and a soft whine.

"Hawk?"

He growls and there's a snappish sound like he's shaking

his head so hard his ears are slapping his neck. Probably shaking out water but the connection is still good. He must have jumped and not quite made it.

"Careful there," I say. "I don't want to drag a wet dog out of the river tonight." I hear his jaws snap and he growls some more. "I'm sorry. I don't speak wolf."

A steady growl comes through the phone for nearly a minute before he finally subsides and races on. His red dot slowly changes direction and heads for a big empty space of woods.

A faint howl reaches my ears. I pull the cell phone away to muffle the sounds of Hawk's passage to listen. The howling is distant but steady. Soon the sound of Hawk moving stops. He must be listening too.

"One of the teenagers, maybe?" I say. "Calling together a party with his friends?"

Hawk doesn't make any indication that he's heard me or is paying attention anymore. His red dot holds steady but then abruptly takes a turn and moves fast.

"Hawk? What's going on?"

More howling starts close by. I get partway out of my seat and grab the door handle so hard the edge cracks. Movement up at the farmhouse catches my eye. Something big is crawling along the roof and jumps down to sprint away into the woods.

"Hawk, I just saw Ben go out his window," I say urgently into the phone. "If Ben's here, who are you tracking?" No response. "Ah, crap."

Just my luck. I track his dot and run my finger in a hurry down the marked map. There's a road close to his location. I throw the truck into gear and lurch past the driveway. The road rolls away under the truck's tires and I keep an eye on my cell phone, watching the red dot continue to sprint away. I can almost hear Jefferson's voice in my head telling me how stupid I am for not following orders. Would he have those tranquilizer darts in this truck? I dig in the glove compartment, my eyes flicking between it and the road, but there's nothing in it except maps, mace, and an old bag of beef jerky.

When a dark shape darts across the road, my heart jumps into my throat and I slam on the brakes. I jerk forward hard against the seatbelt and a horrible squealing sound fills my ears. Adrenaline pounds through my veins, making me sharp, and I catch enough of the shape to realize it's a reddish timber wolf.

"Hawk!" I shout. I scramble out of my seat belt and throw myself out the door, leaving the truck running in the middle of a deserted road in the woods. Then I'm flying after my brother. I can hardly see with only the little flashlight for guidance and more than one branch snaps me in the face. Hawk has all but disappeared and I can't hear anything over my pounding feet and thumping heart. Whenever I try to glance at my cell phone and track his dot, I stumble and run into brush. Twigs and tall grass wrap around my arms and legs and after a bad misstep I fall on my face.

Spitting out dirt and groaning, I crawl up out of the brush on all fours, my hands sweeping the ground for my cell phone and flashlight that tumbled away from me. I grasp the flashlight and as I get to my feet, its beam illuminates a face in the darkness. I clamp a hand over my mouth to cover my scream, but my shock quickly subsides into surprise.

"Jefferson?" I gasp. "What the *flaming hydra dung* are you doing out here?"

"Watch your language, kid," he grumbles and hoists the

end of the shotgun he's carrying so it's not pointed at me any-more. "And I could ask you the same thing. What on earth do you think you're doing running around in the middle of the night?" He shifts the shotgun to one hand so he can grab my arm and shake me. "You just learned there are werewolves the serum isn't working on so you decide to *chase them?*"

"We can handle ourselves," I grumble and wrench myself out of his grip. Ignoring the look of death he's giving me, I stoop to find my cell phone under a bush. The red dot isn't too far away and it looks like it's stopped. "Hawk's this way. Come on."

Jefferson follows in my wake. I move more cautiously now that Hawk's indicator isn't speeding away from me anymore. Branches appear out of the dark under the glare of my flash-light and soon I can hear the panting and rustling of some-thing big. Pushing out from the trees, we reach a small clearing. Hawk circles round and round, clearly agitated, in the center. As soon as he sees me, he rushes forward, pushes his head into my gut, and whines. I sink down to wrap my arms around his furry neck.

"What the heck were you doing?" I say and lean back to grab either side of his muzzle and shake him a little. His eyes are wide and he's breathing hard. Burs, leaves, and twigs stick out all over him and his legs are quivering. More howling starts in the distance and he tenses.

"Don't you dare run off again," I growl. "You deranged maniac."

Jefferson stands over my shoulder. "Get him to the truck and go back to the cabin. And don't take any detours. You're in enough hot water as it is. Now, *git.*"

I rise and Hawk limps beside me. Before we get far more howling begins and a chill runs down my spine. I think of Ben running out of his house because of the howling earlier. Werewolves are attracted to wild instincts but Hawk has never run off before like he did just now, never before has he been so compelled by what other werewolves succumb to.

"Who's out there?" I ask aloud, almost to myself.

"Not who," Jefferson says and tucks the butt of the shotgun tight into his shoulder, securing one hand on the pump and one on the trigger. "But *what.*"

8

Hawk is still whining when he climbs into the bed of the truck. I'm tired and angry and pretty sure my face is bleeding. So, I slam the gate of the truck and almost catch the end of his tail. He's still whining.

"Okay, either transform and tell me what's wrong like a normal human being or shut up!" I yell and jump into the driver's seat, throwing the door shut so hard it shakes the entire truck.

Once inside I grip the wheel, take several deep breaths, and close my eyes. The truth is I'm not angry. Well, of course I'm angry, but I'm angry because I'm scared. It's not a feeling I'm used to. Anger is a regular companion, but this? My arms are shaking, my heart is racing, and I feel like something is crawling down my spine. The night doesn't bother me, that thing out in the woods I can deal with, but Hawk actually acting like some kind of animal? That frightens me.

After another deep breath, I open my eyes to find I've made

handholds on the old wheel. It groans when I release my fingers so I hastily try to smooth out the ridges. It's not like clay, unfortunately for me, and my ten digits remain permanently a part of the wheel. Just one more thing Jefferson is going to kill me for. I glance in the rearview mirror to make sure Hawk hasn't taken off again. His dark eyes catch what little light there is and his ears flatten against his head. I quickly look away. I can tell he's embarrassed, but I'm also still angry.

I crank the old rust bucket into gear and the engine roars. I take my time driving to the cabin. I'm not eager to face Jefferson's wrath. The headlights pave the way and my anger starts to seep out of me, leaving coherent thought in its place. It finally registers in my head that Hawk had been limping. I should have cared more. I glance back again to the bed of the truck but I can only see the top of Hawk's furry head as he watches the road behind us. A pang of guilt goes through my chest. Some sister I am.

I blow out a puff of air, pushing the stray hairs out of my face. I can only remember one other time Hawk ran off and truly acted like the werewolf he is. It hadn't been long after he was bitten and our parents had . . . well, after we were taken to Underground. We had both been terrified and Hawk started to change. They had the werewolf serum at the time and gave it to him but he hated needles and freaked out. We were shepherded by adults because we were little children. They took us where we needed to go, got us clothes, gave us food, setup a place for us to stay with other children our age of which there weren't many—just kids of agents left behind while the adults went to work.

Hawk never whined despite the frequent injections but I

could always see the pain in his face. When he got a year or two older, they entrusted him to start giving himself his own injections. All werewolves have to account for everything they do themselves—keep logs, make notes if anything goes wrong, and always, *always* go to the clinic if you miss an injection. Hawk took his for a short while under my tenacious supervision but then he started saying he had already taken his injection before I had woken up or while I was in the bathroom or otherwise when I hadn't been watching. He'd show me an empty syringe, but I knew. Hawk became more aggressive. He had outbursts. And one time—I shudder to think about it even now—he changed and didn't keep his mind. He became a wolf—*was* a wolf—and attacked me.

I roll my hands over the steering wheel a few times before I slow down coming up to Jefferson's driveway. I vowed to keep my brother safe from others and from himself. I just hope I'm not losing that battle now after everything. But maybe this is only a one-time accident, a fluke. Hawk isn't stupid or weak enough to let his instincts get the better of him. I have faith in my brother, and if I don't have that, and we don't have each other's back, then what do we have?

The truck's brakes let out a long squeal as I come to a stop inside the ring of rust flakes that marks the truck's usual parking space. I hop out and find Hawk sitting like a normal human being in the back, his legs pulled up and arms crossed over them. He looks pale and almost ghostly in the darkness. I don't say a word but wrench open the tailgate and make a sweeping gesture to indicate he's free to leave. He remains sitting a moment longer before grabbing the side of the truck and rising unsteadily to his feet. His limp is much more pronounced than I thought.

He grimaces and makes it to the tailgate by himself as I look on anxiously and settles down on his butt, swinging his legs over the edge. The second before he touches the ground I'm at his side and grab one of his arms to wrap it around my neck to take his weight.

"I'm fine," he grumbles.

"Just shut up and walk." I mean to say it as playful banter to lighten his spirits but the words are a little too bitter on my tongue. "Come on, you gimp."

Halfway to the door of the cabin there's a loud slam and I jerk to a halt. Jefferson stalks across the open space from the barn, somehow able to reach the cabin before us. His face is purple, his beady eyes livid, and every muscle in his jaw is tense. He gets to the door before us and yanks it open to allow us through. I keep my head down and guide Hawk to the chair inside.

Hawk lets out a huff when he sits and bends down to peel up the hem of his jeans that are ripped and bloody. I bite back my sudden surge of panic and kneel to take his foot in my hands. There's a gash bleeding freely above his ankle and the skin is warm to the touch.

"What did you do?" I ask.

He glowers. "I was running through freakin' brush, what do you think happened?"

"Well, maybe if you hadn't taken off like a five-year-old chasing candy—"

"*You* were the one who said we should go out there!"

I can feel my face turning red. "It wasn't just *my* idea! And I wasn't expecting you to—"

"Enough!" Jefferson bellows behind us. Hawk jerks his foot out of my hands so suddenly he almost kicks me in the face.

"Stop talking! Just sit there. Be silent. Not another word or I swear I'm going to bury both your bodies in the backyard."

I bite my bottom lip to stop myself from giving a snappy retort and settle on the floor to lean against a stack of file boxes crammed underneath the table. Jefferson continues to mumble under his breath as he fishes through a cabinet under the sink and digs out a first aid kit. When he pulls out a roll of gauze I hold out my hand. It's automatic. I've been patching up Hawk since we were kids. I know what to do.

"Seriously?" Jefferson snaps. "You think I'll give you any job right now so you can mess that up too? Get up."

I'm fuming. I jump to my feet and shove at the table to let out my anger so I don't shove Jefferson instead. The legs screech against the floor and the thing slams against the wall with a resounding crash. A few papers flutter and land on the floor. Before I can move out of the way, the old man gets right in my face and points a finger that almost touches my nose.

"*That's enough!*" he shouts. "Don't you think you've done enough damage for one night?"

He looks pointedly at my brother then back at me. My face burns and I move to stand in the relative darkness of the entry-way to face the wall. Jefferson cleans up Hawk's leg and I try to ignore the sharp intakes of breath from my brother at the pain. I cross my arms and lean against the log wall, absently toeing a pair of boots in front of me. I feel like a five-year-old in trouble—then realize I *look* like a five-year-old in trouble pouting in the corner. I straighten, turn about to face them, and stand still, trying to resemble something of a proper adult. How I've made it this far through life, I'll never know.

Jefferson closes the kit after Hawk's lower leg has been

wrapped in white and puts it away before leaning against the kitchen counter. He runs a hand down his face, tugging at his wrinkles and fuzzy beard before slapping his hand back to his side.

"I don't know how things went for you two back in Underground," he starts, voice low and strained. "I'm assuming there was a lot of mayhem, destruction of property, throwing elves out windows, that sort of thing—but out here, if you go off the rails you aren't going to get spanked and sent home with a warning. Two things could happen—either the agency throws you out for good, or you end up getting yourselves killed before your next birthday. You seem to think werewolves are just a game and you know what you're doing, but you're wrong. You have no idea what you're facing out here."

My impulse to spit out words and my desire to become an agent war inside my head. Hawk and I *do* know werewolves. Hawk *is* a werewolf, how could we not? We know the lore, we know the symptoms, we know how the infection spreads. I want to throw Jefferson's words back in his face.

Hawk speaks before I can say anything. "We can handle werewolves."

"Can you?" Jefferson leans in towards him. "Because from what I just saw, you can't even handle yourself."

"That's—" Hawk pushes his lips side to side. "That's never happened before."

"Why don't I believe you?"

"It's true," I say. "Hawk's different. I mean, he doesn't even—" Hawk shoots me a sharp look and I catch myself before letting our little secret slip. ". . . take walks on the wild side," I finish lamely.

I try to keep up my poker face but Jefferson's beady little eyes lock on me like they have the ability to peel away my mask with some telepathic power. Lucky for me, Jefferson is a normal human being, not Blessed with such a power, and can't see what I'm hiding.

Eventually his eyes draw back to Hawk. "Well, I don't care if you've been Mr. Goody-two-shoes-werewolf up until this point. I don't trust you—either of you. You're only still here because the IMS can't afford to lose kids like you. But if you push that button long enough, they *will* kick you out."

I guess I can't argue with that. I always knew Hawk and I were hanging on by a thread in the junior agent program. If the IMS could pull anyone off the street and train them like the FBI, we never would have gotten close to entering the program, but regular people tossed into our world don't take to it very well. Going from thinking criminals are the most dangerous beings on the planet to coming up against a five-headed hydra can really shake a person up. Not that I've come up against a hydra myself but I've seen the footage. Hawk and I grew up amongst the legends and the monsters. When we see a giant or a harpy, we don't flinch and that's what the IMS needs more than anything.

"So . . ." Jefferson combs a hand through his shaggy hair and takes his time exhaling. "From this moment on, there are no more screw ups, no more midnight jogs through the woods, and no running off after werewolves. You do what I tell you. You toe the line, and maybe, *maybe* if you're lucky, you might actually live long enough to see an IMS badge with your name on it."

He stalks past me to the door and is about to leave when he pauses and turns around. "And just because I don't know you doesn't mean I don't care if you die or not." With that he retreats into the night and slams the door shut behind him.

The silence echoes between Hawk and me.

My brother looks up with comically wide eyes. "I had no idea he cared," he says and sniffles for dramatic effect. I roll my eyes and make for my bunk bed. Midnight has crawled away and I'm exhausted. Hawk stays out in the main room a moment longer so I dig through my things and find a hard black case at the bottom of my travel bag. I ease it open to make sure the pair of werewolf serum injections are still there.

Hawk hasn't taken one in years, not since that time he went after me, because after that day when I vowed to save him from himself he changed. We ran off for a short while after it happened and hadn't brought the serum with us. Hawk managed to change and change back without any side effects and kept his mind. He's one of a kind—the one werewolf who doesn't need the serum to stop from being a monster. And Hawk *hated* the injections. So we falsified his logs, bought the serum but never used it. The IMS would have our heads for that, or steal Hawk away to experiment on and find out what makes him different. It's our secret and one we have to keep.

I stare at the injections a moment longer, thinking that maybe we've made a mistake. I hear Hawk's footsteps behind me and hastily tuck the case out of sight where he won't find it.

Hawk stops in the doorway and leans his head against the wood frame. "We're okay, right?"

I stand to face him. "I don't know. Are we? Are you?"

He nods slowly. "Yeah, I'm okay. When I'm with you, it's . . ." He swallows and averts his eyes, not wanting to lay any mushy feelings or anything on the table. I don't want him to either. I hate chick flick movies. I just want him to be okay. "It's easier to be regular ol' me."

"Good." I nod and stand with my hands planted on my waist, adding to the awkwardness in the room. To break the tension, I step forward and punch him in the shoulder with a grin. "No more howling at the moon tonight though, right?"

"I got it all out of my system."

"Then I'm going to bed. I'm bushed. Come on, Balto."

I grab his arm and push him at the lower bunk before kicking off my shoes and climbing up into the top bunk. I don't bother changing. In fact, a part of me thinks it's a good idea to be prepared in case Hawk decides to take off again. Easier to run after him in jeans than pajamas.

Light catches my eye and I look to the window. Jefferson is out in the barn again and his shadow passes across the light that seeps out the bottom of the doorway. That intense curiosity of mine returns and I slowly drift away watching the light flicker around Jefferson's shadow.

I don't stay asleep for long. Out here in the country it's too quiet and every little sound and twitch Hawk makes in his sleep wakes me up. I'm used to a thrum of white noise in the background from living in Underground, of fauns singing softly, the hiss of steam from Old Man Two's shop, elves cranking up hip-hop tunes to practice their breakdancing moves late into the night. Now just hearing Hawk shift his blankets throws me awake. I'm too on edge, expecting him to get up and leave again, or hear howling in the distance. Jefferson doesn't come back inside before dawn so I begin to suspect he has a mattress out in that barn. He's insane. It's too cold to be sleeping out in a barn with October quickly coming to an end.

I can literally feel the bags under my eyes when I finally force myself to get out of bed and change in the bathroom. I glance into Jefferson's room but he's still not there. I put on some coffee and raid what little there is in the fridge. I cook up eggs and settle into my spot at the table to finish organizing what's left of the paper disaster, but I start nodding off. I try taking a nap at the table to see if I can squeeze in some more sleep but end up sitting there with my head on the desk and my brain buzzing. Aggravated, and choosing consciousness over idle drowsing, I change into my running clothes and head outside.

The air is chill and a breeze nips at my nose, but the sky is clear and blossoming in colors like a watercolor painting. Before taking off I step carefully over to the barn. I stand at the door and decide barging in isn't a good idea. It didn't go over so well last time. Instead, I knock twice. When there isn't a response, I yell.

"I'm going out for a run!" No response. "Not running away, just running. Exercise! You know . . . ah, forget it."

I pop in the earbuds of my mp3 player and jog down the long gravel driveway. My feet pound along to a techno song Hawk and I once danced to in a competition against a group of feisty elves. They had challenged us because I had to open my big mouth and say we could take them. That first time they cleaned the floor with us. Then Hawk and I came back after months of practice. *That* time we won. I smile to myself as I run along the shoulder of Soldier Road. I can still picture the look on those elves' faces when the crowd pronounced us the winners. Best. Day. Ever.

A hip-hop tune comes on next when I realize there's an echo to my footsteps. I slow my pace to look behind me. I jump to the side with a startled yelp and stumble across the pavement when I find a wolf running beside me, its deep reddish fur glowing in the morning light.

"I am going to *smack* you into next week, Hawk," I shout at him. I kick up my pace and he trots along beside me, tongue lolling out and everything. "You're a freakin' puppy, you know that?"

He just pants and keeps his head down. I turn up the volume of my music and start running faster. It's really a stupid thing to do because a werewolf can easily out pace me but I get competitive. He keeps up with me easy as you please which only makes me angrier.

"I can't be seen running with a wolf, you moron!" I shout, make a sharp turnabout, and run as fast as I can in the opposite direction. He catches up again. I hear the rumble of a car. "Oh, crap."

A minivan pulls out of a driveway directly in front of me. It's too late to jump into the bushes and pull Hawk along with me. Instead I slow my pace and try to look like I'm merely walking my dog—my stupid, huge, wolf-like dog. I smile and wave at the woman in her fifties that swings onto the road and stares at me as she passes. She's driving slow and, if she's smart, she'll realize I've got a wolf glued to my hip.

"Go, go, go!" I say under my breath and we take off towards Jefferson's place. I glance over my shoulder but the van has moved on. I come to a stop and plant my hands on my knees to suck down air. Once I've got my breath back, I whip about on my brother. "You—"

I'm alone on the road again and hear the faint snapping of branches through the trees. I throw up my hands.

"Oh, now you wise up?" I shout after him. "Ugh!"

Too angry to continue my run, I complete the short distance to Jefferson's and jog down the driveway. Hawk is standing outside the door of the cabin holding a plate with a few scraps of eggs left on it. He lifts it up for me to see once I'm in range.

"What, none for me?" he scoffs.

"Are you an idiot?"

"Depends on who you ask, but not generally, no."

I gesture to the road. "Then what was all that about!"

He looks wide-eyed from the driveway, to me, to his empty plate, then back to me. His face is blank. "What? I'm lost."

"You've been careful for how many years, then you just strut along the road like a stray husky? What's wrong with you?"

He squeezes his eyes shut and holds up his hand. "Wait, wait, wait." He opens his eyes and points very deliberately to me. "*You* think that *I*—" he points to himself, "—went out *there*—" he points to the road, "—as . . . my other half?" He narrows his eyes at the empty plate. "Was there something in these eggs? Because you're crazy."

"I just saw you out there! You were running beside me!"

"Uh . . . no, that's a negatory. I woke up like two minutes ago and you didn't leave me any eggs, you hog."

I throw my hands up. "It was you! Reddish fur, werewolf, about yea high . . ." I freeze with my hand hovering at the right height. Thinking back, the wolf was a little short for Hawk, the

121

red fur not quiet reaching all the way down its back. My eyes snap up and I drop my hand.

"It wasn't you?"

He shakes his head very slowly so I can't misunderstand him. "Looks like you've got a stalker friend. A furry, shapeshifting, stalker friend."

9

I pace in front of the cabin, eyes darting to the woods every other second. Jefferson sits in the front seat of the old truck pouring over a map and muttering to himself. He dials multiple people I don't know and I can't hear what he's talking about. He's been that way since he came out of the barn. I told him about the mysterious running companion I had but he just waved it off. He seems to have a few new wrinkles on his forehead though so maybe it perturbed him more than he let on.

Wolf-Hawk trots out of the woods after having been gone for fifteen minutes. He nods in my direction then disappears behind the barn, returning a minute later as his usual slim, upright self. He musses his hair and avoids direct eye contact. Crap.

Once he reaches me, he shakes his head. "Your friend must be a ghost." He crosses his arms. "Or got into a car somewhere. The trail vanished at the end of Soldier Road. No luck."

He glances in Jefferson's direction who lets out a choice

swear word after hanging up his cell phone for the umpteenth time. Hawk quirks an eyebrow at me and I shrug. As if Jefferson would tell me what he's doing. We're the slaves to his whim, not his confidantes. I pick at the seam of my *Go Fire Sprites!* sweatshirt and debate asking Jefferson what he's doing. Does he know who that random werewolf was? Not that I'm afraid or anything—just creeped out. Does that werewolf randomly run alongside people for kicks or does he or she know that I know about werewolves? Was it the one howling out in the woods last night?

I start walking towards Jefferson when Hawk throws out his arm and stops me. He gestures to the driveway and I hear the rumble of an engine. My stomach plummets when I see the bar of red and blue lights on top, the reinforced grill, and the brown and white paint job. When it stops in the turn-around I read *Carlton County Sheriff's Office* across the side. I self-consciously stand at attention and straighten my sweatshirt. This can't be good.

A deputy unfolds from the driver's seat and straightens to a good half foot over my head. He could have been the son of a giant—tall, broad-chested, and strapping. His tan uniform stretches across solid biceps and when he takes off his wide brimmed hat, brown hair falls past his ears. He's young, but his size is menacing. His dark inquisitive eyes peer down a pointed nose at us. His gaze moves past us to Jefferson who finally exits the rusted truck.

"Deputy Graham." Jefferson shakes hands with the deputy like he's an old friend.

Deputy Graham smiles and it changes everything about him immediately. He's suddenly warm and approachable and a giant ray of sunshine. I let myself relax a little. He fiddles with the brim of his hat and shifts his weight onto one leg, throwing an eye over all of us.

"I got a call this morning." The deputy clears his throat and he's back to being deadly serious. "Mrs. Swenson thought she saw a young woman being followed by a wolf on your road. I told animal control I would look into it. You wouldn't happen to know anything about that would you? Happened right past your driveway."

Jefferson glares in my direction. "It's handled, Jared. Just some teenage miscreant causing trouble and bothering our girl here. We'll handle it."

It takes me a second to process what Jefferson just said, and the fact Deputy Graham doesn't even flinch or look confused. He knows. He *knows* about the werewolves. I've been told there are officers in law enforcement all over the globe that work with the IMS but it feels strange knowing this man is one of them. An ordinary guy in the ordinary world dealing with your usual delinquent teenagers, suspicious reports, and, oh right—werewolves. Just another day at the office.

"I've been catching a number of calls," Deputy Graham continues. "Wolf sightings. Something going on, Jefferson?"

"It's nothing." He waves the comment away. "But, uh, if you hear anything about a black wolf, let me know."

The deputy looks like he wants to ask more but doesn't. Instead he turns his attention to me and Hawk. "So, trainees?" He moves with easy grace for such a big guy and gives both our hands a firm shake as we exchange names. "I guess I'll see you around town then. Holler if you need anything, Jefferson."

He puts his hat back on, tips it at us, and then squeezes

himself into the squad car. Jefferson gives a short wave as he pulls away. I'm bubbling over with questions and suspicion.

"He was nice," I say offhand before moving onto what I really want to talk about. "So, *is* nothing going on?"

"No, something is." He looks at me out of the corner of his eye as if deciding if he can trust me. It's hard to look trustworthy when all I've been feeling lately is guilty. I hold my chin up and try to at least look the part of an adult who has it together—apart from the fact my brother's a werewolf, I probably have powers I don't even realize, and at least one strange werewolf is stalking me.

He flips his cell phone over and over again in his hands before stuffing it into his pants pocket. "I went through the information you two organized and I've been calling the werewolves around town. There have been other odd dosages of the werewolf serum. A lot more people than just Ben are taking extra shots, but none of the werewolves in town want to talk to me. They're claiming amendment rights, and blah, blah, blah. Then Deputy Graham says we're getting wolf calls? The people here know the dangers of discovery and they've never wanted anything like that to happen. Something's changed and it worries me."

"But no one's talking to you," I say aloud, talking to myself.

"That's what I said."

Hawk holds up a finger. "But they would talk to another werewolf."

Jefferson's beady eyes get even smaller if that's possible. "What, you want to go knocking on people's doors hoping for a wolfy group hug and answers? Kid, they still don't know you. You aren't from around here. They won't talk to you. And honestly, I don't trust you to talk to them. Remember the last time I took you two to someone's house?"

Hawk holds up both hands. "I get that, but isn't it better if someone like me tries to find out what's going on? If you plan on plowing into someone's house demanding answers with an IMS badge, do you really think it's going to go better that way? Or hiding cameras out in the woods and spying on them?" He taps his palms on his chest. "*I* know what they're going through. I can help them."

I hear the grasping need in my brother's voice, that urge to do something for his fellow kind. It's something I can never help him with even though I've tried. There are just some things you can't understand if you've never been in that person's shoes. This magical disease is one of them.

Jefferson rolls his shoulders, looks to the woods, and then leans his head back to face the sky. This decision must be agonizing for him—trust us two rotten scoundrels or try to fight his way through the brick wall the wolfy residents have put up around themselves. Hawk gives him a wide smile.

"Come on, Agent Barnes," Hawk says. "I've even got a plan."

"Oh, why is that not at all reassuring?" Jefferson massages the bridge of his nose. "All right! What's this plan of yours?"

"The W.A. meeting. There's got to be one here, right?"

Jefferson makes a kind of growling noise from the back of his throat. "You're kidding."

"Only on Tuesdays, and luckily for you it's Saturday," Hawk says and winks. "That's right. I'm going to Werewolves Anonymous."

~

We all cram into the front seat of the truck and make our

way noisily along the road to the W.A. meeting on Sunday night. I've heard of these meetings before. Hawk went to one once. When he came back to the apartment he made a face and said he'd never go back. It's a support group for those that have problems coming to terms with what they are or can't handle the issues that come with shifting into a furry creature. Hawk, apart from the injections, has taken being a werewolf in stride. It doesn't seem to bother him in the least with the exception of when others in the legendary community isolate him for it. To some, werewolves are second-class magical citizens—humans with magic that don't belong with the rest. Thankfully, we haven't encountered too much of that in Underground.

It's dark out by the time we reach our destination. I stare out the windshield confused as we turn into a cemetery and slowly wind our way past tombstones.

"Seriously?" I say, breaking the silence. "They meet here?"

"Welcome to Riverside Cemetery," Jefferson says and rolls the truck to a stop outside a little caretaker's shack. Dark trees rise up behind it dropping away into a forest, and when Hawk pushes open the door I can hear the rush of a river close by.

"Isn't this a little . . . creepy?" I ask, my eyes roving over the tombstones and neat stretches of grass on a rolling hill. "And counterproductive to having a happy 'feel better' sort of meeting?"

"It's secluded, next to an easily accessible road, and where someone won't accidentally stumble onto it," Jefferson explains as if it's all quite plain and I'm an idiot. "You don't exactly want a group of people talking about the urge to rip apart cattle to be overheard."

"Okay," Hawk sighs. "Let's do this."

Jefferson reaches over me and pats Hawk on the chest. The friendly gesture is a little odd considering Jefferson has made it a point to tell us how much he doesn't like us. "Hey, do a good job in there, all right?"

"Well, duh," Hawk says then hops out and disappears into the shack.

Once he's gone, Jefferson pulls around on the little dirt track and exits the cemetery, finding a nice secluded side road a ways down to sit and wait. In the darkening cabin of the truck I'm about to ask Jefferson if he brought a deck of cards for something to do when I hear people talking faintly. I look out the back, to the side, but don't see anybody around us. Then Jefferson pulls a cell phone out of his pocket and turns up the volume.

"What—" I start but then catch Hawk's voice on the phone as he introduces himself to some woman. I put two and two together and glare at Jefferson. "That was some nice sleight of hand, sticking a phone in Hawk's pocket just then. What do you think you're doing?"

"Did you really think I was going to let him go in there alone and take his word for whatever he tells us when he gets out?"

I can't believe this. "*Yes*," I say forcefully. "He wouldn't lie. Why would he?"

He leans back from me, one elbow propped up on the steering wheel. "Have you *ever* been around other werewolves? Of course they lie! They lie to protect themselves. Do you honestly think your brother has shared all the gory details of what it's like to be what he is? If you were in his shoes, you would do the same. Anyone would. They're not pure human, and they protect their own."

I turn away from him and stare out the windshield. I hug my arms and curl my fingers around my biceps. I feel uncomfortable and a chill crawls up my neck. "This is wrong. They go to this meeting because they need to talk freely. We can't just eavesdrop. Isn't that breaking the law or something anyway?"

"If you haven't noticed, the IMS gets a bit more flexibility than most because we have bigger secrets to keep than anyone." Jefferson ups the volume on his cell phone and I hear a rumble of voices mixing together. "Think of it this way. Someone in there might know what came over your brother the other night when he ran off. Maybe it's something he won't want to talk about and hides it from you. Wouldn't it be better if you knew what happened? What if you could protect him from it but he didn't give you the chance to because he didn't share what's being said in that room?"

I face away from him to the passenger side window. There's nothing I wouldn't do for my brother. I still feel this is wrong and we'll end up paying for it later if Hawk or anyone else finds out, but that part of me twisted up with anxiety for my brother drowns out my morality. I don't stop Jefferson or tell him to turn off the phone. I sit silently and listen curled up against the door acting like I can't hear.

The mingle of voices over the small speaker quiets as a woman asks for everyone to take their seats. Her voice is gentle and her words patient—exactly what I imagine a therapist would sound like.

"I want to thank everyone for coming out tonight," she says. "I know it can be difficult finding the time to meet with us, and I appreciate your courage in bringing your thoughts to the table."

"That's Dr. Rosewell," Jefferson says quietly so we can both still hear the conversation buzzing through the phone. "She's the one that feeds me the medical and injection data from the clinic. She's the werewolf doc."

I don't acknowledge Jefferson has told me anything but continue to listen. The group starts to share their stories one at a time. A woman with a high thin voice talks about her urge to chase a squirrel that keeps coming to her bird feeder and says she accidentally tore off the screen to her kitchen window. A man in a booming baritone that causes reverb on the phone goes into a tirade about teenage werewolves running across his territory and quickly corrects himself, across his *property*. When a young girl with a quivering voice talks about how painful the transformation is and nearly breaks down into sobs, I bite my lip and squint my eyes.

Once the group has calmed the girl with reassurances, there's a long pause before a familiar boy's voice begins next.

"Hello, my name is Ben."

The room echoes back, "Hello, Ben."

"And I've been a werewolf for a month."

I can't help myself. I find Jefferson's eyes in the dark. "Is that Mrs. Ferguson's kid?"

He nods. "Yeah, the one you harassed."

"I didn't *harass*—"

"Quiet. Listen."

I resume my previous position but keep my head tilted so I can hear better.

Ben's voice remains steady as he continues. "I don't know what's changed but . . . there's something wrong. I don't know if it's me or . . ." There's a moment of quiet and I can hear the previous girl sniffling in the background. "I haven't been able to control myself like I'm supposed to on the serum. I've been angrier than ever and it's like anything can flip the switch. I've had blackouts and I'll come back to my senses lost out in the woods. I—I'm terrified. And I know I'm not the only one."

I sit straighter and cock my head even more, intent on Ben's story.

"I have friends at school that have been feeling the same way but they refuse to come here and talk about it. I felt like I needed to say something. I just—*we* just all feel so alone and confused because we thought the serum was supposed to stop this from happening." He stops and doesn't go on. He doesn't mention the extra doses he's been taking. Maybe he feels it would make him look weak.

Dr. Rosewell speaks next. "I acknowledge your frustration, Ben, and I'm glad you were open with us. We're here for you, and if you need support during this difficult phase, we will help in any way we can. It's also important to have encouragement from family members. Does your mother know what's been going on?"

I can hardly hear Ben when he replies, "I told her, but she doesn't know what to do."

Dr. Rosewell makes a kind of cooing sound like she's trying to comfort Ben, but it sounds awfully odd to me. "Would anyone like to volunteer as a companion to support Ben? We all need to rely on each other."

"I volunteer." It's Hawk.

Another pause with static over the cell phone. The werewolf doc speaks and sounds a little uncertain when she says, "Would you like to introduce yourself to the group?"

Hawk clears his throat and I imagine him running a hand through his hair, maybe leaning forward eagerly in his chair. He's a people person after all. That part of him I've never understood.

"Hello everyone. My name is Hawk." A murmur from the group repeats his name back to him with a hello. "And I've been a werewolf for fourteen years." There's actually some surprised muttering in the background this time. I'm sure Hawk is soaking in the attention. "I was bitten when I was very small and don't remember much of the incident itself. It's been really hard at times accepting what I am and who I am. I think I would have tossed in the towel more than a few times if it weren't for my sister."

My cheeks grow warm and I stare at the cell phone held out in Jefferson's hand.

"She's the one thing that's kept me from drifting away. She's not just my family, she's my best friend. Even when I've been acting like—well, like a dog—" Gentle laughter meets his little joke, "—she pushes right back and reminds me that I'm not a monster. I'm not a freak. I'm her brother. I'm someone that matters. And I think that's something everyone needs in their life. Everyone needs a family, a pack. They don't have to be an actual blood relative. Otherwise a lone wolf is just that. Alone."

I bite my lip so hard it hurts and face the passenger window again as if I've discovered something immensely interesting out in the black night where I can hardly see a thing. Warmth swells in my chest and I could lead a parade, become president, save the world. I never thought I had made much of a difference for Hawk. I sort of always felt like a stone around my brother's neck that held him back and kept him grounded. I didn't think he needed me as much as I needed him.

I miss part of the conversation and zone back in as the meeting breaks up. A few people say farewell to each other, and there's shuffling and the scuffling of chairs being moved. We listen to footsteps and the crunch of leaves underfoot. Hawk must be outside again.

"Hey, Hawk!" It's Ben. "I need to talk to you."

The footsteps stop. "Yeah, okay."

"Look, man, you don't need to be my support. My mom would freak if she knew an IM—"

"Not here, Ben," Hawk says sharply. The footsteps continue and Jefferson and I exchange a look. I guess we didn't really think about Ben ruining everything. He and his mother, apart from Deputy Graham, are the only ones that know Hawk and I work with the IMS. Like Jefferson said before, the werewolves wouldn't be so willing to talk to someone working for an agency with *slayers* in the name. We need to be flying below the radar if we want to figure out what's happening to the werewolf population.

Hawk's voice echoes through the speaker. "I want to help, Ben. I really do. This isn't about me being with the IMS. This is about me being a werewolf and knowing what it's like to be afraid of what's inside you. If you need to talk, I'm here."

"Okay, yeah," Ben says uncertainly. "Thanks, man. I gotta go. My mom didn't know I came to the meeting tonight so I need to run."

"Okay, I'll see you around. Take it easy."

There are more crunchy footsteps, shuffling, then button beeps. I almost jump out of my skin when the cell phone in my pocket starts to ring. Jefferson quickly cuts off his call as I pick up mine.

"Hello?" I ask even though I know it's Hawk.

"Hey, Phoenix. Meeting's over. Where are you guys?"

"Down the road about a quarter of a mile."

"Hang tight. I'm coming."

I hang up, shove the phone back in my pocket, and exhale sharply. It dawns on me that by listening in on the W.A. meeting I am harboring a secret, one I can't share with my brother without causing a rift. I want him to know he can always trust me. Lying to him is going to be hard.

We don't have to wait long before Hawk opens the passenger door and slides onto the seat beside me. Jefferson cranks the truck into gear and we head to the cabin.

"So?" I prompt. "How'd it go?"

He watches me for a long moment. Oh, no. He must already know. He knows and I'm a terrible person. He musses his hair and blows a raspberry. "It was about as fun as the last meeting I'd been too. Everyone's got problems and everyone seemed too on edge. They're becoming territorial and instinct driven. I sort of agreed to support Ben. He's still having problems."

He doesn't say any more. I wait for him to continue and explain what we already know. I don't want Jefferson to be right that Hawk won't share everything with me. We're supposed to be in this together. Then again, I'm not exactly telling Hawk everything either. I have no idea how Jefferson is going to get the phone back from Hawk without him noticing. My eyes are magnetically attracted to Hawk's pocket like I'm waiting for it to explode and announce its presence. The fact Hawk hasn't noticed it yet surprises me. I thought he might have felt the weight of it or something.

"So . . . anyone else having problems like Ben?" I ask, deciding to prompt it out of my brother and prove Jefferson wrong.

Hawk sighs. "He said some other teenagers were having the same symptoms."

"We should check it out," Jefferson says and strums his fingers on the wheel.

My brother's eyes are hard as he stares at the old man. "That'll sort of be a problem since no one wants to talk to you."

"Not to me, no." He brings the truck to a stop outside the cabin and the engine stutters into silence. "But they would talk to you and probably your sister now, too, after that little performance."

The blood drains out of my face and I sit very still with my hands in my lap. Hawk doesn't tense or make any sort of exclamation and I realize he *does* know about the phone in his pocket. I brace myself for the explosion waiting to happen. Hawk slides the cell phone out of his pocket and tosses it at Jefferson.

"It's no wonder none of them trust you," Hawk snarls. He yanks open the door and steps into the night.

I'm frozen to the seat, the blood flooding back into my face until it feels like it's on fire. Jefferson lets out a little sigh. I want to punch him so bad my hand cramps clenched in a fist.

"What was the point of all that?" I shout, my voice ringing inside the truck. "Sneaking it on him then telling him anyway?"

"Because I wanted him to know," Jefferson says calmly. "I wanted him to know I was listening despite his little tantrums earlier about werewolf rights. Werewolves are dangerous and I'm going to do my job however I need to. Trying to hide the real problem is only going to make everything worse. There's something out there in the woods and those werewolves are hiding it."

I'm disgusted and let it show on my face. "What are you talking about? Do you know something we don't?"

"I know a lot you don't," he snaps, wrenches the door open, and then slams it behind him.

I feel like I've been slapped in the face. I let out a frustrated growl inside the truck before heading into the cabin. Jefferson isn't there. He must have hid away in that stupid barn of his. I find Hawk sitting on his bunk stripping off his socks. He ignores me completely. I stand in the doorway unsure of what to say.

"That was all really stupid, wasn't it?"

"Understatement," he mumbles.

"I'm sorry, Hawk. I didn't know what Jefferson had done but then I . . ." Then I what? Played into it? Let it happen because of reasons? I have no good explanation to give him.

Hawk throws his shoes into the corner of the room but they tumble back across the floor. "What? You didn't trust me? You thought we'd be discussing our secret evil plans to take over the world? What were you expecting, Phoenix? Did you get a kick out of listening to those people's problems?"

"No!" I slap the doorframe and dust falls from the ceiling. "I just—I just wanted to know you were okay! Yeah, it was stupid and I should have thrown that phone out the window but you haven't been acting like yourself ever since we got here. I was worried."

He rolls his eyes and flops down onto his bed facing away from me. "Whatever."

I stand there for about a minute trying to summon the words for an apology before gathering up my pajamas to go change in the bathroom. When I come back, I grab my mp3 player and bring it with me into the top bunk. I find the song I'm looking for, *Ain't No Mountain High Enough* by Marvin Gaye and Tammi Terrell, and hit play. Twinkling notes and soft drums play through the speaker.

It's an older song and one of the only things I remember of my parents. Whenever I think of them, I remember them singing this song to Hawk and me when they put us to bed. All my other memories of my parents and childhood are foggy except for this song. I've listened to it thousands of times whenever I've had an especially hard day, as if my parents were there singing it to me to let me know everything was going to be okay. I play it for Hawk now. I want him to remember. We're all we've got, and there's nothing I wouldn't do for my family. Surely he can understand that.

Hawk doesn't ask me to turn it off. Instead it plays through to the end and the room falls silent again. I hear his steady breathing and can't be sure if he's asleep or not.

"I'm still angry at you," he says.

"Okay. I deserve it." I exhale slowly and stare up at the ceiling. "As long as you don't hate me for eternity."

"Only if you borrow my socks and lose them again."

I can't help it. I let out a goofy giggle and Hawk laughs under his breath too. The tension breaks and I can breathe easier. Once the fit passes, Hawk prods the underside of my mattress, poking me in the back. I slam a fist down and he stops.

"I don't trust Jefferson, though," he says more seriously. "Listening in wasn't your idea, it was his."

I think about what Jefferson said in the truck and the bitter malice in his voice every time he brings up werewolves. "This is personal for him. I get the feeling he really, *really* doesn't like werewolves."

"You don't say."

"And he's hiding something. He knows . . . something."

"Wow, that was specific. You've really opened my eyes to the whole problem."

I roll onto my stomach and hang my head over the edge of my bunk. "Oh, shut up." He tries bopping me on the nose but I slap his hand away. "Well, what are we going to do about it? We're already hanging on by our fingernails to stay with the IMS. You heard Jefferson."

"How do you hang on by your fingernails? That sounds painful, and gross." He wrinkles his nose at me.

I roll my eyes. "Whatever. Answer the question."

He tucks both hands behind his head. "Well, we need to talk to Ben's friends in such a way that we can control the situation and Jefferson still thinks it's a brilliant idea."

"How in the world do we do that?"

"Oh, you know exactly what I'm talking about."

"Know what?"

"Where can a bunch of teenagers gather together on a daily basis where the parents are excluded and Jefferson won't get in the way? Here's a hint. It includes a meal with a side of harassment!"

My stomach drops. "*Pixies*, no."

"We're still young enough to be seniors."

"No! No, no, no, no, *no*." My palms turn sweaty from the mere thought of it. Hallways stuffed with pushy students, crabby teachers, terrible lunches served on plastic trays, home-work, cliques, those vampire book fangirls—living hell. "I would rather eat a salted slug from Old Man Two's."

He smirks. "Well, I'm sure they'll serve something similar at lunch time."

10

The following morning Hawk and I go over our plan behind the closed door of our bedroom. It's simple enough. We need to make Jefferson think this is all his idea because then he'll be more willing to go along with it. Hawk will play the melodramatic werewolf and I will be the conspirator with Jefferson. I'm feeling pretty excited.

I walk out first and poke my head into Jefferson's room. He isn't there. Big surprise. I check out the window and see him walking towards the cabin from the barn.

"He's coming!" I hiss. Hawk pokes his head out of the bedroom door for just a second, gives me a thumbs up, then disappears.

I pretend to be digging through what little is left of the venison when Jefferson walks in. I hear a crinkly thud on the table and can't resist but look to see what it is. There are a couple of subs from the shop again in their green wrapping.

"Good morning," Jefferson says in his usual gruff way.

I straighten from the fridge, surprised. He's being nice? Something is definitely up. "Good morning?"

He pinches the bridge of his nose. "Get your crab of a brother out here, would you?"

I want to stick to the plan but he's screwing everything up. I guess the gig is up for the moment. I walk over, slap the doorframe to the bedroom twice, and call, "Hawk!"

He struts out. I guess his grim and dour pretense isn't going to come into play. Dang it, we had a plan and everything. Jefferson slides the subs toward us and keeps his head down.

"Consider it a peace offering," he says. "We've really gotten off on the wrong foot."

"Yeah, for like a straight week," Hawk mutters but grabs the subs before Jefferson can take them back. He hands me one.

Jefferson takes the chair, giving us the high ground. We stand shoulder to shoulder uncertain. This is a trick. Did he hear us scheming?

"I'm not used to working with trainees, especially kids."

"Young adults," I automatically correct.

"*Fine.* Young adults." He pinches his nose again like I'm about to give him a nosebleed. "I'm supposed to be training you but I realize I've been pretty strict. I haven't been as fair as I should have. I want to make it up to you. I want to give you some real work."

My eyes slide to Hawk momentarily. Coming from Jefferson, "real work" could mean anything, and by anything I mean duct taping fences, filing more paperwork, or shoveling manure for all I know.

"I want to give you both a mission."

Well, that's unexpected. I wield my sub like a club and hit it into my hand a few times. I seriously doubt Jefferson would change his mind so quickly and give us what we've wanted all along.

"Okay . . ." Hawk says, drawing out the word. "What kind of mission?"

"I need you two to go undercover and find out what Ben's friends know. I want you to infiltrate the high school."

He makes it sound so much cooler saying it like that. And he's also stealing our line. Weren't we supposed to be convincing Jefferson to let us go into the high school and not the other way around?

"I really don't know," Hawk says and gives a little sigh, hamming it up. "I mean . . . *high school*? Really? You think that would work?"

Jefferson actually laughs. "Well, I'm certainly not qualified to get inside. The parents won't talk to me but the teens might talk to you. Besides, the youngsters are always the most impressionable." He stares off darkly and mutters almost to himself. "They're always the first."

"Sorry, what?" I say and lean forward. "I didn't catch that."

He blinks and shakes his head. "Nothing. I just mean the adult werewolves usually have better heads on their shoulders. You teens tend to go bananas and do stupid things when you have the opportunity."

"Hey!" I point my sub in his face. "Mind who you're talking to."

He brushes the sub aside and stands. "Yeah, you've got no right to protest. So, are you two in or not? Or do I have to go buy more subs to bribe you?"

Hawk scoffs. "Well, I'll definitely stall if it means more food."

"Okay, then no more subs unless you're in."

"Then sign us up, maestro."

Jefferson claps his hands together. "Great, then we'll get right to work. You'll need some supplies. Grab your money, we're going to the thrift store."

He hustles out the door, not even waiting for us to enjoy the subs. Hawk gives a sharp laugh.

"Well, look at us" he says and throws his arms wide. "We smoothed him over like pros."

"Yeah, we're geniuses." I smack him upside the head. "Come on, weirdo. We're going to the thrift store!"

I shake my hands with exaggerated excitement then unwrap my sub. We both shove our sandwiches into our mouths and grab our wallets before running out the door. I don't know why I'm excited all of a sudden. I'm going back to a place I've hated all my teenage life. School sucks. Just ask anybody. Maybe it's because this feels like an actual mission. I'm doing something instead of sitting around Jefferson's cabin and cataloging lives.

We run to a local thrift store and pick up a few clothes along with backpacks, college-rule notebooks, and cheap mechanical pencils. I know we need to look the part but I really don't plan on doing any schoolwork. I've already been over all this. I got my GED from the centaur homeschool teacher in Underground after getting kicked out of high school in Minneapolis. I passed with flying colors. I just didn't handle the school environment well. It was unhealthy for everyone else around me. I don't mention this to Jefferson though. His faith in us is shaky enough as it is. I don't need to let him know my brother and I locked students inside the bathroom before for harassing Witty.

"Oh, shoot. Witty," I spit out. We're in the middle of walking across the parking lot to Moose Lake High School when I stop in my tracks. "I haven't called him to report in. I'm surprised he hasn't called me."

Jefferson waves a hand absently. "I've been reporting in to him, don't worry. I'm telling them *everything* about you two."

I gulp. He chuckles in a rather creepy way under his breath and keeps moving for the doors of the school. Hawk gives me a sarcastic thumbs up. I try to smack him but he jumps out of the way and jogs ahead. I wish I hadn't forgotten to report to Witty but I've been caught up in the secrets Jefferson's hiding about Moose Lake, what's out in the woods, and the fact that the teenagers are *always the first*. What a creepy guy. No wonder IMS headquarters stuck him out here by himself.

I stop at the top of the five steps leading to the entrance and gaze up at the two story bricking building, light brown window coverings, and chalk graffiti on the lower walls. It's around ten o'clock in the morning so all of the students are already inside. I take a deep breath and shake the tension down my shoulders and through my arms.

"You okay?" Hawk says. He waits holding the door open for me. "Having a seizure? Let's get going, you walking panic attack."

I stalk past him and shove the side of his face against the glass of the door. "Shut up, dog breath."

Thankfully the hallways are empty for the time being. We walk down smooth, off-white cement floors flecked with dots of color bordered by rows of worn yellow lockers. The place smells like feet, books, and strong lemon cleaner. My palms are sweaty again.

Jefferson and Hawk enter a glass door on my right and I hustle to catch up to them in the office. A tough-looking old gal wearing cat eye glasses and a pink sweater sits behind a long counter and talks quickly to Jefferson. The place is decorated with your usual motivational posters, school schedules, and framed pictures of the current principal and superintendent. I rub the toes of my shoes against the beige carpet and wipe my hands on my jeans. This part of a school is probably the most familiar to me. I spent enough time in the principal's office at my last high school to grow familiar with the setting.

The pink-sweater lady directs Jefferson to a side office and the three of us go in. A great mahogany desk littered with paper fills up most of the room and a double pane window lets in light from behind. There are bookshelves on either side bearing binders, leaflets, textbooks, and framed certificates in between. It reminds me of the office at Werevine Pharmaceutical where I had the run in with the shapeshifter. Somehow, in my own deranged way, that calms me a little. I can deal with monsters. But kids and teens my age? That's a whole different animal.

The pink-sweater lady drags in another folding chair so there are enough places for all three of us to sit and then we're left to wait. A clock on the wall ticks out the excruciating seconds before a man in a pinstriped suit walks in. He's tall in a peculiar way—sort of elongated like he's supposed to be a foot shorter but was stretched out to his current height. Even his face is thin and the odd bob of graying hair on his head wobbles at each step he takes to the chair behind the desk. I bite hard on my lower lip trying not to smile. He's like a skeletal crypt keeper with Elvis hair.

"Sorry to keep you waiting," the man says, his voice stronger than I'm anticipating and booms in the small office. "I'm Principal Tom Tippen. The kids just call me Principal Tippy."

He reaches his abnormally long arm across the desk to shake each of our hands. His fingers are thin and papery. Jefferson introduces all of us. Tippy sits down, nodding the whole time, and goes over our paperwork.

"So, Uncle Jefferson Barnes, is it?" Tippy says, a listing hum filling in his pauses like he can't stop his baritone from oozing out of him. "No parents to speak of?"

I'm a little offended how he just throws it out there, and not very gently at that. I remove my hands from the arms of the chair before I break the furniture.

"They passed a long time ago. I'm their legal guardian," Jefferson says. "They were staying at my sister's but moved up recently to stay with me."

"Yes, yes," the principal says under his breath, that constant baritone hum continuing in the silence while he reads our paperwork under his breath. He lets out a stuttering cough that escalates in volume until I'm leaning back in my chair away from him. The fit passes and he raps his bony fingers on his desk.

"Things look to be in order." He leans to the side so he can look out his door. "Mrs. Krat! Please summon our guide for the tour." He sits back and clasps his hands neatly on top of our papers, giving us a wide smile to reveal his yellowing teeth. I grimace a little and feel Hawk squash my toes with his heel. I lose the grimace and smile back at the principal.

Before I have to endure a minute more of awkward stares and silence in Principal Tippy's presence, a girl about my age pops into the room. She's relatively short and has a bounce in her step that jogs her blonde ponytail. There's a wide and energetic smile on her face when she looks at us like she just found old friends. Definitely too much energy for me.

"This is Ashley," Principal Tippy says, gesturing wide to the new girl. "She's one of our student aides. Ashley, would you please give these three a tour of the school?"

"Of course!" Her voice is high and chirpy.

I hold back a sigh and we rise to follow her out into the hallway. I notice she's got pink flip-flops on even though it's October and a pink ribbon in her hair. Her black shirt boasts a picture of a shirtless vampire and werewolf from those *Love Moon* movies. I fight back a gag. I can tell the second Hawk sees the same thing because his face goes from being open and friendly to stiff and grumpy. Hollywood portrayals of werewolves and the like get pretty ridiculous and, on occasion, annoying. I mean, it's good for us—if anyone overhears us talking about werewolves we can just say we're talking about a movie—but it does sting Hawk's pride to hear girls pawing over shirtless guys in cheesy romance stories about werewolves.

"So!" Ashley starts, her flip-flops slapping on the floor. "These are the hallways where the lockers are."

"Thanks, Captain Obvious," I mutter under my breath. It earns me an elbow in the ribs from Hawk.

He leans in to whisper in my ear. "This is why you never got along with anyone in high school."

I glare at him and whisper viciously back, "You were thinking the same thing and you know it."

"Yeah, but I don't say it *out loud.*" He raps his knuckles on the top of my head and I give him a good shove away from me. Jefferson reaches over and puts a hand between us. I ignore them both and continue to follow Ashley who's either oblivious with her back to us or pretends not to notice our short-lived scuffle.

"So, are you two brother and sister?" Ashley asks over her shoulder.

"Twins," we answer in unison.

"Oh, that's adorable!" She giggles and paws her hand at us like we're already besties. I want to turn around and run screaming out the front door. I start repeating a mantra in my head. Don't punch anyone, don't fight, stay on mission. Don't punch anyone, don't fight—

"This is the auditorium," Ashley says and leads us into a shallow down-slanting room filled with rows of chairs leading to a stage. She starts rambling on about some play but then quickly herds us out and we're taken through the cafeteria, gym, one of the currently unoccupied classrooms, the science lab, and nurse's office. By the time the tour is over a bell rings directly above us and I jump. Doors fly open and students flood into the empty space. I tighten up next to Hawk so I don't get run over. Ashley spearheads the way through the noise, the crowds, and the dizzying amount of body spray back to the office.

"And that's it!" she announces over the echoing hustle and bustle going on behind us. "I guess I'll see you two soon. We'll probably be in a lot of classes together. You're seniors, right?"

"Right on the edge of freedom," Hawk says with a smile. Her own smile grows in response. I roll my eyes.

"If death doesn't take us first," I add and Ashley's face freezes for a minute before she gives an uncertain laugh.

"Okay, then. See you later!" And with that she's lost in the crowd.

Principal Tippy is waiting for us back inside the office. We're shepherded to the guidance counselor and have a long uncomfortable chat figuring out what classes to put us in. Jefferson apparently redacted our last year from our school records so it looks like we just finished our junior year. The counselor, a pretty young woman with shoulder length brunette hair, taps the end of her pen on her desk and studies her computer, pointing out our options. Hawk keeps trying to get us into separate classes which only makes me feel more desperate than I already am. Eventually we're settled to have only three classes together. I'm completely on my own for the other four.

The second we leave the building I punch Hawk in the shoulder. He recoils with a nasty look on his face but I don't care.

"What was that about?" I demand. "I thought we were doing this together."

"Relax, you psycho!" He rubs his shoulder and glares at me. "We can cover more ground if we split up. So, throw on your lovely, raging social skills and suck it up. We're here to work, remember?"

"I hate you sometimes."

"Yeah, you're going to make *lots* of friends here."

We glare daggers at each other until I catch Jefferson chuckling behind us. He pushes past us to the truck.

"You two have problems," he says and keeps laughing.

11

I have bags under my eyes, my Go Fire Sprites! sweatshirt on, and a "I'm gonna burn the whole world down" kind of attitude as I step out of Jefferson's truck in front of the high school the next morning. Hawk steps down looking like he owns the universe. He's all confidence and wears a plain gray shirt with a black leather jacket he won from an IMS agent in a pop trivia contest. He only brings it out for special occasions when he wants to make an impression.

"Ready, grumpy?" He smirks at me and slings his backpack onto one shoulder.

"Jerk."

"Oh, get off your cranky high horse." He starts walking backwards and mimes putting on a crown. "Wear your optimism like a crown and you will find yourself on a throne of success!"

I stalk after him and frown. "Really? You're quoting Fredrick the faun now?" That faun was the most annoying teacher we ever had in Underground. "Is your arsenal of wit running low or something?"

He just laughs and impersonates the faun's high squeaky voice when he says, "A smile is the window to a kind soul."

"I'm going to hurt you. Stop it." He wiggles his eyebrows at me and I fight back a smile despite myself. "How do you even remember all of his stupid motivational one-liners?"

He points at me and squints. "Admit it. You like random flowery nonsense. You *like* it."

"Says the tough guy that just quoted the random flowery nonsense."

He shrugs and readjusts his backpack. "At least it wasn't *Love Moon*."

I grab his shoulder dramatically and say, "Only true love falls under the moon."

He puts his hand between my shoulder blades and pushes me forward so hard I almost fall over. I stumble and throw my hand out for a second before I regain my balance. I give him my best "seriously?" face.

"Sensitive, much?" I grumble.

Hawk grabs my arm and yanks me to the side. I'm about to complain before I realize he just saved me from being run over by a pack of boys wearing jerseys emblazoned with the school's mascot.

My brother spins about and throws a fist in the air before calling, "Go Rebels!"

Most of the jocks ignore him but a few other people in the hall stop and stare. Hawk smiles and gives a small wave to his audience.

I shake my head. "*I'm* the weird one?"

"Hey, weird can work. Funny works. Being crabby doesn't."

"How about self-deprecating? I can handle that."

We stop in front of our lockers and I swing mine open to shove my bag inside. There's a stumpy boy next to me with loads of acne clutching a physics textbook like it's the meaning of life. I can't help but sneak looks at him and the contents of his locker while I slowly pull a notebook free of my bag. There's a poster for a game I recognize called Mystic Universe with an axe-wielding orc roaring front and center. When the boy tries to swap out textbooks, a slew of comic books fall to the floor.

Hawk nudges me in the back and nods to the boy trying to hastily pick up his collection. I suck in a breath then bend down.

"Let me help," I say and pick up a comic depicting Pale Knight, a zombie in plate armor, throwing a sophisticated lance. The boy snatches it out of my hands before I even get the chance to offer it over. I clear my throat and try my best to be friendly. "Hey, the Pale Knight is pretty cool. I loved the movie they made based on the comics."

The boy grimaces and glares at me like he's disgusted by what he sees. "You're one of *those* fans. You don't know Pale Knight."

I'm left squatting on the floor in shock as he shoves the comics into his locker, slams the door, and stalks away. I get to my feet and throw up my hands.

"What did I say? Seriously?" I turn to my brother and he's trying to hide laughter behind his hand. "What? It was awesome."

Hawk gasps, pretending to be scandalized. "You're one of *those* fans, aren't you? I can't even look at you right now."

"I read some of the comics too!" I slam my locker door shut and the metal screeches at the force. I grimace and work at carefully inching the door forward out of its jam. While I do, a pretty girl walks up to the locker on Hawk's other side. He immediately strikes up a conversation, says he's new in town, makes a witty reference to being a rebel, she laughs, he laughs, and I throw up in my mouth a little. At least he gets directions from her for our first class. When she leaves, he turns back to me with a smug grin.

He winks. "And that's how you interact with human beings."

"In my defense, I think that boy was part troll."

"Or you're just part kelpie." He snatches a pencil from his locker and starts to walk away. "Come on, Fifi."

I stand there for a second trying to work it out in my head before jogging after him. "That doesn't even make sense!"

The hallways clear and we make it into the classroom seconds before the bell rings. The room is cramped with student chair-desk combos. A single metal desk sits off to the side that Hawk makes a beeline for to chat up the teacher. When I approach he passes back an English textbook and keeps one for himself. The teacher, a plump woman with short hair, lets us sit in the back without making a fuss of introducing us to the class, which I'm thankful for. I slide into a chair next to my brother and inspect the students in front of me. I page open my textbook to appear like I'm paying attention while the teacher goes to the front to talk about Shakespeare.

I casually pull a piece of paper out of my sweatshirt pocket and lay it flat in line with the pages of my textbook so I can study it and look like I'm reading the assignment at the same time. It's a list of names that I've gone over a hundred times already. Last night our lonesome trio went through Jefferson's records and identified all of the teenage werewolves in town. There's a good fifteen of them and Jefferson is sure there are others not yet identified. I double-check the names against the brief physical descriptions I had scribbled down, but it's a little hard to identify anyone from "tall, dark hair, male." That describes about five boys in front of me in this class alone. I'm sort of hoping the teacher will do a roll call but she doesn't.

So, I lean back and wait for the tedious minutes to crawl by. My mind wanders and I scribble a line on my notebook then push it to the edge of my desk towards Hawk. He discreetly leans to the side and props his chin in his hand so he can read it.

Wish we were fighting a berserker right now.

He smirks and pulls the notebook over when the teacher has her back turned. After taking a good long time writing something down, he pushes it back onto my desk.

If we get in trouble our first day, I'm sure Jefferson will be able to play the part quite nicely.

A little drawing of Jefferson bulged out with enormous muscles and crossed eyes follows underneath. I hide a laugh behind a cough and clamp a hand over my mouth. The teacher's eyes find mine so I force the cough a bit more into a convincing fit and hold up a hand to show I'm okay. She moves on and explains our homework assignment. I jot it down quick as the bell sounds.

We move out into the hallway and Hawk taps me on the shoulder. He points to the side and leans in to say, "There's Ben."

I stand a little straighter to see over the crowd and spot Ben by himself. His shoulders are hunched and he looks exhausted.

Hawk immediately moves through the foot traffic to reach him but I hang back when I notice something odd. There's a very tall boy wearing a baggy, black hoodie and beanie at the end of the hall watching Ben intently. In the opposite direction about half way down is another boy, this one in a sweater vest and thick glasses watching Ben as well. Two completely different people keeping their eyes on Ben like they're waiting for him to react. The next second they turn away, walk in opposite directions, and disappear.

The number of students in the hall thins so it's easy for me to track hoodie-boy at a distance and see where he goes next. I keep my footsteps light and stay in a straight line behind him so he doesn't catch me in his peripheral vision. He passes the classrooms and makes a beeline for the rear exit. Soon it's just us in the hallway. I guess I'm not as quiet as I imagine and he spins around. I automatically move for a water fountain nearby and take a drink like that's what I meant to do the entire time. I don't dare look in his direction again but hear him continue on. The door creaks open then thunks closed. I straighten in time to see him jog across the rear parking lot and to the forest on the far side. Who comes to first period then ditches immediately after?

But I've taken up too much time. The bell overhead rings and I cringe away from it.

"Ah, crap, crap, crap."

I sprint back the way I had come, shove my English textbook into my locker, then take a left, run some more, and skid into the classroom at the end of the hall. Everyone is already seated and a beach ball of a man, whom I assume is the teacher, stands at the front of the room. He's wearing some freakish sweater with all the colors of the rainbow and the whole thing looks like it's about to rip off him at any second. His graying mustache quivers and his pinprick eyes behind his glasses put me under a laser beam. I'm on my own for this one. Hawk's in a different class this period.

"You're late," he says in a thin voice. "I take it you're Phoenix Mason?"

As I expect, when he says my name there's some soft laughter from the room. I guess Phoenix isn't a real common name but I still haven't figured out what's *funny* about it. The teacher looks me up and down just like comic-book-boy had. I'm not sure if I'm supposed to go find myself a seat or remain where I am to be scrutinized. At last he hustles to his desk, picks up a sociology textbook which he then shoves into my hands, and makes a shooing motion.

"Well, what are you waiting for?" he says. "Take a seat."

I grind my teeth together and walk down the narrow aisle between the desks. I'm trying not to look at anybody but my eyes fly up when I see a sweater vest and thick glasses. It's the same boy that was staring at Ben earlier. He locks eyes with me. I hold his gaze for just a moment, noting the faint golden ring around his brown eyes, before gliding past him to an empty spot at the very back. I sit down and immediately pull out my list of werewolf names while the teacher begins to drone on about criminology. There are five boys on my list who have brown eyes, and only one of those wears glasses. I make a note in parentheses next to the name Adam Glass.

(loves his sweater vests, prep)

It's not a particularly nice notation but at least I know I'll recognize him from the description. I lean to the side to get a better look at Adam and make a few more notes.

"Ms. Mason."

My head snaps up. Mr. Beach-ball-jerk is staring at me down the row of desks and several of the students have turned around in their chairs to find me.

"Yes?" I say uncertainly.

"I hope the doodles you're making are pertaining to our study of the FBI and that you are, in fact, paying attention."

"Of course, sir." I tap the end of my pencil on my notebook for emphasis. "Just remarking on how Hoover institutionalized the training of FBI agents and created Hogan's Alley at Quantico for that purpose."

The teacher's mouth thins and color dashes his cheeks. "I haven't mentioned that yet."

I can't stop myself. "I'm sure you were working up to it."

"That's enough lip from you unless you want detention."

I clasp my hands together on top of my paper and don't say another word. His mustache trembles and he turns back to the chalkboard. I mouth "wow" to myself and slide my list into the safety of my pocket before he can chew me out some more. The rest of the period ticks by as slow as my previous class. I keep an eye on Adam whenever possible. Two times he glances back at me. I wonder if he knows who I am, then I remember what Ben had told me when we first met. I smell different. I assume that's part of me being Blessed. Hawk's never mentioned anything like that before but it could be he's just used to my scent being what it is. Can werewolves really sniff out the magic in me?

Finally, I'm saved by the bell and file out last. As I pass the teacher, he sniffs twice. I pause but he gives me the stink eye and shoos me out. I'm bumped and pushed in the sea of students on my way to my locker. I sincerely hope that teacher was just being weird and isn't actually a werewolf too. That would mean I might have to interact with him at some point. What a pain.

Hawk meets up with me and boasts about finding five of the werewolves on our list already. I don't even bother pointing out that he can probably sniff them out. I'm in a sore mood already and anxious to have this whole thing over with. I honestly wish someone would jump up and say "The problem's solved! The serum is working fine again! You can go home." I miss my old friends. I miss Celina helping me with my homework. I miss Old Man Two telling me stories of Scotland. I miss talking tech with Witty. I consider calling Witty after school. I should chat with him and see how he's doing. It'll take my mind off how I'm doing.

I share my next class with Hawk and am, thankfully, not late again. We make it through biology without any difficulty and then on to physics. When the bell rings and it's time for lunch, my hands are all sweaty again. It's one of those times during the day where it feels like everything is chance. The food could be good or bad, there might not be any good places to sit, and you could end up being separated from your friends. So, as usual, there's an intense rush to get to the cafeteria first.

The instant we reach the open lunchroom, it's easy to pick out the cliques. A group of four girls in what I'm sure is considered "high fashion" have already claimed a table. I have no idea how they got here so fast in those high heels. The group of jocks we passed this morning are in line together having a shoving match. Behind them are a couple of boys and girls wearing gamer shirts. I spot what you might consider your regular "preppy geeks" wearing sweaters and slacks, one even holding a calculus textbook, and I expect to see Adam Glass the werewolf with them but he's not.

Gathered at a table in the farthest corner is Adam along with Ben, the crabby comic-book boy, and a number of others. Preps, jocks, Goth types, nerds, and drama queens all sit together like ambassadors from their respective stereotypes. I count fifteen—the werewolves assembling together like a pack. Despite the tendency of werewolves to congregate, it's odd for them to be so unified. Werewolves are still individuals and normally stick to their usual human patterns. It's only when they're in wolf mode that they really have the pack mentality.

Hawk and I get our meals dished out on plastic trays—foot-long hot dogs, thank goodness—and we gravitate toward the werewolf table. Once we're close enough, several of them wave Hawk over to join them. I follow in his wake only to discover there's only one spot open. The only way I'd fit is if I put my tray at the end and either kneel or stand to eat. Either option is embarrassing and not worth it.

"We can sit somewhere else," Hawk suggests.

The werewolves are looking up at us expectantly and listening to every word. I swallow and fake a smile.

"No, it's fine! You can hang out with your friends." I'm fighting back social anxiety, but Hawk needs to blend in with the pack. He needs to know who's having symptoms like Ben and if they know about that black wolf. And if I'm honest with myself, he'll do better if I'm not there ruining his conversations anyway. I make the sacrifice and start to walk away. "Go ahead. I'll find somewhere else."

Hawk doesn't look remotely happy about forcing me out but he eventually sits down among his kind. I take ten steps back the way I came before I stop and realize I have no idea where I'm going. One of the most uncomfortable moments in high school is standing with a tray in your hands, visible to everyone in the room, glancing around at every table with empty spots, but not knowing where you can sit because those open spots might be reserved for friends. It's obvious you don't know where you belong and lacking that surefire confidence can single you out instantly. Unfortunately, without Hawk as my wingman, I become an easy target.

I tread slowly forward and pause at an open end. A boy purposefully slides his tray down to make it clear the space is reserved—or he just doesn't want me there.

"Right, it's cool," I say, my face growing redder by the second. Fighting monsters feels less hostile and complicated than this. I move to another table and all conversation silences at my presence so I move on again. I have a horrible sinking feeling that I might end up eating alone in the bathroom or hiding down a hallway somewhere when someone calls my name.

"Phoenix! Sit with us."

I'm drawn to the voice like it's a beacon in a storm and find myself sitting down next to Ashley. She's got a smile and a t-shirt proclaiming "I fell in love under the *Love Moon*." Two other girls with mousy hair sit opposite wearing similar screen-printed shirts professing love for some pretty-pretty boys I don't recognize. I'm grateful for the friendly invitation to escape attention but I'm terrified what their conversations might involve.

"Thanks," I mumble and rip open my cardboard container of milk.

"No problem," Ashley says. "You looked a little lost."

I nod and decide it's best not to elaborate on how accurate that is.

"I like your sweatshirt," she says, clearly trying to keep a conversation going. I glance down at myself. I've forgotten what I'm wearing.

"Oh, yeah. Thanks."

"Are the Fire Sprites the mascot from your old school?"

They're actually elemental beings that compete against the other sprites in a sport like polo except with glass stones, fireballs, tidal waves, earthquakes, and hurricanes. Aetherball is a thousand times more exciting than sports like basketball when you throw natural disasters into the game.

I smile to myself. "They're a team. It's from a game."

"Oh, you mean like Mystic Universe?"

I'm shocked she even knows what that is. It's both a computer game and card game based on a fictional fantasy world. Hawk and I have used it frequently as a cover when we've been overhead talking about our world. Everyone buys it without a second thought. Although *Love Moon* and Mystic Universe both technically have monsters, there's an enormous gap between the two. From my experience, fans of one or the other can't even look at each other.

"Exactly. It's from Mystic Universe," I say, happy I don't even need to make up a story since she's provided the perfect one for me.

Her smile brightens. "I used to play with Jason." Her eyes travel to the werewolf table and she lets out a sad little sigh. "But he doesn't care for it anymore. Or me, I guess."

I shift about so I can see where Hawk is sitting. "Which one is Jason?"

"Oh, the tall dreamy one."

Yeah, like that helps. I have no idea who she's talking about but she doesn't elaborate and gazes wide-eyed with one hand propping up her chin.

"It's okay," she says. "I abandoned Jason for true love." She points to her shirt for emphasis and all three of them giggle. "The guys from *Love Moon* wouldn't keep secrets like Jason does."

Considering Jason is a werewolf, I can't blame him for keeping his secrets. I would like to know what Ashley thinks, though. Maybe she knows more than she realizes.

"What kind of secrets?" I ask and finally start on my hot dog. It's freakin' delicious.

She shrugs and pushes her baked beans around on her plate. "I don't know. We used to hang out every day but then all of a sudden he changed friends and it's like he doesn't even know I exist anymore. I heard he's passed out a few times and can't remember the night before. Sounds like he's turned into some kind of alcoholic and gets himself blackout drunk. Idiot. My stupid, beautiful idiot."

Blackouts. Missing memories. Yeah, this Jason could be getting drunk. That, or he's having the same problems as Ben.

"I'm sorry to hear that," I say. "When did all this happen?"

"Oh . . ." She purses her lips and squints up at the ceiling as if the dates are written up there somewhere. "It hasn't been that long. A couple of weeks? Maybe three?"

So the change was recent. If it's because of a defect in the serum caused by those shapeshifters, that would make sense. They couldn't have been at Werevine Pharmaceutical for long. I definitely need to call Witty after school and discuss this. Maybe they've gotten some answers from the shapeshifters by now.

"Hey, do you need any more help navigating the school?" Ashley prompts. "I kind of noticed you were late for Mr. Webster's class."

"Webster?" I realize I never caught the teacher's name. "Looks like a beach ball? Hideous sweater? About yea high?" I hold a hand about two feet above the floor.

Ashley laughs and gives my arm a friendly swat. Her laugh is kind of high but at least it's genuine. "Yeah, that's him. If you need a buddy to show you around so you aren't late again . . ."

"I'd really appreciate that," I say and mean it. She may be a little much but she's been the friendliest person here so far.

Suddenly there's a high pitch screech directly behind me. I hunker down automatically, brace one hand on the table and spin about on my seat ready to launch into action. I expect some werewolf to have changed in the middle of the lunchroom, but instead I find myself face to face with three muscly boys sporting jerseys.

"Oh my gosh!" one of them screeches and claps his hands together like an over emotional fangirl. It takes me a minute to realize they're making fun of Ashley and her friends. I'm probably lumped into that group as well. "It's a vampire! Bite me, I'm a loser, and want to love you forever!"

"Seriously?" I say and give them an exaggerated roll of the eyes. "You're going to buy into your stereotypes and be the bully jocks? Why can't you be jocks *and* intellectuals with a fetish for chess or something? Or maybe have a secret desire to become a chef?"

Their apparent leader bites back, "Oh, go cry to your vampire boyfriend, Red."

"I wouldn't want to disturb your 'male-bonding' time with him. Wait, don't tell me. You're actually Team Werewolf."

In my previous high school experience, associating your aggressor with the material they're picking on you for tends to make them blue in the face. It seems to work here and he goes into a tirade of how he's not a fan and how I'm really the fan and blah, blah, blah. I hold up a hand and turn back to my uneaten food.

"Too long, did not listen."

"Leave us alone," Ashley snaps. She's red in the face. Clearly the insults *did* get to her. "Find some other way to fill that empty feeling in your jock strap."

We turn our backs to ignore the bullies—I'm silently congratulating Ashley in my head—but then one of the three passes over his milk carton to their vocal leader who then "trips" and spills half of it down the back of Ashley's shirt. She gasps and sucks in a sharp breath, her hands shaking. Tears instantly spring in her eyes and the cold malice of the bullies' laughter fills my ears. Something inside me snaps.

Hawk shouts as I rise. "Phoenix, stop!"

I pull back my arm and throw my fist into the jock's face.

12

I manage to control myself enough so I don't break his jaw with the force of my punch—there's enough magical strength in me to do it easily—but he stumbles back and falls into a table, arms flailing and everything. My hand throbs and I try to shake it off. For a split second there's dead silence. Then a teacher's aide is shouting at me, the jock's two friends are pointing their fingers in my face, and fevered talking breaks out all over the cafeteria.

Ignoring the commotion for the brief moment I'm allowed, I check on Ashley.

"Are you okay?" I ask.

Tears run down her face as well as a little bit of snot forced out by her violent sobbing. The back of her shirt is drenched in chocolate milk. Protective rage burns through me and I would be happy to beat the jock into a slimy pulp, but I'm already in enough trouble as it is. Ashley's other two friends rise from the table and escort her to the bathroom.

The teacher's aide rushes up to me and then there's a lot of confused shouting between all of us. The jocks, of course, blame me for attacking unprovoked. The spilled milk was an accident they say. They're the victims here. I shout right back unafraid and try to explain what happened but the aide saw me clear as day decking the boy. A few teachers show up and I start to get embarrassed. Mr. Webster arrives only to make matters worse. He escorts the jock away to the nurse's office and my English teacher goes to check on Ashley in the bathroom.

I, in the meantime, am escorted to the principal's office. Score: high school, 1; me, 0. They're going to tell Jefferson and he's going to give me the boot. I screwed up. I can't deny that. Jefferson's pointed it out and Hawk's mentioned it before—I don't control myself. Now my reaction is going to get me suspended. I won't apologize for hitting that jerk, though. He definitely had it coming.

I wait in an uncomfortable chair outside the principal's office for a couple of minutes before I'm let inside. Principal Tippy adjusts his hair as I enter, literally pulls it from side to side. I knew his hair was too perfect to be real. It's a piece. I take the offered seat and the door closes behind me.

Tippy temples his fingers. "One day," he sighs. "One day here and you're already starting fights."

"No." I try to say it respectfully like my brother might but it comes out aggressive. "I didn't start the fight. I was defending a friend."

"You threw the first punch."

I hold up a hand. "Okay, maybe literally but not figuratively."

"That doesn't matter."

"It matters to me."

"You are not in a position to be talking back." He sucks in a nasally breath and leans all the way back in his chair. "So, in your words, what happened?"

"I thought I'm not supposed to be talking back." I'm going to get detention at the least. Suspended possibly. Jefferson called at worst. I'm sour and pretty reckless at the moment. Might as well enjoy the ride down, right? Then some better part of me, my conscience maybe, retorts that I'm supposed to be making this right and not worse. What would a true IMS agent do? They'd protect their cover. I blurt out, "I'm sorry. I didn't mean that. I'm just angry."

He lifts his chin and makes a face a bit like a sturgeon fish. "All right. What are you angry about?"

Grateful he's giving me a chance, I quickly summarize what went down in the cafeteria. He nods now and again and his listing hum continues in the background like white noise. I finish, but before Tippy can pronounce judgment, there's a commotion outside the door. I angle myself towards it trying to hear what's going on. Then the door suddenly flies open and the jock I sucker punched fills up the doorway. There's a nice red mark on his jaw.

"Principal Tippy, it's all my fault," he announces. "I started the fight and she was just protecting a friend. I was harassing them all. She shouldn't be blamed."

We both stare at him. I can't believe what I'm hearing. He's *defending* me? He's willing to take the blame? From all of his talk in the lunchroom, that's the very last thing I would expect from him. Then again, I don't even know him, but still.

"I'm surprised to say the least, Mr. Jones." Principal Tippy gestures to the other empty chair. "Take a seat."

He has Mr. Jones explain what happened and asks me not to interrupt. I wouldn't even have the words if I wanted—Mr. Jones says basically the same thing I did but ends up spinning a picture of how very evil and maniacal he was and how I was the avenging heroine. Maybe not that dramatic but that's the image it conjures up for me. There's no way this guy pulled a 180 from spilling milk down a girl's shirt on purpose to conceding everything in my favor. I just decked him five minutes ago, for crying out loud.

After his story, Principal Tippy lets out a sound like a dying wheeze. I watch him carefully to make sure he isn't really kicking the bucket right then and there. He massages his forehead and smooths a hand over his fake hair.

"Physical confrontations are completely unnecessary and not allowed. However . . ." He holds up a spidery finger. "Given the circumstances I will be somewhat lenient. Detention for both of you. You will take it over your lunch hour for the remainder of the week. I want to keep you both away from a situation in which you may be tempted to reenact another scene of violence."

"Thank you, sir," I say and sincerely mean it. I can't imagine if I had to explain this to Jefferson. Tippy's saved me from a world of pain.

We're dismissed and the second we're outside the office Mr. Jones takes off and doesn't give me a backward glance. I get a hall pass from the receptionist who is wearing yet another pink sweater and move out. The hallways are already empty because fifth period's started. I hustle to my next class and when I get there I try to explain in an undertone to the teacher why I'm late. She raises her voice so the whole class can hear anyway and I'm set in the back in shame. I spend the rest of the period glaring out the window and trying to figure out why Mr. Jones helped me out.

I trudge to my locker after I live through that hour of misery and find Hawk leaning against it, a smile lurking on his face because he clearly knows something I don't. He winks and moves to the side.

"You're welcome by the way," he says quietly and his words are almost lost in the noise around us. "I heard Mr. Jones spun quite the story."

My mouth goes slack and my brother stands in a new light before me. "*You* got that guy to vouch for me? That's impossible."

He rummages through his locker like this is an everyday thing for him. "Like I said, you're welcome."

"But . . . *how?*" I shut his locker door so he's forced to face me directly. "You can't just smile and laugh your way into the good graces of some random guy in two minutes, then convince him to take the fall."

He looks to the left, to the right, behind him, then leans in close and whispers, "Not all forms of persuasion are polite. It's a secret."

Hawk winks again, gives me a thumbs up, and jogs to his next class. I'm left dumbfounded. Did my brother blackmail someone to get me out of trouble? A swell of gratitude stirs in my chest for a moment before worry kicks in. I seriously hope whatever Hawk did doesn't blow up in his face. I gather my books and move in the opposite direction for my sixth period class.

Like all the others, it's wretched and boring and I want to slam my head against the wall. I do notice a number of students shooting me looks over their shoulders. I guess I've become a hot topic of conversation since the lunch hour. I haven't seen Ashley again since and hope she's okay. That friendship is probably burned to the ground already. I prop my chin in my hand and stare out the window for the next forty-five minutes.

The bell rings and there's only one more class to go. Hawk gives me a low five when he passes me in the hall and it gives me a little boost as I walk in, early for once, to my history class. There are only three people here besides me so far and I have the option of seats to choose from. I start walking towards the very back when I'm summoned.

"Ms. Mason?"

The teacher waves me over to his desk. Unlike most of my other teacher encounters over the course of the day, he starts ours out with a genuine smile. I instantly think he's a pretty handsome guy, in a completely aesthetic way. He's one of the youngest teachers I've seen and he sports short black hair that sticks up a bit in the front, a five o'clock shadow, and the bluest eyes of bluest blue. He's got regular jeans on, a gray button down shirt with the sleeves rolled up to his elbows and a dusting of chalk over everything he's wearing.

I stop in front of his desk and shove my hands in my pockets. "Yes?"

"I've got your textbook here for you." He passes it over and I run my hand over the embossed letters, *Advanced European History*. "My name's James Krushnic. I like to keep things open so students feel more comfortable asking questions and interacting so please call me Jim, or if you're feeling dramatic, Captain Krush."

I laugh a little at that and his smile widens.

He gestures to me with both hands. "See? It's working already. Now, we've been working through the politics of Greece lately so you might be a little behind. I'm sure you can borrow some notes from one of your classmates to catch up. If no one wants to lend out their notes, then Captain Krush will make sure someone gives you their notes anyway. Any questions?"

"No, I think I'm good."

"Excellent! Take whatever seat you like," he says then bends over a paper he's grading.

Some of the tension eases out of my shoulders and I slump into a chair furthest from the door near the windows, leaning my head back as far as it can go. At least I'll be able to end the day on a relatively okay note. Before the class begins I notice a couple of students approach "Captain Krush" and chat with him. I guess his social tactics work. Class begins and Jim stands at the front. He's energetic and engages with everyone in the room, even walking back to talk one on one with people. Then he runs to the front to write down an important name or date concerning Greek history. He cracks jokes, pokes fun at himself, and we're laughing throughout.

At one point he comes over to me and asks, "Okay, so you have their politics, their economics, their customs, but what stands out as being the most memorable part of Greek culture to you?"

I don't need to fumble for an answer on this one. There is something that came out of Greece that all IMS agents know. "Their mythology."

Jim throws up his hands in victory and exclaims. "Their mythology! Exactly! Their stories, their lifeblood, the tales that have been passed down and remain well known even to this day."

He bounces up to the front and scrawls "mythology" across the chalkboard. Unfortunately, the bell rings just then and he lets out a big comedic groan. Everyone laughs and starts to rise. He holds his hands out towards us.

"Wait, wait! Before you go, homework!" Now the rest of us groan and he laughs. "Oh, it's not that bad! Just find a Greek myth. Find your favorite story and we'll discuss tomorrow. Now, go! Run wild in the streets."

I pick up my book and dash out as fast as I can. I dump everything into my backpack and walk alongside Hawk to the entrance.

"So, we survived," he says.

"No, *I* survived. You thrived." I study the toes of my shoes and the cracks in the pavement beneath me as we move into the parking lot. "And thanks."

"Hey, I've got your back. Just like you've got mine."

At the end of the last row of cars I spot Jefferson waiting in the truck. Even from here I can see him glancing at his watch and rapping his fingers on the steering wheel impatiently. The second Hawk and I slide onto the bench seat Jefferson throws the truck into gear.

"We've got a problem," he says. His face is drawn and his hair a bit askew.

Crap. He couldn't possibly have heard about my little incident today, could he? Principal Tippy didn't say anything about calling my "uncle" to report the fight. Jefferson could have other connections, though, or has tapped the phones or something. I wouldn't put it past him.

"What's wrong?" Hawk asks.

"I got a call from Deputy Graham. There's been another

cattle mutilation. I've already taken pictures but I could use your help on this, Hawk." He maneuvers the truck onto the main road out of town. "I was hoping you might use your abilities to catch a scent. Maybe figure out who it was."

"Where are we going?"

Jefferson is silent for a moment and broods. "The Fergusons' farm."

The road flies away beneath the tires. A cattle mutilation at a home housing two werewolves can't be a coincidence. Either one of them lost control and did it themselves or another werewolf is targeting them. Both cases are bad.

"Did it happen during the day?" I ask.

"Sometime this morning. Mrs. Ferguson went out for groceries and came back to find one of her cows scattered across her back field."

"So it wasn't her, and Ben was in school the whole day." I catch Hawk's eye. He's thoughtful and grim. "They're being targeted."

Jefferson nods and turns us onto a side road. "Territorial instincts. Another werewolf must feel threatened by them and isn't under the control of the serum."

"The serum isn't working," I say. "Ben said it himself and from what I learned today, all of this started around the same time those shapeshifters infiltrated Werevine Pharmaceutical. They must have done something."

"It's possible—by a long shot—but I don't think that's what's going on."

"And why not?"

He doesn't answer. It's infuriating. We sit the rest of the ride in silence and pull up the rutted driveway to find an empty sheriff's squad parked out front. Mrs. Ferguson stands at the top of her steps, her arms crossed and her face pinched. We exit and her expression sours even more.

"Oh, it's you," she growls. She's glaring directly at me when she says it. Clearly I haven't been forgiven for intruding on her son before. She stomps her cowboy boots on the ground then jerks her head to the side. "It's this way."

She doesn't speak again even when Jefferson attempts to ask her how she's doing. We just march through a gate in the wooden fence to her back fields, past a barn, over a hill, and to a horrible scene of gore. Entrails, flesh, and organs have been ripped apart and scattered across the hillside leading towards a forest of evergreens and poplars. Thankfully there's enough of a chill in the air to dampen the smell somewhat but it's still strong enough. I hold the edge of my sleeve over my nose and step carefully forward through the mess.

Blood taints the yellowing grass and chunks of pink matter spread in lines like the parts of the cow were dragged. I almost step on an eyeball and nearly gag. Hawk walks lightly beside me. There's a darkness in his sweeping gaze as he inspects the carnage. It puts a chill down my spine. Sometimes it's easy to forget about the monster inside of him. He contains it better than any werewolf I know, but it's always there. Moments like these I can't tell if a part of him likes the smell of blood soaking into the ground, the sight of butchery and destruction, or if he's as disgusted by it as I am.

I manage to keep my lunch down and watch Hawk sniff the air before making his way towards the trees. Mrs. Ferguson follows in his steps and the pair of them stop at the edge of the woods taking deep breaths.

"I don't recognize the smell myself," she says. "And I know most folk in town."

"So, it must be someone from out of town or new to the area?" I say.

"Or more likely someone who's been recently changed," Hawk corrects me. That darkness continues to linger in his eyes and shadows fall across his brow. "A person's smell changes after they've been bitten."

Jefferson lets out a huff. "Well, that's just great. That means we've got an unchecked werewolf running around and we don't know who it is."

There's a shuffling in the woods and Deputy Graham emerges from the trees. He brushes himself off and marches forward to tower over everyone in our group.

"I followed the trail for about a mile to the road but they disappeared at some tire tracks, so no point trying to sniff them out." He gestures behind him to the trees a little out of breath. "It was definitely a werewolf."

"Thanks, Jared." Jefferson pulls up the collar of his jacket and retreats towards the farmhouse. We all follow in his wake and I end up walking beside Deputy Graham. He picks a path between the gore but manages to stain his massive hardy-man shoes with blood. His face is a little green.

"Are you okay?" I ask.

He nods and forces a strained smile. "Yeah, I'll be fine."

"Spooky stuff, huh?"

"You're telling me. I never imagined it would get this bad again, though."

I frown and hold out a hand to slow his pace. The others

continue on and we fall behind out of earshot. "Again? What do you mean?"

"This same sort of thing happened about fourteen years ago. I was just a teenager back then." He stops and inhales the fresh air brought to us on a cold breeze. "A bunch of people were bitten, cattle started getting ripped to shreds, the city almost caved in on itself, and a good part of the population just disappeared. I, uh . . ." He clears his throat and adjusts the gun holster on his belt. "My little sister, she was . . . she disappeared with the others, but not before I saw her turn. That's how I know about all this."

We start walking again and it's difficult to keep up with his long stride.

"I'm so sorry," I say.

"I swore I'd find her one day. Maybe I still will."

I nod and bite my lip. After fourteen years I doubt it's possible but I'm not one to step on someone's conviction.

"So what happened?" I ask. "Did the IMS intervene?"

He squints down his long nose at me. "No. It just stopped."

"But what stopped it?"

"I don't know," he says and shrugs. "One day wolves were out in broad daylight and attacking folk. Next day, the town was back to normal and everyone returned to their old selves. I'm surprised Jefferson hasn't mentioned it to you."

"Wait, he was around when all that happened?"

Deputy Graham reaches his squad car and opens the door to climb in. "Of course. He's been here since the beginning."

13

I find it incredibly difficult to not say anything on the ride back to the field office. I let Hawk and Jefferson talk uninterrupted about the scene of the crime and Hawk assures us both that if he catches the scent again he'll probably be able to recognize it, but I know his sense of smell can be wonky. It's always easier for werewolves when they're in their wolfish form. I keep my mouth shut but my fingers tug at the bottom of my sweatshirt and play anxious drums on my kneecaps. I know Hawk notices but he doesn't say anything about it.

When we reach the cabin I assume Jefferson will give us free time but the second we put down our backpacks he hustles us outside to work on our firearm skills. We go through fifty rounds each using the rifle, then the handgun, and even get a feel for a shotgun that kicks hard into my shoulder. Then he runs us through tactical drills on a little obstacle course he set up inside the edge of the forest. Jefferson shouts at us if we do anything wrong or even slightly off. We did a good deal of this during our training in Underground but there's a completely different vibe out here where we know there's something lurking in the woods that could be watching us even now.

Once the light fails Jefferson brings us inside only to give us blank report forms. "I want you to account for everything that happened today at school. I want to know every little thing about the werewolves in that building—what they looked like, what they were doing, what they ate, who they sat with, *everything*. Each detail is important."

Hawk and I sit at the table to start. Jefferson hovers in the background to make sure we actually do the paperwork before he disappears outside. A quick check out the window lets me know he's holed himself up in the barn again. I race through my report of the day, obviously leaving out the bit about the lunch fight, and set my pen down. Hawk is still working on his by the time I finish.

I nudge him anyway to make him stop. "Jefferson knows a heck of a lot more than he's telling us."

"Didn't you already say that before?" he grumbles, focused on what he's writing.

"Yeah, but there's more," I lean in closer and put a hand on his report so he's forced to stop. "Deputy Graham told me all of this strange behavior has happened before. Fourteen years ago." Hawk's eyes widen and a muscle in his jaw twitches. "Jefferson was there. He knows about it but he's never mentioned it before."

"Fourteen years," Hawk mutters. He massages his jaw and his gaze grows distant. "That's an eerie coincidence, don't you think?"

I know exactly what he's thinking because I've been thinking the same thing. Fourteen years ago exactly in five days' time on Halloween—and incidentally our birthday of all days—Hawk was bitten and changed into a werewolf. The same day our parents died. The same day I became one of the Blessed. I never knew the full story. I was four at the time and only remember a great black shape and Hawk screaming. I remember the blood and the terrifying snarl of a wolf. Then I remember punching that werewolf in the nose to save my brother. After that is only bright light and suddenly I was in Underground.

I know a dragon was involved somehow, that he saved us and gave me his magic, but beyond that there's only black ink. My parents' file is classified. I've tried to get Witty to crack the files but there were measures put in place that stopped him. I don't even know where I used to live before I went to Underground. I was too young to remember. For all I know, I could have grown up right here in Moose Lake.

"Should we ask Jefferson about it?" Hawk says quietly. His fingers curl around the pencil in his hand and the wood begins to splinter in his grip.

"If he hasn't told us already, he's not going to if we ask him point blank. He'll deny it or side step it like everything else we've asked him. No, I say we comb through these files ourselves."

He frowns. "And what? Find a report about our parents in all this? Phoenix, we've gone through everything and neither one of us has found anything about our parents *or* me."

"Hawk, this is too big of a coincidence to ignore! And Jefferson could be hiding the files on our parents—"

"Phoenix . . ."

"Don't *Phoenix* me," I snap. "He's taken and hidden a report before."

"What are you talking about?"

I gesture angrily to the mountain of boxes in front of us. "I was going through stuff and found a police report about some little girl being bitten. I think the mother was killed but the rest was a mess of coffee and I couldn't read it." I'm talking fast and one of Hawk's eyebrows is slowly rising. "The point is, I left it right here, I went to sleep, and when I woke up the next morning it was gone. *Jefferson took it.*"

"But it was a little girl bitten," he argues. "That doesn't have anything to do with us."

"No, but it does prove Jefferson has hidden stuff before and is hiding things now."

Hawk exhales sharply and runs his hands through his hair. "What are we supposed to do about it? He's an agent. Maybe it's classified. Maybe he took that report and stuck it in the right file when you weren't looking. All we have are conspiracy theories."

"Then we have to keep looking."

He puts his hand on top of mine and gets real quiet. "Phoenix, I know you want answers. So do I. But let's do this the right way, okay? If you get yourself too worked up about something—"

"This is our mom and dad we're talking about." My voice escalates in volume along with my temper. "Of course I'm going to get worked up about it!"

"I know and you have every right to. Just keep a level head, okay? We'll be smart. We'll go through the files and see if there are any werewolves that were bitten back in 1996. Then we keep up the mission at the high school and see if there are any more similarities. Don't rush into this blindly."

I glare at him. "And do what? What do you honestly think I would do?"

"For our family?" He scoffs and shakes his head. "Anything and everything, even if it ends up hurting you or someone else."

I don't know if it's meant as a compliment or an insult but it sort of feels like a punch to the gut. So, I ignore him and pull the closest file box towards me. Hawk finishes his report then grabs a notebook and brings it to the table.

"Okay, but we also need to do homework in turns so *you* don't get in trouble again." He prods me with the eraser of his pencil and offers a smile.

"I can live with that," I say and keep digging through the files.

The last time I went through these papers I was mostly skimming. I put names together and what not but I didn't really analyze anything. Now I know exactly what I'm looking for. There are a number of werewolves that have relocated out of the area but quite a few stuck around Moose Lake or Carlton County. The bite incidents are scattered through time, across months and years. I make a ledger in the notebook Hawk brought me with names and dates. If there were any associated cattle mutilations or territorial displays I note those as well.

Three hours and two boxes later, a pattern has started to emerge. Hawk nudges me out of my chair and passes over a plate of eggs so I can take a breather. He settles in and adds his own neat handwriting to my list. I try to work on my Shakespeare quiz and math assignment but it's difficult to concentrate. I plug in my mp3 player and crank up some old hip-hop songs Hawk and I used for dance competitions. I soak up the music for a solid twenty minutes before I'm able to focus enough to write about Romeo and Juliet, then abstract equations.

My mythology assignment is a piece of cake. I know the Greek lore because a good deal of it refers to actual monsters that roam the earth and have been classified by the IMS. I'll discuss the story of Lycaon, one of the many origin stories of the werewolf. It's always interesting, and informative, to see how other people react to such legends because to them they're just stories.

The second I'm finished I push Hawk out of the chair and pick up where he left off. He disappears into the bedroom for a while and I'm lost in dates and police reports. Scanning through the notes he left on the ledger, I see "black wolf?" circled next to the date of infection for several people. I go back to those particular files and page through them until I find Jefferson's handwritten notes. There's a lengthy report of his discussion with a girl freshly infected. She said it was too dark to see the creature exactly but knew it had great yellow eyes. Jefferson has "black wolf?" circled in the margins of the page.

Then I notice something else odd. He says "we followed the trail into the woods." Plural. I keep reading and it definitely indicates Jefferson had been working with others before. He doesn't say any names but then I see other handwritten notes that don't match his hasty script. Someone else made notes in this file. I have to squint at the initials on the bottom of the page for a good two minutes before I decide they're R.M. My fingers brush the letters as if I could feel them.

R.M. My father was Robin Mason. Both he and my mother had been agents. Was it possible? Did my parents work with Jefferson here in Moose Lake? Did they die here in 1996 during the last uprising of the werewolves?

I realize I'm breathing hard. I press the heels of my hands against my temples and fight something ugly in my chest.

"Hawk," I wheeze out. "Hawk!"

He races out of the bedroom. "What? Did you find . . ." He puts a hand on my shoulder and kneels down so he's looking up at me. "Are you okay?"

I push the paper towards him. "Did you see this? Look at the bottom."

He slides it off the table and his eyes scan back and forth. When he reaches the very bottom his eyes slowly narrow and his eyebrows knit together. "I just skimmed over it before," he mutters. "I guess I wasn't paying close enough attention. Two people wrote this."

"The initials, Hawk. R.M."

His eyes jump to mine. "You don't think . . . Dad?"

"There've been too many coincidences. It's got to be him."

He frowns and reads the paper over again. He rolls his lips and sticks his tongue out a little. "We need to talk to Jefferson."

"Okay." I start to rise but he pushes me back down.

"Let's go through some more files first," he says. "See if we find R.M. anywhere else or more bites in 1996. I want to be able to prove something to him. That way he can't deny the facts. He's clever and I'm sure he'll try to avoid answering otherwise."

"But *why?*" I say louder than I mean to. "Why hide the truth about our parents if they were here? If they worked with him?"

"Well, let's figure it out. Hand me a box, will you?"

We bend our heads over the files together. My brain is fevered and I can't stop. I don't care that it's getting late. Each time I see another reference to 1996 or a black wolf or see R.M. anywhere, it drives me on. We also spot a third set of handwriting with the initials M.M.—Mary Mason, our mother. It has to be. Our list grows and a greater pattern emerges. There were at least thirty people bitten within a three-week period in the beginning of October of 1996. Then people started going missing like Deputy Graham said. In fact, I see his name mentioned in a report on his sister. After that there were attacks during daylight and livestock was being slaughtered all over the place. Then after Halloween everything just stopped. The werewolves calmed down, a task force from the IMS stuck around for a while to make sure the situation had settled, then life moved on. There have been only sporadic biting incidents since then from random people going off the serum injections.

Our list is made and it's 1:30 a.m. but I don't care. Hawk and I take our information and march through the darkness to the barn where light spills out from under the door even at this hour. I knock three times and wait. Hawk cocks his head and I'm sure he can hear movement inside that I can't. He nods to me and I knock again, harder this time so the whole door shakes. Seconds tick by and I'm ready to wrench the door off its hinges when it swings open.

"I told you not to come in—"

I cut him off. "It's about what happened in 1996."

The color bleeds out of his face. I put my hand on the door to make sure he can't close it again. I'm ready to push Jefferson aside and storm his secret base.

Hawk must sense my impatience because he inserts himself between me and Jefferson. He snatches the list out of my hands and holds it up for Jefferson to see. "We know about the previous attacks. Deputy Graham said you were there so we looked into it. We've got questions and I think we've got a right to have them answered if we're going to work as a team here. The more we know, the better we'll be able to handle the current situation. Don't you agree? Or are we going to keep hiding secrets until people start to disappear like last time?"

Smooth talker. Jefferson squints at the list and a muscle in his jaw twitches. I can almost smell victory. He doesn't look at us but holds the door open wider and gestures us inside. I walk in first to survey what I never got the chance to the last time I came in uninvited.

The dirt floor has a thin scattering of hay across it and the place smells like mildew and alcohol. Directly in front of me is a tan tarp covering what is obviously a car with four tires peeking out underneath. There are some file boxes stacked on wooden pallets beside it and a workstation covered with hammers, crowbars, screwdrivers, glue, and cans of oil. I go up an open flight of stairs next to the draped car to the loft. The first thing that catches my eye is an enormous map of Moose Lake taped to the wall and marked by a hundred little colored pins. There's a bookshelf on the right stuffed with more files and boxes, and a little hook on the wall holds car keys. A plain table in the center holds a few open files, photographs paper-clipped to the covers. A picture of Hawk sits on top.

"What is this?" I ask. I walk over and point to my brother's picture. "And this?"

"What does it look like?" Jefferson says gruffly. "I was given files on you two when you first got here, remember? I was re-familiarizing myself with your case." He glances over his shoulder at Hawk who emerges at the top of the stairs and soaks it all in. "Bitten in 1996. Son of Robin and Mary Mason. Both parents killed during the incident. Sister marked by a dragon. Both siblings rescued by said dragon. The werewolf was never caught." His eyes lose focus as he gazes at the open file. "It was a bleeding nightmare."

My heart thunders in my chest. He says it like he was there and witnessed it firsthand.

"Where?" I breathe.

His beady eyes are pained when they meet mine. "You don't know, do you?" He massages the side of his face and pulls a hand over his beard. "They classified the files since that dragon got involved."

"Where?" I demand, my voice steady this time.

"Here," he sighs. "Or more accurately, right here." He walks to the massive map and points to a blood-red pin near the edge of town. "Right here in Moose Lake fourteen years ago."

14

I had already convinced myself of the facts. I was the one pushing Jefferson to confirm all my theories. Yet the moment he tells the truth, a gaping hole rips open in my chest. So it's true. Hawk and I used to live here when we were kids. Neither of us can even remember it. I walk to the map and put my finger on the pin that marks where our lives changed. Where our parents died. I can't speak. I just stand glued to that map as Jefferson continues to talk.

"Robin and Mary were my co-workers." He clears his throat. "And they were my friends. Back in 1996 something began happening to the werewolves in the area and we investigated it together."

"A population explosion," Hawk says quietly.

"Exactly. But not just that. Their behavior changed. They got aggressive. They stopped taking the serum. It got to the point they started biting people in the streets. We called in the IMS because something was seriously wrong."

I don't turn around. There's a prick behind my eyes as I stare at that horrible red pin.

"Things got bad. Real bad. Then we started piecing the puzzle together. There were sightings of a huge black wolf all over town. The other werewolves were drawn to it and protected it. And—" He clears his throat again, louder this time. "It was directly involved in several incidents."

"You don't know who it was?" Hawk asks even though the answer is obvious.

"No, but your folks called me Halloween night. Said they might have a lead before the line went dead. I went to your house but by the time I got there . . ." He trails off. He doesn't need to fill in the blanks for us to understand but that twisted part of me needs to know. Answers have eluded me for so long and I want the truth no matter how gruesome at this point.

"But what?" I say roughly, still facing the map.

There's a long moment of silence before he answers. "By the time I got there a dragon was already cradling you and Hawk. He said the black wolf had been there, then he took you two and vanished. Robin and Mary didn't make it. The wolf had killed them and from what I could make of the wreckage in the house, they died trying to protect you two."

I worry my lower lip and stare at the little red pin. I never knew my parents. I just have that old picture of them in their IMS jackets, happy and smiling. I never knew what kind of people they were. I always imagined them to be brave and selfless and heroic and I was proud. Now hearing how they died, trying to protect Hawk and me, all I feel is guilt. There's a bubble swelling in my chest but it's cold and dark. That black wolf killed them. Had it been after Hawk and me the whole time? Had our parents simply gotten in the way? Or were they killed because they had figured out the identity of the wolf?

"Why didn't you say anything?" Hawk says and the tremble in his voice breaks my heart. "You knew all this time and never said a word."

"I didn't say anything because I was ashamed," Jefferson says quietly. "They died on my watch and I've never been able to catch the *schweinhund* that did this. I didn't want to confront the kids of my dead friends only to say I had nothing to offer them. I *failed*."

I glance at Hawk before I wipe the back of my hand under my eyes. Normally we would both be jumping to arms at someone calling a werewolf a vile 'pig-dog' but I think this black wolf deserves it. I take a deep breath, and move away from the map to face Jefferson. "But it's happening again. It's got to be the same black wolf as last time. There've been too many similarities. We have a chance to stop this before it gets that bad again. We can find that black wolf."

"He's a slippery dog," Jefferson says and runs a hand over his face again. I just now notice the heavy bags beneath his eyes. "I've been going through all the paperwork, setting up cameras wherever I can, using every one of my contacts, but this wolf is a ghost."

"No, he's not." I curl my hands around the collar of my shirt and tuck my chin down to rest on my knuckles. "He came here that one time, remember? I saw him when we were out shooting. He wasn't hiding himself then."

Jefferson braces his hands against the table and nods. "Keeping tabs on us no doubt."

"Why not attack me right then and there?" I ask.

"I don't know."

I'm exhausted but my mind is buzzing. I take the single chair at the table and puddle into it. I plant my elbows on the tabletop and set my forehead against my palms. "So that's why you hate werewolves so much."

"I lost people," Jefferson says hardly above a whisper. "Everyone did."

Hawk goes to inspect the map and points to the pins. "Biting incidents, I take it?"

"Yes," Jefferson says. "The red pins are all back from 1996. The yellow are the random attacks in the between years. The blue are those happening now."

There's a large mass of red pins scattered through with yellow. There's already a significant number of blue but they aren't concentrated anywhere. They're all over the city. Whoever this black werewolf is, he's careful.

"There's no pattern except for one," Jefferson continues. "Random people are bitten but the teenagers are the first to really start acting out, then the parents—aggression sets in followed by attacks and disappearances."

"Why would a werewolf do this?" I mutter to myself.

"There is no such thing as a lone wolf," he says. "They always need a pack. I've known others to create their own packs out of desperation and loneliness, but this . . . it's almost like a militarized operation. Like this wolf is building an army."

From the number of pins on that map, I believe it. But an army for what?

"Shouldn't we call in the IMS for something this big?" I ask.

At that Jefferson ducks his head and works his jaw. If I didn't know any better I'd say he's embarrassed.

"There's a reason I'm out here by myself," he says and starts shuffling through the loose paper on the table. "I may have used questionable judgment and acted recklessly in the aftermath of 1996. They don't exactly trust me at my word anymore."

"You? Questionable? Reckless?" Hawk says and scoffs, sticking his hands in his pockets. "I wouldn't believe it for a second."

After how often Jefferson has yanked on our chains because we've "misbehaved," I'm curious to know what he did to make the IMS isolate him on purpose. "What did you do?"

He waves his hand dismissively. "It doesn't matter."

"Of course it doesn't," I mutter. Disappointed, I let my attention float back to Hawk's file in front of me. "So what now? How do we help?"

Hawk stands at my shoulder and we wait for an answer. Jefferson gazes between the pair of us and a sad smile adds fine wrinkles to his face.

"You two look just like your parents," he says. "I mean, Robin was the red head, but Mary was the stubborn one. Guess you both got those genes." He suddenly slaps his hands together, making me jump. "Well, I guess I owe you both an apology for keeping you in the dark. Hold on a minute."

He shuffles over to the towering bookshelf and hauls down an old box covered with broken evidence tape. I swallow when I read the label on top. *CLASSIFIED: Case File 1996-W5-44207; Robin Mason; Mary Mason.*

"The original un-redacted case file." Jefferson pats the top of the box. I realize it's not dusty like some of the other boxes.

He must have been going through it recently, probably because of the current situation in town. "I know it's supposed to be classified but you have a right to know. I'll be downstairs if you need me."

It's suddenly very hard to breathe. I have a crazy irrational fear that if I open the box everything inside will disintegrate and this precious gift of answers will be gone forever. It's Pandora's box. It'll be everything I ever wanted to know, but at what cost? Will there be secrets about our parents we should never learn? Will there be something about Hawk in there? My mouth is dry and my palms sweaty.

Hawk reaches past me and tugs the box towards him so it's between us. He lifts the lid and I stand so we can inspect the contents together. There's a great thick manila file on top and plastic bags of evidence beneath from the crime scene. Hawk pulls out the file and begins to unwrap the string holding it shut but I'm drawn to the plastic bags sealed with red evidence tape. I lift out the largest to find a leather bomber jacket. The fluffy, tan insulating layer inside the collar is a little sun-bleached. My fingers tremble as I read the label. *Mary Mason's bomber jacket; found next to Phoenix Mason's last location, under dining table; blood sample taken from lining.*

This was my mother's. I've never had anything of my mother's. All I had was that single photo. I don't even know how I got that much. My eyes are swimming. I want to touch the leather, I want to know if it still harbors what my mother smelled like, I want to know if I would fit her size, if I'm anything like her at all. I hold the bag out to Hawk.

"Do you think we can . . ." My voice cracks so I clear my throat. "Do you think I can open it?"

He doesn't even look up. He has the police report clutched in his shaking hands. A single tear splashes on the paper but he doesn't seem to notice that either. I clutch the evidence bag with my mother's jacket to my chest and start to read over his shoulder.

The caption at the top lists our parents' names and our old address. Then my name and Hawk's follow with a little indicator for minors. No suspect is listed on the page. A report created by Agent J. Barnes follows under the IMS insignia.

The report starts at the same place Jefferson said—on October 31, 1996. He goes to their house after getting a call that they might have a lead on a suspect but the call cut out. When Jefferson arrives he finds a gaping hole where the front door used to be and debris scattered throughout the inside. Jefferson unholsters his bio-mech gun and makes for the dining room because he hears crying. Just before the entrance he discovers Robin's body—

I stop and suck down a sharp breath. Images are being seared into my brain that I know will never go away. This is my father I'm reading about, his corpse on the floor being described in cold unmitigated detail. I wipe the back of my hand under my nose and have to find the spot where I left off. Hawk passes it to me as he reads on to the next page, his breathing ragged.

Jefferson stops to check Robin's pulse but it's obvious he's gone. There's too much blood and deep gashes down his side. Jefferson continues forward and discovers Mary next. She's dead with a gun still clutched in her hand. Blood trails on the floor indicate she was grabbed from behind and pulled away from underneath the dining room table where Jefferson discovers

Hawk and me hiding. Also there is a man Jefferson recognizes from previous contact—not a human but a dragon in human form. Draco, a majestic class dragon. Jefferson notes Hawk has a large bite mark beneath his shirt that is bleeding profusely. He also observes three talon marks through the torn sleeve of my shirt left by Draco after passing on his dragon magic.

After a quick conference, Jefferson and Draco decide to take Hawk and me to Underground where we can both be safe and looked after. The dragon vanishes in a flash of white light along with Hawk and me, transported off to Underground. The report goes on to say Jefferson is contacted shortly after by Draco who says he saw a black werewolf fleeing the scene but Draco's first concern was to make sure Hawk and I were okay. The werewolf got away. The rest is a summary of Jefferson attempting to find leads but they go nowhere. The report ends.

Hawk walks away sniffling and braces himself against the wall with the map. I take a seat, hardly feeling the tears running down my face, and keep going through the rest of the papers in the file. There are photographs taken of the scene. I page through them as quickly as I can but I can't unsee the ones of my parents lying lifeless in pools of blood. I shove the pictures away from me and fight back a sob crawling up my throat. I put my face in my hands to collect myself before I keep going.

There are a number of call logs with notes from Jefferson regarding a black werewolf. The monster seemed to come out of nowhere then vanish as soon as Draco showed up. Why the dragon showed up in the first place is beyond me. Any appearance by one of them is extremely rare and unheard of for something as trivial as a werewolf.

But it was Draco that saved us. Draco that made me one of

the Blessed. And then it was Draco again that fought against Director Knox to keep us in the IMS. Always just out of sight, always watching over us. It doesn't make any sense.

I read through the rest of the extensive notes of the investigation and linger over the handwritten pieces by my mother and father. I have the same jotting scrawl as my father whereas Hawk has neater penmanship like our mother. Hawk eventually comes back over to look at the bags of evidence and stands there staring at our mother's jacket for the longest time. I go through the rest of the bags, dreading what I might come across. There are a few shreds of fabric, cut-outs of carpet with bloodstains, and in the very last is a pearl-handled .45. It was the gun clutched in my mother's hand as she was dragged away from protecting her children.

In my dreams I always see a great black shape biting Hawk, and then myself punching the werewolf in the nose. Now I can almost hear a woman's screams in the background—my mother screaming.

I shudder and have to leave. I hustle down the stairs so fast that I trip at the bottom. I'm unable to catch myself but Jefferson grabs my arm to keep me upright. I didn't even see him there. I hastily wipe at my face and avoid eye contact.

Jefferson lets me be and takes a step back. He plants his hands on his waist and hangs his head but I can feel his eyes on me.

"It might not be the same werewolf here now," he says.

"But it could be."

"Yes. It could."

I swallow past the lump in my raw throat and force myself to stand straight. "Then we find it."

"That's not going to be easy."

"It doesn't matter." Because Hawk is right. I would do anything for my family, and I will do whatever it takes to find my parents' murderer, the person that passed their sick disease on to Hawk.

"The problem with finding a wolf is knowing their human half," Jefferson says. "And right now, that devil could be anyone."

15

I can't sleep. I check my phone thinking an hour has passed only to find it's been ten minutes. I lay that way for the longest time and keep checking my phone until eventually I sit up, hug my legs to my chest, and stare out the window. The full moon is out so I can see everything outside in shades of gray.

The light in the barn eventually goes out but Jefferson never comes inside. I check my phone again. It's 3:00 a.m.

Reading the file on my parents has given me some answers but has also led to more questions. Who was the black wolf? Was it Draco's presence that stopped it? If so, why has the wolf come back now? Why was Draco here in the first place? I know he's one of the founders of the IMS and a majestic class dragon, one of only six on earth. I've never actually seen Draco in his dragon form. In fact, I've only seen him twice that I can remember and each time was as a human looking to be about in his forties—tall, slim, and overall rather average looking apart from something in the way he held himself that made all eyes turn in his direction. But as a majestic class, in his dragon form he would be about the size of a house and an enormous source of magical power. What would a werewolf be to him?

Then again, what could *I* possibly be to him? My hand automatically touches my shoulder where the three talon marks are hidden under my sleeve. I never understood why Draco chose me to bear a piece of his magic. So far it hasn't really given me any astounding gifts. I don't call my strength amazing by any measure. Sure, it comes in handy for kicking in doors and hauling Hawk out of trouble but it's not like I'm shooting lasers out of my eyes or tossing around buildings with the power of my mind.

It certainly hasn't made me able to handle the current situation. If only his magic had given me exemplary social skills, that would have been helpful—or something to track down this monster roaming in secret somewhere in Moose Lake.

Jefferson hadn't let me open the evidence bags and right now I wish I could hug myself to my mother's jacket. He said we can open them when the case has been solved. I'll hold him to that. I try to block out the image of those crime scene photos but they keep coming back to me. I wipe my face a few times. I could really use a hug but I don't want to disturb Hawk. So I grab my pillow and hug it to my chest. I curl up like a five-year-old with a security blanket but I don't care in the darkness of night where no one can see me. I let myself fall apart so I can put myself back together stronger.

My mind continues to process the rest of the night and I only catch an hour, maybe two, of sleep before I'm jolted awake by nightmares. The sky is beginning to lighten outside so I slip out of bed and pull on my running clothes. I have a brief moment of panic when I realize Hawk isn't in his bed and rush out into the main area only to find him stretching on the floor in his own exercise clothes. His eyes are red rimmed.

I silently take up the space next to him and start stretching out my hamstrings. We don't say a word to each other but we don't need to. There aren't any words sufficient anyway. After a few minutes Hawk rises and holds the door open for me. Sunlight touches the tops of the trees and our breath mists before us.

Darkness lingers in the underbrush and I watch it with nervous disdain. Anything could be hiding out there watching us or ready to attack. I mean, we just learned the truth about a black wolf that's probably back in town, has murdered before, and targeted us specifically.

"This is probably a really stupid idea," I say quietly.

"Yeah, probably. Let's go."

He takes off down the driveway and I race to catch up. Once I reach him, we match our pace and keep together as we turn onto the roadway. We run in the middle of the right lane since there's no one out at this hour. Hawk swivels his head this way and that, occasionally sniffing at the air. I keep an eye out as well, but being out here and getting my blood moving starts to shake me out of my reverie. I'm still alive. I can make a difference now. I have my brother and together we can work this out.

The burn in my legs starts to satisfy the pain surging through me by letting it out in a physical way. I push harder and Hawk does the same. We reach the end of the road and turn south down the next. We race each other and I'm sucking in sharp breaths of chilly October air. We reach the end of the road and the sun is climbing in earnest, dappling the asphalt with light. I tap my wrist to indicate the time and Hawk nods.

We turn back and challenge each other to go faster on the way to Jefferson's. We're almost to Soldier Road when Hawk throws out his arm to stop me, then grabs me by the shoulders and hustles me off into the ditch to duck down. We both try to stifle our loud breathing and I follow Hawk's line of sight.

Farther up the road a group of four wolves cross the pavement in a single file line. The one at the very end with a distinctly reddish hue—possibly the same wolf that had jogged beside me that one morning—stops and sniffs in our direction. We slip down lower to hide in the ditch. Thankfully we are downwind because we stink from running hard and would have been easy to locate otherwise. Right now the thought of being confronted by a pack of werewolves and not knowing their current state of mind terrifies me. Who knows if they're in their human minds or working off pure instinct? If they feel threatened by us while we're in their territory, they could attack.

The reddish wolf eventually trots after its fellows and they disappear heading west into the woods. We stay hidden for another minute before Hawk helps me to my feet. Together we move at a more cautious pace east on Soldier Road and then sprint down Jefferson's driveway to the cabin. Jefferson pulls up in his rusty truck fifteen seconds later.

"You two just take a run?" he asks as soon as he steps out with a cardboard tray holding three cups.

"Yeah," I say.

I'm expecting an angry response, a lecture about safety, and how we were reckless. Instead, Jefferson slowly nods and brings us the drinks he's carrying. I take one, unsure what to say, and inhale the fragrance of coffee.

"I figured you could use some," he says. His tone is a lot kinder than it's ever been and I realize he understands what we're going through. He's being nice to us, and suddenly it's like we're actually on the same team.

"Thanks," Hawk and I say in unison.

Jefferson takes his own and leads the way inside the cabin. "Are you two going to be okay going to school today?"

I didn't even realize sitting on the bench is an option. "We need to work."

"I get that." He sips at his coffee and leans against the kitchen counter.

"I've been thinking," I start, happy to share my thoughts with Jefferson for once, "We should really keep trying to get the teenagers to talk. I noticed quite a few of them are children of those attacked in the last . . . incident. They might be able to share something."

Jefferson nods. "Good idea. I'll try talking to the parents again directly but things are getting more and more hostile. The second I try leaning on them with IMS authority, I'm not going to get anyone to open their door for me. You two are our best chance of getting the inside scoop. Maybe one of them has seen a black wolf."

We get ready and Jefferson drives us to the school. Once there, I feel like I'm on a different planet and speaking a different language. With what I know now, every student, teacher, cook, and staff member looks like a suspect to me. That girl laughing down the hall? Could be a murderer in disguise. That couple making out? They probably attacked someone yesterday.

Those boys playing cards in the middle of the hallway? They could be the masterminds of the entire operation.

A change has come over Hawk as well. He looks beat and I know I do too, but for him it's a huge turn around. He's always been the social ray of sunshine, but I see the effort it takes him to smile at the girl beside his locker.

We head to English together and take up silent sentry posts in the back of the room. This isn't school anymore. It's an infiltration mission. Hawk discreetly points out one of the known werewolves sitting in the middle of the room. I watch the unassuming boy closely. He works on meticulously ripping one of his notebook pages to shreds beneath his desk and clearly isn't paying much attention.

He's got black hair but that's hardly an indicator that he's the black wolf. For one, anyone can dye their hair. Second, the human physical appearance doesn't necessarily equate to what their wolf half will look like. Sure, Hawk has red hair and is more red colored. Then again, I once knew a werewolf that visited Underground who was an African American with jet black hair that would change into a pure white, arctic wolf.

Class ends and I'm forced to attend Mr. Webster's class. The second I walk into the classroom his beady eyes find me and I'm greeted with a sour frown. I ignore him and move to find a seat. Someone waves a hand in my face so I stop only to realize Ashley is in this class with me. I hadn't even noticed before.

"Hi!" she says and pats the empty chair next to her. "I saved you a spot."

"Thanks, Ashley. I appreciate it." I sink down next to her and rub at my eyes. Despite the coffee this morning, my brain is starting to slow down to drunk giant pace. It takes me a while to register she's exceptionally happy this morning, although it could be her default setting. I don't really know her but she does seem pretty perky considering. "You look like you're doing better."

"Oh, yeah. I'm great. You on the other hand . . ." She moves her hands up and down gesturing to all of me. "You look like you got hit by a bus."

That's a pretty accurate description. "Yeah, bad night."

She pats me on the shoulder and is momentarily distracted as a boy pushes his way between us to another seat. Then her smile is back in place and she leans towards me.

"Hey, I wanted to say thanks for sticking up for me yesterday. I can't believe you decked that jerk but, wow, that was awesome. You must work out or something because he got *hammered*." She slugs me lightly in the shoulder and I can't help but smile a little. "He's been so embarrassed. I think he's actually 'out sick' today—" She mimes quotation marks in the air, "—to avoid everyone."

That catches my attention. "He's not in today?"

"Yeah, I overhead some of his buddies." It's funny how often she's overhearing things. "He was supposed to hang out with them last night but he never showed and he's not returning their calls. I'm sure he's just mad because they were calling him a wuss, getting beat up by a girl and whatever."

Mr. Webster clears his throat rather loudly to get our attention and starts the class. I lean back but there's no way I'm able to focus on his current lecture. It's true the Jones-wuss could actually be out sick today, or avoiding the usual high school ridicule—or something more sinister could be going on. He could have been bitten. If he was, he would be extremely susceptible to another werewolf's influence. He would need the serum and soon. I never did catch his first name.

I scribble *"What was the jerk's name?"* on a scrap of paper and pass it to Ashley. She unfolds it under her desk, writes something underneath when Mr. Webster's back is turned, and discreetly passes it back. Apparently not discreetly enough because Mr. Webster points down the row at me.

"Give me that," he huffs.

I ignore him and read it before he can take it away. *Matt Jones.* Mr. Webster waddles between the tight desks towards me. I rip the note to shreds before he reaches me then drop the bits into his outstretched hand. His face turns purple.

"Go to the principal's office," he snaps. "You're getting—"

"Detention," I say over him. "Right. Thanks. Going now."

I grab my book and hop over the other side of my desk to avoid trying to pass him. Everyone's staring so I wink and jog out of the room. A part of me really hopes Mr. Webster is the black wolf so I can have the pleasure of taking him down myself. Once in the hallway, I check both ways before pulling out my cell and dialing Jefferson.

His surly voice answers. "Hello?"

"It's me. I think you need to check up on someone. A Matt Jones?"

"You have a lead?"

I walk towards the end of the hall away from any classroom doors. "He's not in school today and my gut tells me something's up. He might be a fresh pup, if you know what I mean. Could you check his house to see if he's there?"

"Yeah, I know the place. Now get back to class before you get detention again."

I stop short. "Wait, you know about that?"

He actually laughs and then disconnects the call. I grumble under my breath and shove my phone into my pocket.

I don't go to the principal's office. I decide I don't care about detention and that I need a moment alone. I go out the rear exit and slide down against the brick wall to sit on the ice-cold cement surrounded by silence. It's a clear and beautiful morning with the surface of Moosehead Lake sparkling through the trees past the football field.

If I leaned my head back, I could probably fall asleep. Instead, I pull out my phone again and the small beeps of the buttons sound loud out here in the relative quiet. It rings for a short time before a familiar voice answers.

"This is Wallowitz."

"Hey there, Witty."

"Phoenix! Hey, I haven't heard from you in forever. What's going on?" There's a constant squeak barely audible on the other end. He must be moving around in his wheelchair somewhere in Underground. A strong wave of homesickness sweeps over me, which only reminds me of why Underground is my home. Moose Lake could have been my home if only it had gotten a chance.

"Oh, I just . . ." Why am I calling? If I ask him about the shapeshifters or the werewolf serum he'll probably clam up. "I just needed to hear a friendly voice, that's all."

There's dead silence for a long time on the other end of the line. Even the squeaky wheels have stopped.

"You still alive over there?" I ask.

"Yeah. I'm okay. Are you?"

I bite my lower lip and rub the palm of my free hand around my knee. "I've been asking myself the same question."

"Phoenix, if you need anything . . ."

"Yeah, actually." I clear my throat to get the sticky emotion out of it. "If I ask you about those shapeshifters, will you answer? Have they talked? Do they know anything about the werewolf serum being tampered with?"

"I, um . . . yeah. I don't know how to tell you this." Over the line I hear him tapping his fingers on the arm of his wheelchair.

"Tell me what?"

"They looked into the serum. Nothing's changed. It wasn't tampered with."

"But that—" I clamp a hand to my forehead and squeeze my eyes shut. "That doesn't make any sense, Witty. They must have done something to it. The wolves here are taking extra doses and it's doing nothing for them."

"Then if there was tampering, it wasn't on Werevine's end."

There's too much anxiety and caffeine in my system. Suddenly very antsy, I get to my feet and start to pace. "What are the distribution channels for the serum? Tell me what the steps are from it leaving the lab to the werewolves getting it."

"Hold on." There's more wheel squeaking and then fevered tapping which could only mean he's in front of a keyboard. "Okay, from Werevine Pharmaceutical labs it's sent out to clinic centers. From the centers, the serum passes directly from the attending physician to the werewolves who need it. The clinic in your area is—"

"Northwoods Family Clinic. Doctor Rosewell."

"Yeah, that's right."

The wheels are already turning in my head. "Thanks, Witty," I say and end the call.

It has to be the werewolf doc. She has direct control and access to the serum. She could be tainting the stock in town. Could she be the black wolf? Hawk could set up an appointment to get some of the serum and then we could send it off to the IMS for testing. I'm about to call Jefferson next when I see a shadow move on the edge of the football field. It's large, has four legs, and turns tail as soon as I spot it. Best guess, it's a werewolf, but it's the middle of the morning. Why on earth is someone out now and transformed?

I consider running back inside and finding Hawk but what would I say? Oh, sorry teacher but I have to pull my brother out of class for a second to track a werewolf? I shove my phone into my back pocket and sprint to the field. Yeah, now I'm reckless. I hop the chain link fence and go diagonally across the field, hop another fence, and reach the woods. The cold nips at my face and I rub the tops of my arms. I've only got a long sleeved shirt on and hadn't bothered grabbing my jacket earlier.

Very large paw prints are visible in the soft, exposed soil inside the tree line. A swath of leaves are pushed aside beneath a line of broken twigs and underbrush. I pick my way carefully forward following the trail deeper into the woods. I stop now and then to listen. In the distance I can hear panting and the occasional whine of a dog. Correction, a wolf. A great big, gray timber wolf twenty yards ahead of me. Its tail is tucked between its legs, it stands awkward like it's not used to standing on four legs, and looks lost. A freshly turned werewolf would be my guess.

I run through the procedure in my head. When approaching a new werewolf that has just turned, it's best to stun or tranquilize it first and inject the serum as soon as possible. Otherwise, if the wolf feels threatened, it may attack and bite. Whoever this is will be confused, disoriented, and prone to violence. I'm about to back pedal to a safe distance and call Jefferson to get him over here as fast as possible when it rings before I can reach it.

The sound is loud and the wolf whips around at the noise. I wrench the phone out of my pocket and hit the answer button to stop the sound but it's already too late. I bend slightly at the knees and slowly back away holding one hand out towards the wolf. Its eyes lock on me, its hackles rise, and its lips pull back in a vicious snarl. I bring the phone up to my ear nice and easy and try not to make any sudden movements.

"Phoenix, I checked Matt Jones' house." It's Jefferson. "He's not there, but I found a trail of wolf tracks leading into the woods."

"Yeah," I whisper. The wolf starts to creep towards me. "I think I found him."

16

I try to keep distance between me and the werewolf but I end up backpedaling into a tree.

"Jefferson, hurry," I whisper. This isn't going to end well.

"Where are you?" he asks sharply. I'm touched. He's concerned. Hopefully that will make him move faster.

"The woods past the football field, not too far in. Please hurry. This wolf's pretty angry."

"Hang on." The truck rumbles to life in the background. "Stay on the line. Take it easy. No sudden movements. Don't be aggressive."

"Aye aye, captain."

I stand like a statue but the wolf keeps inching closer, snarling and saliva flying. I really, really, *really* don't want to get bitten. Hawk almost bit me once when he first went off the serum but I held him off. Ever since we got to Underground and our caretakers knew what we were, a werewolf and Blessed, they drilled it into my head that the worst things would happen if I was ever bitten. I've heard the horror stories of other Blessed that have gotten bitten on the job. The magic in their veins was too potent, a hundred times more potent than the serum, and the combustion of their magic trying to fight the disease either ending up killing them or turning them into an unstable mess. The lucky ones simply changed into werewolves but they couldn't take the serum and were closely monitored by the IMS. So, would I turn into a super strong werewolf? Would the magic in my veins twist me into something different? Or maybe the disease and magic would react so violently it would kill me straight out. *Pixies*, I need to stop being a pessimist.

The wolf is maybe ten feet away. One good leap and he could flatten me to the ground. If things get really hairy I might be able to grab him by the fur below the jaws then curl in my knuckles and cut off the blood supply to his brain to make him pass out. I nearly had to do it to Hawk before. It was unpleasant to say the least. Now, a strong blood choke might be my only option.

"Sorry, Jefferson," I mutter and drop the phone on the ground so I can make full use of both hands if I need to. I hold my palms out to the werewolf. A part of him is still human. Hopefully, that part can hear me through the beast. It might be enough.

"Listen to me," I say in my best commanding voice, low and forceful. "I'm no threat to you. I'm a friend. I can help. You just have to let me help you."

It lowers its head even more and puts another paw forward.

"This isn't you—not the real you. You can *fight* this." I speak louder. "You've got to stop or you're going to regret this. We both will, I think."

It comes closer and my heart is trying to leap out of my chest.

I take a deep breath and try to remember what my instructors taught me. Keep a level head, know your surroundings, know your strengths and weaknesses, know your opponent's as well. I maneuver my feet into a better stance and bend my knees to resist the impact I know must be coming.

I don't want to hurt this werewolf who in all likelihood is Matt Jones. True, I did punch him yesterday but that seems like a lifetime ago. Matt's life is going to change forever and starting out like this isn't going to make anything easier. I know I can stop him but I could also accidentally crush his bones.

"*Stop*, Matt," I practically snarl. "It's you in there, isn't it?" Now that he's closer I can just barely make out the faint lines of what could be a jersey. "You may be a prick and a bully but you're not a monster, are you? Prove me wrong. Stop, Matt. *Stop!*"

My skin feels like it's on fire and I hold out my hands willing him to stop. The yellow in his eyes is vivid—the sign of a werewolf without any control. When he's within five feet, he pauses and takes a step back. Those great big wolf eyes stare up at me and he tucks his tail again. He whines. He takes another step back, then another, and shakes his head as if trying to expel water from his ears. I don't believe it.

There's a gun blast and I jump so hard I hit my head against the tree behind me. The wolf jerks, stumbles to the side, then falls over into a pile of leaves. I hold a hand over my heart trying to keep it from popping loose and watch Jefferson step between the trees carrying his hunting rifle.

"He's not . . .?" I point to the unmoving wolf.

"No, just sedated."

I heave a huge sigh and slump to the ground with one hand

grasping at my chest and the other massaging the back of my head. Jefferson kneels next to the wolf and plucks out a tranquilizer dart before coming over to me. He grasps my arm and pulls me up out of the grass.

"Are you okay? Did he bite you?"

I shake my head and feel lightheaded. "No, he backed off."

His face goes blank. "What?"

"I told him to stop and he did. I must have gotten through to him somehow."

The disbelief in his face is clear enough but he doesn't press the issue. "We need to get him out of here. And what on earth were you doing out here in the first place? You're supposed to be in school."

"I was taking a quick break outside and spotted him watching the school."

His gaze travels over the large canine body sprinkled with dirt and leaves. "Odd."

"Yeah."

"Help me get him into the truck. I want to see this super strength of yours."

I glare at him out of the corner of my eye. More like he doesn't want to help carry a big heavy wolf. I bend down and carefully grasp the front paws, then the back paws, and after some awkward maneuvering get Matt the wolf over my shoulders in a fireman's carry. I rise a bit unsteady and have Jefferson lead the way. I can take the weight easy enough but I was already exhausted at the beginning of the day and my feet start to drag.

Jefferson whistles once we reach the truck and he folds down the back gate for me. "That's pretty impressive, Phoenix."

"Thanks, do I get a cookie?" I grunt as I tip Matt to the side and ease him into the truck bed. Jefferson helps a little here and makes sure his tail doesn't get caught when he closes the gate.

"How about I bring you coffee after I drop him off at the doc's?"

I grab the edge of the truck to keep him from walking around me to the cab. "Wait, Doctor Rosewell?"

"The one and only."

"You can't do that." I quickly explain what Witty told me over the phone but Jefferson shakes his head.

"That's just it, Phoenix. Doctor Rosewell's clean as a whistle and has been my friend for a long time. She's not tainting the werewolf serum."

I follow him as he slips around me. "But how can you know that for sure?"

"Because she's human for one and wouldn't fall under some kind of instinctual calling like the werewolves. Two, I've already had some of it tested and it passed muster. Third, do you even know how the serum is made?"

Science isn't really my strong suite. "Well . . . no, but—"

"Each vial of that serum starts in a lab, then is processed directly by a dragon. It's their magic that gives werewolves their minds back. Magic can't be tainted." He gets into the cab and shuts the door but keeps speaking to me through the open window. "It's not even a real cure. It's just one kind of magic fighting another kind of magic inside the werewolves and keeping the disease at bay long enough for them to keep their heads."

"So what does that mean?"

"It means there is something in this town that is making the disease in the werewolves stronger than the serum." He turns

the ignition and the truck roars to life. "Get back to school before you get into any more trouble. Better run."

I stand back so he can drive away. Then I start to run. By
the time I reach the school I'm sweaty, out of breath, and my
shoes are covered in dirt. The bell rings and I race to my locker.
The second Hawk finds me he looks alarmed. I wave him off
and say breathlessly, "I'll explain later."

I'm fidgety through biology but at least it's easy to pass
notes to Hawk since the table we sit at is connected and we're
supposed to be doing a lab assignment together. We talk in
whispers but the things I don't dare even to whisper I write
down for him to read while I pretend to look through the microscope in front of me.

"You've got to get your wolf friends talking," I say urgently
under my breath. "Someone's got to know who bit Matt."

"He might know when he comes round," Hawk whispers.

"No, he'll remember a wolf. So unless the person transformed right in front of him, it's doubtful he'll have a clue who
it was."

We fall silent and keep our eyes keen on the other werewolf
in class. It's the preppy one, Adam Glass, and he's absentmind-
edly chewing on the end of a pencil. Not just chewing, but actively gnawing and the thing is starting to fall to splinters in his
hand. He's about as twitchy as the werewolf in my first class.

Biology passes and we head to our fourth period class. The
teacher is explaining a rather difficult physics equation but I'm
concentrating on the girl two seats in front of me biting her fingernails. She's scratched off her bright red nail polish and flecks
of it are stuck to her teeth. Her nails are in nasty shape and
will no doubt begin to bleed very soon. No surprise, it's another

werewolf going off their rocker. So far the only werewolf that hasn't been acting strange is Hawk. He's moving a bit slower than usual and rubs at his eyes but I'm doing the same. Neither of us exactly had what you would call a good night's sleep.

At lunch I'm forced to grab my food then head out to serve my detention in Captain Krush's classroom. On my way out I notice the werewolf table is concentrating solely on their food and not speaking a peep. I give Hawk a single wave then walk down the hallway carrying my tray. The door at the end of the hall swings open and Jefferson enters the school bearing a cup of coffee. I meet him halfway and he sets the cup in the open space on my tray.

"You actually brought me coffee?" I say. "I thought you were joking."

His eyes scan both ends of the hallway and he leans in. "Matt's been injected and is sitting at a remote farm with the doc. He's still not quite with it but from what I got out of him, a group of wolves came for him. He was heading out to some party and they surrounded him by his car. Then one bit him."

"That sounds coordinated."

"That's not all. The one that bit him? It was a black wolf."

I swallow involuntarily. "When did this happen?"

"Last night. His parents are out of town so there wasn't anyone to report him missing when he fled into the woods."

I soak it in. The wolves really know what they're doing. "That's clever."

"I need to get back there so I can fill Matt in on his new life. You keep safe."

"Yeah."

He jogs out of the building and it takes me a moment to remember I'm supposed to be somewhere too. I reach Captain Krush's classroom and knock on the door. Krushnic is sitting at his desk going through some papers and gestures for me to come in without even looking up. The room is empty except for the two of us so I pick a seat right at the front and plop down. Despite the steaming temperature of the coffee, I chug it. It has a nice kick but I'm getting to the point where I don't know if I'll be able to keep my eyes open if I stay in one place for too long.

"You don't look so good." Captain Krush sets aside his papers and cocks his head, studying me. "You okay?"

I drag both hands down my face. "Yeah, I'm getting there."

He stands and walks to the podium at the front of the classroom to lean against it. "Not quite fast enough though, eh?"

"Guess not." I start to eat but the food is basically tasteless after the scalding coffee and my mouth doesn't really want to chew right now.

"Yeah, that seems to be going around."

"What do you mean?"

He scratches the back of his head and ruffles his dark hair. "I've noticed several students out of sorts. Kind of distracted or a bit ill. Some of the staff too."

"Really? Like who?"

He cocks his head again and gives a crooked smile. "I shouldn't talk about the other teachers and their personal problems. Let's just say more than one person has been having difficulty the last couple of nights."

I'm about to pester him when he throws up a hand and faces the doorway.

"Aha! Here's our late comer," he says.

Ben walks in carrying his own tray of food. There are dark shadows under his eyes and his feet are dragging like he's gotten the same amount of sleep I have, which is basically none at all.

"Take a seat." Captain Krush ushers him to a chair next to me then glances at his wristwatch. "Well, this is detention so I forbid you from having fun. That being said, I'm hungrier than a hippo so I'm going to run to Submart but I'll be back before the hour's over. Don't move you two or you'll get me into trouble."

He winks and hurries out the door.

I'm left dumbfounded. "Did he just . . .?"

"Yup," Ben says and starts devouring everything on his tray.

"Wow. I wish detention was this slack at my old school."

Ben gives a single dry laugh around the food in his mouth. "You were a problem child? I thought you're supposed to be, you know, an agent of the law?"

I glower at him and pick unenthusiastically at my own food. "Yeah, well, you're in here same as me. What did *you* do?"

That brings him up short. He sets down his fork and his face pales. He avoids my gaze altogether. "I just, uh, got into a little trouble."

Considering how all the werewolves have been acting lately, I have a sense it wasn't as minor as Ben is implying. He might also be hedging because I *am* with the IMS and he wouldn't want to get into more trouble.

"You can tell me, Ben. Come on. What'd you do? Blow up a toilet? Key a car? Slap Mr. Webster? Please tell me you slapped Mr. Webster. I'd be your best friend for life."

He doesn't laugh but gives a heavy sigh. He starts rubbing his hands together absently and cracks his knuckles. "No, I sort of started a fight with one of the boys in first period. It was over something stupid."

"How stupid?"

"He took my pencil and wouldn't give it back. I've been so on edge that I blew up and slugged him good." He continues to knead his hands and taps one foot rapidly on the floor.

"Yeah, you look pretty twitchy." I pat him on the shoulder. "It sounds like all of the—all of the people like you have been having problems lately. You just need to take your mind off it."

He rolls his eyes. "Easier said than done. You don't know what it's like. You're not like me."

"No, but I've been with my brother every single day since he was infected. Trust me. Sometimes you just need someone to talk to and take your mind off things."

He eyes me doubtfully. His gray irises are still rimmed with a yellow tint. Hawk had been there once—the one and only time he acted out. His green eyes had been tinted and he transformed and attacked me. That was the first time I felt the power in me. My strength blossomed out of nowhere and I was able to hold him back. I talked him down until he finally relaxed and was able to shift back. He's been in control since that moment on. Well, up until he took off that one night when we got to Moose Lake.

Ben's the same now and if nothing's done he'll lash out like Hawk had. It's my chance to do some good. I shift in my seat so I'm facing him.

"Okay, here's how it's going to go," I say and lean forward

with my elbows resting on my thighs. "I'm going to ask you a series of questions and you're going to answer as honestly as you can."

"What is this? A therapy session?" He shakes his head and finishes what's left on his tray.

"Sure, why not, if therapy sessions involve loads of *awesome*."

He actually laughs this time. "What?" He shifts around so his arm is slung across the back of his chair and he's facing me.

"Okay, here we go." I clasp my hands together in front of me. "Here's the first question. You ready?"

The smile slowly spreading on his face puts a little color in his cheeks. "I'm ready."

"Who would you bet on in a fight? Unicorns or giants?"

"You're joking."

"No, I'm completely serious. I used to do this with my brother all the time." I slap his knee. "Come on. Don't be scared."

He narrows his eyes and purses his lips as he thinks. "Unicorns."

"Really? Unicorns? I thought giants smashing things into splinters would be more your thing."

"You kidding? It's a horse with a sword on its head that can impale its enemies."

I hold up my hands. "I concede. Good choice."

"Next question." He leans forward eagerly and has stopped tapping his foot but he's still wringing his hands.

"Who would you rather play poker against? A vampire or a berserker?"

When he laughs this time he throws his head back. "Who comes up with these kinds of questions?"

"Crazy awesome people like me." I tap my chest twice with

my fist. "Come on. Vampire or berserker? Who do you think you could beat in a card game? Or do you just suck at card games?"

"Hey!" He points in my face. "I will have you know I once won a pretty *epic* poker tournament me and my friends held."

I prop my chin in my hands. "Oh, do tell."

"Okay, so let me set the scene. I had won three rounds and made it into the finale. You wouldn't believe the hand I got. It seemed rubbish at first but then . . ." Ben rattles on for a good five minutes and I interject with the appropriate reactions to each twist in the plot. He stops wringing his hands and talks animatedly. The color is back in his face and he looks loads better than when he had first walked into the room.

"So you beat your friends," I say. "But you still haven't told me if you'd rather play a vampire or a berserker! Stop stalling, Ben."

"I don't even know what a berserker is!" He throws up his hands.

Hmm, I guess I tend to forget how little everyone else knows of monsters. They're just stories to people like Ben. Even if he is a werewolf, he doesn't know about the rest of the universe.

"It's a rage monster," I say and puff out my arms to convey the size of one blown up into full red-rage mode. I keep poking taunts at him to keep him talking. He laughs and I laugh and I'm pretty sure he's completely forgotten he's sitting in detention because the disease inside him made him act out. That taint is gone and if I look closely, I can almost see the yellow in his eyes thinning.

"Stop, stop!" he says after a long heated debate and is rocking in his chair because he's laughing so hard. "I can't argue this with you! Bloodsucker or rage machine, what difference does it make if they can play poker?"

"Oh, they're both cheaters," I say and lightly punch him in the shoulder. "Only, if you beat a berserker it's likely to tear your arms out of your sockets."

His laughter slowly dies but his smile remains. "You're not bad, Phoenix."

"Oh, good." I wipe the back of my hand across my forehead. "Thanks for clearing that up. I was really worried."

It's his turn to punch me in the shoulder. "I'm serious."

The door to the classroom opens and Captain Krush comes in with a half-eaten sub in his hand. He points it at the pair of us.

"Hey, I said no fun," he says around a mouthful and goes to his desk. "What were you two laughing about anyway? I could hear you cackling all the way down the hall."

"Hey, Captain," Ben says. "What kind of monster do you think you could beat in a poker game?"

"Intriguing proposition. Let me think." He chews thoughtful and doesn't even bother to ask why on earth we're talking about monsters and poker in the first place. Once he swallows he says, "A sea serpent like in the story about Hercules."

"Oh, come on!" I say and slap a hand on my desk, shaking my empty lunch tray. "A sea serpent? How is a sea serpent supposed to play poker?"

"Exactly," Captain Krush says and winks. "It can't because it doesn't have any *hands*." He glances at his wristwatch. "Any way, no time to debate the point. Detention's almost over. Now, I hope I've stressed enough how very wrong you two were during this detention and urge you not to get into any more fights."

At the mention of fights, Ben starts to wring his hands again, undoing all the good that happened over the last forty minutes.

"Yeah, you've gotten a reputation now," Ben says to me.

I point to myself. "Me? What?"

"I've even heard it," Captain Krush says from his desk. "Kicking butt, taking names—the girl with the legendary bird name. Oh, and that last part I just added. No one else has said that bit. Apparently no one knows what a phoenix is anymore. It's just a city nowadays."

Ben waves him off and starts tapping his foot again. "Nah, all the people that play Mystic Universe do." He turns to me and whispers rather loudly. "They think your name is pretty cool."

The bell rings and we both stand reluctantly. Ben sighs and I can clearly make out the bags under his eyes. We walk back to the cafeteria together to deposit our trays. He's looking downcast again and twitches a bit. What is going on around here? Once at our lockers, I grasp his arm before he can move away.

"Hey, if you ever need a friend," I say, "you know where to find me. Any time."

He nods and pulls away to head in the opposite direction. "Yeah. Sure."

Like a switch has been flipped, Ben is back to being a haunted, unstable werewolf. And I've failed again.

The rest of the school day passes in a hazy blur. I'm super tired and can't concentrate. When Captain Krush calls on me in my last class of the day I can barely even pronounce Lycaon for our mythology discussion.

"Lycaon?" he repeats back to me. I nod and he goes into a whirlwind as usual. Apparently he knows the story in and out. I don't really need to participate and fall into a stupor in the back of the room while he waves his arms around, asking questions of students up front. They talk about the myths of werewolves for a while, some other Greek legend involving the mother of monsters, and a mention of *Love Moon* garners a few laughs.

When the bell finally rings, I'm a sloth getting up from my chair.

"You aren't driving yourself home are you?" Captain Krush calls to me.

"No," I slur back and he gives me a thumbs up.

I find Hawk and we walk into the parking lot. Jefferson's truck is nowhere to be found. I try to call him but it goes to voicemail.

Hawk shrugs. "We could hop the bus?"

"*No.*" School is enough of a nightmare but the bus is a whole different animal.

"Then what? Walk?"

I throw up my hands and take a seat on the curb, then put my head on my arms curled over my knees. "Just let me sleep right here."

A car rumbles close by and from the sound of it, stops directly in front of us. Hawk nudges me with the toe of his shoe. "Hey, it's the deputy."

I jerk my head up and sure enough Deputy Graham is leaning towards us from the driver's seat of a regular gray sedan, not his squad car.

"Deputy?" Hawk says and bends down to see him through the passenger side window.

"Jefferson asked me to come pick you two up. There's a situation." He pushes the door open. Hawk and I both reach for it at the same time and get stuck in the doorframe together. Hawk holds out his palm and plants his other hand in a fist on top of it. I growl under my breath and play a game of rock, paper, scissors for the front seat. Hawk beats my rock with paper and slides into the front, sticking his tongue out. I shove the side of his head before getting into the back. Deputy Graham shakes his head and puts the sedan into gear.

"So, what's going on?" Hawk asks from the front. I put a foot on the back of his seat and push.

"That Matt Jones kid might not have been the only one bitten last night. Two of his friends have gone missing. Their parents called the sheriff's office to report they've been gone since yesterday evening. Jefferson's covering part of the state park since that's where Matt thinks they were last."

"Why would he think that?" I interject.

The deputy gives a cold laugh. "Because he was going to meet his buddies in the park to have themselves a little illegal drinking party. Kids these days . . . Anyway, Jefferson was hoping you two might be able to cover another section and I'll drive on the trails, see if I can find anything."

I groan and settle back into my seat. Of course this had to happen now. More people bitten, more people missing, and I'm functioning with half a brain.

"You all right back there?" the deputy asks and finds me in the rearview mirror.

"Super. I'm running on hardly an hour of sleep. Could we get some caffeine, please, before we go racing through the woods? I'd really appreciate that, kind sir."

He chuckles and salutes. "Yes, ma'am."

We swing by a coffee shop called Java Jitters and the deputy is kind enough to buy Hawk and me large double espressos. I thank him profusely and the stimulated energy wakes me up enough so I can function. We head out of town and cross the interstate where the woods are all we can see. We take a quick right and enter the small parking lot for the Moose Lake State Park. Jefferson's truck is already here.

"Why were those guys out here in the first place?" I ask. "Drinking at home wasn't cool enough or something?"

"Oh, a lot of teenagers come out here for parties and to drink where they think no one will catch them."

"Lot of good that did them," I mutter.

Deputy Graham cuts the engine and opens his door. "Wait here a second. I'm going to have a word with the park ranger."

I guzzle the rest of the scalding contents of my espresso, my brain buzzing. How long that will last, I have no clue. Hawk and I step out to stretch our legs and roll our shoulders. The sky's overcast and darkening by the second.

Hawk grimaces. "Smells like it's going to rain."

"Well, that's just great. We better get moving then if we want to find anything and not get completely soaked in the process."

A howling wind answers in reply blowing cold rain droplets into our faces. Deputy Graham emerges from the small park headquarters and walks to the trunk of his car. We follow him and he lifts the lid to reveal an arsenal inside. He glances at the sky then passes us two identical handguns. He drops out one of the magazines and shows it to us.

"Tranquilizers only." He snaps the magazine back into place then gives us each a spare as well. "The range is crap with these though. You've got to be pretty close, within fifteen yards probably. And do *not* accidentally shoot yourself. Humans can overdose easy on these but they're just the right dose for werewolves."

Hawk clears his throat and takes the offered pistol. "Right. I'll keep that in mind."

The deputy pulls out a couple of flashlights and walkie talkies for us as well, then shuts the trunk and spreads out a map of the park on top of it. He snatches a red pen from his pocket and starts to circle a wide swath of area. He taps the circle with the end of the pen.

"Jefferson is out covering this area. You two take this section." He makes another big circle to the southeast. "There are campsites around the edge of the lake that way but it should be mostly empty this time of year. If you see anything or need assistance, give a holler." He holds up a walkie talkie for emphasis and twists the dial. We quickly test them and Jefferson buzzes in as well with nothing to report.

"What about you?" I ask.

He runs a finger along some marked trails going around the lake. "I'm going to borrow a four-wheeler from the ranger and take a quick loop around. Okay, that's it. Be careful out there and good luck. Oh, and don't let anybody catch you carrying those pistols. You're still under twenty-one and aren't supposed to have them."

With that friendly little warning, he jogs to the rear of the office building and disappears. I fold the map into a square and stick it in my pocket before tucking the pistol into the waistband of my pants and buttoning my military jacket up the rest of the way.

"Ready?" I ask. Hawk nods, having done the same, and we march out in the direction we were instructed along a narrow gravel road. It's quiet out here with only birdcalls for company. We keep the silence and head deeper into the trees.

I touch the walkie talkie attached to my belt now and then to assure myself it's there. The woods are too quiet for my liking. I'm still getting used to the country where I'm surrounded by trees and a hush instead of sky scrapers and the sounds of humans close by at all times. The left fork in the road takes us down a hill and to a wide gravel parking lot alongside the lake. A couple of canoes are stacked up next to a small dock. The waves lap at the nearly nonexistent beach and a breeze rattles the dead leaves above us.

Hawk sniffs at the air a few times then jerks his head to the left so we keep moving. It's slow going, scanning the ground for tracks or waiting for Hawk to catch a scent. He eventually guides us off the gravel road and into the trees following some trail I can't see.

"If they were bitten at the same time as Matt," I whisper, "would they really still be here? It sounds like Matt went home right after. They could have done the same."

He shrugs. "Either way, there must be a trail here. If they were disoriented they might not have gone too far or maybe they went seeking out others like them."

"The black wolf."

He nods and a chill goes down my spine. That's been happening a lot lately. You'd think after all this time living among impossible creatures, searching for the same kind of thing wouldn't scare me. But this isn't just a couple of werewolves in the wild. This is personal and more dangerous than we had first suspected. If the same thing is really happening again like in 1996, then everyone in town is in danger. Our parents' murderer could be lurking out in these very woods.

I keep looking over my shoulder and click on my flashlight as the clouds grow thicker and darker. Beneath the trees it's already twilight. Hawk does the same and our beams scan the underbrush and yellow grass. The wind picks up and the trees whistle and creak. My cheeks and nose are already ice cold when it begins to sprinkle.

Static crackles over my walkie talkie and I pull it from my belt.

Deputy Graham's voice comes over a bit distorted. "Come in. I found dozens of wolf tracks crossing about fifty yards south of the campground area. They look pretty fresh."

"I'll head your way," Jefferson responds. "Masons, keep checking your area."

"Copy that," I say and clip the radio onto my belt.

We keep walking, Hawk stopping every now and then to sniff closer at the dirt like a hound. We've gone about a mile through the woods heading southeast when Hawk stops again and sniffs at the wind as tiny droplets of water prick my face. He frowns and messes the back of his hair.

"What's wrong?" I ask.

"I could have sworn I just smelled Ben."

"What would he be doing out here?"

"Well, that's the question isn't it?" He keeps rubbing the back of his neck and stares out at the lake. We're on the top of a hill and it's just visible in the distance. The rain picks up even more and I start to shiver in my jacket that clearly isn't warm or dry enough for this weather.

Hawk spins around without warning and draws the pistol from his waistband. I follow his motion a fraction too slow. He lets out a shout as a great big gray wolf slams into him from the side. I'm clipped in the shoulder and stumble sideways, unable to raise my pistol in time. Hawk and the wolf going tumbling and roll end over end down the hill. Halfway in their descent another werewolf rushes out of the trees to chase after them.

"Hawk!" I shout. I'm so focused on the three of them that I don't see the one directly beside me.

I pull up my pistol but too late. It lunges. I let off a shot but the tranquilizer goes high over its brownish head. A cry escapes me as it bites down on my forearm and its teeth tear right through the sleeve of my jacket. The werewolf jerks its head backwards and I can feel every single one of its sharp teeth rip through my skin. I cry out in pain but have just enough sense to stick the pistol into the fur of its throat with my other hand and fire twice.

The wolf whines and its grip loosens. I pry its jaws off me and cradle my arm to my chest. It teeters for a moment, sways side to side, then collapses in a cloud of dry leaves. I breath hard between my clenched teeth and groan through the pain of the bite. I get to my knees and look down the hill for Hawk but he and the other werewolves are gone.

I shuffle on my knees to a thick oak tree and settle on the roots with my back to it. Wheezing and my fingers going numb, I fumble with the walkie talkie on my belt and press the speak button.

"Jefferson," I force out through gritted teeth. "I need help."

"What's wrong?"

I groan and try to focus through the burning pain in my arm. "We were attacked. Hawk's gone. I don't know where he is."

"I'm coming right now. You gotta tell me where you are."

Rolling my head one way then the other to locate some kind of marker, I spot the top of a camper in the distance behind me. "I'm just north of the campers I think. I can still see the lake from here. Hurry."

"I'm on my way," he says.

"What about Deputy Graham?"

There's a long pause before he answers. "I can't find him."

"What?"

"I found his four-wheeler but he's gone."

I lean my head back against the trunk of the oak and grimace. This is terrible timing. I'm about to start panicking. I need help but maybe it's already too late for me. "We can't just leave him out there."

"Do you think you can hold on by yourself?" he asks.

"I . . . I don't know. But we can't leave Graham out there alone."

"Phoenix, are you hurt?" he demands.

I bite my lower lip trying to distract myself from the pain spreading in my arm but it doesn't work. "I . . ."

"Are you hurt?"

"Jefferson, I've been bitten."

18

Trying to peel back the edge of my sleeve to inspect my arm is much more difficult and painful than I'm hoping it'll be. The material isn't exactly stretchy and doesn't want to give. I grimace and pant and pull back the edge of my sleeve one burning inch at a time. Blood runs down my arm and soaks into the chest of my jacket where I clutch it to myself.

"I'm coming straight to you," Jefferson says and the loud growl of an engine causes reverb through the speaker. He must be taking the deputy's four-wheeler. "Hang on. Keep your pistol up."

"Yeah, yeah, just hurry," I growl. I settle my injured arm against my stomach and set the walkie talkie next to it to free up my other hand to hold the pistol at the ready, balancing the butt of it on top of my upraised knee.

The rain and wind picks up. I'm not really protected by the oak I'm sitting against so I'm quickly soaked through and water drips into my eyes. At least the cold numbs the surface pain in my arm.

My teeth start to chatter but all I can think about is Hawk. Is he okay? I know he can take care of himself but if a pack ganged up on him, so help me . . . I thump my head against the trunk of the tree. I'm supposed to have his back and I let him down. I should get up and look for him. Who cares if I get turned into a werewolf? My brother is out there somewhere and in trouble. I can't leave him alone.

I set the pistol in the wet grass beside me and pick up my walkie. "Jefferson, I have to find my brother."

"Phoenix, stay put."

"He's my *brother.*" My throat feels raw. "I can't lose him."

"You're not going to lose him. He's a tough kid."

"He's all I've got, Jefferson."

"Stop it, Phoenix! Getting yourself killed out there isn't going to help him either. Don't get yourself hurt any worse."

I clip the walkie to my belt, pick up the pistol, and push myself up using the trunk of the oak. Breathing hard, I stagger to the top of the hill. It's gotten so dark that it's hard to make out anything apart from the tree trunks.

"Dang it," I mutter and shove the pistol into the waistband of my pants. I yank the flashlight out of my pocket and gingerly hold it in my injured hand, then hoist the pistol in my good hand. I carefully start to make my way down the rather steep hill. The flashlight beam sweeps over the underbrush but can't illuminate it all. I slip on a rock but at least I fall backwards. The breath is knocked out of me and I wince.

Deciding on a different approach, I scoot down ever so

slowly until I reach the bottom then push myself upright. I scan the ground but it's hard to make out anything. I'm no tracker like Hawk. My chest constricts and it gets harder to breathe.

"Hawk!" I shout and spin in a circle. "Hawk!"

The pain in my arm starts to intensify. I wonder if it's the pain of the transformation starting to sweep over me or the magic in my blood trying to fight the disease. I'm suddenly terrified—if I change how can I possibly protect Hawk anymore? Or what if this simply kills me? That seems more likely because I'm burning up and the pain is staggering. It's building up and I groan, falling to my knees in the wet soil. I bend over and breathe harshly. No, this can't happen. I can't change, not now. I don't want to die either.

A rumble approaches then stops. Branches snap and I hear loud shuffling. I force myself to straighten enough to raise my pistol and squint through the downpour.

"Jefferson? That better be you!"

A flashlight beam points directly at my face and hurts my eyes.

"It's me!" Jefferson shouts. "Don't shoot!"

I let the pistol drop to the ground and the pain in my arm grows so unbearable that I double up and fall to the side. Jefferson rushes over and kneels beside me. He tries to peel back my sleeve but it pulls at my feverish skin. I let out a loud cry and he stops.

"I need you to stand, Phoenix."

"Argh . . ." I squeeze my eyes shut. "I don't think I can."

"I've got you. Come on."

He pulls my good arm across his shoulders and hauls me

to my feet. He wraps his other arm around my waist to keep me upright and starts to walk me forward. My toes catch the ground and I stumble along almost blindly.

"Hawk's still out there," I manage to say.

"We'll find him after we treat that arm."

"No! I've got to . . . got . . ." A wave of dizziness sweeps over me. This isn't a typical reaction, is it? I know the werewolf disease can be painful, but this? This is torture. The woods spin and I slump forward. The world begins to hush as if someone has put headphones over my ears. My legs are hoisted up and Jefferson carries me in his arms back to the road.

I don't remember being set on the four-wheeler, getting in the truck, or driving away from the park. I don't remember returning to the cabin or being set on a mattress but it must have happened because when I wake up I'm lying on a cot in Jefferson's barn. Dusty rafters come into focus above my head, there's a smell of hay and alcohol, and my jacket's gone, replaced by a worn quilt blanket. I'm shaking and my whole body is feverish. Jefferson's voice reaches me from downstairs.

"Yeah, she's all right . . . I took her back to the barn. Can you make it? Okay, we'll be waiting. It's going to be fine."

I push myself onto my side and sit up. Jefferson walks up the creaky wooden stairs and once he sees me rushes over to grasp my shoulder.

"You need to take it easy," he warns.

"Where's my brother?" I mumble.

"I just talked to him on the phone. He's okay. He's coming back right now." Jefferson grabs a chair behind him and pulls it up to the side of the cot. "What about you? How are you feeling?"

"Like I've got a fever."

He places a weathered hand on my forehead and frowns. "You're burning up."

I run a hand over my frazzled hair and close my eyes so I can press the cooler back of my hand against my burning eyelids. "Is that normal? I can't remember."

"Well, sort of. After being bitten it takes about half an hour for the disease to spread through the entire body, causing a fever and intense pain. For a normal kid, if a serum injection is given within that narrow window, it can keep them in their right mind before they first change."

I hang my head and rub the back of my neck. "For a *normal* kid."

He clears his throat. "With you being a Blessed, there's no telling what's going to happen. You could turn into a werewolf and the natural magic in your blood could make it so you don't have to take injections. Or . . . well, we'll just have to wait and see what happens. I'm sorry."

Or the two parts of disease and magic might rip me apart from the inside and kill me. The IMS might like to think of the werewolf problem as a minor thing since the invention of the serum, but the disease itself is still one of the most dangerous things out there to a Blessed.

I exhale slowly and trace my fingers over the thick white bandage Jefferson put on my arm. "It's not your fault."

"Yes, it is," he says quietly. He bows his head and clasps his hands together in front of him. "I had a chance to stop this fourteen years ago but I couldn't. I couldn't save anyone."

For the first time Jefferson sounds fragile. He hasn't ever shown much emotion, unless you count anger and grouchiness. He's vulnerable and there's moisture gathering in his small eyes.

"You mentioned you lost people the last time," I say. "Who did you lose?"

He rubs his hands together slowly and doesn't look up. "My wife. It was around the same time your parents were attacked. A werewolf came into our house while I wasn't there. I, uh . . ." He pauses to hastily wipe at his eyes and sniffs loudly. "My wife was killed and my daughter was bitten. After it happened, despite how much I tried to protect her, my daughter disappeared along with the others."

And there it is—the cause for Jefferson's hatred of werewolves. I would be inclined to hate them just as much if it weren't for the fact my brother is one. With the serum cure, I've learned werewolves can be good and bad just like regular people. They aren't all one and the same but unfortunately, if the current situation is any evidence, they can be held under some dark sway.

"I'm so sorry," I murmur.

He pats me on the shoulder twice then walks away. I'm left alone which isn't good because then all I can do is think. I can't imagine what my life will be like if I change. Then there's that other possibility hanging on the horizon. I might not live to see Thursday. Hawk would be alone. I clutch my wounded arm to my chest and will it not to happen but, being the pessimist that I am, I start forming plans in my mind. I need to tell Hawk it's going to be okay. I should make some kind of arrangement so my brother always has a home somewhere. I should call Witty too, but I don't. What would I even say? I've been on a mission for three days and I've already screwed up so badly that I'm going to kick the bucket?

I stay curled up on the cot and pull the quilt up to my chin. I shake with fever chills and my eyes droop shut more than once. That short bit of unconsciousness was the most rest I've gotten in thirty-six hours and I'm burned out. The pain through my arm won't let me sleep though, and I use that to keep me awake until Hawk shows up. I need to know he's okay.

I don't know how much time passes until I finally hear the door creak open downstairs. There are muted voices and then someone is thundering up the stairs. Hawk emerges on the landing and when he spots me he comes to a halt. He's drenched and his hair is plastered to his forehead. Mud is dabbled on his face and he's pale but he doesn't look injured.

"Phoenix." The word comes out in a rush and he races over to wrap me up in a hug. I wince as my arm is jostled but I don't pull back. I tuck my chin into his shoulder and my face twists up. I keep trying to fight back the terror inside me but in my brother's arms I start to fall apart. I hold onto him with my good arm and heave a shuddering breath.

"I'm scared," I whisper.

He runs a hand over my hair. "You're going to be okay. I'm here. It's my turn to watch over you now."

I hiccup back a sob and take a deep breath. I'm not going to cry. I'm not going to succumb. A few tears escape anyhow and I wipe my face on my brother's already wet jacket.

"I hope that's not snot," he whispers.

A sharp laugh rips out of me and subsides into crazed giggling for a few seconds. Count on my brother to make me laugh even now. He pulls back and grasps both of my shoulders to look me directly in the eye.

"We're going to be okay," he says. "I want you to say it back to me, Phoenix. You need to believe it. Go on."

I swallow past the lump in my throat. "We're going to be okay."

"See? The truth will set you free." He offers a smile and I try to return it but my mouth keeps turning into a frown.

Jefferson comes up the stairs. "Can you watch her until I get back?"

"Where are you going?" I ask.

"Deputy Graham is still missing out there somewhere. I have to try to find him." He picks a flashlight off the table and twists it in his hands a few times. "I put in a call to the IMS for backup. They're supposed to be sending in a team tomorrow morning to assist. You two stay put." He reaches into his waistband and pulls out one of the tranquilizer handguns which he leaves on the table. "Just in case."

Then he leaves us behind in the barn. The rain drums against the roof and a draft blows in through the wall. Hawk peels off his wet jacket and starts up a space heater near my cot. He runs to the cabin for a minute and returns with a few more blankets and my *Go Fire Sprites!* sweatshirt.

"Thanks," I murmur. He sits cross-legged on the cot next to me and I lean against his side. "What time is it?"

"Almost midnight I think."

"Shouldn't I be going to Underground or something?"

He rests his head against the top of mine. "There's nothing they can do for you there except watch."

I guess I already knew that but needed to ask the question anyway. I close my eyes and mutter, "Do we ever get any sleep around here?"

He laughs under his breath. "How about you sleep and I'll keep watch?"

I don't say my fears out loud. The irrational part of me doesn't want to fall asleep because I fear I might wake up a twisted monster or never wake up at all. But I'm exhausted and I ease off right then and there.

When I wake again I'm lying down and hear fast shuffling, the cocking of a gun, and labored breathing.

Hawk stands a few paces away, the tranquilizer gun hoisted in his hands and aimed at the stairs. Staggering up the steps comes a reddish timber wolf which, if I'm not mistaken, is the same one that has been dogging me. There's a bloody gash on its shoulder and it's limping.

"Don't come any closer," Hawk warns. "If you want our help, you have to transform for me to trust you."

The werewolf whines and carefully lies down. It rests its head on the floorboards and curls its tail around itself. Water and blood drip onto the floor.

"That's real cute," Hawk growls. "Transform. If you can't, then I know you're like the rest and there's no way you're getting any closer to my sister. I'll put you down first."

The wolf huffs and lays its ears flat before curling up even tighter upon itself. I sit up, my head swimming in the fever spell, and watch as the wolf starts to shift. It whines as its fur tucks into itself, the muzzle and tail recede, the arms and legs stretch out, and the torso narrows. Within thirty seconds, the wolf whine changes to a human's cry and a boy is curled up on the floor in the same black shirt I saw him in earlier today.

He slowly uncurls and his tortured gray eyes lock onto mine.

"Ben?"

19

Ben sits up and sucks down air like he's been running hard. There's a great bloody bite on his shoulder and a terrible gash on his right arm. He's dripping wet and his dark hair is plastered to his skin.

"What . . . *you* are the wolf that was stalking me?" I say and point my good hand at him.

The present circumstances pass me by in my indignation. Hawk on the other hand lowers the gun and kneels to inspect Ben's injuries.

"Why did you come here, Ben?" he growls. "You should have gone to the hospital."

"I wanted to make sure you two were okay," he pants and clutches at his bleeding shoulder. "You disappeared during the fight."

"Wait . . ." I frown and think back to the state park. I remember Hawk rolling down the hill fighting the one werewolf when another went chasing after. I can't be sure but it could have been reddish. "That was you in the park?"

He nods and winces. "I followed you out there—"

"Oh, good to know you're still stalking me."

"I wasn't *stalking* you."

"Yeah, following me around wherever I go is basically the definition of stalking," I bite back. "You haven't been watching me sleep too, have you?"

Hawk holds a hand out to me. "Would you shut up for a second? Ben saved my life back there." I roll my eyes and he focuses on Ben again. "Why were you following us?"

"I've been sick, man. I told you that." His eyes flicker to me. "But I felt like I could control it better when she was around. She's got some kind of . . . I don't know, *aura*. She's different. I wanted to know why, so yeah, I was watching her. Sue me."

I don't know how I feel about that. Creeped out is probably the best way to put it. I hug my good arm around myself. "Please tell me you didn't get yourself into detention just to talk to me."

He glares at me this time. "No, that was a lucky accident."

"Huh. *Lucky*. Whatever." I shake my head.

"Anyway, I saw you two get attacked so I jumped in to help." He lets out a groan when he tries to move his arm. "Lot of good that did me."

"Stalker, creeper, hero, whatever," Hawk says. "We need to get you to the hospital but Jefferson's got the truck."

"We can't ask him to come back either," I add. "What he's doing is too important. We've got to call your mom."

"Ughhh." Ben rolls his head around. "No, just let me die instead."

Considering what my own circumstances are, I don't find

it very funny. Hawk pulls out his cell phone and shoves it into Ben's hand.

"Make the call," he says darkly, "or I'll give you something to whine about."

Ben rips the phone away from Hawk and jabs at the buttons. He glowers the whole time as he tries to explain to his mother where he is and what's wrong. I can hear her shouting through the phone from here. When he finally hangs up, he tosses the phone hard at Hawk but my brother catches it easily.

"She's on her way," he mutters.

"Good," Hawk says. "Then while we're waiting you're going to tell me everything you know about that park, who those other wolves were, and what the heck is going on around here. Everything you know. Go."

"I don't know what to tell you."

"Anything," Hawk says. "You tell me something we can use."

Ben starts to lean to the side clutching his shoulder and shakes his head. Hawk suddenly grabs him under the open wound and squeezes until Ben cries out.

"Hawk!" I shout. "That's enough!"

Instead of letting go he ignores me and keeps hurting Ben. He leans in and bares his teeth, snarling. "My sister's been bitten and I want to know who did it. I want to know who was out there tonight. What happened to Matt's buddies? What happened to Deputy Graham? You've got to tell me something!"

I scramble to my feet and lurch towards the pair of them. Ben's mouth is open in a silent scream but Hawk is unrelenting. I grab my brother's arm and wrench him back. I misjudge the amount of strength needed and end up flattening him to the floor. He lets out a huff and struggles to get up but I hold him down.

"Are you out of your mind?" I hiss. A wave of dizziness hits me again and I'm breathless. The room starts to sway and I'm falling. Hawk catches me before I hit the floor and holds me upright. We stay that way for a long moment while my head evens out. The exertion has made the fire in my arm kick back into life and I'm panting against the inferno crawling under my skin. Hawk pushes himself upright so we're sitting awkwardly on the floor but I'm too tired to move anymore.

"You've really been bitten?" Ben asks quietly.

I tap the white bandage on my arm. "What does it look like, Sherlock?"

"But you'll be okay. You'll just turn into one of us."

"You idiot," Hawk snaps. I put a hand on his arm to try to keep him under control. Funny—this situation is usually reversed. "She could die."

"What?" Ben waves his hand gesturing to the pair of us. "It's just a bite. It'll heal."

"No." Hawk sighs and rests his chin on top of my head. "No, it might not."

His words are hollow and wistful. My heart hammers in my chest as it really starts to sink in. I haven't transformed yet and it would have happened within the first couple of hours. If I'm not changing then that means . . .

"They were a couple of boys from school," Ben says, breaking the silence. "The one that bit Phoenix must have been Jason."

Why does that name sound familiar?

"Why did they attack us?" Hawk asks.

"Why have any of us been doing anything? It's that calling in our head. Haven't you heard it?"

Hawk clenches his hand and I feel the rest of his body tense too. "There was . . . something."

Ben sighs. "I don't know what else to call it. It's not like there's a voice in my head or anything but I keep getting these urges like there's something I'm supposed to be doing. At times it makes me so angry I've got to—" He throws a fake punch with his good arm. "Sometimes it's gotten so bad that I blackout and when I come to I don't have a clue what's just happened."

"What about the missing people?" Hawk presses.

"I don't know. I'm sorry. If they're missing, maybe it's because they've been changed and followed the call somewhere."

"I guess that would make sense if we had any idea what this 'call' was." Hawk grasps at the back of his hair and lets out a low growl. "It'd be nice to know *where* the missing people are going if they are following some kind of instructions."

"What have all the werewolves been doing?" I say. "They've been spreading the disease. Those people could be missing because they're widening the field and going to other towns." I shake my brother's arm. "Hawk, when you ran off that one time do you remember why?"

He shakes his head slowly. "I just knew I had to find someone. I don't know who."

"I bet we can guess. The black wolf. He's got to be controlling the werewolves like some mega alpha werewolf."

Ben looks startled and jabs a thumb at his chest. "I've been dreaming about a black wolf. That's got to be it."

"Have you met it?" Hawk asks.

"No. I don't think so. I could have when I blacked out though, I guess."

"Then we've got nothing. Again."

There are four loud knocks on the door downstairs that shake the whole barn and we all jump.

"Where's my son?" Mrs. Ferguson bellows.

"Coming!" Hawk shouts. He helps Ben to his feet and they make their way carefully down the stairs. I return to my cot and lay exhausted. Mrs. Ferguson shouts some more below but her words are incoherent noise to me.

I close my eyes and try to think around the pain and lack of sleep. I try to listen past the shouts and wait for some urge to grab hold of me, but there's nothing in the darkness. Of course, why would I hear a call when I haven't turned? Sure, I've been bitten but nothing else. The shouting stops and a car engine rumbles in the distance. The stairs creak and I open my eyes. Hawk comes up rubbing his hands together anxiously and his mouth presses into a thin line.

"Now what?" I sigh.

"Now we wait, I guess. You should get some sleep."

"Yeah." I almost laugh and want to cry. "I'll probably get some permanent sleep soon enough."

"*Don't.* Don't you dare. Don't you ever think like that." He glowers at me and he's furious but his voice cracks when he speaks. "You've always been the strong one. You never allowed me to give up or give in. Don't you dare stop now. You fight this and you keep fighting. You're all I've got, Phoenix."

He paces away from me and around the backside of the table. I watch him and decide I want to ask for something I can't have.

"Can you bring me Mom's jacket?" I whisper.

He doesn't even hesitate. He cracks open our parents' evidence box and pulls out the plastic bag with the leather bomber jacket. There's not a second's hesitation for worry of Jefferson's inevitable reprimand. He tears apart the tape, strips the bag away, and holds it up in front of himself. We both stare at it. Hawk presses it to his face and squeezes his eyes tight as he breathes in the smell of it.

Walking stiffly, he comes to the cot and drapes the jacket over me. I pull it up higher so I can smell it too. I inhale old leather and the faintest flowery smell of perfume in the lining of the collar. I picture my mother wearing it, fighting the good fight alongside my father, and being every bit the heroes I imagine them to be.

I want to fight to the very end like my parents did. They died protecting us. Now it's my turn to do whatever it takes to fight the unavoidable end and stay here where I belong—with my brother.

A song starts to play from my mp3 player that Hawk must have fetched from the house earlier. It's our parents' song telling me that everything's going to be okay. I fall asleep to the music played on repeat, my brother's hand wrapped around mine.

~

My eyes open to warm light filtering in between the boards of the roof, down the dusty rafters, and soaking into the blanket across my feet. I get a sense something is wrong. I'm awake. It's daylight.

I'm not dead.

I am NOT dead.

That thought bounces around inside my head and takes me two full minutes to absorb it. I made it through the night. I survived. I wiggle my fingers and wait for extreme pain or something worse to happen but I'm normal. I'm still me. I didn't even change. It's like the disease is gone completely but that can't be right. No one's ever done that before. No one has simply resisted, not changed, and come out the other side. Okay, so something must have changed. Do I still have all my fingers and toes? Are my hands now paws? Does my nose have whiskers? I absent-mindedly pat myself down as if I'm going to find an extra appendage or a tail. No, it's just me. Seventeen-year-old Phoenix Mason with a snarky attitude, obsession with movies, and sudden urges to dance.

Ouch. My arm still hurts. Dang it. Why couldn't that have healed over? Well, that's a good sign I guess. No accelerated healing like a werewolf. I sniff but the barn smells the same as before. No super nose either. Wait, I do smell coffee.

I sit up and find Hawk asleep with his head on the edge of the cot beside me, his hand extended towards mine. The song has stopped playing and I really can smell coffee. I sense I'm being watched.

Jefferson sits in the only seat at the table, a cup of coffee held between his hands, hunched forward with his elbows on his knees, and stares at me. There's confusion in his face, sadness, and darkness in his eyes. I can't be real is what his expression is telling me. I can't be real and this is some trick.

"You're alive," he murmurs.

A smile bursts on my face. "I'm alive!"

"That's not possible."

"Well, it is now."

Hawk stirs but doesn't wake. I'm impatient so I grab his shoulders and shake him until his hair's flopping. He jerks to and freezes when he sees me. Then he throws his arms out and smiles wide.

"Fifi! You didn't die!" He wraps me up in a hug and we're both laughing, giddy little children. We're cackling madly and I'm on a sort of sugar rush. But over Hawk's shoulder I see Jefferson frozen stiff in his chair, eyes dark and his mouth a thin smile.

"Just like a real phoenix," he says drily. "But this is still impossible."

We pull apart and Hawk sits on the floor with his back to the mattress. I sit cross-legged on the bed and tug my mother's jacket onto my shoulders.

"You keep saying that, but I'm proof that it's not." I hold my hands out, palms up to show him nothing's changed. "I'm fine."

"There is no cure, Phoenix. Do you have any idea how long I've searched for one?" He sets his coffee cup on the table and looks everywhere except at me and Hawk. I think of the story he told me about his daughter. I imagine he would go to the ends of the earth to find his daughter and a way to cure her.

Jefferson stands and paces back and forth before facing me again, gesturing with both hands. "There is no medicine that can cure a magical disease, and other magic only combats other magic. They destroy each other. That's why the serum isn't a true cure. It's just enough magic to stop a portion of the werewolf disease without killing the host. Phoenix, don't you see?"

He rushes over and puts his hands on my shoulders. "What's in your blood cleansed it without killing you in the process."

"But that means—" If they could somehow process my blood and keep the magic intact, mass produce it, and send it out . . . "If it worked for me, maybe it could work for others."

"You could cure the entire werewolf population."

20

I throw on my long-sleeved junior agent shirt. There's no logo but it's specially stitched, flexible, and made for an agent in action. I carefully tug the one sleeve over my bandage to hide it. Over top I wear my mother's bomber jacket. Jefferson wasn't exactly what you would call pleased that Hawk had opened the evidence bag but I think he understood why we did it. He didn't shout at least.

Wearing the clothes that are each a piece of who I am, I walk out to the truck where Hawk is arguing with Jefferson.

"I'm not leaving!" Hawk shouts. His cheeks are flushed and he slams the truck's cab door shut.

"*Yes*, you are," Jefferson counters. "I need you out in the field."

"She almost died last night."

"But she didn't. She's going to be fine but we've still got a werewolf situation, no clue as to the identity of the ringleader, and at least a handful of people missing now." Jefferson opens the door again and tries to pass over the keys. "The IMS backup team will be coming but until they get here, I need you to go out there and do your job. Find the kid that bit your sister. See if he knows who the black wolf is. Can you do that?"

Hawk doesn't move to take the keys. He's upset, shifting from one foot to the other, and I want to help him.

"It's not like we've gotten any great intel from the high school," I interject. "Seems kind of pointless."

"Trust me," Jefferson says. "It's not. Hawk, I need you out there. It's vital. And you know what Phoenix and I are doing is too important. We need all hands on deck."

I guess I can't argue with that. Jefferson's right. We need an eye on the werewolves with everything going down the tubes. What if others have been bitten or are missing? That also makes me worry about leaving Hawk on his own, but testing my blood as soon as possible is something that can't wait either.

"Hawk, I'm fine," I say. "Honest. I'm not going to suddenly drop. Pretty sure we're past that point."

He glares at me for taking Jefferson's side but snatches the keys. "Fine, but you better be sending me texts every hour to let me know you're okay."

I shrug. "Fine, as long as you do the same."

"I'm not the one we should be worried about."

That's debatable but I don't argue. Hawk gets into the truck, cranks the engine, and drives away. As soon as he's gone Jefferson pulls another set of keys out of his pocket, tosses them in the air, and catches them again.

"Let's go," he says and leads the way to the barn. Instead of going in the side door he throws open the massive double doors to reveal the car he's always had covered up. The tarp is gone and I let out a low whistle.

"Why don't you drive *this* beauty instead of that piece of crap truck?" I say.

I don't even know what kind of car it is but it's one of those old muscle cars—a sleek piece of mechanical splendor. Its deep, forest green paint is buffed to an impeccable sheen. The chrome shines and there's not a speck of dirt to deface it. I run a hand over the hood and up to the hardtop. It's obvious this is something Jefferson values since the rest of the cabin and barn are held together by duct tape and rough repairs—they're more practical than pretty. This is on a whole different level.

"She's a 1970 Oldsmobile 442 with four on the floor," Jefferson says with the first real smile I've ever seen him wear. He bends down with hands braced against the roof so he can gaze inside the interior as if he's never seen its pristine beauty before in his life. "This baby's got a 455 big block that's been balanced and blueprinted, and pumps out loads of torque. She can blow the doors off most any factory-equipped car. It's all about the acceleration. I save the Green Monster only for special occasions."

The technical talk goes right over my head but I grin and ask, "The Green Monster?" We look at each other across the hardtop. "You named it?"

"Of course," he says a little defensively.

"Jefferson, I'm not beating you down. I just want you to know how *awesome* you are." I've got that giddy feeling again. I'm no car expert but this thing is making me excited. "This looks fierce."

"Wait until you hear her thunder," Jefferson says with the

same excitement and we swing the doors open at the same time to slide into the bucket seats.

The inside is dressed in black leather and green trim. When Jefferson turns the ignition, it roars to life—it's not the groaning roar of the truck like an old grouch trying to get out of bed. The Green Monster lives up to its name because it's pure thunder in the mountains. I actually laugh as I buckle up.

"Hit it!"

He shifts into first and we roll out of the barn. The Green Monster is a thousand times cooler than the truck could ever attempt to be. We hit the road and the engine revs up along the open stretch. I brace one arm against the door and imagine what we must look like to everyone else driving by. Then I wonder how many of those people looking on are werewolves. Moose Lake is crawling with the supernatural but I can fix it. I can cure my brother. There's still the question of how, but right now I'm just grateful the magic in my blood even exists.

The city appears out of the trees like a curtain being pulled back and we turn onto the main drag. Once through the heart of the city, we turn off onto another county road to the hospital and clinic. The two buildings loom ahead and are clearly the largest in town. The clinic is maybe a fourth the scope of the hospital but it's still a good size for Moose Lake. Jefferson picks a spot next to the doors. It's fairly early and the parking lot is less than half full.

I keep one hand in the pocket of my bomber jacket to keep from jostling my injured arm too much. Jefferson leads the way in through two sets of doors to your typical secretarial counter. The young girl managing the desk smiles.

"Oh hey, Jefferson," she says.

He leans forward with one elbow on the counter. "We're here for Dr. Rosewell. Is she in?"

The girl's smile falters. "She's actually running late. A personal emergency, I'm afraid."

"Nothing too serious I hope."

"No, she said she'll be in as soon as she's done managing it. You're welcome to take a seat and wait until she arrives."

He gives her a casual two-fingered salute and guides me over to a wide waiting room. Chairs line the walls and sit back to back down the middle. Jefferson goes all the way to the far end next to some kiddie play area and we take up two of the comfy chairs.

"Personal emergency doesn't sound good," I say.

"No. No, it doesn't." Jefferson glances at his wristwatch then picks up a *National Geographic* off the table next to him.

I ignore the stack of outdated magazines and instead watch people start to bleed in from the outside one at a time. There's your typical pack of elderly probably in for their checkups and prescriptions refills, but then there are a few teenagers I recognize from school bouncing on their toes, wringing their hands, or fidgeting with their keys. They snap at the lady at the front desk, each and every one, then take a seat only to tap their feet or rap their fingers on the arms of their chairs. Then it's not just teenagers but men and women all in a highly agitated state.

"Jefferson," I say under my breath. He looks up from his magazine. "Are they all . . .?"

He surveys the room bustling with agitation and people pacing. "Yeah, I think so. There's quite a few more werewolves than I know about it seems." He sits up, closes the magazine, and tenses, which makes me tense too. "The infection rate is increasing faster than last time. A lot more."

"Do you think they're all here to see Dr. Rosewell?"

"Must be. She's the only doctor they can see." He turns about in his chair to look out the window at the parking lot then back to the room that's crowded with anxious werewolves. "She's still not here. I'm starting to get a bad feeling about this."

"Yeah, no kidding."

He leans to the side so he can pull his cell phone out of his back pocket. He dials a number, waits while his face draws into a frown, then snaps it shut.

"She's not picking up either," he says under his breath.

The crowd continues to grow and nearly all the seats are taken up. Across the room I spot Mr. Webster, the crabbiest teacher alive, staring at me. He's white knuckling a *Sports Illustrated* and just . . . staring. There's a shift in the room and I find a lot of eyes watching me, as if they know what I am. I could be the cure to the disease—and, in their eyes as pawns of the black wolf, a threat to his power.

"Jefferson."

He tosses the magazine onto the table. "Yeah, we're definitely moving. Follow me."

We rise together but instead of heading through the crowd and back the way we came, Jefferson leads me down a hallway into the clinic, leaving the crowd behind. We pass door after door after door until a nurse comes around the corner. Jefferson grabs my arm and we slide into a room before she looks up from her clipboard. He shuts the door and we stand next to it listening for her to pass.

"What are we going to do?" I whisper. "What about drawing my blood?"

A muscle in his jaw twitches and he surveys the little room we trapped ourselves inside. There are a couple of plastic chairs, a big cushioned bed thing with crinkly paper covering it. In the corner is a sink and cabinets topped with a jar of cotton balls and box of tissues. Jefferson locks the door then starts to dig through the cabinets. I stand guard at the door listening while Jefferson finds a locked red box with some kind of warning label on top. He reaches into a hidden pocket in the lining of his jacket and pulls out a pair of thin metal picks.

"You're kidding," I say. "You have lock picks?"

He doesn't even respond but goes to work on the lock. After thirty seconds he cracks the box open to reveal rows of syringes in plastic bags. He takes a couple out before putting the box back. I watch mesmerized as he finds a bottle of alcohol, grabs a cotton swab, tears a rubber band off a stack of papers in the cabinet, and unwraps the syringes.

"Take a seat," he says and points to the cushioned thingy. "We don't have a lot of time."

I plop down, pull my right arm out of the sleeve of my jacket, and roll up my long-sleeved shirt. Jefferson wraps the thick rubber band around my upper arm and dabs at the inside of my elbow with alcohol.

"Have you ever done this before?" I ask. "I mean, I'm not afraid of needles or anything, but you do know what you're doing, right? I'm not going to sit here while you figure out how to fill a syringe or find a vein or—OUCH!"

The needle finds its mark and pinches sharply as it slides under my skin. Jefferson holds a finger to his lips for silence then eases the top of the syringe back. My blood fills into the empty space, vibrant red. I avert my eyes while he fills one syringe then another. He takes my hand and has me press a cotton ball to the sore spot. Easy as can be, he unwraps the rubber band from my arm, caps the syringes, tucks them into the hidden lining of his jacket, and slaps a bright pink Band-Aid on me.

"Suits you," he says quietly and gestures for me to get up.

It's something my brother would say. Jefferson's not so bad once you give him a chance. I tug my arm back through the sleeve of my jacket and meet him at the door. We pause to listen, then escape from the patient's room and walk steady and upright down the hallway as if we were meant to be there the whole time.

Jefferson must know where he's going because he takes us straight to a rear entrance. He smiles and waves at a nurse passing in the opposite direction and we slip out before she can say anything. We pick up the pace once we're outside and jog to the parking lot. Through the windows I watch the mass of werewolves waiting to see the doc inside. Their eyes find mine like magnets and I'm quick to look away. This is getting way too creepy.

The Green Monster is waiting for us and we gun it out of the parking lot at full speed. I run a hand over the top of my head.

"Well, now what?" I ask. "How are we supposed to analyze my blood or whatever? Wasn't this kind of pointless without Dr. Rosewell?"

"She's not qualified to check out your blood. I only needed her to draw it and I was going to ask her about the serum supply. If she's gone, that's really going to slow up the distribution.

There's going to be a lot of werewolves off the serum," he says and gives me a sideways glance. "No, we're taking your blood to a dead drop to have an expert check it out."

"Seriously? We're going all CIA on this?"

"I need you to understand something, Phoenix," he says and swings onto a road off the main drag. "We need to get this out right away so it can be processed immediately but a cure is going to be a long ways off. We aren't going to save this town through your blood. Not right away."

"*What?*"

"I'm sorry but it's going to take time. You can't just inject your blood into a werewolf and hope it works. It might counteract with the serum and kill the host."

"*Or* it could cure them."

We come to an abrupt halt as he parks outside a small building with an even smaller sign pronouncing *Moose Lake Public Library*. He faces me with one hand resting on the back of the bucket seat. He smells like coffee and pine trees. I didn't notice until now with him practically breathing on me, giving me a hard stare.

"Would you be willing to test that on Hawk without knowing for sure?" he asks.

My cheeks warm. "No."

"Then consider the same for every other werewolf out there. The only way we're going to win this is by getting this out—" He takes out the syringes and wiggles them in front of my face, "—stopping the black wolf, and giving ourselves time to get the cure and get it right. I know it's the last thing you want to do, but you've got to be patient."

I glower and reach for the door. "Fine."

We get out and Jefferson hides the syringes in his jacket again. I follow him through glass doors, a tiny lobby, and a set of heavier doors to the library. It's quaint and, like any library, has that smell of old paper, dust, and cleaner. A very tall, slender woman with arms like toothpicks stands behind the counter. Her mousy hair is pulled back into a tight bun that makes her severe facial features that much more pronounced. Her eyes are sharp on us when we enter.

Jefferson walks up to the counter and raps his fingers. "I'm looking for the first edition of *Apollodorus*."

The woman appraises me with those razor eyes and then glides into a backroom. Moments later she returns hefting a large book bound in brown leather. Its pages are yellowed with age and *Apollodorus* is embossed in gold on the cover.

"Thanks." Jefferson takes it over to a computer cubicle and checks around us to make sure we're alone before opening it. A square notch of space is cut out of the very middle—the perfect place to hide items. Jefferson carefully places the two syringes into the massive book, tears off part of a page, jots down a note to sit with the needles, and eases the cover shut. He returns the book to the librarian and hustles me out the door.

"Is it really safe to just leave those there?" I cast an anxious look at the library. "Who picks that up then?"

"It'll make its way into the hands of my expert. Don't worry about it. It's safe." He waves me over "Come on. We've need to get to the cabin before the IMS backup team arrives."

A lingering sense of disappointment weighs on my shoulders as I climb into the Green Monster and Jefferson guns it out of the lot. In my mind things were supposed to happen a lot faster. The cure would be instantaneous, the full might of

IMS resources would be behind it, and the entire world would be rid of the disease forever. But now my magic blood is sitting in a dinky little library in a small town waiting with no sense of urgency for some mysterious "expert" to examine it and decide if it's the real deal or not.

The trip back to the cabin is done in silence apart from the roar of the engine. I watch the trees flicker by out my side window, keeping a hand on my wounded arm. We pull into the driveway and Jefferson backs into the barn. I walk outside to a cool breeze in my face as Jefferson shuts the big doors.

A rumble comes up the driveway moments later and a black SUV emerges from the tree line. I can make out a man driving and a woman in a black coat in the passenger seat. They're expressionless but their eyes lock on Jefferson and me instantly.

"That's them?" I ask.

Jefferson leans in really close until his mouth is at my ear, freaking me out a little, and whispers, "Don't say anything about being bitten or about your blood or a cure. Don't mention a word of it to them."

I jerk back, startled. "What? Why?"

"To protect you."

"From what?"

His eyes are deadly serious and he straightens to his full height, hands shoved into his jacket pockets. His gaze drifts to the SUV as it stops in front of us.

"From them," he says.

21

I don't even get a chance to ask Jefferson what on earth he meant about not trusting the IMS before the agents exit their SUV and introduce themselves. I'm so distracted by Jefferson's last comment that I miss their first names and just remember two of them are Agent Smith and one's Agent Moore. I don't even know which are the two Smiths.

They aren't a happy bunch and I get the distinct impression they're looking down on Jefferson and me. They aren't polite either but Jefferson glosses right over it and gets to business. He leads them into the loft of his barn and gives them the rundown of what's been happening in town—the agitation stirring through the werewolves, the cattle mutilations, the disappearances, Deputy Graham vanishing in the woods, the high number of bites, and the possibility that Dr. Rosewell has vanished as well. When Jefferson finishes, the team doesn't seem impressed and the woman sits there cleaning her fingernails with a pocket knife as if she couldn't care less. I wait for her to accidentally cut herself and can't look away.

"Okay, the situation seems straightforward enough," their leader sighs—Agent Moore, I think. Everything about his appearance says average—average height, regular cropped brown hair, not too skinny, not too muscular. He's someone easy to forget.

Jefferson lets the first crack of irritation show through his polite mask. "Oh, really? Nothing about this seems odd to you?"

"Werewolves are a low key problem. This isn't as bad as you think it is," the agent assures him like he might a small child. I want to punch him. Jefferson catches my eye and shakes his head a fraction of an inch.

Agent Moore waves to the other two agents to get their attention back on track. "Okay, let's get this taken care of. Agent Smith, I need you to go to the Carlton County Sheriff's Office and see where they are in their search for Deputy Graham as I'm sure they've already figured out he's missing. We need to know how involved they are so they don't interfere or come across something they shouldn't." His eyes flicker back to Jefferson, clearly accusing him of bringing cops into the mess. "Agent Smith, go through Barnes' files and trace the point of origin. I'll go to the site of these *disappearances* and do some first-hand investigation."

I note they don't call Jefferson *Agent* Barnes. Just Barnes. I'll admit, I wasn't Jefferson's number one fan in the beginning by a long shot but what can I say? He's grown on me, and when people pick on those I care about, I don't like sitting by and doing nothing. Not speaking out takes all of my self-control.

"We'll go with you," Jefferson says. "Phoenix and I can help with the door to door stuff. I know the area and Phoenix is getting the hang of the place. People will talk to her."

I'm touched by the vote of confidence on my behalf but Agent Moore cracks a smile that is in no way friendly.

"No offense, Barnes, but I think you've done enough already. Stay here and help Agent Smith go through the files." His gaze turns to me and he gives me a crude up and down. "And there's no way I'm letting the girl who blew the Werevine operation go anywhere near my investigation."

It's a slap in the face. I probably deserve the insult but Jefferson certainly doesn't.

"Don't be an idiot," I snap. That gets everyone's attention fast. "There are a *lot* more werewolves out there than three people can manage. You—"

"Obviously," Agent Moore interrupts, and I realize I just kind of dismissed my own team of three. We haven't exactly been handling things well ourselves and I inadvertently pointed that out.

"What I meant is that you could use our help," I continue. "We know the area. We know what's been going on."

"That may be true, but I can use a map without your help and Barnes filled us in. I think we're good."

He doesn't give me a chance to keep arguing because he walks away and the other Agent Smith follows him out. I start to storm after them but Jefferson holds out an arm to stop me.

"Don't," he warns under his breath. "That's not going to help anything."

The other Agent Smith, a squat man with round glasses, claps his hands together then spreads his arms wide. "Okay, where are the files? Where do I start?"

Jefferson gestures for him to follow and we all head to the cabin. Once inside the cramped main room, he points to the stacks of boxes upon boxes Hawk and I sorted when we first got here.

"I've been meaning to move them to my command center, as it were," Jefferson says.

Agent Smith squints at the boxes and lifts the lid off the closest to peer inside over the rim of his glasses. "Where are your digitized records?" he asks.

Jefferson and I share a look and laugh. I move over to the dinosaur of a computer and knock twice on top of the dusty monitor.

"We aren't exactly high tech here," I say.

"You either take the hard copies," Jefferson says and lifts a box to push into the agent's arms, "or you point at a star and wish away into the dark."

Well, that's a phrase I haven't heard in a while. It's one of the charming sayings of the unicorns who aren't very mystical themselves and frown upon whimsical magic users like fauns.

Agent Smith purses his lips and hefts the box out of the cabin. Jefferson winks at me and picks up a couple of boxes himself. I reach for one too but he shakes his head.

"You're going to strain that arm."

"I can lift a *box*."

"And if that wound starts bleeding again? Don't draw attention to it." He nods to my arm since his hands are full. He walks out with the boxes and I'm hot on his heels.

"Why are you so worried about them finding out?" I whisper at his back. Agent Smith is far enough away that he can't overhear. "They could help with a cure."

"Yeah, help you right into an early grave." He stops and turns around, drawing me up short. "They'd bleed you dry for a cure, Phoenix. You'd be dead before you could see your brother cured."

Now I'm the one shaking my head. "They wouldn't bleed me like a vampire."

"Or they'd stick you in a lab somewhere in the dark, alone and hooked up to so many machines and needles that you'd *wish* they'd bleed you out."

I've lived among IMS agents for years. I've heard the stories of their bravery and the lengths they go to in order to protect their legendary charges. The picture Jefferson is painting doesn't add up.

"They wouldn't. They couldn't."

"You'd be surprised," he says darkly. "Don't say anything. Please."

I'm too confused for a moment to realize he's trying to protect me. He's been searching for a cure all this time and now he's willing to push it aside in order to save me from that imagined pain. So, I shut my mouth and march behind him into the barn.

My phone buzzes and I see a text from Hawk wanting to know I'm okay and mentions there are several more people missing from school today. I send him a quick message letting him know it's been uneventful. I don't mention the creepy situation at the clinic. No point worrying him when nothing really happened.

Jefferson goes back and forth from the barn to the cabin to bring in the rest of the boxes while I point out how the files are organized to Agent Smith. His face is tight and he kind of pushes me to the side the second I'm done explaining. I hold up my hands and walk away to stand next to Jefferson on the other side of the table. The agent has clearly claimed the space as his, despite it being Jefferson's home, and spreads out the boxes to his liking. He licks his finger to turn pages and I cringe. It rankles my inner pet peeve and I want to slap his fingers each time he does it.

With the table and chairs commandeered by Agent Smith, I sit sprawled on the cot in the corner dismantling a tranquilizer gun and cleaning it. Jefferson combs through the files with the agent for a while before he's pushed aside like I was. He brings over another gun from his safe in the cabin, a Remington shotgun, and cleans it beside me. I'm almost hoping the sight of us cleaning guns will unnerve the agent but we've obviously become invisible to him once out of the way.

"I can't stand this," I mutter.

"Yeah, well, they're a bunch of hot shots that don't like being called out for werewolf duty," Jefferson says absently. "It's like detectives being kicked down to mall cops for them."

I roll my eyes. "That's just stupid. What's going on here is *not* normal werewolf activity."

"I know."

"But it's more than that." I snap the slide on the gun back into place and set it down. "I get why they don't like me—Werevine was not exactly my shining moment. You, on the other hand, I don't get. What did you do, Jefferson?"

He pumps the shotgun and pops out a shell but doesn't answer.

"What did you do?" I repeat. "I'm going to keep asking until you tell me."

At that he raises his narrowed eyes. "I inappropriately used IMS resources. That's what's written in my file."

"Okay . . . but inappropriate how?"

"Any sign of a black wolf and I called in the cavalry," he mutters. "I was desperate and I needed their help. One time Draco actually showed up after I sounded the alarm but it wasn't the right wolf." He clears his throat. "That didn't go over well."

"Wait, Draco as in *the* Draco? Majestic class dragon? Founder of IMS?"

He sets the shotgun down and scratches a spot behind his ear. "That's the one. And, trust me, dragons don't like to be summoned unless there's a darn good reason. Pretty sure that's why I've been stuck out here by myself without any of the normal resources. It's punishment for ticking him off."

I can't help but notice Draco's interest in the case. He was the dragon that saved Hawk and me and scared off the black wolf in the first place. Then he came back again when Jefferson thought the black wolf was around? Why is a dragon so interested in a werewolf, one of the least substantial beasts out there? Dragons go after leviathans, hydra, and level five monsters, not *werewolves.*

"Barnes?" Agent Smith raises his hand to catch our attention. "Could you come here a moment?"

Jefferson's eyebrows jump up into his shaggy hair and he puts the gun parts aside to see what the agent wants. I sit quietly polishing gunmetal and listen as the agent asks Jefferson to explain the amount of werewolf serum going out above the norm. When Jefferson tries to explain, once again, that he believes the black werewolf is behind it, the agent won't have any of it and states the werewolves must be harboring the serum for other wolves unaccounted for as of yet. The implication is Jefferson doesn't have a clue how to do his job.

After the agent rudely dismisses Jefferson from the table, he marches back over to me with a sour expression.

"I can't stay here," I growl. "If I do, I'm going to end up punching somebody in the face. We should be out there tracking the black wolf down."

"There's not much we can do," he says and sits on the cot next to me to inspect the tranquilizer darts in the magazine. He holds it out to me and says under his breath, "Tempting."

I smile and take it from him to snap into the gun. He returns to his shotgun on the table opposite me and finishes putting it back together. I can't sit still any longer so I rise and tuck the gun into the back of my waistband. So, we can't go do our jobs but there's no way I'm staying here either. There is one place I want to go, though.

"Jefferson, what ever happened to my parents' old house?"

That catches him off guard. His beady eyes jump to me and he sets the shotgun aside. "It went into limbo. Something about legal paperwork and the IMS preventing it from selling. It's just been sitting abandoned."

I shift my jaw back and forth then bite my lower lip. "I want to see it."

"Are you sure that's a good idea?"

"I need to see it."

He rises and sets his hands on his waist so he can look down at me properly. "I don't think it's a good idea."

"Okay, fine. You don't have to come. Give me the keys." I hold out my hand.

He holds up a finger in my face. "First off, no one drives that car except me. Two, you aren't going anywhere alone. Not now. Three, I still don't think this is a good idea. You don't know what kind of memories this could trigger."

Any would be welcome, considering I only have two about my parents that I can actually recall. I need to see the place I spent the first four years of my life, the place my parents had called home—where a dragon gave me a gift I can never repay.

"Well, I'll be as stubborn as I have to in order to see it," I say. "I'll walk."

"No, you won't," he growls. He runs a hand through his hair then tugs his car keys out of his pocket. "You kids are annoying."

"Young adults."

"Teenage rebels," he mutters and starts down the steps.

"You know us so well," I say and follow in his wake.

We hop into the Green Monster, ignoring Agent Smith calling after us to find out where we're going, and peel out. Jefferson winds off Soldier Road, down Aspen Road, then we head up north along Highway 61. A twisted knot of anxiety forms in my stomach. What will the house look like? Did the cops leave the place just as it was in the crime scene photos? Will there be furniture knocked over and bloodstains on the floor? I don't normally chew on my fingernails but I start to worry my thumb between my teeth.

We drive for a few minutes on the old highway before Jefferson turns off onto a long gravel driveway. At least I think it used to be gravel. It's so overgrown with wilted high grass that I can barely see the two ruts that mark where a driveway had been. We cross a large open field bordered by a wooden fence falling apart. An enormous willow tree rises before us. Its bare branches reach towards me like skeletal fingers and a tire swing hangs from one of the lowest ones. When we pass I see the nest of some creature nestled in the bottom of the tire.

Pine trees and poplars close in around the colonial style house that draws my gaze. The front porch is sagging and the storm door hangs at an odd angle. Its light blue paneling is faded and worn. The tall grass reaches up to the front stairs and some even peeks through between the steps. It's a lonely and ruined monument of the life I never knew and the horror I wish I could forget. I'm clutching onto the seatbelt strap for dear life, frozen in my seat and unable to move.

"You don't have to go inside," Jefferson says quietly.

That's true. I've seen the outside and that could be enough. Then my hands are fumbling with the seatbelt latch and I get shakily out of the car. I force myself to walk slowly through the high grass and not trip. The front stairs groan under my weight and the storm door just about falls off its hinges when I swing it wide. I grasp the tarnished brass door handle and push my way inside.

For some reason I expect to hear ghostly noises, a creepy wind whistling, or sinister sounds, but it's quiet. The front entrance is littered with leaves and debris dragged in by animals. Stairs climb directly before me and a living room opens up on my left. I take careful steps into the room and recognize it from the crime scene photos. This was where my father died. Something catches in my throat. I try to swallow past it with some difficulty and stand where he fell. The floorboards are dark all around me but there's discoloration even darker right where I am. Blood.

I exhale sharply and keep moving to the dining room. The table is still here, the one Hawk and I hid underneath. There's another stain where my mother died trying to protect us. I hug her bomber jacket closer to myself and crouch down to look under the table. A support beam runs down the middle and is so familiar. I duck and wiggle my way underneath to sit grasping the bar.

I close my eyes and can hear the wolf, feel Hawk's hands on mine, and my mother's arms wrapped around our shoulders keeping us down and out of sight. I hear my father shout and vicious growling. My mother is whispering something, touching the bottom of the table. Then my mother being wrenched away and the explosive sound of her gun firing twice. Screaming, I'm screaming. My mother's gone and the wolf's head slips under the table. Black and terrible as death. It's jaws take hold of Hawk's side and drag him from under the table. I'm screaming for my brother and crawl out after him. Before the wolf gets too far I throw a punch into its nose with all the strength my tiny four-year-old self can muster.

There's blinding light and Hawk falls to the ground. I can't see anything. Light cascades and surrounds me. The next thing I know there's a man standing over me who touches three fingers to my shoulder where the sleeve of my shirt had ripped off. I feel pain and tingling but I ignore it to clutch my unconscious brother to me.

My eyes snap open and I take a deep breath, still clutching the bar underneath the table but no longer that little girl. I flinch away from it and scramble backwards, surge to my feet, and trip backwards into a wall where I catch myself only to sink to the floor upon scattered leaves and dirt. I clamp both hands over my mouth to hold back the hysterical sob that wants to rip out of my chest. I breathe sharply through my nose and fight it and fight it until my chest stops shuddering. I hastily run the back of my hand across my cheeks and under my nose. I'm not allowed to fall apart. I can't. Not ever.

I rise and force myself to think past the nightmare to the facts. My parents contacted Jefferson because they had a lead on the black wolf's identity. Jefferson never figured it out, so how did my parents? What did they know?

I decide to check out the rest of the house even though I'm probably not going to find anything that the cops or Jefferson didn't. When I turn to leave the kitchen I find Jefferson standing in the entryway and jump.

"You all right?" he asks.

I cough to clear my throat in case it's raspy and say, "Yeah, I'm fine. Or I will be, anyway." I run a hand down my face one more time to make sure there aren't any traces of tears. "So after the . . . incident, I assume you searched the house?"

"Yeah, I picked over this place in case your folks left a clue behind. I never found anything. All the notes they had were with the file at my place."

"Hmm. Yeah. I guess. Maybe." I plant my hands on my waist for a second before I march past Jefferson and start exploring the house.

There's a quaint little kitchen—at least I'm sure it was quaint before the animal droppings, cobwebs, and smell. I throw open cupboards and drawers and screech when a squirrel leaps out of one. I knock on panels and push things aside looking for hidden nooks or crannies. It's just a normal old house, not some spy's lair with compartments to stash weapons or secret messages. I know that but I keep desperately searching for something—what exactly, I don't even know. I move upstairs and find what must have been Hawk's and my room. Wallpaper of zoo animals peels off the walls. There's no furniture left except a busted dresser sitting lopsided in the corner.

I smooth out the edge of wallpaper that's hanging off the wall and smile at the zebras, lions, and tigers dancing across the paper. Jagged markings on the wooden paneling along the bottom of the wall grab my attention and I bend down to see what they are. I run my fingers over a terrible rendition of a cat or a bear. I can't quite decide which. Yeah, I can picture us carving into the wall—little psychotic four-year-olds with knives going at the fixtures. I don't remember it but it seems like something we would have done. I see another one farther down that is much more visible and easily identifiable. It's a wolf.

The crude carving makes me uncomfortable, a message left behind like some eerie foreshadowing of our lives, and I'm quick to slip away from my childhood room. I check the master bedroom but it's bare unless you count the garbage that animals have brought in. But my parents must have left something behind. They wouldn't risk it to chance and wait until Jefferson showed up to tell him what they found. Why couldn't they have just told him over the phone? Were they being watched? If they were, where would they hide something?

"They didn't have time," I mutter to myself. Jefferson continues to lag behind me as I wander and scuttle past him back to the dining room table.

"What was that?" Jefferson asks.

"They didn't have time to leave a proper message. They called you and then were attacked. What if that wolf was watching them?" I duck under the table and inspect every inch of it. "What if my mother wasn't just trying to protect us but was hiding something at the same time? Leaving behind a clue?"

"Phoenix . . . I know you're hoping for answers but I think you might be grasping at straws here."

"No, she whispered something to me. I can't remember what she said. I was so scared then." I twist around so I can run my hands under the bottom of the table. "She did something here. I know she did."

Jefferson keeps trying to dissuade me but I'm not listening anymore. My fingers have found a crack between the flat top and the support leg. Stuck in between is something white and dusty—a slip of paper. I ever so carefully start to tug it out. I wince when the corner begins to tear.

"No, come on," I mutter. "I've got you."

After much wiggling and gentle persuasion, the paper slips free and it's mine. I push out from the table and hold it aloft for Jefferson to see. That shuts him up fast. I unfold its creased edges and find the riddle my mother left behind in her last moments for us to follow the trail.

Lycaon.

22

"Lycaon." Jefferson gives me a sideways look as he pulls onto Soldier Road.

"Lycaon."

"*The* Lycaon?"

I fold the one word note and stuff it into my pocket. "Who else could it be? It's not like it's a popular name or anything." I stare out the windshield. "I actually picked that as my Greek myth for class the other day."

"But that's not possible. Unless . . ." He rubs at his beard. "I suppose if this really is the original werewolf, the father of the race, he could have greater abilities than any other werewolf."

"Like immortality?" The story of Lycaon dates back to ancient Greece—the man who offered up a butchered human to Zeus and was turned into a werewolf for his horrid act. Of course, with it being an old Greek myth, the details are mixed. Some say it was a guest roasted up and served to Zeus, other stories have Lycaon sacrificing children, and some even say he killed his own child as the sacrifice. Whatever detail is true, the core of the myth is horrific. The man was a monster and was therefore literally transformed into a beast.

"Let's hope not," Jefferson mumbles. "Immortal or not, I'll be emptying a clip into his face whenever I find the schweinhund."

I silently agree. I'm not usually the one to say shoot first, ask questions later, but for this werewolf I would make an exception. Blood lust is in my veins this time. My parents were murdered. My brother is cursed. I'll do whatever I have to in order to avenge them.

"Well, now what?" I ask. "Should we tell the three stooges?"

"Honestly? I don't think they'd believe either of us. I'm the crazy old guy and you're the loose cannon, both with vengeance issues. I've cried wolf a few too many times. No, we do this ourselves." We pull onto the driveway and the barn door is still open so we park inside. Jefferson peers up through the windshield to the loft. I can just make out the top of Agent Smith's head from here.

"And the plan is?" I ask.

"Call your buddy in Underground."

"Witty?"

He turns off the engine. "That's the one. See if he can pull anything up on Lycaon in the IMS database. They might have an idea on whether it's a myth or an actual person. I'll distract Smith for you, Agent."

A grin spreads on my face. "Did you just call me Agent?"

"Nope. Let's go."

We hop out of the car. Jefferson heads to the loft while I

make for the cabin. As soon as I'm alone I dial the number and scrounge for paper and a pen while I wait for it to ring.

"This is Wallowitz."

"Witty, it's good to hear your voice."

"Oh . . . hey, Phoenix." His tone is strained.

Silence stretches on for what seems like forever. "Everything okay, Witty?"

"Of course. Yeah. Everything's fantastic."

"You're a terrible liar."

More silence. I wish I could hear something in the background but it's quiet for once. He must be sitting still and alone. This can't be good.

"Witty, you've got to talk to me," I say and press the phone tighter to my ear. "What's going on?"

He heaves a sigh. "Look, you didn't hear this from me, okay? You promise me you aren't going to tell anyone. Promise me."

"Okay, now you're scaring me."

"*Promise me.* I want to give you a heads up, Phoenix— you've always been a good friend—but I can't get in trouble and be pulled down into this."

That definitely doesn't sound good. "Into *what?*"

"Promise me!"

"Okay!" I shout back. "I promise. Cross my heart, knock my hooves, paint my antlers, the whole schebang."

His voice hisses static through the line. "The backup team they sent? Well, they reported in saying you guys have made a mess of things and aren't doing your jobs. As soon as they've caught the ring leader of the werewolves, they're pulling the plug on you, Hawk, and Agent Barnes."

I turn to stone. After everything I've been through in the last week alone, I can't handle it. A switch flips in my brain and I want to burn the world down.

"What?" I say, my voice dead.

"I'm sorry. I wasn't supposed to say anything but . . . you deserve to know."

"What do you mean *pull the plug?* What does that even mean, Witty? Shutting down the Moose Lake Field Office? Replacing us and sending us back to Underground?"

"Well, sort of," he hedges. I want to reach through the phone and shake it out of him.

"*Witty.*"

"Director Knox plans to take all three of you off the force and stick you in civilian jobs where the agency will keep an eye on you," he says in a rush.

I have to put the phone down. I brace both hands against the tabletop and hang my head, focusing on breathing in and out. No, not now. They can't do this to us. Hawk and I are just getting started. Jefferson was going to turn us into proper agents. Now all of us are going to be canned and stuck in dead end jobs. I slam a fist on the table and the wood cracks in a spider-web pattern across the surface.

They'll let us stick around to apprehend the black wolf but then we'll be shipped away and I'll never get actual answers, like why the wolf killed my parents. It'll be in a cell somewhere and I'll be roasting slugs at Old Man Two's for the rest of my life—unless they eventually kick us out of Underground too. Then I'll probably end up flipping burgers at a fast food joint in Antarctica. Jefferson will never be allowed to find his daughter or know why his wife was killed.

I'm suddenly thankful Jefferson sent my blood to his expert and not directly to the IMS—I'd wind up in a lab bleeding out like he said instead of a fast food joint at the end of it all otherwise.

I want to rip the walls down. I'm winding up to start punching holes through everything around me when I hear Witty's voice from the phone on the table so I pick it up.

"Yeah, I'm still here," I manage to mumble. I close my eyes and keep a fist pressed tight to my forehead. I've quickly forgotten what I was supposed to be calling Witty about in the first place but I'm going to find out everything about this black wolf if it's the last thing I do.

"Witty, look up the name Lycaon for me."

"Pardon?"

"You heard me," I snap. "If this is the last job I do then I'm going to do it. Look up the freakin' name."

I've never been this mean to Witty but I've lost it. He'll be sitting easy as can be in Underground while my life falls apart all over again. That stupid black wolf took away my parents and forced me into the legendary world and now because of him I'll never become the only thing I've ever wanted to be.

I hear the familiar squeak of wheels and rush of air as Witty rolls along a hallway. The sound eventually stops and he taps at a keyboard. Then there's some seriously fast typing and a choice swearword muttered under his breath.

"What is it?" I ask.

"The name's flagged."

"Meaning?"

"Anyone looking it up gets reviewed because it's been classified." More fast typing. "An alert went to—oh, you've got to be kidding me."

I grasp at my hair. "To who? Who got the alert?"

"Draco," he groans, defeated. "It went to *Draco* as in—"

"One of the dragon founders of the IMS. Yeah, I know who he is." Geez, this is getting complicated. "If they start hounding you, send them directly to me. They won't drag you down with us, Witty. I won't let them. They've got to go through me first."

I end the call and toss the phone onto the table. Well, I guess that answers Jefferson's question at least. Lycaon is definitely real, otherwise a dragon wouldn't be getting a warning if someone tried to look up the name. Why the crap does everything have to be classified?

Okay. Think. I need to think, and not about the inevitable, sticky end waiting for me, my brother, and our grouchy mentor once this is over. Lycaon is real. My parents figured it out. Lycaon is here and, from what we know so far, building a werewolf army. Why? No idea. How? Well, obviously by biting them and having other werewolves go around biting even more people. But how is he controlling the werewolves? I can't imagine charm on its own could do so much. Maybe some super special wolfy power he has by being the first?

I snatch up my phone and march out to the barn. Agent Smith has his own laptop on the table while going through files, Jefferson standing over his shoulder. They both look up when I storm the stairs. I'm fire and wrath and my mind is clearer now than it's ever been before. If this is to be my last shining moment, then it's going to be finding and bringing my parents' murderer to justice.

"Jefferson, I need you," I say.

He doesn't even question my attitude or why but meets me at the map on the wall full of colored pins.

I throw out my hands to gesture to the whole thing. "These mark locations where people were bitten, right?"

"Yeah."

"Were they all teenagers or a mix of ages?"

He glances at the board and massages his beard in thought. "There was a mix but maybe two-thirds were teenagers."

"Okay, was there a werewolf population here before the big incident in 1996?"

"Yeah, a small one."

"Mixed ages?"

He watches me out of the corner of his eye. "What are you on to, Phoenix?"

"Just go with me on this one. I'm assuming there was a range of ages for the werewolf population before 1996 so there would have been a fairly wide sampling of werewolves in the area during that year?"

Jefferson angles more towards me and even Agent Smith is listening over his shoulder. I take a moment to glare at him before returning my attention to the only person I care to talk to in the room.

"Jefferson?"

He nods. "Yeah, we had children, teenagers, adults, even a few senior citizens."

"But you said it's always the teenagers that go first—this time and last time. Not being bitten but behaving weird even with the serum."

He cocks his head, clearly starting to catch on. "Yes, I did. You're right."

"And if we had, say, a really old werewolf, maybe even the *original* werewolf, don't you think he'd have kind of an alpha complex? The first of the monster breeds are the strongest, right? What if the other werewolves start acting odd because he's nearby? What if it's not about being young and naïve? What if it's about proximity?"

Jefferson taps a finger on the map near the edge of the lake. "And where do we know large groups of teenagers regularly gather and would therefore be affected all at the same time?"

I snap my fingers. "The black wolf is *in* the school."

"What?" Agent Smith asks and we turn on him. "Original werewolf? What are you two going on about? Proximity?"

Seeing he has nothing to offer us, Jefferson and I turn back to each other.

"So, he's got to be one of the teachers or staff," I say.

Jefferson taps his pointer finger against his chin. "Or *she*, and not necessarily. If this werewolf is immortal, who's to say he or she still doesn't look like a teenager? They could pose as a student."

"Well, that could be problematic. We need to be able to narrow down the field somehow." I bite my lower lip and gaze at the red pins on the map. "Do we have some kind of census records or something? Can we find out who was here both in 1996 and now? Would the school have a listing of previous staff and students we could get our hands on?"

"Census records would take too long to go through without a functioning database to search." His eyes flick to Agent Smith. "But school records might be a better idea. Principal Tippy won't just hand those over though, and showing up to demand the records might tip off our wolf."

"*You* could come in handy for that," I say and point at Agent Smith.

He looks less than enthused. "My team is handling this case, not you. I'm not going to storm the school, flash some credentials, and pull records for you. And you have no proof of some *original werewolf* running around."

I'm on edge and with the promise of nothing to look forward to after the case is closed, I storm forward and get into the agent's face. "How can you ignore the facts right in front of you? Jefferson laid it out, I've laid it out more, and you still won't accept anything we have to say? What the crap is wrong with you!"

Jefferson grabs my arm and hauls me back. I shake him off. So he puts both hands on my shoulders and steers me towards the stairs.

"Come on, you need to cool off," he says.

"*What?*" I have to say it over my shoulder because he's walking me down the steps to the ground floor. Once there I spin about on him. "They can get us what we need! I'm not going to stand by and let them walk all over us!"

"*Phoenix,*" he says so sharply I lean back. "You've got to calm down."

"Don't tell me to calm down! This is the monster that murdered my parents and your wife! I'm not going to calm down when we're finally onto something!"

"Get in the car!" he shouts and points to the passenger door. "We're going for a ride and you're going to clear your head."

I don't move.

"Now!" Then he winks. He *winks*.

Oh. I glance up to the loft railing where Agent Smith is leaning over and watching us. I keep up my angry façade, now that I realize Jefferson is playing me along, and get into the car. He opens the doors to the barn, gets into the driver's seat, and guns the engine. Once out on the driveway he shoots me a dark look.

"Was going crazy really necessary back there?" he says.

I run both hands over my head. "Sorry," I mutter. "I didn't mean to."

"I know how upsetting this is but dial it back."

Jefferson doesn't know the half of it. I almost spill what Witty told me right then and there but think better of it. What would be the point of telling Jefferson the bad news? It's not like there's anything either of us can do about it and we need our heads in the game.

"So, what did you find out about Lycaon?" he asks.

"That it's classified and an automatic alert went to Draco when we tried to search the database for the name."

"What is it with that dragon?" Jefferson mutters. "Okay, so obviously Lycaon is a major player, and if a dragon has been searching for him then he's even more dangerous than we thought. We need to find him."

"Jefferson, if Lycaon really is at the school . . . Hawk's there." I pull out my phone and send my brother a quick text to see how he's doing. When he doesn't respond immediately I start to freak out.

"He's a smart kid," Jefferson says. "I'm sure he won't let anyone get the jump on him."

"You weren't that confident before."

He shifts in his seat and gives me the impression he's uncomfortable. "School will be out soon enough anyway. We just need to be patient and get the records we need."

"And how are we going to do that? You said yourself we can't go grab them from the school."

"You know, they have these funny little things called *year-books* we can look at. The library keeps copies." He tosses me a snide smirk.

I fight the impulse to roll my eyes. I've been doing that too much lately. "Who knew libraries had such cool things? Dead drops for magical blood, yearbooks of werewolves . . . don't tell me there's a secret bunker underneath, too."

"Don't be stupid," Jefferson says gruffly and gives me a sideways look. "That's beneath the movie theater in town, not the library."

Mention of a movie theater, of all things, makes the reality of everything hit me the hardest. Going to the theater in Underground had been my one place of normal. Sure, I went to watch movies with a faun and a giant, surrounded by elves, centaurs, and a slew of other fantastic creatures, but for me it felt normal. I was a normal girl with a normal brother watching movies with friends, training to be their protector. Now, if they even let me and Hawk stay in Underground, that'll be all we do. There won't be any grand adventure waiting for us anymore. We'll be useless.

"Maybe we can catch a movie some time," he says.

I lean to the side window. "Yeah. Maybe."

Hawk texts me back letting me know he's fine by the time we reach the library for the second time today. There's that at least. We enter the building and Jefferson nods to the sharp-eyed librarian. He apparently knows exactly where he's going and heads for the furthest shelves. The lighting is dimmer back here and a haze of dust floats around us.

"Sheesh, when's the last time someone came back here?" I say and wave a hand to expel the dust cloud in front of my face.

There are great leather bound volumes, thin booklets, ones about taxes, others about government, but tucked away in the corner is a section on local history. Jefferson combs through it and pulls a narrow, worn yearbook from the shelf. He flips it around so I can see the cover: *Moose Lake High School Year of 1996.*

"I told you," he says. "And the newest ones . . ."

He and I pull out the previous two years. The most current one won't come out until the end of the school year so we move to one of the computer terminals and look up the school's website. While I bring up pictures of the staff, Jefferson dumps the other yearbooks on the desk and spreads them out. I scroll through the website and he flips through the pages one by one. I'm okay with faces and names but no one is jumping out at me as someone I've seen at the school recently. We double-check the staff and teacher pages first. I'm expecting to see Principal Tippy but he's not here. He's about as old as a dinosaur but he must have transferred from somewhere else. But there is one face on the page I recognize, one face I'm likely to loath for all eternity.

I tap my finger on his face. "Him. It's got to be him. Mr. Webster."

23

Jefferson doesn't want to be too hasty in pointing the finger at Mr. Webster even though I'm all for it. So, instead we spend the next several hours comparing photos from the yearbooks to make sure none of the students look too similar incase our werewolf is immortal. Between the two of us, our search comes up empty and only one suspect remains.

While the librarian is busy shelving books, Jefferson and I smuggle out the 1996 yearbook. We don't want anyone to know that we've taken it, and that we're on to the black wolf's identity. A part of me had wished it would be Mr. Webster—that sly, judgmental, little weasel—and now the evidence is beginning to point to him. He's the only staff member present in 1996 and now. True, the black wolf could have skipped picture day, but he's the best lead we've got.

Despite how much I don't like the backup team, we have to tell them what we've found. By the time we return to the barn, the black SUV is back and so is the truck. Oh, good. I let out a sigh of relief. Hawk's here. Cheesy as it sounds, I miss my other ginger half. We park in the barn and I hear voices in the loft. The tenor doesn't exactly sound cheerful.

At the top of the stairs I find Hawk with his back to me being interrogated by all three of the agents. He's tapping his foot, rubbing his arms, and running his hands through his disarrayed hair. That's definitely not a good sign.

"Are you sure you didn't notice anything odd about him?" Agent Moore demands.

"Yes," Hawk snaps. "I've already told you, the only thing noticeable about him is he's a lousy teacher and a jerk. That's it."

Agent Moore spots Jefferson and me sneaking up the stairs. His eyes narrow. "I thought I told you two to stay here."

I move forward to stand by my brother and give him support against whatever the agents are accusing him of. Hawk's eyes are fierce and there's something off about him. I lean in closer to make sure and I can just barely make out a ring of yellow around his green eyes. It's easy enough to miss at a distance but I know Hawk too well not to notice. I don't want to point it out to the agents in the room so I lean back and squint at them all, trying to make it less obvious I was squinting at my brother's eyes.

"We were following up on a lead," I say to keep them focused on me and not Hawk. What happened to him today? I want to ask but I can't. I have to wait until we don't have IMS agents breathing down our necks. I hold my hand down and out hoping he'll give me a low five to let me know he's okay but he doesn't even seem to notice. He's only got dagger-eyes for the agents in front of us.

"That doesn't matter," Agent Moore says and crosses his

arms over his chest. I lift my chin to show I don't care what he thinks and I'll stand my ground. "We got a lead of our own. One of the werewolves I talked to said he saw the black wolf and knows his identity."

"Wait, what?" Hawk and I say in unison.

Jefferson steps forward as confused as we are. "Someone talked to you? Who?"

"A boy named Jason." Agent Moore gives him a disgusted look. "And if you had been doing your job properly, maybe you would have talked to him sooner."

"Jason?" I ask. "But that's the boy who—"

Jefferson backs into me and misses crunching the toes in my right foot by centimeters. Oh, right. I forgot I'm not supposed to mention being bitten or the cure or anything.

Unfortunately, I have Agent Moore's attention now and he's staring at me waiting for an answer. You could have heard crickets in the silence.

"The boy who I met at school," I finish but Agent Moore isn't buying it.

"Who did he say it was?" Jefferson asks before it can get anymore awkward.

"A teacher at the school. Mr. Webster."

I run my tongue over my teeth and hold back some snappy responses. I'm irritated. Jefferson and I figured out it was Mr. Webster first on our own without their help. I still can't believe he got someone to talk, though. The whole town has been under a self-imposed gag order concerning the black wolf. How in the blazes did he get Jason to spill his guts?

"So, now what?" I ask and toss my hands up. "Do we go interrogate him? Lock him up?"

"*We* have a plan in place already." He acknowledges the two agents behind him with a nod. Clearly, Hawk, Jefferson, and I are not included in the *we*. "We're going to setup surveillance on Mr. Webster and make sure we've got our man before moving in. We don't want to spook him or he might run."

"Okay," Jefferson says, the calmest of our merry band. Hawk is still twitching and I'm a powder keg ready to explode. "How can we help?"

"You can help by staying out of the way," Agent Moore says. "We'll take it from here. Now, if you don't mind . . ."

He turns his back on us and the agents huddle around the table to make their plans. Hawk is the first to leave, storming down the stairs. I'm quick to follow and Jefferson is on my heels. We escape from the hostility of the barn and regroup at the old grill-table thing on Jefferson's duct tape gun range. Hawk has both hands in his hair and is more agitated than I've seen him in a long time—well, apart from the night before when he freaked out on Ben.

"Hawk?"

He paces and ignores me, so I grab his forearms to wrestle his hands down and hold him still when he tries to pull away from me. The yellow in his eyes is taunting me.

"Hey, snap out it," I growl. "You aren't helping anything. Calm down."

"I *am* calm!" he practically shouts in my face.

"Yeah, wow, that was super convincing. How about you try that again, psycho."

He's not acting like himself and I know why. He's been at the school all day in the presence of the black wolf, Lycaon, the alpha werewolf. He's acting more like Ben had been—a loose cannon. But Hawk never got this bad during the other days we went to school together. This is new. This is—

Oh, I'm such an idiot. Maybe the black wolf isn't the only one whose powers work in proximity. Hawk has always had *me* around, all his life, including the other days we've gone to high school, and the times between.

All the time except today and that one night when he was off in the woods by himself while I stayed in the truck. I'm the cure. Hawk never had special powers of his own to be able to live as a normal human without the serum. He had *me*.

"I've got you, brother," I say quietly. "I've got you."

He's tense as a bowstring. I managed to calm down that jock, Matt, and stopped him from attacking me in the woods. How? How did I do it? How have I kept Hawk's animal side sedate all this time? I stare my brother down. I've always wanted him to be okay, and I urged Matt to remember who he was when he went after me.

I want Hawk to remember who he is, to remember I'm his family and that I'll never give up on him. My face gets warm just thinking how badly I want him to be my brother again.

The yellow rings in his eyes start to fade away. His breathing evens out and he gazes at my hands like they hold the answers to the universe. I loosen my grip and let go. His arms are a bit red from my tight grip but he flexes his forearms and lets out a genuine, pure Hawk laugh.

"What did you do?" he asks, his smile reaching his eyes.

"It worked?" I say breathlessly. I jump up and down unable to contain myself and throw up my arms. "It worked!"

Hawk grabs me by the shoulders and shakes me, continuing to laugh. We're both little kids again but I don't care. I've finally figured it out. I literally worked my magic and was able to save my brother. I never would have known it if Hawk hadn't gone off by himself today. It's a miracle that . . .

My laughter dies and I face Jefferson. "You knew, didn't you?"

His eyes are so small they're nearly lost beneath his eyebrows. "Let's say I had a sneaking suspicion. I know Hawk hasn't been taking the serum."

Oops. Wasn't expecting that by a long shot. Hawk and I share a worried look, and I even take a step back, one hand grabbing at Hawk's sleeve, ready to run into the woods with him, to protect him if I have to. I know what happens to those werewolves that refuse the serum. They're locked up and the key is thrown away. The same thing might happen to some of the werewolves here in Moose Lake after all that's happened. Jefferson has slowly proven himself to me but I'm not taking any chances when it comes to my brother.

"I also know," Jefferson continues, "that he's in control of himself despite that. Well, apart from the few occasions when he wasn't around you."

I'm struggling with the implications in my head. "But how? How did you know? *When* did you know?"

"Last night," he says and shrugs, as if uncovering our most guarded secret is the same as talking about the weather. "When we discovered your blood is the cure, I realized Hawk never has the redness or scars on his arms from taking the injections, and he doesn't monitor the days like most werewolves. I assume you've been without the serum for some time now?"

Hawk shrugs and keeps his eyes on his feet. "Never really started I guess."

"Well, isn't that something." He points between the pair of us. "And you two never thought that might be something worth looking into?"

"We did the usual checks," I say defensively. I keep a grip on my brother's sleeve ready to run, still unsure if Jefferson is going to turn on us. "They checked Hawk's blood and nothing ever came up. I always thought it was him, you know? I never thought I could be the one that—well . . ." I don't want to say *controlled* my brother because I don't think he'd like that. It's the whole reason he never liked the serum in the first place.

"Kept him human?" Jefferson shakes his head and combs his fingers through his shaggy hair. "You two better stick together like glue until this is over. We aren't going to be any use if Hawk gets brainwashed like the rest. I think you two should go back to school tomorrow and—"

"Wait a second," I interrupt. I can't help myself. I need to know. "You aren't going to rat us out?"

"Why? What would be the point? So the IMS can slap some penalties and cuffs on your brother for not taking a serum that would have been pointless anyway given your unique situation? I think we're past that point."

Hawk's mouth drops open. "Really? You aren't going to bust our chops?"

Jefferson shrugs again. "Like I said, what's the point? I mean, if you didn't have your magic sister you would have been taking the serum otherwise, right?"

There's no need to point out Hawk went off the serum and attacked me that one time before my gifts kicked in. Hawk never would have taken the serum regardless.

"Of course," Hawk answers. I don't say anything because I'm afraid I'll give that secret away.

"Anyway, as I was saying, you two should go back to school tomorrow." Jefferson glances up at the barn where the agents are gathered and clueless about what's going on. "Phoenix, see if you can do the same thing you just did with Hawk. Calm the other werewolves and it may draw the black wolf out. He won't like someone being able to disrupt the spell he's putting over the town."

"Got it." I give him a thumbs up before tucking my hands into my jacket pockets. I'm feeling jittery and can't help but smile. "Secret missions, defying orders—it's kind of exciting isn't it?"

Jefferson gives me a dark look. "We aren't defying orders. You two are enrolled and it would be suspicious if you stopped showing up. Plus, the IMS should be using all available resources. You two have more convenient access to keep an eye on Mr. Webster than they do."

Hawk rubs his hands together and bumps my shoulder with his. "Looks like our team has finally assembled." He suddenly grows serious. "We should have a name."

"We do," Jefferson says. "It's called the Moose Lake Field Office."

"No, that's boring and it's just the location anyway." His face screws up in thought. "How about Team Awesome?"

Jefferson groans and turns away to the cabin. Hawk chases after him and I jog along in his wake, happy to see Hawk back to his normal crazy self.

"How about a mash up?" Hawk continues. "Team Magic-old-wolf, because Phoenix is magic, you're a geezer, and I'm a werewolf. Or Old-magic-wolf."

Jefferson doesn't even turn around when he responds, "How about team shut up?"

"That's not very catchy," Hawk scoffs.

I rush up and grab his shoulder. "Team Rebel. Rebel Team. Team Rebellious."

"*No.*"

"Hey, it's got school spirit!"

We continue to argue over team names, more to poke fun at Jefferson than anything, but it's levity that I need. I've still got that bomb to drop about all of us getting the boot, but for the time being I'm keeping it to myself.

The next morning, after the three stooges have left in the black SUV to start surveillance, "Team Thunderstruck" rolls out in the old truck to the high school. We had bugged Jefferson all last night until he agreed on a team name as long as he picked it—so he picked his favorite AC/DC song. After saying the name about a thousand times, we agreed and even abbreviated it to T2. Jefferson's had a stony expression ever since.

The black SUV is already parked in the lot. Jefferson drives past it to stop behind the line of buses in front of the doors.

"Everyone know the plan?" he asks.

"Calm werewolves. Draw out Mr. Webster. Don't die," I list off.

"Yes. Don't die." He leans over Hawk to point a finger in my face. "Glad you added that last bit."

"I thought it was relevant."

Jefferson switches to Hawk. "Watch her back. If Mr. Webster does make a move on Phoenix, you need to back her up."

Hawk shoots him a dirty look and starts to push me out of the truck on the passenger side. "You don't need to worry about me keeping my sister safe. If anyone messes with her I'll tear them in half."

We're out the door and moving to the school when Jefferson shouts at our backs, "That's what I'm worried about!"

Walking through the door with my brother at my side and my mother's jacket wrapped around me, I'm a new person. I know what I am now. I'm a recluse and loose cannon, reckless and abandoned, but I've got one mission left to do and I'm going to see it through. This is for my parents and Jefferson's family. This is my moment to shine.

Passing down the hallway I spot several of the known werewolves glance in my direction. A few frown and quickly look away like they don't know why they looked in the first place. It's a bit creepy, but maybe it's a good sign. Are they feeling a change sweep over them by my mere presence? How far does my range of proximity extend? And do I have to concentrate on a single person for it to really work? Guess it's time to experiment like Jefferson said.

We reach our lockers and eye the corridors swimming with students. Hawk sniffs a few times and frowns. He opens one of his textbooks and points at something random on the page so we can have a private conversation without drawing too much attention. No one wants to listen in on a conversation about homework.

"Lot of new scents, even from yesterday," Hawk says under his breath. "Someone's working overtime to change the population—" Hawk's locker buddy shows up on his other side, practically materializing out of the wall. ". . . *of Canada*, yeah, you're right. Population is really thin over here." He carries on louder. "Oh, look! Vancouver!" Then flips the page with a side-ways glance at the girl.

"Yeah, Canada's fantastic," I say and nod, flipping to yet another page. "*Polar bears*. Enough said."

The girl leans over to see what we're reading. I guess we're being a little too loud. Her eyes scan the page and she gives us an odd look.

"You guys realize that's a physics textbook, right?" she says and wrinkles her nose because we're clearly the stupidest peo-ple on the planet.

"What, they don't have physics in Canada?" Hawk replies and tosses a smile.

The girl giggles loudly and walks away with a pronounced bounce in her step. Hawk and I roll our eyes before bending our heads over the mathematics equation. Just looking at it makes my head swim.

"If this pace keeps up," Hawk mutters, eyes flicking up to students walking past, "this wolf is going to end up converting the entire town."

"Give me an estimate," I say under my breath. "How many out of ten would you say are werewolves in the school at the moment?"

"Eleven," he grumbles. "I don't know! You think I can pick scents apart like they're nametags? And, oh, that national an-them! I love maple leaves too." He gives a lazy smile to another girl coming too close and she moves on. "But with this many wolves around, I have a feeling you're going to be drawing a lot more attention."

"Enough to draw out the black dog?" I mutter. A boy drops

his book bag right in front of us and scatters paper everyone. "Gotta love hockey, am I right? Hockey's the best in Canada. I love me some Canada. Mountains . . ."

"Snow," Hawk chimes in.

"Eskimos."

"Universal healthcare."

Wow, this kid is taking forever to move it along. I shuffle a few papers in his direction and he finally takes off. The hallways start to clear. I absent-mindedly grab my textbook and a notebook.

"And you're sure you can't just sniff our black wolf out?" I ask offhand.

He levels a glare at me. "Don't you think I would have if I could? Remember that time he showed up in Jefferson's backyard? I couldn't smell a thing."

"Stupid freakin' alpha wolf powers."

"Or something."

I sigh. "Where do you think the dream team is hiding?" I ask and search the corridor to see if one of them had the balls to come in dressed as a janitor.

Hawk grabs his things too and we walk to first period. "They probably set up cameras and mics around the building. If they were clever, they could have two younger agents sneak into the building posing as students—oh, wait! That's right."

"Go Team Thunderstruck!" I hold up my hand for a high five.

Hawk almost goes for it but then leans back. "*Pixies,* no, you are not doing that again."

"Doing what?"

"The last time you high fived me you fractured my wrist, you animal."

I raise an eyebrow at him and drive my shoulder into his. He almost teeters into the lockers. "*I'm* the animal? Let's go, party pooper."

We jog to English and slide into our seats seconds before the bell rings. During my first English class there was a single werewolf. Now when I enter the room seven heads turn in my direction. Passing by I make sure to hold each of their gazes long enough to see the yellow rims in their eyes. We position ourselves in the back and I sit forward in my seat, ready to give my powers a go.

Our teacher starts class and, to the cheers of the students, wheels in a television so we can watch a film adaptation of *Romeo and Juliet*. That's perfect actually. The lights turn off and it's action time. Hawk slides me a piece of paper I can barely read by the thin light coming through the blinds and from the television screen. It's a layout of the chairs and he's marked where each werewolf he's identified is sitting. He faces the television screen but watches me out of the corner of his eye.

I take a deep breath and focus on the closest werewolf two seats in front of me. It isn't hard to pick him out of the crowd. He's chewing the plastic on the edge of his binder and ripping it off with his teeth. Yeah, I'd say this guy's a bit on edge. At least it should be easy to tell if my power works. If it does, he'll hopefully stop going at the plastic like it's a steak.

My movie knowledge surfaces and I think of all the times I've seen the hero stretch out their hand, close those eyes, and move objects, twist metal, or levitate people. Slowly, so hopefully no one will notice, I extend my fingers and inch my arm off the desk towards the boy. My arm tenses and I concentrate—actually I don't even know what to concentrate on except the back of the kid's head and my disgust of him devouring a binder. At least he's not actually eating the plastic but spitting it to the side.

I stay that way for a couple of minutes but nothing happens. Frustration creeps up on me because I don't have a clue what I'm doing. I drop my hand, and at Hawk's questioning look I shake my head. What worked last time? I managed to calm Hawk. I kept stupid Matt from biting me. Why did it work then and not now? I didn't really concentrate or focus either of those times—I was terrified. Terrified of losing my brother. Terrified of being bitten. Terrified of Matt turning into a monster. Was it the fear or the raw emotion?

To test my fear theory, I imagine binder-chewing-kid suddenly transforming in the middle of the classroom, hackles rising and a deep growl churning out of his wolf throat. Then him losing control and attacking the blonde girl behind him, ripping into her, killing the kid wearing a band sweatshirt to his left. Hawk and I would rise to fight the wolf. I would try to use my power but Hawk would jump in first. He would move to protect me. My imagination soars and I'm feeding myself grisly images of my brother being torn in two.

I shudder and force the image away. The basc instincts buried deep in my bones catch fire just thinking of someone hurting my brother. I would stop that werewolf. I would stop it in its tracks.

I hold out my hand to direct my focus towards the boy. Imagined scenario or not, this werewolf could fly off his leash at any moment and I won't let anything happen to my brother. Not ever.

The boy stops chewing, wipes a sleeve across his mouth, and sets the binder aside. He glances around as if embarrassed then ducks his head, sets his chin in his hand, and focuses on Romeo fighting someone on the screen.

Hawk is staring at me, mouth agape but lips transforming into a smile. He holds his hands out towards me and shakes them for emphasis. *You did it*, he mouths.

I know! I mouth back and duck my head when the teacher stands on her toes to see what we're doing. We sit still long enough so her attention is drawn back to the movie. The coast clear once again, I set my sights on the next boy. I've got a better idea of what I'm doing this time. I stretch out my hand and focus that intense energy I harbor, that protective instinct. After a few minutes the boy stops shredding the bottom edge of his shirt and sets his hands calmly on top of his desk.

One by one I set my sights on each werewolf in the room until their anxious tremors and twitches disappear. My skin is on fire and my face burns. By the time the movie stops and the lights are turned on, I've got a headache and feel feverish. My long-sleeved shirt is suddenly too thin and I curl my arms around myself. The wound on my arm throbs so I hug it even closer.

The bell rings and it's time to leave. I rise and flash Hawk a big smile. I'm doing it. We give each other a low-five and walk to our lockers. My next class is with Mr. Webster and my rush of victory quickly ebbs to be replaced by something much darker. If Mr. Webster really is the black wolf, then he killed my parents and has been controlling the entire town. This is going to be my boss battle. I've got power running in my circuits—I just hope it's enough to take him down. I pull on my mother's jacket to hide in its warmth.

"I'm going to skip my next class," Hawk whispers to me. "I'll be hanging out right outside if you need me, okay?"

"Yeah, okay." I swallow and my eyes are drawn to the classroom door.

Hawk shifts his jaw back and forth. "I don't like leaving you alone in there with him."

"Well, tough luck," I say even though I'm of the same mind. "Pretty sure if you marched in there we'd end up having a confrontation in the middle of the school. We definitely don't want that."

"Now who's the party pooper?" He claps me on the shoulder and pushes me towards the door.

It takes everything in me to step through the open door calmly. My eyes instantly go to the teacher's desk and the rest of the room fades away. Mr. Webster sits in his chair easy as you please in a revolting brown and orange striped sweater. My feet are lead and I don't move for thirty seconds until someone bumps into me from behind. I ease between the desks and when I look back up my eyes connect with Mr. Webster's. Every inch of me burns and the world could catch fire right there. The pulses I had let off for the other werewolves now come off me in a tidal wave. Heat shimmers in the air around me.

His eyes narrow and he cocks his head ever so slightly like a dog before tilting his chin down until he's watching me through his eyebrows. A smirk lifts the corner of his mouth.

He knows. He knows exactly what I am.

24

Sociology plays out in a staring contest but I'm not willing to flinch. Mr. Webster fumbles through class while exchanging shots with me via eye contact. I never thought a glare could be so potent or used as a weapon but he manages to do just that. My skin lets off heat like a furnace. Fever chills set in and I wrap my mother's jacket closer to myself and prop up the collar.

My phone buzzes in my pocket and I sneak it out to read a text from Hawk. *Krushnic caught me standing around. Got kicked to class. Hiding in bathroom down the hall. U ok?* I stare Mr. Webster down again until he looks away then text Hawk to let him know I'm fine so he doesn't come storming in.

There are a few werewolves I recognize in the room. A couple are from my first class and they're already back to fidgeting, tearing at paper, ripping apart loose strings on their clothes, and close to pulling out their hair. Focusing once again, I try to calm them.

For a short while I have success. The werewolves manage to pay attention to the stumbling lecture but eventually regress to their anxious states. I spend the rest of the class split between trying to burn a hole through Mr. Webster with my eyes and sending out pulses to the werewolves in the room. My chills increase and my hands start to shake.

Near the end of class, Mr. Webster gives us free time to start on homework in groups. I remain on my own, ignoring the two people that try to invite me into their group. Once the rest of the class is preoccupied, Mr. Webster walks back directly to me. I grip my arms hard so I'm not tempted to reach up and strangle him.

"What are you doing?" he asks quietly, leaning in so our conversation can be carried in relative seclusion.

"What are *you* doing?" I shoot back. "You know, you're pretty unassuming. I'll give you that much. The whole hideous beachball look really throws off suspicion. I was expecting something more like Arnold Schwarzenegger."

His face turns puce. "*Excuse me?* You are out of line."

I lean forward. Anger makes me dangerous and reckless. This wasn't supposed to happen but now I can't stop myself. "Is this how you get your kicks? Enslave a generation?"

"You have some *nerve*, Ms. Mason, and I've had quite enough of your radical views on homework. I see you've neglected your own and refused to use this time to work with your peers. I'll be speaking to Principal Tippen about your attitude."

"You do that."

Before he can get another word out the bell rings. I don't move. He doesn't move. It's another staring match until he slides away to his desk at last. Why we can't just arrest him immediately is beyond me. I pick myself up on shaky legs and march out of the room. My head pounds, fever chills rack me, and my skin is sensitive to the touch. Feeling wretched, I clutch my arms to my chest and tuck my chin into the collar of my jacket.

"Hey hey hey," Hawk says as he rushes towards me to grab my upper arms. "You look terrible."

"I'm fine."

"Uh-huh. You need to work on your delivery if you want to be a convincing liar." He peers into my face so I push away from him.

"I'm fine. We've got work to do."

I swap books and walk with Hawk to our next class. Before we get there he takes me by the arm on a detour to a candy machine near the lunchroom.

"Seriously?" I grouse. "You've got the munchies?"

"Shut up." He buys a chocolate bar, bag of chips, and Skittles. Instead of keeping them for himself he pushes them into my arms before putting his hand on my back to guide me to our biology class.

We sit in the rear and I unload the snacks onto our combined desk. I rip open the Skittles first and realize I'm starving. The teacher hardly pays us any attention and sets the class to work on a lab inspecting cells on glass slides. The Skittles disappear within the first five minutes. Hawk doesn't even try taking some for himself—usually he's sneaking part of my snacks constantly.

"Thanks," I mutter and move onto the chips. I munch noisily while Hawk manages the slides on the microscope.

I'm eyeing the rest of the class to identify the werewolves when Hawk puts his hand on mine and leans in close.

"Don't. Not right now."

I pause with a chip en route to my mouth. "Why? Isn't doing *that* the whole point of being here today? It's been working."

"Yeah, a little too much I think." He gives me his best impatient parent look. "I think you need to take it easy. You're burning yourself out."

"What?" I shove the chip into my mouth and talk around it. "No, I'm not. I can handle a little hocus-pocus finger waggling if it means no one else goes bananas and snacks on people like they're fried chicken."

"Just eat your chips, you moron." He moves towards the microscope for only a second before apparently changing his mind and leans towards me again. "You remember the Pale Knight comics, don't you?"

I shove two more chips into my mouth. "Well, duh. The zombie knight."

We both got into comic books a while back after one of the agents in our apartment building, Tory, raided a troll's hoard and in the mess found an extensive comic book collection that he kindly gave to us to read. I always liked Tory.

"Don't you remember how much he had to eat because of his ability to throw those magic lances? He had to eat like a gazillion of those mystic flowers a day because he was always using that power. *He burned up all of his energy.*" He raises his eyebrows at me and gestures to my face. "You've got bags under your eyes like you haven't slept for a month, I can see you shaking, and are you cold or something? Because it's like 72 degrees in here and you're wearing a winter jacket."

I glower at him and eat a few more chips as loudly as I can. "Are you really basing this on something out of a comic book?"

He smirks at me and raises his hand to get the teacher's attention. I sit up straight and push the bag of chips away from me as our balding middle-aged teacher comes over in his plaid shirt.

"Yes? Questions?" he asks once he reaches our table.

"Yeah, a little off topic," Hawk says. "Isn't it a basic fact that the more energy you burn up, the more fuel you need?"

"Well, yes. Of course."

Hawk turns to me smug. "*Of course.*"

The teacher chuckles and shoves his hands in his pockets. "Does this have to do with the food consumption over here?"

"Totally," Hawk says with exasperation.

"Yes, well, human metabolism continuously needs energy in order to meet the demands of the body. The more you exert yourself, the more fuel your body needs. Otherwise, the body starts digging into other resources for energy. You don't feed yourself, your body's going to feed off *you.*" He lowers his eyes to look at us quite seriously through his eyebrows as if this is a major concern.

"Great," Hawk says. "Thanks for clearing that up."

"Okay, any more questions?" the teacher sighs. "Or can you two actually work on the assignment?"

"Sure thing, sir."

The teacher moves on and Hawk winks at me. I roll my eyes and snatch up my bag of chips. I scowl for the rest of the hour, wanting to keep doing what I came here for, but Hawk shoots me dirty looks if I even appear to be contemplating stretching out my hand and calming the few werewolves I see twitching around the room.

"What I don't get," I say after finishing off the chocolate

bar and feeling considerably better, "is why you aren't like the rest. Chewing binders, shredding your clothes. I'm not actively trying to do anything to you."

He shrugs and keeps his eyes on the microscope. "Maybe because we're twins? Because we've always been together? I mean, what if it's a link that's easy to pick up once it's already been made?"

I laugh at that. "Like wifi? Hard to make the connection, but once it's made you pick it up automatically?"

"Exactly." He winks at me again. "Just like wifi. I think you've been hanging around Witty too much. You're spitting out tech references as if they were in a movie."

"Yeah, because movies never mention computers or anything like that," I say sarcastically.

"I deny your logic and submit my own."

By the time the bell rings my chills have eased off. I do feel better and accept the fact that Hawk's reasoning might actually make sense. I certainly hope I don't have to keep munchies on hand all the time though if I want to keep calming werewolves and, in the future, even cure them. Hawk stops at the vending machine again and gets me another bag of Skittles. This time we split the bag in the back of physics class and Hawk allows me to give it another go. I calm a couple of wolves before the exhaustion creeps up on me again. I try to hide it from my brother so I can keep going but he grabs my hand and holds it down the rest of the period.

Lunch couldn't be more welcome. It's spaghetti with breadsticks and I'm famished despite the snacks earlier. I get my tray and scan the lunchroom for a place to sit. Hawk stands beside me frowning at the scene before him. The werewolves aren't at their own table anymore. They're everywhere, at every table, talking with every clique under the roof. It hits me that the werewolves haven't just changed tables, they've literally infected every group. How many more werewolves are there since the last day I was here? And with Dr. Rosewell missing, how many of them are even taking the serum?

"Phoenix. Hey."

I turn at the sound of my name and find Matt Jones behind me holding his own tray. His shoulders are hunched, he's got a black eye courtesy of my fist, and he stands there like he's waiting. I wonder if he remembers almost attacking me in the woods behind the school.

"Yes?" I ask.

"You coming?"

"Coming where?"

He starts to smile like he thinks I'm joking but then stops. "Detention. We've got lunch detention the whole week, remember?"

"Detention?" I draw a blank until I remember my first day. I punched Matt. Right. "Oh. Yeah. We should do that, I guess."

Now's not the time to be separating from Hawk but I can't just bring my brother along to detention. He nods once, giving me leave to go, before he stalks between the tables—a wolf on the hunt.

I reluctantly follow Matt out of the lunchroom to Captain Krush's classroom. He's sitting on top of his desk with a foot propped up on a student's chair, reading some kind of essay. When we enter he tosses the report to the side.

"That kid's not going to Harvard anytime soon," he mutters in an undertone. "Hey! Well, if it isn't my delinquents. Take a seat."

Matt sits at the very front and pats the desk next to him hopefully, motioning for me to join him. I clench my teeth and take the offered spot as politely as I can. I really don't want to talk to Matt—the last time we "talked" he spilled milk down Ashley's shirt on purpose and I knocked him flat.

Captain Krush crosses his arms over his chest and comes to stand in front of us. "You two all right? I missed you in class the other day. You're looking a bit rough around the edges."

"Nothing some spaghetti won't cure," I say and dig in.

"You sure it's nothing serious?" he presses. "I caught your brother hanging around outside your class earlier. He looked worried."

"Oh, he's just like a loyal puppy sometimes," I say, cherishing my inside joke. "We're good. It's all good."

"And you, Matt?"

Matt talks around a mouthful of spaghetti. "Fantastic, Captain."

The teacher glances at his watch and starts to backpedal to the door. "Well, as long as you two behave yourselves, I need to go get myself a sub."

"Don't you ever eat here?" I ask. You'd think bailing on supervising detention would get him in trouble too.

He looks shocked and holds a hand to his heart. "And eat with the other teachers? Nonsense. We substitute teachers never join the throng. Now keep put. I'll be back."

Captain Krush jogs out of the room leaving us alone.

I'm not left to eat my meal in peace. Matt ignores his food and spins around in his chair to face me directly, like Ben did during my last detention. I wish the werewolves would ease up around here without so much effort on my part.

"Hey, so . . . I'm sorry," Matt begins. "I almost—" He swings his head to sweep his hair out of his eyes dramatically. The self-absorbed gesture makes me want to punch him. Again. "I almost attacked you and I know I must have really freaked you out. I guess watching those *Love Moon* movies really made you okay with the whole werewolf thing, though, huh? You're handling it super good."

My face falls flat. He did *not* just say that. I hold up a finger for silence as I collect my thoughts and try not to be offended.

I clear my throat and shake my head. "First, I'd be handling it *well*. Check your grammar. Second, I'm not a *Love Moon* fan. I've never read the books and I only watched the movies to get up to date on the latest pop culture references for werewolves as required. Third, I'm cool with the whole *werewolf thing*—" I make air quotes. "—because my brother's been one for years. Fourth, and this is very important, you never, ever, *ever* start up a conversation about werewolves in public, you idiot. Didn't Jefferson talk to you about this crap?"

He leans away from me, one arm over the back of the chair, and throws on an air as if it's no big deal. "Yeah, he mentioned some stuff."

"Geez, it's a wonder nobody's discovered this place yet. Teenage wolves are morons." I run both hands down my face and fix my attention on my spaghetti.

"So, you're not into *Love Moon*?" he says sounding utterly surprised. "You were hanging with the team whatever crowd."

"I was hanging with the only people that were nice to me," I grumble. "That's it. That does *not* mean we've read all the same books, braided each other's hair, and bonded over vampire romance."

"Hey, I'll be nice to you. We could hang out. Talk about other stuff. Want to go somewhere with me tonight?"

I glare at him. "Are you trying to hit on me?"

"Maybe. Is it working?"

"No. Gross." I try to keep eating but he snatches my injured forearm and I let out a pained hiss. Instead of letting go at my reaction, he squeezes my arm until tears prick in my eyes from the wrenching pain of it.

"Let go," I wheeze out, "or I'll break your hand."

Matt's eyes have gone crazy and the yellow rims in them flare. I've never seen a werewolf's eyes react like that before. I grab his wrist and twist it hard. He yelps and hastily draws away clutching it. My breath comes out in rasps and I hold my arm gingerly. It's sure to have started bleeding again.

Before I can try to calm Matt down he lunges at me. My good hand goes straight for his throat. He scrabbles at my grip, giving me an opportunity to send a knee to his groin. His legs buckle. When he crumples, I step to his side and send my heel into the back of his leg. He sinks to his knees with a groan and I release his throat to shove him in the chest. He falls backwards into the hard desk and hits his head. Once he's dazed, I hold my hand out like I did for the others.

"Calm down, you maniac, or I'll put you face first into the floor," I growl.

He gasps for air but stops trying to fight. He sags and slumps into a sitting position on the floor between the desks, one hand holding the back of his head. Adrenaline makes my heart pound and my skin's ablaze again. Matt's eyes jump around the room like he doesn't recognize it.

"What just happened?" he asks breathlessly and his eyes finally settle on me. "How did you do that?"

"You have no idea who you're dealing with," I snarl. "Why did you attack me?"

"I don't . . . I don't know what came over me."

"Stay there," I order and jog to the door, throwing it wide.

If Matt is telling the truth and just received wolfy orders from his alpha, the black wolf could still be close by. I rush into the hallway and look both ways.

I spot a hideous brown and orange striped sweater move around the corner at the end of the hall.

Mr. Webster.

25

Jefferson picks up on the first ring. "What's going on?"

"Mr. Webster, that's what," I whisper into my cell phone while pacing outside Captain Krush's door. "He had Matt Jones attack me during detention."

"You know for sure?"

"I saw him walking away down the hall after Matt had a sudden *urge*."

"Hmm."

I tap my foot waiting for a more definitive answer. "Can we arrest him now?"

"That's not up to me anymore, Phoenix, but I'll tell the backup team what happened. Are you okay, though? Matt didn't hurt you, did he?"

"He tried," I say darkly. "He's regretting that decision."

"What did you—"

"Don't worry, I didn't kill anyone. I just twerked his wrist."

Jefferson's disapproving sigh is clear through the phone. "Keep your head down. You've definitely caught his attention and he's making his move."

"Yeah, so how long do we wait?"

"We'll get him," he assures me. "You've done your job so take it easy. We'll talk soon."

I stuff the phone into my pocket and storm back into the classroom. Matt has gotten into his chair and is alternating between massaging his head and wrist. No sympathy rises in me at his pain. My arm is throbbing horribly. I peel off my jacket and try to lift the sleeve of my shirt but it sticks to the bandage soaked through. I kick a desk in my anger and send it flying into the one behind it.

Matt jerks away from me. Good. He *should* fear me.

"You're going to say nothing happened. You're going to straighten out this mess." I point to the spaghetti that landed on the floor during our struggle. "It was an accident. You got up too fast. You got that?"

He nods. When I snatch up my mother's jacket and start to leave, he calls after me.

"Where are you going?"

"Tell him I'm cleaning spaghetti off myself," I say over my shoulder and march to the nearest girls' bathroom. Once inside, and after making sure there's no one else around, I don't bother to cover up the pain in my wheezy breath. I ease back my sleeve and carefully lift the edge of my bandage to inspect the damage. Blood drips down my wrist and into the sink.

"*Pixies*," I say under my breath and pull out my cell.

I'm in the middle of texting Hawk to come help me when the door swings open. I freeze with my phone in one hand and my bloody arm hovering over the sink. Ashley stops in the doorway, the face of a smirking vampire splashed across her shirt, and her mouth falls open.

"Uh, it's not what it looks like?" I say.

"Oh my gosh!" she squeaks and rushes forward. "What happened? Are you okay? Are you *bleeding*?" She holds her hands close to her chest like she's afraid to touch me.

"Oh, I'm fantastic," I say between clenched teeth. "Just a dog bite, that's all."

"Good thing it wasn't a werewolf, huh?"

My head jerks up. Her sad attempt at a smile quickly fades. Then it sinks in she's joking. She *is* a *Love Moon* fan.

"Yeah. Good thing." I laugh weakly.

"You need to see the nurse," she says.

"No. I'd really rather not." I can't risk the IMS team somehow figuring out I've been bitten. That would raise a lot of awkward questions. "You can't tell anyone, Ashley. Please."

"Did you at least see a doctor before? You could have rabies!"

That makes me laugh. "I definitely don't have rabies."

"Well, that looks bad."

"Yeah, I could use a fresh bandage. I can handle it from there."

She jabs her thumb at the door. "Well, the office staff likes me. I could get some from the nurse's office for you."

Ashley's full of surprises. "You'd do that for me?"

"Well, I'm not going to let you bleed out in a high school bathroom. *Gosh*, that would be an embarrassing way to die." She pats my shoulder. "Give me two minutes. I'll be right back."

She sweeps out of the bathroom, her hair fanning out behind her in her haste. I tuck my phone in my pocket. Hawk doesn't need to know. He'd just worry. If Ashley pulls through for me, then no one needs to know. Wish she could get me some ibuprofen too or something. I wince through the pain and start to unwind my red bandage.

True to her word, Ashley returns within a couple of minutes with a bundle of gauze and tape in her hands.

"How did you manage to get all that?" I ask, impressed.

"I said a boy in the lunchroom got a super bad bloody nose."

"And they let you take *that* much?"

She pouts. "I said it was really bad."

"It's perfect. Thank you."

I dump my old bandage in the trash and Ashley leans away to cover her mouth. Her eyes crinkle at the edges and she waves a hand.

"Sorry, I can't stand blood," she says.

"Go get some air, Ashley. And thanks. Really."

She nods but hustles out as fast as she can. After cleaning off the blood that's dribbled down my wrist and hand, I wind the fresh gauze around my arm and rip the tape with my teeth. After I'm patched up, I wring out the bloody sleeve of my shirt and hurry out of the bathroom before a wave of girls comes in from lunch. I shrug on my coat just as the bell rings.

Hawk meets me at our lockers and there's a line between his eyebrows. "Hey, things are getting scary out there," he says by way of greeting.

"Oh?"

"The other wolves are acting almost robotic, not agitated anymore, like they've passed that stage or something. They're . . . odd." He keeps his head down and waits for a group of girls to pass before speaking again. "No sign of Jason in school today but Ben's acting the same as the rest now. And they were watching me, like they know I'm not like them."

"That sounds familiar," I murmur. "I saw a couple of kids doing that to Ben before, watching him from a distance. That was when he was still fighting this compulsion or whatever."

"Think that's why they attacked the cattle at his place? Scare him into giving in?"

I shrug. "I don't know what else to think. He said he had been taking double doses of the serum to help fight it off so he probably held out longer than the others. That could have made them angry. That, and he was advocating for more help at the WA meeting to control the problem."

"Well, either way, he's part of the pack now."

"The dream team needs to move and end this," I grumble and slam my locker shut.

The rest of the day is spent keeping an eye on the werewolves in my remaining three classes. I calm a few more but I'm exhausted. Captain Krush even notices it during the very last class of the day.

"Sure you're okay?" he asks. "Matt didn't get too much spaghetti on you, did he?"

"No, I'm okay."

"If you say so."

We discuss more Greek mythology but I'm not really paying any attention. I'm drained, and trying to snap any werewolf out of their robotic state is taking up way too much energy. Jefferson is right. If the IMS finds out what I can do, they'd have to bleed me dry to get anything worthwhile out of me. There's just not enough power in my blood. Yet.

The bell rings and everyone empties out. I shuffle to my

locker and start loading up my backpack with a sigh. Hawk disappears to get me munchies before we go. When I'm by myself, Ashley comes over to check on me.

"I'm fine, really," I insist.

"Only if you're sure." She blows a few stray hairs out of her face and hugs her notebook to her chest. "I guess you'll still miss the dance though?"

"Dance?" That grabs my attention. "What dance?"

"The Halloween dance! Didn't you see any of the posters around school?"

"But Halloween's on Sunday."

She taps a finger on my shoulder. "Exactly. That's why they're having it tonight on Friday. That way we can stay up late for the dance. I've even been asked to go. You won't believe who asked me!"

"Who?"

"Only the love of my life." She sighs and goes all dreamy mode. "My Jason has come around and texted me asking if I'd go with him. Oh, and it's a costume dance. You get two bucks off admission if you dress up so we're going as a couple of elves. You're going to miss out."

I ease on my backpack. "Sounds like fun. But—wait, did you say Jason?"

"Yeah, Jason asked me to go. Big surprise, you know? He's been so moody and secretive lately but he's finally come around." Her smile is enormous. "But maybe I'll see you there, okay? Gotta go or I'll miss my ride."

She starts dashing away down the hallway.

"Wait, Ashley! Don't go to the dance!"

She waves me off and keeps moving. I'm ready to chase after

her but a hand snakes out of the crowd and wrenches me to a halt. Agent Moore glares at me.

"Hands off," I growl.

His nostrils flare. "You've almost compromised this entire mission. Did you really think provoking our suspect was a good idea? We heard your little fight with Mr. Webster."

"I'm doing what needs to be done to close this case," I respond in an undertone. The hallway is almost clear but there are a few stragglers. "With the way the wolves are behaving around here, you need to act sooner rather than later."

His hand tightens painfully on my arm. "That wasn't your decision to make."

"Hey, I'm willing to work with you guys if you'd *allow* us to."

"You're just a couple of punks and a has-been in over your heads."

I pull my arm out of his grip. "Well, these punks and has-been aren't going to sit on the sidelines and watch."

He towers over me and uses that height to try and make me feel small. "And the lower on the ladder you are, the less anyone's going to care. Get out of here."

I automatically shift into a stance where I can throw a punch or hold my ground. Then I stop. Any other day I might have followed through, and gotten myself arrested in the process, but I see Hawk over the agent's shoulder in the distance. He shakes his head. I back down and move past Agent Moore for the doors. Hawk meets me there and we walk out together. He passes me another chocolate bar but I shove it into my pocket. I'm too angry to eat.

"What was that all about?" Hawk asks.

"Nothing. Just a turd being himself."

Jefferson pulls up as the buses wheel out and we hop in. "So? How'd it go?"

"Fantastic." I pull the door shut. "We've got a problem."

"Yeah, I know." Jefferson puts the truck into gear and we head out. Instead of going the usual way he takes some side streets. "I got Agent Smith to talk to me. They managed to overhear a few things today, like the fact that Mr. Webster is supervising a dance tonight."

"Crap, that would be it." I hold a hand to my forehead. "Jason—the jerk that bit me—invited Ashley to the dance."

"Who's Ashley?"

"A friend."

Hawk pats my arm to get my attention. "I heard a lot of the werewolves inviting people to that dance."

"Could be a coincidence," Jefferson says. "It's a dance. Kids go to those. Doesn't have to be sinister."

"No, but *every* werewolf was asking everyone to go. That can't be good."

I thump my head back against the seat. "So that's what Matt was talking about. He tried asking me out to the dance."

"What?" Hawk looks me up and down. "Seriously? You got asked out?"

"Yeah, shut it."

"What did you say?"

"I said no! He's a jerk and a lunatic and he—" I forgot I haven't mentioned the detention incident and wasn't planning on it. "Well, he sort of attacked me."

"*What?* Why didn't you say anything?" Hawk exclaims.

I hold up a hand. "Relax! It's fine. He didn't *really* hurt me, but I think Mr. Webster made him do it. It was pretty out of no-where and Webster was walking away down the hallway when I checked. On a side note, do we have any ibuprofen?"

Hawk throws up his hands and refuses to look at me any-more. Jefferson stops outside the Java Jitters coffee shop and offers to buy us caffeine.

"We're going to need it," he says. "The other team will be keeping surveillance on Mr. Webster up to and at the dance but we'll need to be there too. A large group of werewolves and stu-dents all together in an enclosed space? Gives me a bad feeling."

We order our drinks and Jefferson stops at the local drug store to get me some pain meds. Once we're jacked up on cof-fee and my arm isn't hurting so bad, we swing by the barn to pick up the tranquilizer guns. The next several hours we spend sitting in the truck on a wooded trail behind the school out of sight. The light wanes and street lamps flicker on around the school, flooding it with orange light. Jefferson has a walkie talkie sitting on the dash and we listen in on the updates from the other IMS team. Apparently Mr. Webster decided to spend his time leading up to the dance in his office grading paper-work and then setting up decorations in the gym.

"It's a costume dance," I whisper in the relative quiet. The only sound is the rustling of the wrappers of our junk food.

"Seriously?" Hawk whispers back. "We're so missing out. Who would you dress up as?"

"I don't know. You could show up as a wolf and people would compliment you on how awesome your costume is. I'm sure that *Love Moon* fan club would fawn over you."

"You could be a troll. You wouldn't need to dress up."

I punch him in the arm and he groans. We start a hitting match until Jefferson hisses at us to break it up. To distract myself, I focus on loading and unloading my tranquilizer gun. There's way too much time to think so I'm considering what jobs I might be doing after this is done. I'm still scared we might get the boot out of Underground too. Director Knox said before that we were special cases so we could stay, but is it possible we could screw up so bad that we couldn't even be trusted there, our home?

"You look grouchy," Hawk whispers.

"It's my default setting," I mutter and pop the magazine out of my gun again, push the darts in and out, pop the magazine back in, and pull on the slide.

The walkie talkie crackles, saving me from having to explain anything. "They're opening the doors for the dance." It's Agent Moore. "A couple of kids are already here. Mr. Webster's still popping popcorn at the concession stand. Agent Smith, you might want to get a better angle on your lenses to see the dance floor."

"This is so stupid," I say. Thankfully the mute button is on at our end so they can't hear me. "They need people in there and not watching on the outside. If something goes wrong and they lock the doors, how are we supposed to help anyone trapped inside?"

From our vantage point I see more students park in front of the school and head in wearing all sorts of costumes. I even spot a boy dressed as the Pale Knight. Ashley will be among the crowd soon—the only person out of the whole school that's been nice to me walking into a possible trap. Right then an old beater pulls up and she steps out of the passenger side wearing a short skirted outfit, has pointed ears sticking out of her hair, and holds a staff. Jason doesn't appear to have dressed up at all.

"That's Ashley and Jason," I say, my hand already on the handle. "I can't leave her alone in there. This is a trap. It's got to be. Jefferson."

He looks long and hard at me. There's some serious internal debate going on behind those beady eyes. We've got orders to keep away and "let the professionals handle it," but Jefferson knows better. He knows we've all got a stake in this. We won't slip up when it really counts.

He rolls his lips then digs into his pocket and hands over some loose cash. "Better put on your glass slippers. You're going to the ball."

26

Hawk and I join the throng of students entering the gymnasium where the dance is taking place. We pass carved pumpkins and walk under fake spider webs and paper skeletons hanging from the ceiling. Near the doors they've set up a little stand where our English teacher is handing out tickets. I pass over the cash Jefferson gave me and we're allowed in.

It's dark inside except for strobe lights from a raised DJ's stand at the back and a disco ball flashing overhead to illuminate the fake fog being continuously pumped onto the dance floor. The music is already blaring to some techno tune and the students have carved out a niche in the middle of the floor to hop around shaking their hips.

"Don't tell me you didn't miss this," Hawk shouts in my face to be heard.

I grin. Yeah, I did miss this. Our performance against the elves in their dance competition gave us some serious street cred in Underground. They hosted it in the water sprites' cavern. The fire sprites even showed up to light the place in a dazzling display of their own and the water sprites created a mist to give the whole place a magical gleam. Then the elves toted in their seriously impressive sound system and we duked it out. The setting here is reminiscent but nowhere close to the spectacle of that day.

Tucked in the far corner with the only normal lights on is a concession stand. Mr. Webster stands at a glass-paneled popcorn machine adding oil and kernels to a pot. I nudge Hawk and nod in Webster's direction. At least we know where he is and can keep an eye on him. I scan the crowd and spot Ashley off to the side with Jason. Her arms are crossed and she's pouting.

I make my way over and wave to get her attention. Her face lights up when she spots me and she jumps up and down in place.

"You made it!" she shouts. "I didn't think you'd come!"

"Me? Miss out on a dance? I don't think so." My eyes move to Jason. He's a statue and hasn't moved an inch except to stare at me out of the corner of his eye. Creepy. Hawk tenses and almost goes after the guy that bit me but I grab his arm to hold him back. We can't even arrest Jason without revealing I'd been bitten, which is a big no-no according to Jefferson. I'm frustrated too but we have bigger things to worry about.

"Awww, you didn't dress up," Ashley says disappointed.

"Can't you tell? I came as a student."

"Ha, good one." She thumbs her nose at me and then tries to tug Jason onto the dance floor but he doesn't budge.

Now that he's really creeping me out, I put a hand on his shoulder and let that protective instinct do its work. I don't want him hurting Ashley or anyone else. His tense muscles thaw out enough so he turns his head to look at me.

"Go on," I shout over the music. "Take the lady for a dance."

His eyes find Ashley and he takes her hand to guide her into the middle of the hip-shaking group. Ashley starts some disco moves so I carry on with Hawk to walk the perimeter of the dance floor. The more the crowd swells, the more people I spot standing robot-like as Jason had. They're on the edges like sentinels to the dancing teens still unaffected by the werewolf disease. More and more the whole situation feels like a trap. Is the black wolf trying to infect all the remaining teenagers at the same time? Why change his strategy now? Picking them off one by one seemed to have been working fine.

To blend in better, Hawk and I move a little ways into the dancing crowd and do an easy side step back and forth to the beat. Time moves on but nothing happens. The werewolves keep standing guard in a ring with some scattered through-out the dancing crowd. My English and biology teachers and Captain Krush walk around to chaperone and occasionally break apart teens grinding together. Students rush back and forth to the concession stand for drinks and soon there's a litter of pop bottles lining the walls and a few students sitting down to catch their breath or talk before joining in again.

Hawk and I separate to keep our eyes on a wider area. I jive my way to the side to check on the concession stand. Mr. Webster isn't there anymore. I stop even pretending to dance and break out of the crowd to find where he's gone. "Monster Mash" starts to play and I'm bumped into from behind. Jason doesn't pay me any attention as he stalks past to the exit. He's not the only one. Two others join him to hang out near the doors—blocking them more like. I jog around to check the other exits only to discover more werewolves are moving for those too.

I whip out my phone and text Jefferson. *Wolves locking down exits. Need assist.*

Hawk finds me a few seconds later, his eyes on the werewolves playing guard dog at the doors. "Webster?" he asks.

I shake my head.

My phone buzzes with a text from Jefferson. *We're moving in. Give us a distraction. No fights.*

I hold my phone out so Hawk can read it. "You thinking what I'm thinking?"

"Way ahead of you," he says.

He rushes around the dancers to the DJ's booth while I push my way to the center of the dancing crowd. I wait there while "Monster Mash" continues for thirty seconds until it's cut off. The students around me groan their displeasure at the silence but then Hawk jumps on a mike next to the DJ.

"We've got a special show for you tonight!" he shouts, his voice booming through the gym. "Clear the center because we're going to blow your minds!"

He jumps off the stage in true Hawk fashion—over the top and flashy—to exclamations and gasps as people move out of the way. He stops fifteen feet away from me and the remaining crowd shrugs back to give us room. The music starts on a strong drumbeat and little else. I can't stop the smile from spreading on my face. Adrenaline hits me in a shockwave. The pain in my arm dulls enough so I might be able to pull this off.

Hawk and I start sliding in opposite directions to the beat, twisting around and back again, slowly coming in closer as techno chirps add to the beat. Even though I haven't done this routine in a while, I still know it by heart. This is how we beat the elves and now it's going to be our ticket to help save the werewolves.

The beat picks up and the techno pulses in loud bursts. We slide together and start doing our synchronized pop and lock moves. The students cheer us on once we prove we're actually good at this and aren't just *trying* to dance. The music hits harder so we enter our trickier hip hop moves. Hawk and I play off each other, grabbing hands and leaning back sharp only to pull ourselves back up. I roll over his back at the same time he pops up so I catch big air and roll out into a breakdance spin when I land.

The crowd is going crazy and all eyes are on us. Hawk and I spread out in opposite directions, rolling in tight spins on the floor then jumping up to catch the beat. We race at each other and jump to twist past within inches, over and under in acrobatic flips. My arm's burning hot and sure to be bleeding again but I manage to pull off each stunt. There's a kind of interlude during the middle of the song where it settles into the bare beat. Hawk and I run around the edge of the circle we've created, raise our arms, and beckon to the crowd with the beat. They eat it up and cheer even louder.

Dimly through the music I hear something crack and see a commotion near the door. Hawk and I get more enthusiastic about whipping the crowd into a tizzy before the techno jumps back in with the beat and we meet in the center for a mix of hip hop and kung fu moves. We stage a sort of mock battle in the center before we both fake punch each other out and spin away on our knees—which hurts like mad on this linoleum floor. The beat surges into its hardest hitting bangs and we do our grandest, most energetic leaps and flips off each other, then the beat slowly eases until it's all that's left. Our moves slow to our original gliding around each other in opposite directions and the song ends. We wave our hands to bring the crowd in and we're practically mobbed.

I'm on a high and jumping up and down. Over everyone's heads I spot Jefferson at the doorway. He's tucking something into the back of his waistband and gives me an O.K. sign with his hand. Danger momentarily averted, I let myself be congratulated by the mob and the DJ hops on the mic to say how explosive that was and everything is right with the world.

Then Mr. Webster's voice thunders through the gym. "NOW'S THE TIME!"

A second later I hear snarls. Then the screaming starts.

Panic sets in three seconds after everyone stops to comprehend that someone is screaming bloody murder. In an instant, the students start to stampede in every direction. Hawk and I, being in the very center, are shoved and hit and I'm nearly run over. Hawk stumbles forward and falls to the ground so I wrap my good arm around his waist and haul him to his feet. We stay put as the crowd disperses around us and look for the source of the mayhem.

It's not hard to spot. Five wolves are rounding up students at the north end. Agent Moore appears out of nowhere with his tranquilizer gun in hand and starts firing, causing even more panic.

"THIS WAY!" Jefferson bellows. "GET TO THE PARKING LOT!"

He waves students over to the doorway he's opened and everyone rushes out in a flood. They scatter in every direction, some out to the woods which might be an even worse place to go. Hawk and I rush to help Jefferson keep the students from falling into more danger.

"Smith and I've got this!" Jefferson shouts at us. "Just stop those wolves!"

He tosses a spare gun and I catch it. I lock and load before sprinting back through the mob of students trying to escape, and nearly trip over someone spread out on the ground. Hawk slides to a stop behind me to help our English teacher to her feet.

"I've got her!" he says. "Go, go!"

I keep on and the second I'm clear of the crowd I raise my gun and fire at the closest wolf. The dart hits it in the neck and it staggers to the side before falling over. A girl the wolf was about to bite lays in the fetal position on the ground. I try to help her up but she screams and ignores me. Another wolf charges us from the side. I drop to one knee to stabilize my body and fire off two shots. The wolf trips over its own feet and skids to a stop, tongue lolling out.

I forcefully grab the prone girl's arm and haul her to her feet so she won't get trampled at least. As she stands there balling her eyes out, I jog on with my gun still raised to help out Agent Moore and the other Agent Smith trying to put down a group of wolves that have students trapped. I smell blood, then see blood on the floor illuminated by the strobe lights. I pop off one shot, then another, then another, and wolves start to drop. But there's no black wolf, no sign of Mr. Webster.

The other two agents are quick to tranquilize the rest and hustle between the furry bodies to pull out injured students. I move forward to help when there's another scream.

"Phoenix!"

I whip around and spot Ashley being dragged out the east exit by a great black wolf, her arm in its jaws.

"Ashley!"

I sprint across the linoleum, gun in hand, as sweat runs down my forehead. I slam into the door and it flies off its hinges. The hallway is empty in either direction and it's quiet apart from the muffled screams coming from the gym. It's hard to see but there's a dark trail of droplets on the floor that lead south. I keep my gun level and follow the path at a jog. It ends outside the double doors to the kitchen. Pressing my shoulder to the first door, I ease it open softly and keep my gun trained ahead of me.

It's pitch black except for the red glow of the exit sign and the little indicator lights on the ovens. If I turn on the lights it'll give away my position. In those few moments I'll be vulnerable, but if I keep going in the dark the werewolf will have the advantage with its better night vision.

I hear sniffling and the quiet groans of a person in pain. Ashley. Taking my chances, I feel along the wall, crouch down to hide behind the stainless steel counter, and flick on the light switch. The glare is brilliant and I squint against it. There's a thunderous crash of pots and pans and I look up just in time to see the black wolf leaping for me. I fire off a single shot but it goes wide over the wolf's shoulder. I roll out of the way as it crashes to the floor where I was a moment ago and try to fire again but the slide locks back in place. The gun is empty.

The wolf snaps its jaws forward aiming for my throat. I kick it hard in the chest before it gets too close and send it backwards into a stainless steel table. Utensils fall around it and a bucket topples down to sit on its head like a helmet, momentarily blinding it. As it untangles itself, I scramble to my feet and sprint past the row of ovens and racks. I grab one and wrench it down behind me to block the way. The wolf snarls and gnashes its teeth as it rips the bucket off its head. At the end of the row I find Ashley lying in a pool of blood clutching her arm to her stomach and moaning. She's alive at least.

The wolf is coming but it's not going to get her—not my one friend in this stupid school. I spin around and plant myself in front of her. I hold out both hands and with every ounce in my body will the monster to stop. It clambers over the fallen rack and leaps for me so I bend my knees and brace myself. My hands meet its throat, I lean my head to the side to avoid its teeth, and then shove as hard as I can. The wolf slams into the wall, dazed. Breathing hard, I stretch my hands out towards it once more.

"Stop!" I shout. "You try touching me or my friends again and I'll snap your neck. You aren't going to hurt anyone else ever again."

The wolf rises and I pour out my heart and soul trying to calm or stop it with what power there is in me. It twitches and shakes it head trying to fight the surge I'm sending it. Fever chills instantly crawl up my back and I'm shaking on my legs. I'm burning from the inside out but the wolf is still coming towards me.

"Stop," I wheeze. "Just stop. *Stop.*"

A loud pop makes me jump and a shudder ripples through

the black wolf. Two more pops. It teeters on edge with three tranquilizer darts in its shoulder, sways left then sways right, and collapses in a lump on the floor. I stumble backwards and catch myself on the edge of the counter. Blood drips into my mouth so I run the back of my hand under my nose to block the flow.

Framed in the doorway at the other end of the kitchen is Hawk slowly lowering his gun. His eyes are dark and dangerous. When they finally meet mine, they're practically sparking. Then the spell snaps and he rushes forward. I sink to the floor next to Ashley and brush Hawk off when he tries to help me first.

"We've got to give her the serum," I say between sharp breaths.

Pixies, she's lost a lot of blood. We need to get her out of here and into the hands of a doctor. Tucking my arms underneath her, I haul her up. I stagger a bit but manage to get my shaky legs under me. It's not that I can't handle her weight but fighting the black wolf really took it out of me.

"Cover us in case there's another psycho around," I mutter to Hawk.

He doesn't argue and guides the way back to the gym. The screams have mostly stopped to be replaced by cries of pain and sobbing. In the distance police sirens pierce the night. Well, that's just great. Agent Moore kneels next to a boy on the floor while talking rapidly into his cell phone. Jefferson walks in carrying a black box. Once we reach the others, I gently set Ashley on the floor.

Jefferson unloads his black box full of serum syringes and pain medication. While Agent Moore and one of the Smiths head off the police in the parking lot, we distribute serum injections to those bitten. We're fast and the injections are applied within the time window. They'll be changing within the hour but they won't be monsters, only terrified. Terror is something we can help them with. The black wolf may have struck a blow but he lost the battle. We got him.

Ashley comes back to her senses after I give her an injection and wind a strip of gauze around her wounded arm. Her eyes flutter open and there are streaks of mascara on her face. One of her elf ears hangs lopsided off her head and the other is simply missing.

"It was a wolf, you know," she breathes. "A werewolf. Our stupid sociology teacher."

"I know."

Her eyes bulge at my acceptance of such insanity so quickly. "You do?"

"I'll explain later, but you're going to be fine. You're going to change but you'll be fine. That's what matters."

She pinches her eyelids shut. "I think I really don't like *Love Moon* so much anymore."

I let out a shaky laugh. "At least some good came out of this then."

27

I never realized how much of a fiasco it is when the IMS clashes with ordinary police. Agent Moore is in a shouting match for the longest time with the sergeant, then the chief when he shows up, and there's a lot of explaining to do. Agent Moore concocts some story about weaponized rabies in a pack of wolves and blah, blah, blah. The ambulances arrive and those bitten are loaded up to be overseen by specialized caretakers when they change. The unconscious wolves are packed in the back of three animal control vehicles which will divert to Jefferson's cabin so they can be processed.

I help load the black wolf in the largest cage. Neither Jefferson nor I are careful about it. I still can't believe we've finally caught him. Everything was such a rush earlier that it doesn't seem real. It almost happened *too* fast. That feeling of accomplishment and justice I'm hoping for hasn't hit home yet. Then again, I don't know if I'll ever get that feeling. The IMS team will be taking him to Underground and we may never know why Webster did what he did.

With this whole thing at an end, it'll only be a matter of time before the bad news is delivered. For now I try to focus on the clean up but it's difficult knowing that each hour is counting down to an uncertain life where I'll never get my badge.

After some more explanations and statements with the police, three black SUVs from the IMS along with a helicopter show up and take over managing the situation at the high school. We're finally excused and the three of us pile into Jefferson's truck. We share a moment of silence and exhaustion before we follow the animal control vehicles back to our base of operations.

It's well past midnight once we get there so Jefferson turns on all of his floodlights outside. Agent Moore and three new IMS agents pull the black wolf out and put him in chains in the barn. We all wait around for him to wake up. Jefferson and I lean against the Green Monster and watch. We're not allowed to participate anymore. More agents show up to drive the other teenage werewolves off to be questioned and checked out at Underground. I wonder how many of them will be charged for what they did under Mr. Webster's control. They don't take Mr. Webster just yet because the Smiths are loading up copies of our files; otherwise, we wouldn't even get to witness this part. One of the specialized caretakers eventually comes to report that those freshly turned are doing fine and more agents are watching over them for the time being.

At last, when the night is deepest, the wolf twitches awake. His yellow eyes appraise us and the chains on all four paws. He gives a great sigh then convulses as his body changes back into human shape. His bulk condenses in spasms into Mr. Webster wearing that hideous brown and orange sweater. I can't believe the black wolf is really him, even after everything. This is the mastermind?

His thinning hair is in disarray and he settles into a cross-legged position with as much dignity as he can muster. He holds up his chin and his gaze passes over us, pausing longer on me than anyone.

"Mr. Webster," Agent Moore begins, crouching down so he's at eye level with him. "You're under arrest for multiple charges of assault, murder, attempted murder, kidnapping, and a string of other federal violations we'll get into later. Under the provisions of the Dragon Pact, you may be held without representation for an indefinite period of time." He rattles off a series of rights Mr. Webster has under the Dragon Pact and Federal Title 51.

"Rights. Powers. *Detention*," Mr. Webster scoffs. "You'll never be safe from me, you fools. I'll come back for my children."

"Why?" I ask and Agent Moore shoots me a dirty look. "What was the point of any of it?"

"Power is power," he sneers. "Those under my command will obey me to whatever end. And those that get in the way . . . well, you know how that goes."

My breathing hitches and I take a step forward. Surprisingly, it's Hawk that holds me back this time. He shakes his head and walks me outside. I'm fuming and grabbing at my hair. I let out a shout of my built up rage and pick up a rock from the gravel driveway to hurl into the forest.

"It's over, Phoenix," Hawk says. "It's over. He's going to be locked up. We get justice for our parents."

"Right. Yeah. Then why doesn't it feel like it?"

I go and sit on the hood of the old truck and stare off to the woods. Hawk comes to sit beside me. We stay there as the agents finally pack up and haul Mr. Webster into the back of their SUV to escort him to Underground. Jefferson walks them out to their vehicle and they exchange frosty farewells. I wait for them to drop the bad news about our termination but they don't say anything. They probably think we aren't worth the effort and we'll get a letter in the mail. They drive away and it's suddenly too quiet.

Jefferson walks over to lean against the bumper of the truck. The only sounds are the birds in the trees and the creak of branches in the cold breeze. The first traces of dawn touch the sky to the east.

"Is that it?" I ask. "Now what do we do?"

"We check on the new werewolves, make sure they get the serum and understand what their lives will be like from now on. Then we need to find Dr. Rosewell, Deputy Graham, and everyone else who's still missing. They'll probably send an agent or two back to help once they take care of the lot they took to Underground."

"Can we at least catch some sleep before then?"

"Yeah, I second that," Hawk says. "Trying to save a city is exhausting."

Jefferson chuckles and we head indoors. For once I'm able to fall asleep immediately but we're not allowed peace for long. In the afternoon we're woken by the Agent Smith with glasses who's returned to help us sort out the mess like Jefferson said. We head to a farmhouse where the new werewolves are currently being housed by another resident werewolf until they've adjusted.

The serum's done its job and without the black wolf's influence, they're in their right minds. Ashley starts jabbering away as soon as I arrive. She wants to know all about werewolves and can't believe Jason was one the whole time and how we need to hang out more.

Once we check that off our list, we spread out in pairs to check on the werewolves we know about that either weren't involved in the attack at the high school or have already been questioned and released by the IMS. Quite a few are detained in Underground after having confirmed they bit people. Hawk insists on putting some distance between him and me just to make sure there's no lingering influence from the black wolf in his werewolf genes and Jefferson agrees. So, Agent Smith tags along with me as we go to visit Ben and his mother. Ben answers the door looking better than he has in a long time.

"Hey!" he says and flashes a smile. "I'm so glad to see you're okay."

"Yeah, I'm peachy," I say and rub at my eyes. "What about you, Ben?"

"Better. Lots better. I mean, I feel horrible about what happened at the dance and can't remember much but, yeah. Better now."

"Good. And your mom?"

He points upwards. "She's in her room. We're all good. Whatever you guys did, thank you."

"Sure thing, Ben. Keep your nose clean, okay?"

He closes the door and Agent Smith and I trot down the steps. He reaches for the car door but misses the handle. He laughs to himself and wipes at the corner of his eyes.

"I could use some sleep," he says.

"Couldn't we all."

We get into his black SUV and he fumbles getting the seatbelt to latch. He swears under his breath and pats his face to wake himself up. We rumble along to the next house on our list where Matt Jones lives.

"So, are you guys going to celebrate?" Agent Smith asks.

"Celebrate what?"

"Your victory! Your help was invaluable during that confrontation. You should celebrate your victories."

I stare at him. He was never this cheerful or nice before. That, and he's making it sound like we should celebrate because it's the last chance we'll have before he has to inform us we're all screwed by the IMS. "Yeah. We should do that."

"We could go see a movie or get some take out or . . ." He's so focused on talking to me that he starts to veer off the road. I grab the wheel and yank us back onto the pavement. He shakes himself and has trouble keeping the lane.

"Are you sure you should be driving?" I ask. I just survived an attack last night. It would be embarrassing to die in a stupid car crash now.

"I'm fine. Really."

It's an awkward rest of the day, going door to door and handing out serum injections that Agent Smith brought back with him from Underground. At least all of the werewolves have returned to their normal lives. Things are almost peaceful. An ideal town full of people waving to their neighbors and smiling. Seems a little forced to me but maybe I'm just crabby. Spending a day on the town with Agent Smith is not my idea of fun.

At last when the sun sets, we all meet back up at the cabin.

We're each shuffling around drowsy. I don't want to sit down because I've got this nagging feeling in the back of mind like I'm forgetting something. Everything is just so . . . *incomplete.* I sit in the lone chair in front of the computer that doesn't work. Hawk sits on the table about to nod off beside me. Jefferson starts a pot of coffee despite the hour. Then there's Agent Smith bouncing up on his toes as he paces.

"Here," Jefferson says and passes a cup to him. Agent Smith takes it very deliberately and sniffs at it. Jefferson passes us cups too and we sit or stand around in silence sipping the steaming coffee.

I spin my cup in circles between my hands. "I don't get it."

"It's coffee," Hawk says pointedly. "You're supposed to drink it."

"Not that, smart alec." I shove at his legs dangling over the table. "I meant the whole . . . the whole everything. The dance, the attack, the building an army, and then giving up so easily. And his explanation. It doesn't sit right with me."

Agent Smith nods. "Sometimes it's hard to feel true closure after you've solved a case. A criminal's motives can be so strange it's often hard to believe that's really all there is to it. But it's over. We caught him and that's what's important. Don't worry, you'll have plenty more cases to solve in the future to keep you occupied."

My coffee cup slips from my hands and splashes hot liquid all over the floor, including the agent's shoes. He jumps back and Hawk hops off the table to grab paper towels.

"I'm sorry, I—w-what did you say?" I stutter. I couldn't have heard that right.

"I said more cases will come to you so don't worry about it."

"But I thought—" I glance to Jefferson and Hawk. They never knew what Witty told me about the plans the IMS had for us, or more like lack thereof. We are the designated troublemakers and were to be tossed away like garbage. "They really want us to keep working cases?"

"Of course!" He smiles and raises his cup towards me. "I said we ought to celebrate, didn't I? Hey, how about you go pick up some snacks, Phoenix? Hawk, you want to run to the video store with me and grab a movie to watch?"

Hawk straightens from mopping up the coffee. "Jefferson, do you even have a T.V.?"

"In back." He continues to sip his coffee. "I think it still works."

"Well, then, yeah. Sure. Why not?"

"Great!" Agent Smith rubs his hands together. "You and I can take my car. We'll race you back, Phoenix. Let's go."

I get up with a sigh and hold my hand out to Jefferson. He passes me the keys to the truck without argument. I guess he doesn't mind the idea of movie night. Despite how tired I am, I don't think it's so bad either. I haven't watched a movie in ages, and *Romeo and Juliet* at school definitely does not count.

Hawk and Agent Smith pull out ahead of me before I throw the truck into gear. It rumbles to life, I tune the radio to an oldies station, and pull out. I've become familiar enough with Moose Lake so I know where to go and make for the closest gas station in town. A light snow starts to fall and flickers in the headlights. Guess the snowstorms will be starting early.

The town's quiet and there's hardly anyone on the main road. I park next to a red pickup at the gas station and browse the aisles for snacks. I load up with Skittles, chocolate, popcorn, and root beer. There's a thin blonde woman I keep bumping into in each row. I think I catch her watching me out of the corner of my eye but when I face her she's reading candy labels. A trucker in a plaid shirt flips through a hotrod magazine in another aisle and his eyes follow me too.

I dump my load on the counter and pay for the snacks, checking over my shoulder to find the man and woman still aimlessly browsing without actually picking anything out. I thank the cashier, a kid I vaguely recognize from school, and hop in the truck. I rip open the Skittles to start eating them and sit with the engine rumbling, keeping my eyes on the people in the store through the windows. They haven't moved an inch since I came outside. I put the Skittles down and throw the truck into reverse.

"Okay. Weird," I mumble to myself.

I try to brush it off. I'm ready to get back to the cabin and have one night of peace and quiet. I'm really sick of everyone acting like creepers around here. Taking North Road, I crank up the tunes and drive about half a mile out of town when a red truck races up behind me. It comes up on my bumper and stays there.

"Oh, come on. Moron."

I squint past the headlights in the rearview mirror and realize it's the same truck from the gas station. It stays right on my tail. I slow a little so maybe it'll pass me but it keeps pace. Okay, this is getting unnerving. I hope it'll turn off onto a driveway soon but then it speeds up and moves to pass. I slow even more to allow it to go around me. That's when I realize it's the lady from the gas station. As I look on, she twists the wheel and smashes the front end of her truck into the side of mine.

I jerk hard against my seatbelt and the truck screeches in protest. I try to straighten out but she comes at me again. The truck trembles and I skid on gravel along the shoulder. She's trying to ram me right off the road. I yank the wheel hard and lean into the next blow. The window on the driver's side cracks but doesn't shatter. I silently thank Jefferson for having such a hardy old truck that can take a few blows.

I'm concentrating so hard on staying on the road and keeping the lady off me that I don't see the headlights in front of me until it's too late. A semi roars towards me and the red pickup blocks me on the left. The only escape is going off the road.

There's nothing for it. I've got a split second to react so I yank the wheel as hard as I can to the right. The semi plows through the back end of the truck, wrenching me against the seat belt and sending me spinning out into the woods. The sound of metal twisting and glass shattering fills every space and I'm hurled this way and that, shards pelting my face until I'm slammed bodily forward against my seat belt as the truck meets a tree.

I black out and when I come to every part of me aches and my head swims. The screeching has stopped but there's still a ringing in my ears. I can't move a muscle. I can only try to blink away the blood beginning to creep into the corner of my eye.

The roar of the semi is what forces me to act. I crane my neck around and see the headlights swing about on the road to find me here, a sitting duck. I claw at my seat belt but it's stuck and won't unlatch. Frantic, I rip the whole thing apart. The driver's door is caved in and won't open so I crawl over the bench seat scattered with glass to the passenger side. I kick and kick at the door to force it open. The whole truck groans and smoke billows out of the engine. Oh *pixies*, please don't let this thing blow up on me.

I wrench open the glove box and pull out the flashlight and mace left by Jefferson. It's a good thing, too, because the second I manage to open the door there's a gray wolf waiting to meet me. I cover my face and spray the mace right into the wolf's eyes. It howls and whines and backs away to rub its face in the thin layer of snow on the ground. I practically fall out of the remnants of the truck and kick the wolf away from me. There's a person buried underneath all that fur but without a tranquilizer gun I don't have any other options.

The semi's engine revs behind me so I dash into the woods before it speeds up and smashes into what's left of the truck. I keep running even though my kidney feels like it's been punched clean out of my chest, my left leg is killing me, and I'm completely turned around.

We got rid of the black wolf, so why is everyone trying to kill me?

Then it hits me. We got rid of *a* black wolf. Mr. Webster confessed too easily for me. Sure, he had been caught but he could have made some excuses. What if he's a patsy? Lycaon could still be out there and know what I am. I've been flaunting my gift to help the werewolves, to cure them—a power that could in theory stop him for good.

He's coming to kill me.

28

I keep running until I run right into a low hanging branch and am knocked flat on my back. Pain reverberates up through my spine and I lay there trying to catch my breath. I've got to get to the cabin and Jefferson and Hawk. If the werewolves came for me, who's to say they won't go after the others too? If they manage to kill me, then they'll probably try to kill Hawk too— if they don't, he will hunt every last one of them down. It's what I would do in the reverse.

Once I think I'm far enough away from the crash, and trusting that wolf isn't able to follow my scent after being maced, I click on the flashlight. It's a good thing I stopped where I did because there's a swamp ten feet ahead that I almost ran into. I dig in my pocket but my cell phone's gone. I must have lost it in the car crash. I swing the flashlight around but keep it low to the ground so hopefully I won't draw attention. I hear a car in the distance and make for that. If there's a car, then there's a road.

If it's a road, then hopefully it's Soldier Road and I can run the rest of the way.

There's a significant amount of brush and I make a terrible racket trying to escape it. Branches cling to me and threaten to tear at my mother's jacket. I push and struggle and trip my way along until it clears away and the ground slopes into a ditch. Pavement painted with yellow and white lines stretches in front of me. I move at a crouch to the edge of the road and look both ways. There are no cars but I see a farm field that I recognize. I'm not far from the cabin.

I clamber onto the road and start to run. My flashlight bobs dizzyingly up and down so I flick it off. It's a beacon for someone else to find me anyway. There's enough moonlight piercing through the light haze of snow that I can make out where I'm going. I wipe my hand across my face to keep the blood away from my eye and pluck a small shard of glass out of my eyebrow. My head is pounding but I can't let up. I'm in danger. Hawk's in danger. Jefferson's in danger. We messed up. We played against someone so clever that we were bound to lose the game. Of course someone as old as Lycaon wouldn't be so tactless as to make his or her sinister plan obvious, having all the werewolves invite everyone to the dance. It was a ruse to make us believe sincerely that Mr. Webster was the mastermind. Now our backup is gone except for useless Agent Smith.

Narrow pines tower over me marking Jefferson's property and I race down the driveway. The floodlights are off but the black SUV is back and parked in front of the cabin. I stagger to the door and fling it open. Agent Smith emerges from Jefferson's room and freezes when he sees me.

"Phoenix? What on earth—"

"I was attacked," I say and move to lean against the table. In the light of the cabin I can make out the blood on my hands and the tears in my mother's jacket. Yeah, now I'm ready to kill someone.

"By who?" he asks.

"The werewolves. I don't think we got the right man. Mr. Webster isn't—" I stop and stare at Agent Smith. "Why were you in Jefferson's room?"

"I was grabbing a cord for the T.V."

"He doesn't let anyone in there."

He shakes his head and pulls out his phone. "How about we forget about movie night and worry about the current situation? I'm calling for backup. If Lycaon is still out there, then we need to stop him."

He dials a number, misses a few buttons and has to redial. I stare as the puzzle pieces fall into place. I had never mentioned the name Lycaon to any of the IMS agents. It was a secret between me, Jefferson, and Hawk. I'm pretty sure none of *them* ever mentioned it to the agents either. Then there's that story about how we'll still be working cases when Witty was positive we were getting canned. Almost like Agent Smith was trying to lull us into a fall sense of security. If he even is Agent Smith anymore.

I've noticed the signs but didn't put them together until just now. He's fumbling for simple things, reaching too far, as if he's not familiar with his own grip, like he's not use to the shape of his own body. It wouldn't be the first time a shapeshifter has worked alongside the werewolves. This all started because a couple were sifting through werewolf records. Were they working for Lycaon?

"Yeah, we need a backup team ASAP at the Moose Lake Field Office," Smith says into his cell phone. "We've got a situation. Our previous plan didn't work. We didn't get our man."

"You're supposed to give your agent identification," I say and straighten. "They won't send a team until you verify your identity."

He cocks his head. "No, this is the direct line to my team leader."

"Oh, okay. You're right."

He smiles and keeps chatting with someone on the other end to confirm we need backup. I twist the mace around in my hand so I have a firm grip on the button. He hangs up and keeps that eerie smile in place.

"So, where's Hawk?" I ask and stay exactly where I am. I let the flashlight in my other hand slide down a bit so I can grip it more like a club.

"Taking a leak." He points to the bathroom but there's no light under the door.

"And Jefferson?"

"Getting some stuff from the barn."

I nod slowly. "I should probably get cleaned up. Jefferson keeps bandages out in the barn."

"I'll walk you out."

"No, I'm okay. Really. Jefferson will help me."

I don't want to turn my back but if he still thinks I'm in the dark, then I need to get out of here and get my hands on a real weapon. If this guy's not only a shapeshifter but a berserker, I'm going to need one if I'm going to survive. I'm in no state for a fight. Besides I need to see if Jefferson really is out in the barn or if he's disappeared. I don't even want to think if Hawk and Jefferson are missing or worse . . .

I turn to the open doorway and start to walk outside when I hear a gun cock. My brain instantly recalls the moments in movies where the hero has their back turned and their ally points a gun at their head. One thing I never got was why they didn't move when they still had the chance. I decided a long time ago that if I ever got in the same position, I wouldn't wait for the bad guy to start his monologue and force me to do something. If I had the opportunity, I would be the first to move.

So I leap sideways out the door as the gun fires. Splinters from the door frame spray over my shoulder but I'm not hit. I pull up tight against the outside wall and lift my flashlight at the ready in my hand. I'm not going to run and hide when Jefferson and Hawk are either captive or—no, they're going to be fine. They're both smart. I just need to find them, and this shapeshifter is going to give me some answers.

The second I see the barrel of the gun peek out the doorway I swing my leg up to redirect the gun to the sky. It goes off again when the shapeshifter's hands slam into the upper frame of the doorway. With his arms up and out of the way for a split second, I slam the flashlight into his face. He's off balance and swings the gun blindly in my direction. I drop what's in my hands to grab his wrist and turn into his body to send an elbow into his gut, in the same motion twisting the gun out of his hands. When I spin back around I send a well-placed kick into his chest to knock him flat and aim the gun at his face.

I put some distance between us so he can't try to kick out my legs. His stunned expression and bloody nose gives me some satisfaction.

"Now," I pant. "You're going to tell me where Hawk and Jefferson are, and what you did with the real Agent Smith."

He smiles and it's really hideous given there's blood covering his teeth. I guess I hit him in the face pretty hard. "You're just a little girl in over your head. I'm not going to tell you anything."

"How soon is your backup arriving?" I press.

He laughs and his eyes flicker to something behind me. I can't help it. I look. Several wolves emerge from the forest. In my very stupid decision to turn my attention away from the shapeshifter, he dashes into Jefferson's room and I hear a window crash. Ballsy escape but I've got other problems to deal with now. I really don't want to shoot anyone so I race the werewolves to the barn.

They bark and howl and snap at my heels as I shoulder my way through the door and take the steps up to the loft three at a time. Lying on top of the table is the tranquilizer gun. My fingers barely manage to graze the grip when a set of jaws grab the back of my shoe and pull. I fall face first onto the floor and start being dragged backwards. This would be a seriously bad way to die. So I kick and kick until I shake the one werewolf loose and scrabble for anything around me. I grab a blanket, roll onto my back, and lift it up between my hands as one of the wolves lunges. It catches the blanket in its teeth and I yank it to the side to throw it off balance. Its body angles enough so I can plant a foot on its chest and shove it backwards away from me.

The next wolf pushes past the others and it's too close. When it lunges I have to grab onto either side of its neck to stop it from ripping my face off. Its hot breath washes over me and I'm covered in dog spittle as it chomps and chomps on empty air. I dig my fingers into its fur and twist in my knuckles to block off its blood supply to the brain. The other two are struggling up and not giving me enough time to knock the one out so I'm forced to improvise again. I get both my feet under the wolf's body and fling it backwards into the other two.

I roll onto my stomach, push up, and grab the gun. Locked and loaded, I spin about and pop one, two, three. The wolves stagger against each other before falling into an unmoving heap. I wish I could relax but a fourth comes snarling up the stairs. It has a reddish coat. For a second I'm terrified it's Hawk but then realize the color's slightly off and he's not quite as tall.

"Ben? That you?" I ask and keep the gun trained on him. "Okay, this is how it's going to work. You're going to help me find my brother and Jefferson. I don't care what Lycaon's done to you."

I keep one hand on the gun but the other I stretch out towards him. Nothing's going to stop me from finding my brother and ending this for good. Ben halts at the top of the steps and continues to snarl but eventually falls silent. I keep pressing and I'm shaking worse than ever. He hangs his head, tucks in his tail, and whines. I get up and walk backwards so I can lean against the table but keep pressing.

Blood is dripping out of my nose by the time Ben finally shifts and kneels on the stairs as a boy. He's breathing almost as hard as I am. I keep the gun trained on him until he looks up and holds out his hands.

"It's me again," he gasps. "Just me. Phoenix, I'm so sorry."

"Stow it." I set the gun down and wipe the back of my hand under my nose, really just smearing the blood around. "As you can probably tell, I'm in no state to put up with crap. My brother's missing, Jefferson is missing, Agent Smith has been a shapeshifter since he came back for all I know, and everyone's trying to kill me. Try and tell me this day doesn't suck."

"Shapeshifter? There are shape—"

"Focus, Ben. Hawk and Jefferson. Do you know where they are?"

He hangs his head and grasps at his ruffled hair. "I'm not sure. It's hard to remember anything."

"Oh, don't give me that. You know. It's buried in that thick skull of yours." I push off the table and stagger over to grasp his shoulder. "*Think*, Ben."

His eyes glue onto my hand. I don't know if it comforts him or freaks him out. He nods ever so slowly.

"I think . . . the park. The state park, close to the lake."

"Well, that's fantastic." I've got great memories of being bitten there and Deputy Graham disappearing out that way. It's the perfect setting for a final showdown, I guess.

I take Ben's hand and haul him to his feet. "Okay, you're coming with me. You're all the backup I have. You don't happen to have a phone on you, do you?"

"No, sorry."

Transportation's the first thing on my mind. The truck's a twisted shell. Jefferson's going to love that. The only option is the Green Monster. I scan the wall and give a sigh of relief when I spot the car keys hanging on their hook. I snatch them up and pass by my parents' open file box. The pearl-handled .45 catches my eye. My mother's final defense. It feels only fitting that I take it with in my desperate bid to save Hawk. I rip apart the plastic bag to check the sliding action and magazine. Its magazine is almost full of red bullets—just missing the two my mother fired in her final moments. Silver harming werewolves is an old wives' tale, but these bullets, coated with a mixture made from wolfsbane, are meant to put a werewolf down for good.

I tuck it into the back of my waistband and pick up the tranquilizer gun. A first aid kit sits on a nearby shelf so I haul it onto the table and start ripping out bandages. I do a poor job wiping blood off myself because I don't have time to take a better assessment of my injuries, but it'll have to do. Ben stands on the stairs watching me and looks helpless. I find another tranquilizer gun Jefferson had been cleaning and load it as fast as I can before shoving it into Ben's hand.

"You ever handle a gun before?" I ask and start pushing him down the stairs.

"Not really."

"It's easy. Point and shoot. Just be close enough because these darts will fall short otherwise."

He tries to turn around to talk to me but I keep moving him along towards the car. "I'm not going to kill anyone."

"Neither am I if I can help it. These are tranquilizers."

I yank the tarp off the car to unveil the Green Monster's flawless green paint job. Ben slides into the passenger seat, holding his gun like it's a grenade, and I buckle into the driver's seat. At the turn of the key the engine roars to life and the last song Jefferson had been playing kicks on. It's "Thunderstruck" by AC/DC.

"Well, isn't that ironic," I mutter and shift into gear.

The headlights flood the driveway as we peel out. I'm forced to go east first to bypass North Road. There's no way I'm taking that road after the semi incident. The snow continues to fall, painting the grass and trees white but melting on the blacktop.

"So, who is he, Ben?" I ask. "Who's the black wolf?"

"I don't know, and please don't punch me, but I really don't know." He keeps his eyes trained on the gun in his hands. "I've only ever seen a black wolf. I swear." He's quiet for a long time as I hit Highway 61 and head west into town. "My mother's out there, I think. Everyone is. We have to help them."

"I know. You just follow my lead, okay? We'll save them all and stop this guy."

"Yeah. Okay."

He doesn't sound like he believes me one bit. I don't know if *I* believe me but I've got to try.

"Are there any payphones around here?" I ask.

"What, here? In Moose Lake," he scoffs. "Not a chance."

"I need to call for backup."

He points out the windshield. "Try there."

It's the gas station I was followed from. "Yeah, that's not going to happen."

We drive past to the next best thing and I scramble out. I rush into the 24-hour grocery store and slam a hand on the customer service counter to make sure I have the cashier's full attention. "I need a phone. Life or death. Just look at me."

He does and I realize I'm still covered in my own blood and bruises and probably a few bits of glass. He doesn't say a word but silently passes over his cell phone. I run out the door before he can stop me.

"Hey!" he shouts at my back.

"I'll return it later!"

The kid will probably call the police but that's the least of my worries. I pass the phone to Ben, throw the car into gear, and race out of the city towards the interstate. I list the IMS number off to Ben while I drive. Once he dials he passes it back to me and I press it to my ear.

A woman answers. "ID number?"

"0919-32, Junior Agent Phoenix Mason. Code black."

"Transferring you now."

I'm put on hold for a good twenty seconds before someone answers. "Phoenix?"

"Witty? Why in the world did they direct me to you? I called in a code black."

"I know!" He sounds affronted. "Phoenix you don't work for the IMS anymore. Agent Smith was supposed to go out there and—"

"Agent Smith turned out to be a friggin' shapeshifter and tried to put a bullet in my head," I snap. "They got the wrong werewolf, Witty. It's taken Hawk and Jefferson and tried to kill me multiple times tonight alone. You've got to send backup ASAP."

"What?"

"*Witty!*" I shout into the phone. "Wheel your butt to Director Knox and tell him if he doesn't send backup we're going to be *dead* before the ten o'clock news, and you're going to have the entire population of Moose Lake eating venison raw for the rest of their lives. You *tell* him to *call Draco*. Tell him Lycaon's here. I don't care what it takes, Witty. They're not going to kill my brother."

"Okay." This time there's no hesitation in his voice. "Where are you now?"

"Heading to the Moose Lake State Park near the—" I look

to Ben for assistance. He mouths *lower lake.* "—the lower lake in the park. I've got an informant saying that's where Lycaon and the rest will be."

"Are you on your own?"

"What do you think, genius? The only backup the IMS sent to us was a shapeshifter. Where do you think that leaves me? Talk to Knox, *now.*"

"I'm going. Don't die Phoenix. I'm sending help."

"Yeah, you better," I mutter and toss the phone back to Ben for him to end the call.

The Green Monster rumbles along the dark road, past the last lights at the bridge over the interstate, and into the night on the other side at the state park. We pull into the deserted parking lot and the headlights sweep over the empty office building. I pause at the edge of the lot where three roads split off into the park.

"Where to?" I ask.

Ben points to the left. "That will take us closest to where I think he is."

"You think? You're not sure."

"No, I'm not, but it feels right."

I glare at him but take the trail on the left. "You and your feelings," I mutter.

We trundle along the gravel path and I lean forward in my seat to watch every angle. Werewolves have excellent hearing and are sure to hear the Green Monster a mile away. I pass the top edge of the lake and the little open fields where campers can park their RVs. It's completely deserted. I reach the last spot and park between a stand of pines. When I kill the engine the silence is palpable.

"Stick by me," I say quietly. "You ready?"

"Um, sure?"

"Good enough for me."

We slide out of the car and I ease my door shut. Ben does the same on his side before we head into the woods together. I flick on my flashlight and hold it up against my tranquilizer gun to clear the way forward. There's hardly any snow here beneath the trees and I can't hear a thing over the rustling of the dead leaves. Ben taps my shoulder and points me to our right. I follow his lead and soon enough we reach the shore of the lake again. We follow its beach until I can hear howling in the distance. I guess Ben's feeling is right after all.

I lower the flashlight some and try to move lighter on my feet. Ben moves at a crouch beside me, the barrel of his gun trained on the ground. Suddenly he stiffens and flinches to the left. I swing about and my beam falls on an enormous gray wolf. My finger squeezes the trigger once, then again as I spot his companion. The pair of wolves fall rather noisily into the underbrush. Crap. I grab Ben by the collar of his shirt and jog him in the opposite direction before more come to check out the noise.

Ben trips in our haste to flee and crashes into a thicket. I turn back for him and find two more sets of eyes watching me in the darkness. Pop-pop. Two more wolves fall unconscious on the forest floor. Ben claws his way out of the thicket and I give him a hand up. My heart's thrumming in my chest. I'm starting to think I should have gone in alone. Ben got me here, sure, but he's certainly not the stealthiest partner for the job.

I keep jogging and lower my flashlight some more, covering it slightly with the palm of my hand. The next time I check over my shoulder to make sure Ben is still following, he's gone. Crap, crap, crap. I take a knee to stop and listen. There's shuffling to my right. I raise my gun and flick up the light to catch sight of three more wolves. I'm not fast enough on the draw this time. I manage to take down two before the third one howls. I put a dart in its neck and rush back to look for Ben.

"Phoenix."

I skid to a stop and wheel around with the flashlight to find Jason holding Ben in a stranglehold.

29

Ben's eyes bulge and his face turns red in Jason's hold. I aim my gun and am ready to put a dart in Jason's forearm when I'm struck from the side. My face smacks the ground as I'm shoved down by a giant, furry body. The breath is knocked out of my chest and I gasp for air as saliva drips onto my neck. The smell of the wolf's breath is disgusting. I try to reach for the gun that's fallen out of my grasp but the wolf snatches it with its teeth and hurls it into the darkness. I'm ready to shrug the wolf off when I realize it's not moving to rip out my throat.

"You're not going to kill me?" I gasp.

Two more wolves move into the beam of my flashlight that's rolled away and I sense movement behind me too. I'm surrounded.

"Get up," Jason orders, keeping Ben in a death grip. "He wants to see you before we kill you since you've made it this far."

"Oh, how kind of him," I wheeze out under the wolf's weight.

He nods to the wolf trying to smother me into the ground and it crawls away. I suck down air with the pressure off my lungs and sit up. I massage my left aching knee and take a moment to catch my breath.

"Get up," Jason says louder. "He's waiting."

"Give me a second, dog-breath," I bite back. "He's waited this long, he can wait a couple minutes more. My leg's killing me."

"*Get up!*"

I hold up a hand and glare at him. "I have been in a car crash, been chased through the woods once tonight already, fought off a freakin' shapeshifter and your pals so you can give me *one* minute to catch my breath or I'm going to feed you your teeth first."

"One minute," he growls. "And don't try anything. You're surrounded."

"Yeah, I got that, Captain Obvious."

I ignore him and keep massaging my knee. So my tranquilizer gun is gone. That means I either have to physically pummel my way through an entire town of werewolves or start using the real gun still stuffed in the back of my pants. At least my strength is my ace in the hole. Even though I'm fatigued, exhausted, and bloodied, I can rally more muscle power than they'll be expecting. No one knows about it except for Hawk and Jefferson. Crap. If Hawk was left alone, could Lycaon have put him under his spell already? Would he have forced Hawk to spill all our secrets? I can only hope Hawk's been fighting to keep control of himself.

So, save Ben, find Hawk and Jefferson, save them too, and then stop the black wolf. I've got goals but not a plan. Awesome.

"Time's up," Jason says.

"All right, all right." I take my time getting to my feet. I'm really going to need a doctor and a nap if I survive this.

"Nice and slow," Jason says. "This way."

Jason tugs Ben around by his neck and pushes him ahead before picking up my flashlight to light the way. A troop of werewolves, ten by my count, surround the three of us. Ben coughs harshly and rubs his throat but he seems okay. We move noisily through the brush without the need for caution.

"So this doesn't bug you at all?" I ask. "You follow this alpha's orders no matter what? Ashley got hurt, you know. She really liked you."

Hard lines form around Jason's mouth and forehead. "She's like us now. She'll heal and be stronger."

"Is that really what you want for her?" I take a wide step over a fallen log that the wolves hop over easy as you please. "So you can go howl at the moon together, drink deer blood, play fetch?"

"It's not like that," he snaps. His eyes catch the glare of the flashlight. The yellow in them is freakishly vivid. "You wouldn't understand. We've been given a purpose. We're connected. We're a family."

"Uh-huh. Sure. Because nothing says family quite like biting a bunch of innocent people for kicks."

At that he launches around Ben to grab the collar of my jacket and clenches it so tightly it gets a little hard to breathe.

"You know *nothing*," he spits in my face.

"My brother's a werewolf, you moron," I wheeze. "I know

more about it than you think. He's managed his entire life without jumping on the crazy wagon. You don't need this alpha to give you a purpose. You find your own. You don't give in to the disease. You aren't animals."

He lets me go and waves us on. "Keep moving."

I hoped I could get through to him but of course I'm wrong. I have a feeling what's in my blood isn't going to be a match for Lycaon, whoever he is. The howling in the distance swells and dwindles and swells again like a tide. We're getting close to the end, and the closer we get the more twitchy Ben becomes. He's clearly trying to fight whatever's tugging on his werewolf instincts but when we finally clear the trees and come to a field filled with werewolves, he straightens and walks like a robot to join the others.

It's no small gathering of wolves either. There's got to be a hundred bunched together and howling in waves like some sort of chant. They fill up the entire field all the way to the edge of the lake where a black wolf stands beside two Jeffersons—wait, *two* Jeffersons? One is on all fours, bloody and beat while the other stands perfectly straight next to him. Well, now I know where the shapeshifter ran off to.

I ignore my escort and start shoving my way through the wolves. They snarl and snap at me but none of them actually bite. My heart is hammering, my head is pounding, my arms feel like lead, and I'm so done with all of this.

"Jefferson!" I shout. I pick up my pace and step on a few tails and trip over paws. Several wolves scratch me with their nails and their teeth rip at my pants. I shrug past them and nearly reach my Jefferson. Two pairs of hands grab my arms just before I break through the edge of the crowd and bring me to a stop. For the moment I don't throw them off, though I think I could, because I still don't know where my brother is.

My Jefferson raises his head and blood drips out of his mouth. I stare at him and he nods once letting me know he's okay. Fake Jefferson steps in front of him to block the real one from view. The black wolf stands calm as can be. He's a good foot or more taller than the rest of the wolves. How did we ever think Mr. Webster's poor substitute of a wolf was this Lycaon? His yellow eyes are nearly luminescent and a thin layer of snow outlines his head and back.

"Where's my brother?" I demand. Fear creeps up my spine but focusing on my objectives helps me keep my head.

The wolf crouches low and his body begins to shift. The black fur recedes, his forelegs shorten and become stockier while his back legs stretch out. When he changes I can make out a navy blue button down shirt with the collar folded neatly, faded jeans, and a ruffled mess of black hair on top. He straightens to his full six feet and gives me a lopsided smile, arms stretched wide.

"Welcome!" he says like this is some kind of surprise birthday party.

No. Not him. It can't be. "Captain Krush?"

He brushes himself off. "Good to see I can still make an unexpected entrance." He tucks his hands into the pockets of his blue jeans and rolls up on his toes before standing still. "Color me impressed, Phoenix. You're a lot harder to kill than I anticipated. I guess I don't have time to make it look like an accident anymore. I didn't want to have the IMS sniffing around after an obvious murder but I'll have to make do."

"But . . . no, you—"

"I was the nice guy? I couldn't possibly be the villain?" He puts a hand over his heart. "I'm touched, but that really only proves how naïve you are. No man is wholly good or evil. The world isn't black and white. And a man like me has more than one face. By the way, I think I'm going to have to give you a C on your mythology assignment. You picked a great story but the facts were all wrong."

"I don't care. Where's my brother?"

He waves a hand to the massive force of wolves behind me. "Oh, he's around but we'll get to that in a minute." He rubs his hands together. "I want to hear your questions. I may even give you some answers. You've earned it by escaping that car crash, getting a leg up on my shifter, *and* culling the boys I sent to finish the job. It's the least I can do before I'm forced to kill you."

This isn't what I'm expecting, not at all. He's smiling and energetic like he's asking for student feedback in the classroom. I had actually liked him. He had been the funny, considerate teacher. Make that substitute teacher—that was why Jefferson and I didn't see him in the yearbook. He wasn't part of the permanent staff or a student.

"So you're the real Lycaon?" I ask. "The original werewolf."

He frowns and rolls his head side to side. "Yes and no. I'm the original werewolf, yes, but the whole story of Lycaon the Greeks concocted was mistaken. I prefer the name . . . Dasc."

"Disk."

"Dasc."

"That's what I said. Disk."

His smile slowly returns but there's a hard glint in his eyes. I'm sure he wants his big name reveal to come with a little more awe but there's nothing I'd rather do than push every single one of his buttons if I can find them.

"So, Disk—"

"*Dasc.*" His eyes flash yellow before returning to their usual blue. Huh. So he can hide that little telling factor at will.

"You're going to have to write it down for me," I say. "So, is it D-i-s-q-u—"

The muscles in his face tense and this time his eyes remain prominently yellow. I tense in response, ready for him to attack, but then he throws his head back with a booming laugh. He holds up a hand to pardon himself until his laughter dies, then clasps his hands behind his back and lowers his head to look at me through his eyebrows. Okay, so blatantly trying to be annoying isn't going to work.

"Ask me the questions you actually want answered," he says. "How about we start with your brother?"

My brain goes blank. "What?"

He beckons with his hand to the wolves. The enormous pack shuffles aside so one reddish wolf can walk through to stand in front of me.

"Hawk?" I gasp.

His ears lay flat and his head bends low to the ground. Dasc, or whoever he is, nods encouragingly to me.

"Go on," he says. "Ask."

"What did you do to him?"

"Aha! There it is." He hoists a finger in the air and starts to pace in a circle around me and Hawk. "Let's just say I have a talent for persuasion. The pack follows me now and me alone. I know you'll probably try to stop it but in your current state I doubt you'd be able to dissuade even your brother. You've lost too much blood, and as they say—" He's suddenly right behind me and whispers in my ear. "The power is in the blood."

I jerk away from him and he continues to pace his wide circle.

"But I have to admit," he says. "I was surprised by your ability. The way you stopped Matt from biting you, how you took away my influence over Ben during detention. Oh, and that was a test, in case you were wondering. After the incident with Matt, I wanted to see the extent of your abilities and you performed beautifully!"

He claps and actually seems quite pleased I had been able to foil him. I get the feeling he's been dying to tell someone every-thing. Psychopaths always want an audience. "Then I had Jason bite you and . . . well. After you didn't turn or die, I realized the true nature of your power. I don't think you realize how unique you are, my Phoenix."

"What are you talking about?"

He steps close again to stand between Hawk and me. "Did you know that dragon magic bestowed on a Blessed isn't a replication of the dragon's own abilities? It's an endowment of power that conforms to that specific individual. No two Blessed are quite the same. There is only one you, the one and only Phoenix, who transformed that power into a way to save her brother."

At this he swivels around on Hawk and lays a hand on his head. I want to rip his arm out of its socket.

"Don't touch him," I growl and curl my hands into fists.

Dasc spins about, jumping a little in his excitement, the same way he reacted when we discussed Greek mythology in class. My brain is having a hard time putting my teacher and this lunatic together.

"There it is!" he exclaims. "It's that drive, that protective instinct you have for your brother. No one before has been in your shoes. There's never been a Blessed on the planet with a werewolf sibling, let alone a twin, that chose to save him and not push him away. It's that bond that's made you what you are! I've seen the way you two jump in front of danger for the other. It's admirable. It really is. And that's what makes this so much harder."

"You mean the part where you're going to kill me?"

He shrugs as if it's no big deal. "I don't want to. I like you, Phoenix. You've got courage and tenacity, but you're a danger to me and my brethren. I'm sorry."

"Were my parents in your way, too?" I growl. "Were they a threat?"

He purses his lips and rubs his hands together slowly. "They were a bit too clever. I meant to turn your whole family but things didn't turn out as expected, and neither did you."

"What about my brother?" I try to catch Hawk's eye but he continues to hang his head. I want him to look up and let me know he's okay. I want to see his normal green eyes untainted by the yellow glint of Dasc's madness in his blood. I want my brother back.

"Oh, him? Once you're out of the picture there won't be anything stopping him from joining my pack."

"He would never."

"Not under his own will, no, but you see I can be *very* persuasive." He winks and marches over to fake Jefferson. He claps him on the shoulder.

I point between the two of them. "Since when are your kind pals?"

Dasc's blue eyes land on me intensely serious for the first time. "When there's a purpose. There are bigger monsters than me. A war's coming, Phoenix. I'm just moving the pieces into place." Then he's light and demented again and points to Jefferson. "I suppose I could always turn you rather than kill you."

"I'd rather kill myself than be your *schweinhund*," Jefferson spits.

"Oh, well, in that case—" He nods to fake Jefferson. "Do you have enough to play him convincingly?"

"I think so."

"Then kill him and toss him in the lake. No one will find the body this time of year."

"What? No!" I start to struggle. Killing Jefferson and enslaving Hawk? Over my dead body. The shapeshifter hauls Jefferson to his feet and tries to wrap his hands around either side of Jefferson's head but Jefferson fights him and fights hard. They thrash against each other on the beach and kick up sand.

"Now, now, no need to get all excited," Dasc says as if he's talking to a toddler.

While they continue to spar, Dasc stretches a hand out palm first towards Hawk. My brother twitches and a deep growl emanates from his throat. Hawk takes deliberate steps towards me.

"You've got to be kidding me!" I shout. "Hawk, snap out of it. You've got to fight it. You've got to help me!"

He flips his tail and keeps coming towards me. Jefferson and fake Jefferson fall to the ground wrestling. Dasc sighs and motions to another werewolf nearby to help the shapeshifter. I'm burning up and shaking at the effort of trying to get through to my brother. I was already weak when I got here. I don't know if I can reach him through the compulsion.

"Hawk, come on! It's me, buddy." I struggle against the hold on my arms. Jason and Ben grunt as they strain to keep me secure. "Hawk, can you hear me? I'm your sister, don't you remember?"

His tail flips again—just once. He closes in and comes within five feet, easy leaping distance. He finally lifts his head and I can see his green eyes. In the faint moonlight I can't be sure, but I can't find a trace of yellow.

Jefferson lets out a cry as the werewolf sweeps its claws across his shoulder and he narrowly avoids being bitten. I'm momentarily distracted but turn back to Hawk just in time to see him leap. I lean to the side and he bowls over Jason, freeing my arm and allowing me to grab the front of Ben's jacket. With the full force of my body, I fling him forwards onto his back.

"No!" Dasc shouts. He storms forward, his bared teeth already shifting into fangs.

There's nothing for it now. I can either let Dasc rip me apart and kill the people I care about or I can take action and use deadly force. Despite everything Dasc has done I don't want to kill him. I don't want to kill anyone, but nothing's going to stop me from saving my brother. And Dasc basically said himself he's the source of the werewolf persuasion. Once he's out of the picture the others should be free.

I wrench my mother's gun out of my waistband, spin about so I'm crouched protectively over Hawk, holding one arm across his furry shoulders to steady myself, and bring the gun up on my other side to level it with Dasc's chest. There I freeze, unwilling to let the destructive force in my hand fire. I'm not a killer. Dasc's teeth are bared and he's partially shifted. His eyes blaze yellow and he's coming to kill me and do who knows what to my brother. Terror courses through me and I know there's only one way to stop him.

The night shatters in the explosion of the red bullet leaving the barrel. Dasc jerks and stands still. His teeth shrink to normal and the black fur on his hands and face recedes or falls away. In an unhurried motion he brushes a hand over his chest like he's trying to wipe chalk dust off his shirt after a long day in class. His fingers come away red. I'm shaking and can't hear a thing except the ringing in my ears. When he takes another step towards me my body reacts automatically.

I fire and fire again until I empty the entire clip into his chest.

This time he staggers, clutches at his chest, then crumples backwards into the sand. Three seconds tick by in silence as the other werewolves look on. Then there's howling and barking and growling. Hawk shoves against my back and forces me towards Jefferson still struggling against the werewolf and shapeshifter. Hawk lunges for the other wolf and they tumble away together into the lake.

Both Jeffersons are bloodied at this point and I can't tell which one is the real one and which is the fake. The real one got clawed on the shoulder but I can't make it out in their struggle and the darkness.

"Jefferson!" I shout. I glance over my shoulder to the wolves snapping at each other but a lot of their focus is on me like I'm fresh meat.

"It's me!" one of the Jeffersons shout.

"No, it's me!" the other shouts before strangling his copy. They kick against each other and continue to roll on the ground.

The one being strangled into the sand wheezes out, "Save *me*, young adult."

Oh. Clever. Only the real Jefferson would remember me pestering him about not calling us kids. I lunge forward and send a kick into fake Jefferson's temple before he can strangle my Jefferson. The shapeshifter falls to the side and the real Jefferson grasps at his throat coughing. I kneel on fake Jefferson's chest and clock him with the butt of my empty gun until he falls unconscious.

The wolves start to swarm towards us as I'm kneeling in the sand and Jefferson remains prone, clutching at his neck. I thought taking out Dasc would solve everything but I guess his hold on the wolves was stronger than I thought. Dasc was right, though. I've lost too much blood and I'm exhausted. There's no way I'll be able to stop any of them.

I hear splashing and out of the lake comes Hawk dripping wet to stand before us. He snarls and snaps at any wolves that come close. His hackles rise and he stretches up to his full height. His ears are flat back and he's terrifying. The other wolves shy away and some even tuck in their tails. Hawk holds his ground and bites those too intent on getting to me and Jefferson. Despite the sheer number of wolves against Hawk, they back down under his fierce display. That, and I'm sure having Dasc out of the picture helps.

We're at a stalemate when a sound in the distance grows louder as it closes in. The field is suddenly flooded with light as a pair of helicopters swing overhead and the air gusts around us at their approach. The wolves whine and a few scatter to the woods. There are several loud pops from rifles held by agents hanging out the helicopter doors, their feet braced on the landing skids. The werewolves trying to flee fall and I'm terrified they've been shot for real.

"Tranquilizers," Jefferson wheezes and puts a hand on my shin as he sits up.

I put a hand on his back and watch the helicopters drop lower on opposite sides of the field to corral the werewolves together to be more easily managed. IMS agents rush the area and it's clear the fight is over. We did it.

"Who ever thought you'd be saved by acknowledging someone isn't a snot-nosed kid?" I say out of breath.

He tries to laugh but wheezes instead as he rubs at his throat and clutches his bleeding shoulder. The werewolves have all but forgotten about us with the arrival of the IMS. Hawk comes over to curl around my back protectively and keeps his head lowered over my shoulder. I allow myself to lean fully against him. I'm all out of juice and ready to pass out.

"What did I tell you?" I pant. "Moose Lake was bound to be boring."

30

Sitting in the back of a specialized undercover IMS ambulance, I'm poked and prodded and have bandages slapped on every inch of my face, neck, arms, and legs. The medic almost changes the bandage on my arm hiding the werewolf bite but I assure her it's fine, an old wound really, and she lets it be. The last thing I need, with IMS agents crawling all over, is for them to figure out what I am and haul me off to a dark room to be tested for the rest of my life. Jefferson's warning has really sunk in and the thought of someone else figuring out what's in my blood terrifies me. The medic finishes patching me up and I look a little like a mummy. At least for now I don't have to fight anyone, stop a psycho's war, rescue a pack of werewolves, or even move for that matter.

The medic straps an ice pack to my knee and I'm allowed a moment of peace for the time being. I'm sure there's going to be plenty of questions to answer, paperwork to complete, and explanations to give. I hope that comes much later though. I've got insane fever chills and I'm wrapped up in a blanket. I wish the medic had left me some candy bars or something. I'm starving. Trying to hold off a horde of werewolves and their alpha has taken everything out of me.

Hawk clambers up drying himself off with a towel and takes the empty bench seat next to my stretcher. He hangs his head and doesn't say anything. I don't think I want him to. From his glum expression I can guess he feels guilty, but he shouldn't.

He ruffles the back of his hair and sets the towel aside. "He tried to use me like a puppet."

"And he failed," I say. "We put him down, Hawk."

"No, you did. You saved all of us."

"Ehh, don't try to make me sound too heroic. It'll go straight to my head." I lean back and try to make myself comfortable. "My hats won't fit anymore."

He smiles and leans forward to set his elbows on the edge of the stretcher. "Thanks, Fifi, for not giving up on me."

"I never will. Not ever."

"Geez, is this the sappy-mobile?" Jefferson says in a gravelly voice as he comes around the open doors. He's got his arm in a sling, almost the same amount of bandages as me, and two black eyes.

"That shifter really cleaned your clock," I say.

"Oh, yeah. We had a grand old time." He sighs and leans against the side of the ambulance. "So what happened to you anyway?"

I lick my lips and try to smile. "Yeah, about that. Your truck is sort of a metal pretzel."

"What?" He straightens and braces his good hand on the end of my stretcher. "What happened?"

"Well, you had a shapeshifter and I had werewolves with a semi. Let's leave it at that."

His face contorts like he's eaten something super sour. His beady eyes are almost lost beneath his furrowed brow but eventually he lets out a sigh and accepts defeat.

"At least it wasn't the Green Monster." He shakes his head then looks me square in the eye. "I'm glad you're still kicking, Phoenix. You did good . . . for a *young adult*."

Coming from him, that's saying something. When we first came here I couldn't stand the guy. Now he's like a grouchy uncle. I never had someone of the sort before. "I appreciate that, Jefferson. Really."

He rolls his eyes. "We don't have to hug now, do we?"

"Heck no. I'm going to lie right here and take a nap. Wake me up when the next crisis comes along. Actually, on second thought, don't wake me."

I'm serious about the nap but someone raps their knuckles on the metal of the ambulance door. I prop myself up to find Director Knox himself standing there. He's in a long trench coat and his expression is deadly serious. Granted, I don't think I've ever seen him with a different expression, but it's certainly a surprise to see him here.

"Agent Barnes," he says and nods to Jefferson. "Phoenix, Hawk."

"Sir," we each answer in turn.

"Thanks to you three, a city's been saved, a major crisis has been averted, and a dangerous criminal's been apprehended."

"The shapeshifter, you mean?" I ask.

"No. The werewolf under the proxy of James Krushnic, or Lycaon, or whatever he prefers to be known as—"

"Dasc," I say. "But he's dead. I shot him. I emptied a magazine of wolfsbane bullets into his chest."

"I know." The director wrings a scarf in his hands before stuffing it into his pocket. "Whatever Dasc is, he's more powerful than any werewolf I've ever seen. He survived, barely, so we're bringing him in. We'll let him heal, then interrogate him. There are still people unaccounted for and questions we need answered."

My gut twists knowing that devil's still alive. I thought I had ended it and avenged my parents. I had been terrified to put him down but I would do it again. Just the thought of him somehow escaping IMS custody makes my skin crawl.

"We're taking every precaution," Director Knox continues. "A dragon has even arrived to oversee Dasc's incarceration."

"Which dragon?"

He gives me a long look and throws the scarf around his neck. "You know the one."

The director nods again and starts to leave.

"Wait!" I call after him.

He walks back into view. "I've got a mess to handle, Mason."

"I know, I just—so we aren't being kicked out of the IMS?"

For the first time I've known him, the director smiles. "Not now." Then he holds up a finger before he walks away and adds, "But don't take that as license to get into more trouble. I expect you to follow the rules. Keep your noses clean."

Warmth swells in my chest and I smile at my brother. He smiles in return and Jefferson even grins a little. Team

Thunderstruck sits around in the ambulance for a while longer watching the werewolves come back to themselves. They shift out of wolf form and I see all the people we saved from Dasc's influence. I watch Ben and his mother find each other and hug before she starts shouting at him and everyone else in the vicinity. A couple of IMS agents in black military gear try to calm her but she shouts at them too. Jefferson laughs at a safe distance.

Deputy Graham is one of the few missing persons to reappear. He walks around dazed in his now filthy deputy uniform and, after being treated, eventually stumbles over to our ambulance. Jefferson shakes his hand and claps him on the back.

"You okay?" Jefferson asks.

His mouth twitches into an uncertain smile. "I'll let you know when I figure it out."

"We tried to find you, Jared. I'm sorry."

"I doubt you would have found me anyway." The deputy smooths back his longish hair and itches at the thick scruff on his face. "After I was bitten that day we went looking for those teens, I went north to Carlton and Wrenshall for a while. He tried to have me turn some other deputies but the further away I got, the less he was in my head, you know? I guess I fought it enough to make him nervous and he called me back."

The thought of Dasc trying to infiltrate law enforcement gives me chills. He really was preparing for a war.

"We're glad you're okay," I say.

"Thanks."

He moves off uncertainly until another IMS agent finds him and offers him fresh clothes and a ride home. Shortly after, the ambulance crew gets their rig ready to go and we roll out of the woods to return to the field office. Early the next morning Jefferson returns to the state park to pick up the Green Monster and we start the huge undertaking of getting things back to normal.

It takes time to heal. I sleep for almost two days straight after the fiasco at the lake. My arm aches like mad and Hawk slaps my hand away every time I want to scratch at my itchy scabs. Jefferson is a grouch as usual but we've got a good team of IMS agents sticking around for at least a little while to help us sort it all out. Deputy Graham helps as much as he can. The rest of the werewolves, now that Dasc has been hauled away to Underground, revert to their normal selves. Regular doses of the serum are administered and Moose Lake is back to being a quiet town in the Northwoods of Minnesota.

Back at school—Jefferson thinks it's a good idea to keep going—the students have plenty to gossip about. Theories over what really happened at the dance, and Mr. Webster's and Captain Krush's disappearances, span from mid-life crisis to military insurgency. Those that do know the truth keep silent. Ashley is back to her bubbly self but doesn't wear *Love Moon* shirts anymore. She's moved on to comic books and superheroes.

"So are you, you know . . ." she says and wiggles her eyebrows at me as we walk to class.

"Am I what?" I ask around a sucker in my mouth that I bought from a vending machine.

"I saw your bite, remember? That was a werewolf bite, wasn't it?" she says and I almost choke on the sucker. I pull it out and toss it into the trash. "Are you a werewolf now?"

"No, I'm not." I shake my head morosely and pat her arm.

"It really was just a dog bite. I promise. But don't tell anyone, all right?"

"Why not?" Her brow furrows so I smile in an attempt to wave her off like it's no big deal even though it's a very big deal. I hold out my pinky finger and wink. She sighs and wraps her own around mine.

"You think those big shot agents would ever let me live it down? Getting bit by a mutt when the town's swimming with werewolves?" I whisper. "I can trust you, right? You're the only friend I have around here apart from my brother."

She wrinkles her nose and giggles. "I promise. You can trust me."

There still hasn't been word back from Jefferson's expert about my blood and the potential it has to cure the werewolves, but he says it'll come in time. I do get updates from Witty on Dasc's recovery progress. It's slow but he's coming around. Then the interrogations will start and we may finally know what happened to Jefferson's daughter and the others that disappeared.

Dasc said a war is coming and he was moving his pieces into place. Now it's time to move ours.

I'll get my answers. I'll become the cure. And if Dasc or his followers ever come for me or my family again, I'll be ready.

THE ADVENTURE CONTINUES...

Get news about the next book in the series at
brightway-books.com and find exclusive content at
bethanyhelwig.com. This is only the beginning!

Listen to the playlist that drove the story at
bethanyhelwig.com/book-playlists
Browse the images that gave inspiration for the story at:
https://www.pinterest.com/phoenixverus/
ims-1-the-curse-of-moose-lake/

Bethany Helwig is the author of the successful International Monster Slayers series. She enjoys writing fantasy novels, composing music, creating art, and participating in various fandoms. She lives in a small town in Minnesota with her dog.

Connect with Bethany:
bethanyhelwig.com

TWITTER: twitter.com/BethanyHelwig
GOODREADS: https://www.goodreads.com/author/
show/7152554.Bethany_Helwig
PINTEREST: pinterest.com/phoenixverus